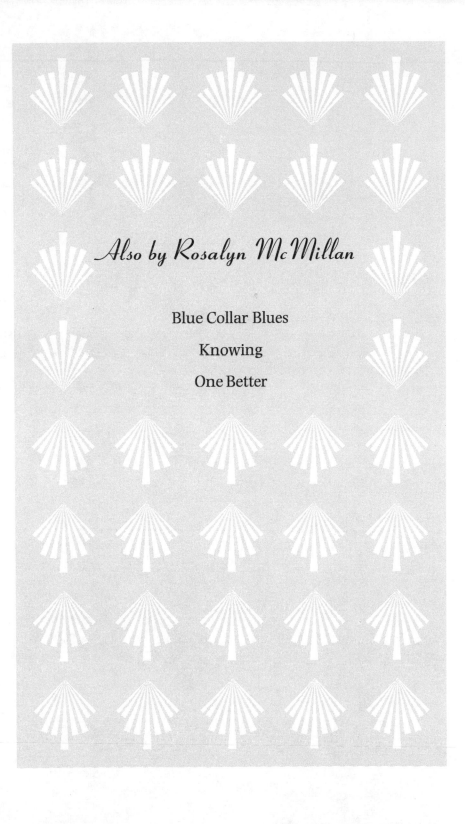

Also by Rosalyn McMillan

Blue Collar Blues

Knowing

One Better

A Novel

The Flip Side of Sin

Rosalyn McMillan

Simon & Schuster

New York   London   Toronto   Sydney   Singapore

SIMON & SCHUSTER
Rockefeller Center
1230 Avenue of the Americas
New York, NY 10020

Simon & Schuster and colophon are registered trademarks
of Simon & Schuster, Inc.

Designed by Jeanette Olender
Manufactured in the United States of America

ISBN 0-684-86287-5

This novel is dedicated to my sons,
Vester Jr. and Shannon Develle.
I love you.

A man, like a book, must have an index; he is divided into chapters, sections, pages, prefaces, and appendix; in size, quarto, octavo, or duodecimo, and bound in cloth, morocco, antique or half calf; the dress, the gait, the behavior, are an index to the contents of this strange book, and give you the number of the page.

—Thomas DeWitt Talmage

Acknowledgments

I would like to thank God for giving me the creativity and heart to write this book. I'd also like to thank God for the blessings and the peace of mind that I felt while writing this story. For those of you who haven't had a child incarcerated, I envy you. For those who have, I understand your heartache and I have cried your tears. May God continue to bless you and yours.

Without the help of special people such as Reverend Lavern Washington, my uncle, this book would not have been possible. He always took time to listen and encourage. He was even the inspiration behind the title of this novel. My uncle Lavern and aunt Ruby have been married for almost fifty-two years and I understand why. The Lord has truly blessed them. I only hope that my husband, John, and I will be so fortunate.

I would also like to give thanks to my sister-in-law, Pastor Allene Jackson: a beautiful spirit who knows the Bible like the back of her hand and who gave me excellent advice about Scriptures any time of the day or night. I wish I had as much patience as she has. I would like to thank Bishop Ollie Robins, my uncle who enlightened me, in depth, on the five chapters of Lamentations. Another family member whom I'd like to acknowledge is my brother-in-law, Pastor James Robinson, who has one of the most beautiful and honest smiles that I've ever seen. Our teenaged daughter loves to hear him preach, and she remembers his wise words, even when I've nearly forgotten them. May God continue to bless him and his family.

I would like to thank Mr. Allen Barksdale, of Elmwood Cemetery in Detroit,

Michigan, who provided the information for the heroic and historic souls who are buried there.

Mary Lamberti, the promotional manager of Pro Brazil in New York, who represents authorities of the cities Rio De Janeiro, São Paulo, and Bahia— thank you. Your knowledge and love for this beautiful country in South America was invaluable. Thank you.

I'd like to thank my agent, Dawn Marie Daniels, and her partner, Imar Hutchins, for their tireless commitment to their clients.

I'd like to thank my publicist, Simone Cooper, a top-notch professional, who has become a very good friend.

My new editor, Dominick Anfuso, has been a great help as well. Thanks. You've made my transition to my new publisher a good experience.

Patricia Bozza, my production editor at Simon & Schuster, helped me look good. Thank you.

Especially key to this book was the months of telephone conversations from my dear cousin, Clifford Washington, Sr.

And as always, saving the best for last, I'd like to thank my husband, Mr. John D. Smith. He read this book at least three times during the editing process. I'm constantly amazed by how well we've come to work together. I don't what I'd do without you, sweetie. And I know, at this stage in our lives, you wouldn't know what to do without me. (I hope other married couples realize, like we have, that love doesn't get old, it gets better.) Throughout the years, it's become harder for me to tell you how happy I am being your wife. But, me being an author, you might expect a bit more. I can only say, like Austin Powers in *The Spy Who Shagged Me*, "You complete me."

The Flip Side of Sin

Prologue

When the cries started, he was sleeping in a caramel vinyl La-Z-Boy. He didn't know how long he'd been asleep, but he could hear Claire from *The Cosby Show*, hollering at Cliff, a few yards in front of him. He wasn't positive, but it sounded like Claire was complaining to Cliff about the mess he and Rudy had left in the kitchen after making chocolate chip cookies. She was as angry as a wet cat!

The Detroit News, the *Detroit Free Press*, and the *Michigan Chronicle*, all opened to their classified sections, were lying on the floor beside him. In the center of the living room, several empty food-stamp packages were haphazardly strewn on top of a coffee table.

He found himself licking his lips, imagining that he was eating chicken and egg noodles, smothered with red and green bell peppers. Dessert was hot chocolate chip cookies and a tall glass of cold milk.

These thoughts transported him to a peaceful place, until the irritating sound disturbed him once more.

He felt someone tugging at his legs and his eyes shot open. Looking down, he saw his son trying to climb up on the reclined chair. His son had a tablespoon in one hand and an empty cup in the other.

Sensing someone else was in the semidarkened room, he lifted his eyes wearily to the left side of the room and was relieved to see that his saxophone case was still in the corner where he'd left it.

"You told me to wake you in fifteen minutes," she said, sitting in a chair across from him in a pale green floral gown. She glanced behind her at the clock on the wall that said it was ten-thirty P.M. "That was two hours ago."

"Will you shut that kid up!" He clamped his hands over his ears, but it didn't block out the growl of his empty stomach. The grumbling seemed to get worse.

"The check didn't come today. Your son's hungry."

He sensed her mood and tried to restrain his anger. He knew what was coming. Following her eyes to his saxophone case, he knew what she was thinking. But even though the scent of bell peppers was still tickling his nose, there was no way he was going back to the pawnshop. Three months ago he'd taken so long to come up with the money, the owner had threatened to sell it. Besides, he had a gig to play at Steve's Soul Food Restaurant on Sunday afternoon. How could he make money without his instrument?

She went over and picked up the little boy, shaking him to silence his hungry cries.

"I ain't the mailman. What you want me to do?" His tone was angry.

She fired back, "You got money to buy shit to keep that saxophone pitched and polished, but you can't buy food for your wife and child!"

A part of him tuned out her angry accusations. He'd heard it all before. She was standing just a few inches in front of him, and he could smell the sweet talc coming from her freshly bathed body. Naturally, he felt a little turned on, but mad at the same time. The outline of her body was so profound through the flimsy gown she wore, he had to stop himself from reaching out to touch it. "I hope you're not walking around the house looking like this all day while I'm out trying to find a job."

She ignored him and went into the kitchen. With his teeth clenched to contain his anger, he kicked the telephone book to the side and followed her.

Once in the kitchen, he sensed that she took pleasure in opening every cabinet. They were all as empty as a shopping cart in the supermarket parking lot. One lonely box of Krispy crackers was in the cabinet above the refrigerator, and a jar of chicken bouillon cubes was on the counter.

Removing a single square cracker from the wrapper and handing it to her son, she said, "I can't live like this no more." Balancing her son on the side of her hip, she bent down and snatched a saucepan from a lower cabinet. "I'm tired of hearing your excuses." In a lower tone that he was positive she meant for him to hear, she added that he wasn't supposed to be staying here anyway.

That pissed him off. Why couldn't she say what she felt out loud like a real woman would?

Fury building in the pit of his gut, he watched her look at him from the corners of her eyes. Reaching inside his pockets, he pulled out a crumpled five-dollar bill. "Look here, I'm going to the store. I'll be back with bread, bacon, and eggs."

She turned her back to him and started filling the saucepan with water. He could hear her unwrap something and drop it in the pot. "It's dinnertime, you fool," she said, turning around to face him. She dropped the empty jar of chicken bouillon in the trash, then sat their son down on the floor and handed him another cracker.

"Baby," he said in a compromising tone, before he felt her harsh push against his chest.

"Just get out!" she yelled, her mouth bunching together like a prune. "Get your always-broke-can't-keep-a-job, sick-dick ass out!"

By now the aroma of the imitation chicken was making him dizzy, followed by his constant companion—anger. "This is my house, dammit!"

His harsh voice made his son spit out the cracker he was eating and begin to cry again.

She was already picking up her son when he moved to a spot inches in front of her. "Don't you touch me," she said, stepping back from him. Tears welled in her eyes when she stopped at the counter. She held her son in a protective embrace and wiped away her tears. "You don't pay the rent here." There was a pause between each word. "Section Eight does. Now, I said get the fuck out!"

He reached out to her, pleading, "I'm sorry, I didn't mean it."

She slid toward the wall where the telephone was located. With a shaky finger, she began to dial. "I'm calling the police. I'd advise you to leave before they get here."

Without another word, he picked up the keys to his 1977 Chevy Nova that were lying on the counter beside the toaster and headed toward the back door. When he stopped and turned back around, she was still dialing. He rolled his eyes at her and went back into the living room, retrieved his sax case, and left, slamming the door behind him.

Outside in the cool night air, blood pounded in his head as a mist of rain settled against his skin. He could almost feel the steam rising from his head as he settled into his car and placed his sax on the backseat.

The ignition whined and groaned like a dry windmill in a fifty-mile-an-hour windstorm. The dashboard lights blinked on and off as he tried over and over to get a spark from the engine. Finally, on the fourth try, it started. Once he put the car in reverse, he noticed that the tank was on empty. He grabbed the steering wheel and took a last look at his house. "Fuck this shit," he said as he backed out of the driveway.

I'll let her sleep it off, he thought. *She'll be missing me by morning time.*

The corner store was three blocks away. He stopped, purchased a jumbo can of Colt 45 and three loose Kool cigarettes. After taking a long swig of beer, he drove two more blocks to the Amoco station and put two dollars' worth of gas in the tank.

"Bitch didn't want me there no way." He took another swallow and headed for the freeway. "Yeah, she think she's slick. Got me out here looking for a job all day long, while she's laying on her back fucking the mailman or who knows who."

Oncoming cars zoomed by him, the glare from their high-beam headlights temporarily blinding his vision as he turned down the service drive that led to the John C. Lodge Freeway.

"She must think I'm some kind of fool or sumpin."

Looking around, he realized he didn't have a destination. He stopped and pulled over on the side of the road. *Where in the hell am I going?* Then he remembered his old friend who lived in Royal Oak, just far enough away from the madness to make him forget a few of his problems. That's where he'd bunk tonight. He passed the exit ramp to the freeway and turned down Eight Mile Road, then went north on Woodward Avenue.

A few minutes later he was navigating his way through an upscale subdivision four blocks off the main drag. For a moment, he nearly got lost before he spotted his friend's bleak beige ranch-style home. He parked, finished his beer, and went to ring the doorbell. No one answered. Hopping off the porch, he went to look through the garage windows. It was empty. He was so tired now, he wished he had skipped the beer. Beer on an empty stomach was making him feel nauseated. Feeling a little light-headed, he went back to the house and decided to sit on the porch and wait.

16

While he waited, he noticed that curtains were being drawn back in the homes across the street. A new Cougar drove up next door. The white couple who exited the car stared at him like he was the broke, homeless-ass bum he was.

Fog was beginning to settle in, and the misty rain was beginning to feel as cold as fear. He knew he would have to get inside the house or leave.

Fuck this shit! I can sleep at the State Fair parking lot on Eight Mile Road tonight if the cops don't mess with me.

Back inside his car, he checked to see if there was a drop of beer left in the bottle. Mad, feeling bad and broke, he threw the empty bottle on the floor. Instantly, he felt stupid for hollering at his wife and son. Knowing all the time that if he kept his cool, he could go back home. Sleeping in the State Fair parking lot was a stupid idea. He made up his mind what he would say to her as he drove hurriedly back toward his house.

Two blocks from Woodward Avenue, he was startled by a police car behind him that had just turned on its pursuit lights. *Oh, shit, I hope I haven't been swerving.* When he turned his attention back around, a white blur flashed in front of his wet windshield.

He felt a big thump against the hood of his car, and within every ounce of air around him, he heard a breathless scream that pierced his ears like the sound of a lost Canadian goose.

Instantly, his knees felt weak. His foot felt numb as he began to hit the brakes. There was a loud thud as the saxophone hit the floor. The empty bottle bounced around hitting loose coins, creating a sound like rattling handcuffs. The nervous sweat pouring down his face felt like grease. His car skidded on the slick pavement, and he slammed harder on the brakes.

As the Nova came to an abrupt halt, his head hit the steering wheel. With the tip of his throbbing tongue, he tasted blood inside his mouth. Slowly, he lifted his head and turned to look over his right shoulder. He froze, temporarily frightened by a lifeless object that appeared to be made of papier-mâché.

Suddenly, he remembered what it was. It was where that scream had come from.

The next scream he heard was his own.

1

The Destruction of Detroit

See Us

Let all their wickedness come before thee; and do unto them, as thou hast done unto me for all my transgressions: for my sighs *are* many, and my heart *is* faint.

—Lam. 1:22

Something Wicked This Way Comes

Isaac went eight years without a kiss. To him, the sheer reverence of such a simple expression of love was like strange star-pulses throbbing through space. It felt as if an eternity had passed since he'd felt the tenderness of such pleasure.

The thought of his wife's last kiss made his heart ache—it throbbed now like a new wound. Isaac hoped that the woman who once, with a simple touch, could make his bones ache would be waiting, so that he could once again feel the ecstasy of her lips touching his.

In the twelve years he'd been incarcerated, he'd learned that the natural flight of the human mind was not from pleasure to pleasure but from hope to hope. If he didn't hope, he believed that he wouldn't find what was beyond his hopes.

With his eyes still closed, he pressed rewind, then turned up the volume on his Walkman, and waited to hear Duke Ellington's "Prelude to a Kiss" one more time. Lying on his back, his took a long drag on a cigarette.

"Say, man. You woke in there?" said a voice from the doorway.

Isaac opened his eyes and waved Wide-eyed Willy inside. "I'm up, Willy," Isaac said, accepting the newspaper that Willy handed him.

Today, like every day, all cell doors were open for breakfast at 6:00 A.M. Inmates were free to walk around during that hour period, as well as at exercise and dinner times. The master head count, where the guards actually have to

21

put their eyes on you, began at 11:30 A.M. Three additional counts that occur in every prison in the United States at the same time every day are conducted at 3:30 P.M., 5:50 P.M., and lockdown at 9:30 P.M. This morning, Isaac elected to skip breakfast and remain in his cell.

With his free hand, Isaac reached for the ashtray crammed with butts and tamped out the cigarette. "You want something, Wide-eyed Willy?" Isaac asked when the man took a seat on his bed.

Wide-eyed Willy opened his mouth, then closed it again. A sad expression came over his face when he finally spoke. "I'm gonna miss you, man," he said. He patted Isaac's knee affectionately, then left. Isaac knew the potent scent of alcohol would linger for hours. Wide-eyed Willy was past the midpoint of a nomadic drunk, moving from place to place in search of a drink. He didn't stagger, didn't slur one word. But it showed in the dazzling white glimmer in his eyes. Isaac shook his head. What a waste; Wide-eyed Willy was a decent man.

His happy mood deteriorated even more when he picked up the paper. Pictures of politicians covered the front page of *The Detroit News*. It was election time. For once, the politicians were getting more press than the criminals. From word one, he didn't like the article that a reporter wrote after interviewing Governor Loren Lake.

The Michigan Department of Corrections has only two goals: providing humane treatment for all offenders the courts send them and providing these services at as minimal a cost as possible. And now, in 1998, the costs are so high, they have become unacceptable to the American public.

For the first time in Michigan history, a privatized prison is being built. According to Governor Loren Lake, this new youth facility in Bad Axe, Michigan, will save the taxpayers at least forty million dollars over the span of a few years. Supposedly, the prison will provide two hundred new jobs and generate millions of tax dollars for the city. Theoretically, these new employees would, in turn, purchase homes and send their kids to college, thereby creating a larger tax base for the community. The private prison is hailed as a win-win situation for all.

Bullshit! Isaac thought. He knew the savings were inflated to make the governor look good. There was no way the establishment could cut costs that much. Isaac, along with the other inmates at Jefferson State Penitentiary, was already eating slop, and their living conditions were worse than those of the homeless.

Most inmates kept cans of chili, green beans, and spaghetti in their cells. In the winter they heated the cans on top of the radiators. In the summer some made illegal stingers to heat their meals. After dropping twenty dollars at the commissary in one month, Isaac calculated how much the prison made off what the inmates spent just buying food—$2,372,500.00. He guessed that they made millions from the furniture factory that made office furniture for the state of Michigan and the cigarette factory that sold knock-off brands to dozens of businesses. He was certain that the biggest moneymaker was in the billions—the license-plate factory, which provided plates for Illinois, Colorado, Ohio, and Michigan. *I bet those figures aren't mentioned in any of their reports.*

Even with the problems of food, sanitation, and low self-esteem, the inmates these days were well informed; they had access to every law that was passed about the prison system. They knew the real truth, unlike the Alcatraz prisoners of the sixties, who were deprived of information about what was happening in the outside world and knew only what the officials wanted them to know.

As Isaac continued to read, the lies became more personal.

"We believe that every criminal who is behind bars is a danger to society. These individuals have failed to realize the love of God or mankind. Therefore, the Michigan Department of Corrections cannot comply with the same laws as society, because the population is not the same. However, we do try and ensure that any inmate can practice any religion they want to," Governor Loren Lake said.

Now, a portion of that statement was true, he thought. Out of the fifty-five hundred inmates in Jefferson, only ten or twelve went to church on Sunday. Going to church was the only time you would get to see inmates from the opposite side of the prison. Isaac had gone a few times himself. Unlike his sister, he didn't believe that going to church on a regular basis defined your spirituality. When he was a teenager, some of the biggest hypocrites he knew sat in the front pew and didn't miss a Sunday. For Isaac, religion was a private matter.

However, living in such a huge complex as Jefferson was anything but private. Isaac believed that few people knew how self-sufficient Jefferson was. The prisoners grew enough vegetables to feed the entire complex, raised their own beef, sewed and cleaned their clothing, and even operated their own utilities. It was like a city within a city, and it took three wardens to run it—some inmates called the wardens "mayors."

"Number 823497," the guard hollered over the intercom, "you've got a visitor."

Checking his watch, Isaac smiled. His sister was right on time, as usual, for their bimonthly visit. *Lord, I can hardly wait to be checking out of hotel happiness,* Isaac thought. Tossing the paper in the trash, he left his cell, then paused by Wide-eyed Willy's open door and heard him snoring heavily. He knew Wide-eyed Willy's number by heart—B811444. The *B* prefix meant this was Willy's second tour in prison. There were a few men on his tier that even had *F* prefixes.

He wanted to tell the governor that the *F* men were the individuals who were a danger to society—he wasn't. And certainly not Wide-eyed Willy, who was a harmless, gentle human being. Wide-eyed Willy needed help, not a prison cell.

As he was being led down from D Block to the visitor's area, he began to count—177 steps. The exact number of steps it took to reach the front gate and freedom. But in six more days those steps would mean nothing. All the counting, waiting, dreaming would end.

Most of the men inside Jefferson Penitentiary would probably agree that the temptation of sin is very powerful. Like Al Capone, they could walk into sin one step at a time, but the longer the step, the deeper the sin. Sooner or later, reparations would have to be made, punishable by either death or incarceration.

Others now hoped that one day the Lord would touch them and help them to begin a better life out in the world again. At least, Isaac thought, with his sister Rosemary's prayers, he had a chance.

As he waited for the final door to be unlocked, Isaac glanced out the grimy, barred window. He saw the same familiar scene: razor wire coiled around the top of the sixteen-foot chain-link fence outside; armed guards posted at four forty-foot-high observation towers, watching the actions of the men below. Just before Isaac arrived at Jefferson Penitentiary in 1994, the prison population had gotten so large, they had to break it up into three prisons, with three wardens to run it. For the past four and a half years, he had resided in the middle section.

"Hey, Coltrane," the security guard on the other side of the gate said as he unlocked the door in D Block and let Isaac pass through. Shortly after Isaac's arrival, his music had become so popular among the inmates, they had dubbed him "Coltrane" after the exalted saxophonist John Coltrane. Isaac nodded hello and continued toward his sister, who was already grinning in her same usual manner, as if it were the first time she'd seen him in years.

Isaac dutifully hugged his sister and kissed her on the cheek. "Hi. It's good to see you. Especially when you're looking so pretty."

Rosemary blushed and smoothed the collar of her celery green linen jacket. She was fifteen years older than Isaac, and had always acted more like his mother than his sister. For as long as he could remember, she had worn her hair parted in the middle with a thick French roll in the back. With a full round face and broad forehead, the style still became her. The gentle look in her eyes and the ever-present smile on her full lips said that she was a Christian woman who loved the Lord. Isaac couldn't have been more proud of her.

The crowded room was full of inmates' families chattering away, touching, kissing, and cherishing the short moments they had to spend with their husbands, fathers, brothers, sons, and lovers.

"Morning, Isaac. I heard you're leaving us this week," one of the guards stationed in the visiting area commented.

Before he could respond, Rosemary, with her Bible pressed against her chest, spoke up. "Yes, indeed," she said, smiling. "Seven days from today. That's May second, isn't it?" she asked Isaac, turning back to him.

"I guess so." Isaac avoided her spirited eyes. He couldn't bear to lie to her. With a wide smile pasted on his lips, he took her by the hand and led her to two empty chairs near the window.

So many lives had been changed because he had failed to put his family before his music. He hadn't realized how selfish he'd been back then. This time things would be different.

"We need to talk," he said after she sat down. He dropped down into the hard seat and stretched out his legs. He stuck his hands in his pockets and drew them out again, keeping his eyes aimed at the floor. "I've got some very definite

25

plans made when I get out of here." *My number-one priority is to never be incarcerated again.* "I never claimed to be a saint. So don't be expecting me to go to church every Sunday. I promise you that I *will* go—just don't pressure me."

After a moment, she said, "Okay."

When she closed her eyes, Isaac knew she was praying. He didn't know that she was reciting to herself Jer. 31:3 when she quietly said, " 'The Lord hath appeared of old unto me, saying, Yea, I have loved thee with an everlasting love: therefore with lovingkindness have I drawn thee.' "

"What'd you say?"

She opened her eyes. "Oh, it's nothing," she said, smiling serenely. "Do you mind if I pray for you?"

"No." For a brief moment he was confused. He was so sure she would disagree with him. The awkward moment passed when he heard her chuckle.

"I thought you were going to cut this off," Rosemary said, grabbing the end of his long mane and giving it a firm tug.

"I changed my mind," he said with a smile that wasn't replicated in his saddened eyes. How could he tell his sister that beneath this façade of youthful jet-black hair were patches of roots the color of deep iron gray? Thirty-nine years old and he felt fifty-nine. No, church would have to wait a while. He had other things that needed to be taken care of first. Reaching inside his pocket, he pulled out a rubber band, then threaded his fingers through his thick-cropped top hair until he felt the longer length. Isaac cocked his head toward his sister and forced a smile. "I know what you're thinking. How am I going to get a decent job with my hair this long?" He shrugged his shoulders and swept his straightened hair, as smooth as his late shave, into a neat ponytail. "I'll manage. Remember, being clean-cut in prison is not a prerequisite for getting a job."

"Jesse told me to remind you about his job offer."

Irritation flickered in his eyes, but Isaac merely nodded. "No offense intended, Rosemary. And I hope you know that I don't want to hurt my brother-in-law's feelings. But I ain't the type of man that can work in a funeral home. Uh-huh." His voice emitted sarcasm. "I've spent the last twelve years of my life coexisting with the living dead. I don't want to be working with the actual dead."

"I'm sorry, Isaac. We won't discuss anything so serious right now." She slid her eyes up to his and smiled. "Regardless of where you work, Jesse is anxious to meet you. He's been such a dear helping me to get your room ready."

Shoving both hands in his pockets, Isaac sank down lower in his chair, then lazily crossed his ankles. "That's just till I get on my feet, Rosemary. I'm too old to be living in your basement." Isaac caught himself in time. "I'm sorry, Sis. I know how crowded y'all are and I really do appreciate the offer to let me bunk there." He kissed her cheeks and placed her hands in his.

A woman giggled. Isaac turned to see the woman intimately embraced with an inmate. When he turned back, he noticed the startled look on Rosemary's face. Until she turned around the woman had resembled someone they both knew extremely well—Kennedy.

A year after Isaac was incarcerated he had received divorce papers. "I don't want you to ever mention Kennedy's name to me again!" he had told Rosemary after he'd been officially served. He didn't tell his sister how guilty he felt for abandoning his family. It was his fault. Just like it was his father's fault for leaving him and Rosemary alone when he was three years old. Except for the pictures that Rosemary kept on the fireplace, Isaac couldn't remember what their father looked like. Therefore, his father remained a mere stranger to him, captured in a time warp. Isaac hoped that his son's proclivity toward him wasn't as keen.

"It's okay, Isaac. And I know what's on your mind. You're blaming Kennedy again. That's not fair. It's not her fault, and you know it."

"We don't need to debate this, Rosemary," he seethed. "You and I don't agree about what happened between Kennedy and me, and there's no use in you trying to smooth things out. It's over. I guess I should be thankful that you have any respect left for either one of us considering the way we acted in the past."

Isaac recalled the soul-shattering argument between him and Kennedy. It was late at night. Peyton was barely two years old and somehow had managed to lift the latch and get out the side door. Their neighbors found him on their front porch, half-clothed and crying. They called the police. Someone else called Rosemary. She was so mad at them, she took Peyton home with her for an entire week, until Kennedy and Isaac cooled off.

"Kennedy's done a good job with Peyton and that's what really counts. I can't wait till you see him. He's you all over again. Just seeing him, listening to him talk, brings joy to this old soul of mine."

Isaac's face filled with pride, then, like a black shadow had passed by, was quickly replaced with a frown. "Then you tell me why Kennedy wouldn't let my son come and see me."

That statement stung Rosemary. She turned away from him like a roach does to Raid.

"Rosemary? What's wrong?"

"I can't speak for her, Isaac. I just know in the eyes of the Lord you are the boy's father, and I hope you'll take care of your responsibilities as soon as you get out of here."

"You mean child support." Isaac laughed. "My God. I'm not even out yet and already half my check is tapped." His smile was wry. "Oh, I'll get a job and give Kennedy money every week, just like I should be doing."

Rosemary chose her words carefully. "That's not what I mean, Isaac. Child support will be the least of your concerns. A lot has changed since you've been gone. I'm sure you know the old saying, Isaac, 'Time waits for no man.' Nor does it wait for a woman. I don't want you to get the idea that everything, and everybody, is the same as it was twelve years ago."

"You've told me a thousand times, Rosemary, about things changing." His eyes roved the visitation room continuously, finally settling on the set of glass doors that led to freedom. "I can handle it. I'll work two jobs if I have to."

Her eyes softened when she looked at him. "Even with your degree, it might not be that easy to find work, Isaac. No one's going to forget what you did. Because of all the press, your release is going to bring back a lot of unpleasant memories for many people."

"I realize that, Rosemary. But I've paid my debt to society. I deserve a second chance. Marion Barry got a second chance and he's making the most of it."

"Isaac, a child is dead because of a mistake you made. Some people might not think you're so deserving of that second chance." Rosemary wasn't smiling. They both knew whom she meant—Governor Loren Lake.

Just then, Paps Bowenstein came ambling down the hall. He gave Rosemary a big hug. "How's my Christian sister doing today?" asked Paps, his long salt-and-pepper hair shining like Lake Michigan reflecting the moon at twilight.

Isaac's dark eyes glinted with jealousy when Rosemary mussed Paps's hair as he bent down to hug her.

"You need a haircut," Rosemary told Paps, smiling. "I didn't realize that *you* were such a bad influence on my brother. The both of you need a good shearing."

Paps smiled and winked at Isaac. "I tried to get him to cut his hair this morning." He coaxed Isaac to move over and let the elders sit down, and took his seat. "I knew what you'd say."

"Stop lying, Paps." Isaac felt relieved. His friend couldn't have timed his entrance better. He had been certain that he and Rosemary would soon get into one of their nice arguments.

Again, Isaac was envious. He couldn't understand it. Nearly five years ago, when Isaac first introduced Rosemary to Paps, Rosemary had coldly extended a hand of fellowship. Isaac had attributed it to their different faiths, Paps being a very religious Jew who welcomed an argument with a dedicated Christian. But over the course of time, Rosemary and Paps seemed to get more comfortable with one another. Still, Isaac never understood how or when they'd called a truce. To this day, their religious beliefs were still as wide apart as the Nile River.

Did it matter now? he thought.

"I am just thankful both of you are able to grow hair." She smoothed down a loose strand from her impeccable French twist. "I'm afraid mine is getting a bit thin." She reached inside her purse and withdrew the June edition of *The B'nai B'rith International Jewish Monthly.* "Hot off the presses, Paps. Enjoy."

"Are you forgetting your manners, Isaac? Go get your sister a cold soda from the vending machine." Paps's tone was brisk. "It's warm for April and I'm sure her mouth is parched."

Isaac kept silent. He knew Paps was merely showing off for Rosemary. Once they were back in their cells, they'd both laugh about the entire visit.

"A Diet Coke, please," Rosemary added.

He quickly looked away before she caught him laughing. "Coming right up, Sis." *You'd think,* Isaac thought to himself, *that she would have learned by now that Diet Coke only increased her appetite.* Living with his sister and her husband was going to be like watching Louise and George in the old *Jeffersons* television series.

He dropped the coins in the machine and smiled to himself, savoring his secret.

Later, as Isaac was led back to his cell, he thought about the amusing visit that he had had with his sister. Soon he would have to face the outside world and deal with some unpleasant situations.

Once inside his cell, he took a seat at the small desk and began composing a letter to Kennedy. From the moment he entered the prison system in 1986 he had written Kennedy faithfully every week. She answered, but, little by little, her letters became scarce. By week fifty-seven, he understood why. Divorce papers requiring his signature were enclosed in one of her letters. He refused to sign. Kennedy said that she would get the divorce anyway. Michigan was a no-fault state.

Afterward, Isaac had been so despondent he couldn't eat or sleep. He lost so much weight that Rosemary was concerned about his health. With a heavy heart, he told her about the divorce and asked her never to mention Kennedy's name again. He wrote Kennedy daily, begging her to change her mind. She never answered. Neither daily prayers nor playing his music helped. He was in a state of depression and nothing could shake it. Contemplating suicide was never far from his thoughts. As the years passed, he was moved from one facility to another. He worked like a madman in one factory after another and kept to himself. He finally ended up at Jefferson Penitentiary and was told he'd finish his time there.

Less than a week later, in the winter of 1994, he overheard someone he remembered from his hometown laughing about Kennedy dating his cousin—a police officer. He got into a fight with that mouthy inmate and was put into the hole for ninety days. It was during those lonely moments that his thoughts of suicide resurfaced.

When he was let out, a guard told him that he'd lost his job in the license-plate factory as he carried his belongings to his new home—cell number 80. There were fifty-three additional single cells, filled nearly to capacity. As time passed he learned that he'd been placed in a cell next to Paps Bowenstein, a religious fanatic who never received any visitors, was neater than a nun's habit, and treated people like breathing corpses.

The cell on his right was empty. He would later learn why.

With each passing day, he kept more to himself, rarely leaving his cell. The heat had been unbearable for the entire month of May. The warden's office and visitor's room were the only rooms in the complex that were air-conditioned. It seemed like eons since he'd seen his only visitor, Rosemary.

Throughout 1994, Rosemary had held the position of vice-president of the national and international foreign mission board. Isaac had hid his disappointment the previous month when she had told him that she'd be in Trinidad for the entire month of May.

By the first of June the heat had cooled, but Isaac was still suffering. He slipped further into depression. Why hadn't Rosemary come to see him? He tried praying, but lost faith. He tried exercise, but lost the energy. He tried prayer one last time and began to feel a slight relief.

He experienced a small setback when he received a letter from Rosemary saying how excited she was—the Outreach Ministry of the foreign mission had been asked to build a church in Trinidad. He wasn't exactly excited about the two additional weeks that would delay her coming home.

Sleep was Isaac's only consolation. He had no idea that he was sleeping more than sixteen hours a day. Only through his dreams could he find Kennedy and peace of mind.

Through sleepy eyes one Friday night he watched the men getting their hair braided, shaving, and sharpening the creases in their jeans in preparation for their morning's visitation. He didn't have the will to press on. He no longer felt the desire to play his sax. This was one of many moments in his life when he prayed for his father to discuss his problems with. He needed someone to talk him out of the evil thoughts that pervaded his conscience.

Feeling the need for absolute peace, he made up his mind about what he'd do. Before breakfast began, his pain would end. He decided to write Kennedy—not a letter, as he usually did, but a poem. He titled it what she'd always labeled his current habitat, "That Place":

*In the calm of Summer's night, **I sleep.** My head bowed low. My eyes shut tight, closing out rays of blue moonlight. And I drift into an endless space, and find a realm, a different place. Where there's no race or creed or face. And I long to be part of that place. In the peace of a Springtime day, **I rise.** My head held* *high. My body upright—bathed in gleaming rays of light. And I drift into an endless space, and find a realm, a different place. Where there's no race or creed or face. And I long to be part of that place. In the still of Autumn's eve, **I wish.** My mind soars high. With the colors of my imagination—and thoughts of beauty of the creation. And I drift into an endless space, and find a realm, a different place. Where there's no race or creed or face. And I long to be part of that place. In the early years of my life, **I love.** My love flows freely. My heart beats gallantly. Driving me on, lovingly. And I drift into an endless space, and find a realm, a different place. Where there's no race or creed or face. And I long to be part of that place. In the setting of my sun, in the dawn of my final hour, **I smile.** Boldly. And praise God, and greet him proudly. And I drift into an endless space, and find a realm, a different place. Where there's no race or creed or face. And I long to be part of that place. In the eternity of my passing, in the realms I seek beyond, **I see** all things that created me. As I drift into the endless space, I find a realm, a different place. Where there's no race or creed or face, and become part of my resting place.*

At precisely six A.M. the following morning, the guards pulled the switch that unlocked all the cell doors. Trustees came down the corridor with mops so that the inmates could clean their floors. In trancelike movements, Isaac headed directly for the rail. Growing numb from the feet up, like someone stepping deeper and deeper into a stream of ice water, he proceeded to climb over the rail.

"Hey!" someone yelled.

Just as quickly, he felt strong hands snatching his shirt, yanking him back to safety. Isaac shuddered. He felt a coldness so strange inside him, it was as if his soul had left his body.

"Heaven help you, son," Paps whispered to Isaac. It wasn't uncommon for inmates to jump from the second and third galleries, falling nearly forty feet to their deaths. Few survived. Usually no one tried to stop them—most felt it was none of their business. Fortunately, today, for Isaac, someone had.

Isaac was taken to the infirmary and put on antidepressants. When Paps came to see him, Isaac was ashamed. "Has anyone contacted my sister?"

"No." He cleared his throat. "Under the circumstances, I thought it was better not to. I'm told that your sister is a very religious woman."

"She is. And suicide . . ."

"Is an unpardonable sin, Isaac." His tone turned even more serious. "Life can be heaven here on earth if only you'll fight for it. The *only* way a man like you can win is through education. Without that, society will feel that you're just another body taking up space."

It didn't take long for Isaac to digest the meaning behind Paps's words less than a month after their initial introduction: "You speak of hope, Isaac. But is hope only a more gentle name for fear?"

Isaac felt crushed. This man had managed to get a quick glimpse of his soul.

"What are your strengths, Isaac? What are your weaknesses?" He paused and looked directly into Isaac's iron eyes. "Always have a contingency plan. The way to assure a secure future is through education."

Paps's words sunk in in no time and Isaac quickly enrolled in a community college that held satellite classes less than ten miles from Jefferson Prison. After two weeks, he felt like a new man. That night, after Paps had begun to snore, Isaac got on his knees and said, "I realize now that as long as I'm alive, there is hope, and as long as there is hope, there is the possibility of change."

Four short years later, Isaac's friendship with Paps had grown. When he received his B.A. in journalism, he knew it was the most important accomplishment he'd made in his life—even more than any feeling he'd ever gotten from his music.

During Isaac's progression back to normalcy, he was startled one day by the erotic scent of musk perfume. "Hey, there, handsome," the female guard said to Isaac.

"Hey," he answered, though she was a sight for sore eyes. Funny, he thought, he hadn't paid too much attention to the guards until now. He felt as if the deep sleep he'd been in was a bad dream and he was finally able to wake up.

Standing before him was a warm-blooded woman. It didn't matter that she looked like Wesley Snipes with breasts; she was still a woman.

She took her time easing by his cell, until she felt sure that she'd gotten his attention. The woman, *fortunately*, had a great body. At this point, though, it really didn't matter.

"Hi. I'm Allison." Her second-skin blouse and seductive smile left little to the imagination.

"Hey. Folks around here call me Coltrane."

"I know," she said matter-of-factly.

Within days, Allison had set up a phony shakedown of his cell.

Isaac finally felt his first kiss. Throughout the twenty-second encounter, Kennedy's face remained as clear as the wind.

One day Allison whispered, "I've got a plan. I know how we can meet."

The following week she put the plan into effect. The empty cell beside him would serve as a rendezvous for their weekly sexual encounters.

He learned later that as the guards were rotated every day through the thirteen blocks, Allison had other lovers, as most female guards did, in each one.

Still, he'd been kissed.

It didn't matter that she had other lovers. It didn't matter that he knew he didn't care about her.

This was prison. Nothing was for keeps.

As Paps said, only your mind could set you free. He envisioned Kennedy's face as he made love to this faceless creature.

When he had filled out the mounds of paperwork needed for a Pell Grant, he had also pictured Kennedy's smile. It had kept him focused. It had given him hope.

Allison called him "Alex Haley" because he wrote all the time. She never knew that he called her "Kennedy" each time he had an orgasm.

Thinking back on that now, Isaac lit a Cruise cigarette, inhaled, then slipped a clean sheet into the typewriter. Allison had gotten pregnant and gone back to the welfare rolls she was on before she became a guard. No matter how deep in passion, Isaac had taken precautions not to impregnate her. Even though he cared about Allison, he knew the child wasn't his and was thankful that the relationship had finally ended. It was time to think about home—about love.

Kennedy.

Even though his ex-wife hadn't answered his letters in the past, he felt certain that she *did* read them.

As he typed, he saw himself sitting at a journalist's desk with a shirt and tie on. He was earning a decent salary and providing a comfortable living for his wife and son. Taking a long drag on the Cruise, it tasted as good as it smelled.

He estimated that it would take about three months to get his plan into action. He felt that he would be reunited with his family by summer's end. But he also realized, with sadness, that he'd be leaving behind the best friend he'd ever known.

The words to Kennedy came easily for him. But how could he ever find the right words to say good-bye to Paps after they had been living together for four years? After he had helped him turn his anger and depression into accomplishments? He wouldn't try, because every con lives for the day when he's leaving or saying good-bye to someone else who's leaving. He was sure that Paps would understand if he was at a loss for words. Isaac was giving Paps his books, typewriter, and twelve-inch color television set.

Upon hearing the sounds of the guards shouting "Lights out in five minutes," Isaac crumpled the paper in his hands and tossed the letter in the trash. He would speak to Kennedy face-to-face. Letters were a coward's mode of communication.

Like the feeling one gets when stepping deeper and deeper into a stream of ice, on his last night of being locked up, the actual realization of finally being released from prison left Isaac feeling temporarily numb.

At three in the morning, Isaac was startled by the sound of a man's screams.

"Please don't do it, man. I'm begging you!"

Less than thirty feet away, Isaac heard the hollow sound of an empty can falling on the cement floor, followed by the unmistakable scent of lighter fluid.

"I thought you was my bitch!" another man hollered. "My main bitch."

Isaac removed the "hawk" from his desk and extended it through the bars. Angling the four-inch-square glass object to the right, then the left, he spotted a small yellow coin envelope lying on the floor in front of one cell. The envelope was nearly flat, with a cartoon character emblazoned on front.

As the arguing became more and more heated, Isaac wanted a cigarette, badly. But he couldn't bring himself to light a match. While he continued to watch and listen, he knew what was about to happen.

Apparently the weaker of the two had snitched to one of the guards the source of his lover's drugs that were coming in from the outside.

"Please, Marv, I didn't mean it. I'm sorry, baby," he cried. "I'll make it—"

"Fuck you! Punks like you are a nickel a dozen."

Hoarse cries, then silence. Isaac could smell the sulfur. The man screamed and screamed as flames engulfed his cell. Isaac removed the hawk. He couldn't bear to watch.

Sure, the guards would come eventually, but not now, they knew better. The cons ran the prison and everybody knew it.

Back on his bunk, he covered his ears with his pillow, trying to drown out the screams that he prayed would end soon.

At some point that night the numbness disappeared and was abruptly replaced with fear. Was he afraid of freedom now that it had finally arrived? He couldn't find the words to define his thoughts, and he felt frustrated.

Seconds later, the smell of burning flesh and fresh spud juice replaced his frustration. He thought he would vomit.

Nearby, Wide-eyed Willy was making up a fresh brew. Spud juice was made in a five-gallon bucket with two large cans of tomato juice, four pounds of sugar, one tablespoon of yeast shaken up in a small container of hot water, and roughly three gallons of water. A lifetime alcoholic, Wide-eyed Willy was never out of spirits. Unlike the old James Cagney movies, in which the concoction called spud juice took ten to fourteen days to ferment, these days the inmate didn't have time to hide the brew for nearly two weeks. The new spud juice took merely forty-eight hours and was 90 proof. It was just like imbibing vodka and tomato juice.

Hearing the man being burned was a horrible experience. But the smell of alcohol made Isaac remember the reasons why he was here. Why a part of him feared going home.

Alcohol.

If he hadn't made the decision to have one more beer and had brought the bread, bacon, and eggs back instead, he might be home with his family today. His entire life had been changed because of his decision to have one more drink.

"Hey, Wide-eyed Willy!" Paps hollered. "I'm getting a contact high over here."

"Shut up, Paps," Wide-eyed Willy yelled. "I'm mixing up a big batch. Me and Tim here thought Coltrane could celebrate with us tonight."

Isaac spoke up. "No, thanks, man. I'll pass. But I appreciate the thought."

"Just like I thought," Tim mumbled. "He thinks he's too good for our shit, man! You shouldn't have offered him a fuckin' thang."

"Isaac?" Paps strong voice came from his cell. "Don't pay them no mind. You need to stay positive. You're leaving in the morning. This stuff tonight don't mean nothing. Remember that the corrections facility is only a prognosis. The powers that be believe that you'll be okay once you get out. Your mind can adapt to anything. Even your environment. Put this stuff behind you. Otherwise, your prognosis for being successful will be just like Dumb and Dumbsheba down the aisle from us."

"Thanks for the advice, old fella."

When he heard Paps shuffle back to his bunk, Isaac turned to his side and removed his framed degree from the wall. He cherished the document—seeing his full name inscribed in the center. It angered him that he'd received his degree in prison and not in the outside world. Seventy-four other inmates had graduated with him. Fortunately, there wasn't a hint that he'd received the document from a prison facility. He closed his eyes and paraphrased a prayer from Hebrews: "God, free me from the bitterness I feel and help me to live this day in gratitude for all the good that has happened in my life." Within seconds, he felt a tremendous chill of fear returning. He wondered if society would give him a chance or condemn him, as if he would always be like the violent characters on the television show *Oz*.

Isaac removed his flashlight from beneath his mattress and took this un-orthodox moment to look through all the pictures he'd accumulated over the years—pictures showing his son's growth from age two and a half to age fifteen, and his new brother-in-law, whom he'd spoken to on the phone but never met. There was even a picture or two of Kennedy that Rosemary had sent him—something else that he couldn't leave with Paps.

By six that morning Isaac still hadn't been able to sleep. He remembered a Scripture from the Bible (Phil. 4:7) that Rosemary often cited: "And the peace of God, which passeth all understanding, shall keep your hearts and minds through Christ Jesus." Tired and decidedly excited about going home, he listened to the easy snores of Paps in the cell beside him—a man who'd sounded so placid when he told Isaac that he would never be free. Paps's sentence was for natural life. Though they had never discussed his crime, Isaac believed that Paps had acted out of poor judgment. Like himself, Isaac felt that Paps was a victim of circumstance. He didn't want to gloat about his freedom in Paps's face and was thankful that the old man was finally able to find solace and was sleeping peacefully. Since Paps was nearly seventy years old, Isaac knew that he needed at least seven hours of sleep. He probably wouldn't wake until eleven or twelve.

At ten minutes after seven, when Isaac returned to his cell after shaving and showering, to his astonishment, Paps was awake and brushing his teeth. *Possibly it was for the best,* Isaac thought.

They exchanged hugs and best wishes, then silently shook hands. They both wanted to keep it short. Just moments before the bureaucracy began at eight A.M., Isaac promised Paps that he would write him when he was settled.

By eleven that morning, Isaac still hadn't been cleared through the system. It seemed that there was another Isaac Coleman incarcerated in Jefferson. It didn't matter that the man wasn't black. Every precaution had to be made, they told him, to make sure the proper man was released. The paperwork had to be completely reworked, and new signatures acquired.

Isaac waited.

He relived the cries of last night.

He relived Becky's cries (the child he accidentally killed twelve years ago).

As a cloud filled with fire, tears of shame filled his heart. He could barely breathe. He thought about Peyton. He thought about Kennedy. But Rosemary's prayers were the blinding force that helped him to pray for patience.

Even though he felt as humiliated as he ever had in his life, he sat there. Silent. Fuming. He felt the bitterness rising like bile in the pit of his stomach. Within seconds he felt torturous sweat build between his toes, inside the waistband on his briefs, between each vein along his inner wrist, in the crevice on the back of his neck, around his collar, and, finally, around the corners of his eyes, and he prayed that they weren't tears. Trying to keep from watching the precious seconds tick by on the clock, he turned to look outside. He told himself that he had to be patient, quiet—and not give them one more reason not to set him free.

Isaac turned around when he heard the turnkey unlocking the barred door. "You're good to go, Coltrane," the man said. "Follow me."

His knees felt as if they would buckle beneath him when he stood up. Finally, he thought, tugging on his shirttail to try and still his trembling hands—it was over. He received his release papers and all of his personal items, including the hundred dollars in cash that the state provided to every inmate once he was released.

By eleven-thirty A.M. a taxicab was called to take him to downtown Jefferson six miles away to catch the bus. Then he was led to the front gate by a guard named Vinnie.

"I'm sure you've heard, Mr. Coleman, that most inmates come back within the first ninety days. If you can make it past that, chances are you'll stay out for life." He extended his hand and shook Isaac's. "I believe you can do it. Take care, man."

Once outside the gate, the cool wind touched his cheeks. Lively birds dove into the heart of the sky. The small faces of flowers floated out of the ground. It was odd, he thought, he hadn't felt this alive in years. Inhaling the freshness, he set down his baggage. It was unbelievable. His first breath of free air actually smelled better than it did in the outside exercise area. It was like it wasn't the same air. He turned around to look back at the building where rats, roaches, bats, and birds also made their homes. It was known as the nation's largest birdcage. Isaac was relieved to finally be set free from Jefferson.

He removed the sax, which was poking out the top of his bag. Turning the instrument over in his hands, he realized that it felt odd to him now. It no longer held the power that he'd felt from it years earlier.

While he was incarcerated, he felt that his music never sounded quite right inside there, bouncing off cinder-block walls. Paps loved to hear him play. He talked about what great talent and potential he had.

It was nearly noon and cloudy out when the taxi arrived, but Isaac still felt a renewed source of energy. He hesitated before getting inside and asked the driver to wait a second. Going over to the trash bin, he reached inside his large bag and tossed every piece of clothing that had his six-digit identification number on it, and decided to chuck the sax as well. He felt as if he'd just rid himself of the devil and the weapons he'd used to hold him hostage.

Alex Haley. Coltrane. Ha! His name was Isaac Coleman. He wanted to shout it out loud. "I'm finally free!"

Ten minutes later, as he was stepping up onto the Greyhound bus, he stifled a laugh. It was the first time he'd ever rode one. He handed the driver his ticket and found a seat near the back.

And he thought once more about Kennedy. A kiss. A long, long kiss—the kiss of youth and love. He realized that it was the passion that was in a kiss that gave it its sweetness—the affection in the kiss that sanctified it.

Two hours and seventy-five miles later, he'd be home and a heartbeat away from his true love.

Thunder Road

With each mile that passed, each stop the bus made, he rehearsed the words to the story he would tell Rosemary when she discovered that he'd lied about his release date.

Resting his head back against the seat, he told himself that it was better to trust his instincts. There was no way that Rosemary would understand that he needed to be alone on his journey back home. It was a selfish act, he knew—and one that he wasn't sure he could explain.

When the bus made its last stop in Belleville, Isaac was down to his last four Cruise cigarettes. Most of the riders got off, stretched, and purchased snacks for their kids. It was just after four, and the sky had turned an eerie dark gray. By the time they reboarded and were back on the freeway, thunder rumbled in the foreground. Within minutes, streaks of silver raced through it, causing fear to the child in the seat in front of him.

As the bus approached the exit sign for Lower Huron Metro Park, Isaac half-listened as the mother's loving words consoled the child. He hadn't heard a child's voice in so many years, he'd nearly forgotten the time that he and Kennedy had last visited the park. It was the Fourth of July holiday weekend back in 1985. Peyton, at two and a half years old, had just been toilet trained. Isaac was so proud for Peyton to put on his first swimming trunks without a diaper. But when he and Kennedy sat Peyton down in the kiddie pool, Peyton hollered like he'd just been spanked.

"I'm cold. Take me out, Mommy!" Peyton cried, clutching his toy against his tummy. "I want out!"

"No," Isaac said. "He's a big boy now. It's time he acted like one." Removing the Batman action figure from Peyton's chubby hands, Isaac climbed into the pool with him. Kennedy's eyes filled with tears as she watched Isaac attempt to help his son adjust to the cool water.

Two other boys who looked the same age as Peyton were swimming like ducks. Isaac was determined that Peyton could do the same.

He was wrong.

A few of the other children near them began to cry as Peyton's screams got louder. Some of the parents appeared irritated as their kids warded off splashes of water from Peyton's constant kicking. Finally, Kennedy had enough. This day marked the beginning of continuous arguments over Kennedy's babying Peyton. Drowning out Isaac's heated words, she picked up Peyton's tiny body from the water and ran back toward their picnic area. Isaac cooled off in the pool for a short while, feeling even more stupid in the matching Batman trunks that Kennedy had insisted he and Peyton wear— trunks that he believed to this day were really underwear.

He laughed, remembering.

Funny, he thought, even as the thunder crackled louder and the rain coated the windows, the woman in front of him had managed to console her child, rocking him to sleep. He had to wonder if Kennedy had been right for being so protective of their son, and if Peyton, now fifteen, had ever learned how to swim.

When the bus passed by the Detroit Metropolitan Airport, the roar of planes landing and taking off grabbed his attention—he'd never been on a plane.

A few miles ahead, he noticed that the sixty-foot-high Uniroyal tire was still there. Less than five miles later, the larger-than-life–sized Marlboro man sign was lit up like smoking was still fashionable and sexy. But the ad was different. It read: I WISH I HAD QUIT SOONER. Isaac had planned on quitting the cancer sticks before he left Jefferson, but he hadn't managed it.

Ten more short miles and he'd be home. His palms felt sweaty, and he reached inside his pocket for a stick of Doublemint gum.

When the bus turned off the John C. Lodge Freeway, he was surprised to see the west end of downtown look totally different. Where was the bus terminal off the Lodge?

A line of new apartments to the right looked like an implant from *The Truman Show.*

While he was looking at the new buildings, the bus turned before he expected it to. Had they forgotten to let him off? Glancing out the window, he spotted the sign for the Detroit Terminal a dozen yards ahead of them on Lafayette Street. The new, larger terminal was located adjacent to the internationally known King's bookstore—the largest in Michigan—where Isaac had spent hours going through boxes of old and rare sheet music.

Getting off the bus at 6:40 that evening, the station was thick with travelers arriving and leaving. Knowing he couldn't smoke in Rosemary's house, Isaac tossed the remainder of the pack of cigarettes in the trash and headed out the door to hail a taxi.

As he passed all the familiar surroundings of home, he paused to wonder if Rosemary was home. Suddenly he realized that not telling anyone he was coming was a stupid idea. What if she wasn't home? Out of town for the weekend? Then what would he do? He did *not* want to spend his first night back in a motel.

Fortunately, when the taxi stopped in front of 17587 Freeland Street, he noticed that several lights were on inside the house, and then he spotted the rear end of Rosemary's white Mercury Marquis parked in the garage. Jesse answered the door. The small man recognized him immediately. Isaac expected a handshake, but when Jesse opened his arms to hug him, the sincere welcome he felt was more than he could have imagined.

Jesse picked up Isaac's bags and led him to the kitchen. Rosemary was sitting at the kitchen table, reading glasses pushed down low on her small nose, which was deep in the Bible.

She blushed. "My God! You're home!" Her hands flew against her heart as she jumped up to hug and kiss him. Isaac let out a long breath. For a brief moment, he thought she would hug the life out of him.

After Rosemary introduced Isaac to Jesse and he assured her that he was neither hungry nor tired, Rosemary excused herself, crying, to use the telephone.

Jesse was smaller in person than he looked in his picture. He was around five-feet-six and maybe 150 pounds. Thick, furry eyebrows nearly hid his deep-set brown eyes that were amazingly gentle. His black-and-gray-streaked hair was nearly bald on top, making him look much older than his thirty-five years.

While Rosemary called every friend she knew to tell them about Isaac's homecoming, Jesse took the time to show Isaac the room downstairs that he and Rosemary had prepared for him. As he did so, Jesse told him about the elaborate funeral he had presided over where no one showed up, not even the man who paid for it. Isaac relaxed. He felt comfort in knowing that in Jesse Jones's version of *The Jeffersons,* all was well in the house.

He had been afraid that Jesse would be an uptight religious freak and he would be ready to move by Monday morning. His fears were unfounded. Jesse was as normal as he was.

By the second day, he and Jesse had bonded like blood brothers. And it was a relief to finally admit to him, man-to-man, about not wanting to work at his funeral home.

"Say, Isaac," Jesse said after a fattening dinner of butter beans, rice, and smoked turkey wings, "I can take the day off work tomorrow and help you with your things."

Rosemary answered before Isaac could. "Mmmm, Mr. Jones, I don't think that's a good idea. Kennedy called here this morning while you two were at Builders Square finding screws for the vacuum cleaner. I told her that Isaac needed to get into her garage to get his stuff. She didn't sound too happy."

"Don't tell me you've stooped to gossiping, Rosemary," Isaac teased.

"No. But I know her a little better than you do right now. Working for the Detroit Police Department has changed her. Hardened her a little. You're probably going to be surprised."

Was she trying to tell him something? Isaac didn't like it. Even though he knew he wanted Kennedy back, he hadn't even hinted at this to Rosemary.

Did his sister know him that well?

Later that night, he checked his stash that he'd hidden between the pages of the photo album. He counted and recounted the twenty-four hundred dollars he had worked for and saved the past twelve years while he was in prison. If he hadn't gone to school, he would have saved at least two thousand more. Until he got a job, he'd have to watch every penny.

With more time on his hands than money, he knew it would take a while to haul his stored belongings from Kennedy's attic and garage over to Rosemary's basement. The following day a neighbor of Kennedy's was there to give him several bags of clothing that Kennedy had brought down from the attic. To his surprise, they smelled like Snuggle fabric softner. He knew it must have taken her hours to wash it all. That pleased him, but he realized, as Kennedy must have, that she couldn't avoid him forever.

Forever turned out to be early Sunday morning.

"Hello, Isaac," Kennedy said casually as she exited her car. He'd just finished with the garage, and it looked a mess.

His words came in slow motion as he stared at her. "I'll be back to clean up as soon as I'm settled." Love, beauty, passion, and lust overwhelmed him all in the same moment. He had on an old pair of khaki pants and a beige and brown muscle shirt that she'd washed and which still fit him well. He didn't have to tell her that they would—apparently she knew him a little bit better than Rosemary did.

Kennedy's gaze studied him from head to toe then back. There was a half-smile on her lips, but she kept silent, watching him.

He had to tear his eyes away from her tender lips.

Isaac could feel new sweat merge with the moisture above his lips. Her eyes held him hostage now, as they always had. Naturally arched eyebrows framed her large, luminous, wide-set cat-brown eyes that were still white with youth. A lovely mole on the right side of her mouth highlighted the deep cleft in her chin. When he was a teenager, his idol had been Elizabeth Taylor. He felt that Liz was the sexiest woman he'd ever seen or would see during his lifetime. When he first met his wife-to-be, Liz began to look like the aging Blanche Dubois in *A Streetcar Named Desire.* Sex appeal suddenly had a new name— Kennedy.

His instincts told him that Kennedy still cared about him even though she hadn't written to him or been over to Rosemary's to welcome him back home. After all, why hadn't an attractive woman like herself remarried? Didn't that mean something?

"What time will Peyton be home? I can't wait to see him." He hid his disappointment that she hadn't brought Peyton by to see him yet. Isaac was certain that Rosemary's first call on Friday was to Kennedy.

She took two strides toward him. "He should be back in a couple of hours. I'll bring him by Rosemary's later, if it's not too late?" She stood so close to him now, he could smell the cinnamon-flavored gum she was chewing. "Will you be finished and cleaned up by then?"

He nodded yes and was relieved when she walked away and went into the house.

The trunk and backseat of Rosemary's car were so full, Isaac could barely see out the rear window as he backed out of the driveway and hurried toward home.

In less than an hour he had unloaded the car and changed his clothes and he was anxiously waiting for Peyton's arrival.

The waiting was like standing before a firing squad. He felt more nervous now than he had before he was let out of prison. What if Peyton refused to see him? What would his son think about him being an ex-con? Smoothing his ten-inch ponytail that was still wet from the shower, he wondered what would his son think about his long hair? So many what-ifs caused him to feel as if he'd been shot in the heart and couldn't die fast enough.

Their meeting was worse than Isaac had imagined it would be. Even though he hadn't seen his son in years, he hoped that the bond of blood between them would bridge the loss of many years of separation. But the moment he first set eyes on his teenage son, his hopes left like a faded watercolor in a painted dream. Isaac could sense immediately that Peyton was an angry young man looking for answers.

"Hey, Isaac," Peyton had said to him, not bothering to shake his outstretched hand.

"Who gave you permission to call me Isaac? You know who I am. Don't you ever address me as Isaac again, no matter what you think. If you don't feel comfortable calling me Dad or Father, just leave the label off until you do."

He looked just like Isaac had imagined that he would, except a little taller.

Peyton stood back, cocky, making the most of the two inches in height he had over his father's six-foot-one-inch frame. "Cool," Peyton responded, his lynx eyes scanning Isaac as though he were a tick on a dog. "No disrespect intended."

"I realize our meeting is going to be a little awkward, but in time we'll get to know each other better." Isaac forced a smile. He thought he'd had it all planned out. What he would say. Instead, Peyton's penetrating gaze made him forget his rehearsed speech. "How about coming downtown with me and shooting some pool? Whatever questions you may have I'll answer as honestly as I can. But I hope you'll give us some time to get to know one another first."

Peyton pretended not to hear him. "Hey, Pops, where's your car?"

"I don't have one yet. We can take the bus."

The look on Peyton's face was one of complete surprise and disgust. "I don't ride the city bus, man. Maybe we can do this later." Peyton shrugged and turned to walk away.

"Peyton, please. I know this isn't easy for you. This isn't easy for me either. But I promised your mom and myself we would get to know each other one way or another." That was a small lie. He hadn't verbally told her so, but he had mentioned it in the last letter that he'd written to her. How he wished he could go back twelve years. Things would be so different now between him and his son.

"Hold up." Peyton swiveled around to face his father. Anger was written all over his face. "You taking time with me because of my mom. I don't need this headache, man. I don't know you. I don't want to know you."

"Peyton—"

"Naw, I'll tell my mom we talked. Boom. We bonded. Boom. Everything's cool between us. But personally, man, between you and me, I really haven't got time. As far as I'm concerned, my mama is my daddy." He turned up his nose like he had smelled burned broccoli.

Isaac held his temper as he watched his son walk away from him. Nothing could deaden the pain he felt at that moment.

Later that night, Kennedy called and cursed him out so badly about his meeting with Peyton, he was speechless. She hadn't even given him the opportunity to explain. Was he crazy to believe that she still wanted him back?

He hurt his sister's feelings when he refused to eat Sunday dinner and elected to retreat to his lodgings in the basement. Once there, he prayed for sleep. He needed a break from the realities of life's daytime dramas. Thankful for his little room in Rosemary's basement—with a twin bed, dresser, table, television, small stereo, and his old record player—he was surprised to discover during the course of an eight-hour period that he couldn't sleep. Several times during the night he rose and went to the bathroom just outside his room. For more than an hour he sat on the toilet seat, listening to the quiet and enjoying the privacy. It was such a pleasure to hear nothing. For the first time in a long time, the silence was beautiful.

For more than a decade he had heard voices throughout the night—screaming, crying, and sometimes just loud conversations. This tranquillity would take some getting used to.

To Isaac's chagrin, that nightly ritual went on for a week, and he couldn't help but wonder how long it would take to free himself from the shadows of his past.

He told himself that if he could keep his mind off Kennedy for five minutes, he might be able to fall asleep. By three o'clock Sunday morning, he'd had enough. Getting out of bed, he moved to the narrow window and opened it. From where he stood he could see a fine silver mist clinging to the neatly mowed lawn. He inhaled the sweetness of the earth's fragrance, and for a brief moment felt as free as the whispering air blowing outside. Now he was where he was supposed to be, away from the madness.

Isaac crouched beside his bed and, reaching beneath it, pulled out the one item from Kennedy's garage that had brought back pleasant and unpleasant memories all at once.

Reaching inside the battered case, he lifted the base of the shiny instrument, attached the neck, then the mouthpiece. As he did so, it began to squeak like a newborn gerbil. Holding the neck in his left hand, he removed the cork rings and applied a drop of cork grease, then put it back together. Giving it a final polish on his underwear, he sat up straight and positioned the sax on the right side of his body. Placing his left and right thumbs in the correct positions he gently curved his fingers along the cool keys. He hesitated before resting his top teeth on the mouthpiece. With his chin flat and pointed, he placed the tip in his mouth and began by first inhaling through the corners of his mouth. After listening to the sound inside his mind first, he began to test the tone of his instrument. He felt as though his whole life were at stake; one wrong note could mess everything up. Music was his life force, and once abandoned life itself meant very little for a dedicated musician. This was his true essence—his own small world where no one could judge him.

The tone was nearly perfect. When Isaac closed his eyes, the cool metal buttons on his saxophone beneath his fingers felt like a wet dream. He licked his lips, placed the mouthpiece near the back of his tongue, then slowly and softly placed his lips around it. The reed's salty taste felt comforting, like a wine connoisseur tasting vintage wine and savoring its bouquet. When his eyes opened, his cheeks gradually filled with air like a 44-D breast filled out a Cross Your Heart bra. The first note made a moaning sound like a virgin's cry at the sensation of her first orgasm. He hadn't realized how nervous he was. The sound suggested a thrust for the power that lay within the body of the man finding harmony within himself, the music vibrating from his flesh and reaching deep into the marrow of his bones. Fresh sweat ran along his forehead, jiggled along his eyebrow, then evaporated into his closed eyelids.

Near his feet as he played was his collection of albums and forty-fives from the sixties and seventies. It was a compilation of music that was priceless.

By now, Isaac was up on his feet. The sweat felt heavy against his forehead. As he played he wished for a lot of things. But how many wishes did God grant one man? he wondered. Surely not the one he had made twelve years ago, that Kennedy would wait for him.

He couldn't give up now, he thought. Lowering the sax to his knees, he began to blow a tune low and deep, so that he wouldn't awaken anyone. He played even lower and the music seemed to whisper to his soul. The peaceful sound nearly brought tears to his eyes, it was so intense. The most eerie feeling came over him then. He remembered the hungry cries, the accusations, the screams, the handcuffs, and then his own silent screams. Tears of shame filled his eyes; he was afraid that bonding with his son would be much harder than he'd anticipated.

All I need is a little time, he thought.

Even though he'd applied for work at the employment office, Isaac found himself with tons of time on his hands. It frightened him. There was no one to tell him what time to eat—what time to bathe—what time to go to bed at night. And he found himself wondering, as each minute passed when he was alone, why each minute seemed like an hour.

But he couldn't help but remember reading a passage by Francis Quarles while he was in prison. It said: "Make use of time if thou lovest eternity; yesterday cannot be recalled, tomorrow cannot be assured; only to-day is thine, which if thou procrastinate, thou losest; and which lost is lost forever. One today is worth two tomorrows." Isaac firmly believed in yesterday, but he also believed in tomorrow. If he hadn't, he would have lost all hope years ago that one day he'd be back home.

Notorious

"Take care of business," Johnnie "J-Rock" Johnson said to Terry "T-Money" McCants, then winked his right eye. J-Rock lit a cigar, then turned around and smiled at Peyton. They called Peyton "Little Caesar" because, at the age of thirteen, he had been the youngest member ever to join the Prophets. "Go with him, Little Caesar." His voice was as cold as Forest Hills in mid-January.

They were parked off Grand River. A dead-end street downtown. The Detroit River looked silver in the darkness, picking up the shadow of the man who stood near the edge of the water.

I don't want no part of this shit.

Peyton was sitting in the backseat of the black Navigator wishing he hadn't come. He knew what was going to happen and was too afraid to say anything. In the past six months J-Rock had begun to change. He no longer treated Peyton like his little brother, as he had in the beginning. J-Rock had gone from being a mentor, teaching Peyton how to become a man—gaining the respect of people, especially since he was so tall—to being an individual whom Peyton barely understood. J-Rock had teased Peyton about his size 17 gym shoes and predicted that Peyton would be six feet ten inches by the time he was nineteen. Those types of things made him feel like the Prophets were good people. A family—they looked out for one another.

Peyton could hear T-Money checking his clip, then cocking it back. "I'm ready."

J-Rock turned his cigar and stared at the tip. "Do it, then."

When T-Money opened his door, Peyton reluctantly got out of the backseat of the truck.

"C'mon, Little Caesar," T-Money whispered, "let's get this shit over with."

49

It happened so fast, Peyton couldn't believe his eyes.

"That you, J-Rock?" the man asked when they approached him.

"No, my man. It's T-Money." He swiftly removed the gun that was concealed at the back of his waistband and fired.

The man merely said, "Why?"

Peyton stepped back, horrified, while T-Money lit a cigarette. He shot the man again in the chest. Smoked. Shot. He continued puffing and shooting, puffing and shooting, until Peyton spoke up.

"Stop it, T-Money." He was backing up as he talked, turning around to see if J-Rock had left them. "The first shot killed him."

T-Money pretended not to hear him and emptied his gun. When Peyton reached the car and saw T-Money bend down and put something in the man's pocket, he knew what he was doing—leaving the Prophets' symbol of six cents.

Peyton got inside the car and slammed the door. "Take me home, J-Rock. I never agreed to no shit like this."

"Times are different, Little Caesar. The Insane Cobras paid Easy Boy to join our group, gain our confidence, and find out how we made our money. I knew months ago that Easy Boy was dirty."

"You didn't have to kill him. You could have taught him a lesson. Cut off a finger. Branded our emblem on his arm. Anything—"

"Are you questioning me? I've been taking care of business since I was sixteen. Ever since the Vice Lords killed my brother. You already know the story, Little Caesar. That's why I took to you so. I treated you like my brother woulda treated me." He hit his fist against his chest. "Like family, man."

Since the moment Peyton had joined the group, J-Rock had given Peyton pocket money and helped him gain the respect of the other eight members, who had balked at letting a youngster join their group. Peyton's mentor had even taken the time to get him his first piece with a seasoned whore on his fourteenth birthday. What a gift!

"We've been doing okay, J-Rock. Stealing money from the numbers man, getting money from store owners to protect their businesses, but nothing—"

The sound of something being dragged over the ground caught their attention.

They heard a splash. Apparently T-Money had dragged the body down to the river and dropped it in the water.

"Serious?" J-Rock eyed him.

How could he explain it, Peyton thought. His past two years in the gang had been the best years of his life. His mom had been too preoccupied with making sergeant to care about his personal life. His aunt Rosemary was also busy, trying to take over her duties as the new pastor. It seemed that everyone he cared about wasn't available. Especially Isaac. And he wasn't sure how he felt about him. He knew he felt hatred. Betrayal. And then . . . nothing.

"Man, we always had fun, shooting pool at the club, doing bodywork on cars." Peyton shook his head, smiling, remembering. "Shit, my mom still can't get over me telling her I took the motor of her new Mustang apart and put it back together." The smile faded.

"I'm sorry to disillusion you, Little Caesar, but we've got the opportunity to make some big money now. Fuck this nickel-and-dime shit we've been doing."

You mean nickel-and-penny, he thought. "Oh, yeah." He tried to sound impressed.

"The big boss wants us to start pushing weight. I'm talking about a G a week for each of us."

"A G a week. Damn!" No. Isaac had just gotten out of prison. He knew there were too many black men there who were in for drug dealing and murders that stemmed from drug dealing.

Peyton wasn't stupid, either. For the first time, he knew that J-Rock was lying to him. The murder tonight wasn't about inside information. It was already about drugs. He'd heard the whispers at school about the Prophets—heard the rumors about the six-cents gang symbol. J-Rock and the other members never discussed this when he was around. But he knew. Yet, he cared for them.

When T-Money got into the car, they were silent. J-Rock started the car and then drove off. Peyton could feel them exchanging glances in the darkness.

"I'll take you home now, Little Caesar," J-Rock said. "Me and T-Money going to the club tonight."

J-Rock was nineteen and T-Money twenty-one—both were able to buy drinks and get into clubs in downtown Detroit, places that Peyton always dreamed about going to. Peyton was the only member who still attended school, even though three of the members were under eighteen.

Peyton didn't bother to answer. He couldn't stop thinking about the murder. He knew then that he would never smoke a cigarette in his life. When T-Money lit up, Peyton felt sick to his stomach.

There was no denying it. He'd witnessed a murder. Would the judge believe him if he told him that he didn't agree to it? Didn't want any part of it? No. He'd heard his mother talk about this stuff too much. In truth, he was as guilty as they were.

My God, he thought, if his mother ever found out he'd been involved in this execution, she'd kill him. It wouldn't matter that she was a cop. His life wouldn't even be worth six cents. And his father? What did Isaac Coleman know about him anyway?

Strange Illusions

Glimmering sunlight from five different angles shone like prisms and came to rest in a sphere of light where Rosemary had had the foresight to place her magical machine that she prayed would take her on a journey back to her golden days. That was ten years ago, when she was a svelte size 10 and weighed 140 pounds. That was also the time when she'd made her decision to go to theology school and become a minister.

And today her weight and waistline weren't what they were back then, but she had indeed become an ordained minister.

Since the age of eighteen she had worked at the City-County Building in downtown Detroit and was able to elevate her position from a clerk to the senior supervisor in the ombudsman's office. This is when she first met her friends for life, Congressman Clyde Miller, his brother, Henry, and Gary Reynolds. She'd also had contact with Mayor Prescott on a few occasions, when she handled complaints against his office.

In January, she retired after thirty-seven years of service. Her plans were already made to begin her second career—one that she and Jesse still didn't agree on.

This morning she was determined to ride six miles on her bike. She chastised herself for being lazy through every one of them. No better than any other sinner, Rosemary finally acknowledged to her husband that she was addicted to sweets, and even more to salt.

She'd put Lawry's seasoned salt on her vegetables, spicy Cajun seasonings on her meats, chicken seasoning on all of her poultry entrées, and splashed soy sauce over her favorite dishes.

At five-feet-nine, the water weight went directly to her abdomen. Rosemary was finally forced to wear what most women her age wore—a girdle.

Jesse would indulge in the confections and spicy entrées as well, but to her constant dismay, as she picked up pounds, Jesse's weight remained the same.

Blessed with an overactive metabolism, she'd never had to exercise on a regular basis. Just fifteen pounds heavier than her high school weight of one hundred and forty, she never worried about her figure until she met Jesse.

Within weeks after she married Jesse, she experienced a severe bout of perimenopause. Her doctor told her she was fortunate that she hadn't gone through this phase in her late forties. She was very late, her doctor kept saying. Very, very late. All of a sudden hot flashes, bouts of depression, and temporary memory loss became her primary problems to overcome. When Isaac would turn forty on Christmas Eve, her goal was to have shed ten pounds.

But Rosemary wasn't feeling like the consummate minister today on this beautiful, sunny morning. She was angry. Angry with her brother, Isaac. And at this moment she was taking her frustrations out on her exercise bike in the middle of her living room. Jesse, as the designated timekeeper, was patiently sitting on the love seat, holding a glass of ice water.

"He's been home a week, and all the promises he made to get his life in order have disappeared like the clouds outside that window."

"There aren't any clouds out today, Rosemary," Jesse commented. "The sun's out. Surely you didn't expect him to go to church the first week he came home."

Ignoring his words of wisdom, Rosemary rode with a fury. You could almost see sparks flying from the spokes. "No, but I at least expected him to respect my home." She slowed her pace a bit. "He didn't come home until five this morning."

Jesse looked at her with mild disgust. "What are you doing waiting up for a grown man anyway? Let the man have some privacy, Rosemary. He ain't like us. Maybe one day he'll get himself together."

"Where's he at, anyway? He can still look for work on Saturday."

Jesse gestured toward the garage, which was visible from where they were. "I let him borrow the car. He had an interview with *The Detroit News*, the *Free Press*, the *Michigan Chronicle*, and one at the new Motor City Grille Restaurant downtown. You know, the eatery down by the Fisher Theater. They've got entertainment now. Isaac thinks he's got a chance. I'll bet he's real good, Rosemary."

"Shhh," she huffed. "Just be quiet! Don't you encourage him. My Lord, Isaac needs a real job first. Then he can play his stupid saxophone." She motioned for him to bring the water, gulping quickly so she wouldn't lose her rhythm. "Is ten minutes up yet?"

"No, baby," Jesse said, limping back to his seat and checking his watch. "It's just been three."

"Jesse, is your leg bothering you?" she asked sincerely, slowing her pace a bit. "You seem to be dragging your left leg more."

"No, darlin'. It's just a little stiff."

She relaxed, then began to pedal faster, her anger building all over again. "Don't get me wrong, Jesse. I respect my brother," she said between pants, "but I don't condone him keeping secrets from me." *Oh, Lord, I'm tired. I'm hurting! Why does staying fit have to be so merciless?* she thought angrily. "He started off wrong, first by lying about when he was being released. I know. I know. He wanted to surprise me. Still, for years I got up at five in the morning, left at six, and traveled halfway across the state of Michigan so I could get checked through that long line of visitors and see Isaac by noon—"

"And usually you had to leave by two to make it back home by eight," Jesse completed.

"You would think I'd be the first person he'd call to come pick him up." Thinking back on Isaac's words, *"Then you tell me why Kennedy wouldn't let my son come and see me."* It killed Rosemary to keep silent. She'd promised Kennedy that she wouldn't tell Peyton where his father was.

54

Nearly a decade ago, Kennedy had begged her to keep Isaac's whereabouts to her son a secret. *"After all the hell Peyton and I have been through, Rosemary, this is the least you can do for us."*

Rosemary had told Kennedy that she understood where she was coming from, but that if her nephew ever asked her where his father was, she would tell him the truth. In twelve years, Peyton had never asked her, and Rosemary regretted the day that she'd made that promise.

"I know how much you sacrificed, Rosemary. Still, it's his life. You got to let him live it. Give him some time."

They'd been discussing Isaac's attitude since he came home from prison. Rosemary felt that Isaac was hiding the fact that he was looking harder for a job playing his saxophone than for a permanent nine-to-five.

"Give him credit for trying, Rosemary. The man's just spent twelve years in prison." Jesse squared his shoulders and, lifting his chin proudly, said, "Frankly, I admire his courage. I don't know if I could make it in prison."

Rosemary frowned. If she didn't know her husband better, she'd think he was lying to take up for Isaac. "How long, Jesse?"

"It's just been six minutes, baby." He leaned forward, nervously rattling the ice in the glass. "Listen, sweetie, I know you want Isaac to be happy. Don't treat him like you're his mother, Rosemary. It'll be your worst mistake."

"I can't talk and pedal, Jesse. Can you go in the kitchen and cut up some celery and carrots for me, please?"

After he left, Rosemary sped up the pace. She could hear him moving around the kitchen, searching through every cabinet for knives and plates, like he couldn't remember where they were. It was his way, she knew, of telling her that he didn't like the way her kitchen was set up.

In the three years they'd been married, Jesse had rarely complained about anything except the kitchen. He claimed that it was set up totally opposite of his kitchen in his old bachelor's apartment. Like her, he enjoyed cooking and had his own way of doing things. She couldn't complain because they both seemed to love to wait on each other. It was strange how well they got along. Her only complaint about her young husband was that she knew he sneaked a beer every now and then. She often wondered how a man could claim to be sanctified and saved and still drink alcohol. Then again, she was guilty of a small sin as well. In all fairness, she never confided in Jesse about her mother and father, who had died so long ago. Therefore, how could he understand that she'd been more like a mother to Isaac than their real mother had been?

When he returned, he brought several vegetables, and even put a few raw potatoes on the side. Her eyes feasted on the potatoes. Rosemary imagined spicy Cajun fries, and could almost smell the seasoned salt. She couldn't help but smile. Jesse could be really considerate when he wanted to be.

"Is thirty minutes up yet?" she asked, feeling like she was about to faint.

"Naw, but you've been working hard enough, Rosemary."

Rosemary stopped pedaling, and was relieved when Jesse came over to stand beside her, wiping her sweaty forehead with a quilted Bounty paper towel.

With a grunting effort, she lifted her worn-out body off the bike. Immediately, she felt an uncomfortable imprint of the seat pressed in the center of her buttocks.

Shaking off the discomfort, she continued with their conversation about Isaac as though there had been no interruption. "I'm going to fix him, though. I received a call yesterday morning from Pastor Fleming at Mount Calvary—he helps ex-convicts find employment when the agencies can't. He managed to get Isaac an interview for a job at Remmey's Hair Grease Company next week. You know, that small factory near Chalfonte Street. Remmey's does millions in business. They even ship to Africa and Germany."

Jesse just shook his head. "Did you have something to do with this, Rosemary?" He spread napkins on the table and sat back down in his chair.

She shrugged. "A little. I know a deacon who knows the brother of the owner who called Pastor Fleming. Working at a grease company sounds a little tacky, but it's a secure job. He won't have to worry about being laid off."

"He wants a job on one of the newspapers. He's certainly qualified. He showed me a copy of his transcripts over the years. I can tell you, he's certainly no dummy. Even in his music—he seems to display an extraordinary talent." Jesse scratched his head. "He's trying real hard to make it. But you know how racist this city is. I can't blame him for finding comfort in doing something that he loves. He plays that instrument every chance he gets. My gut tells me that he ain't gonna give up on his dream to get a record contract."

Rosemary stuffed a raw potato stick in her mouth. "So, you talk to him about his dreams. I'm trying to help him make something of himself, not sign him up to a record deal." She put up a hand to silence him, until she finished chewing. "But I'm fair. The job works four days a week, ten hours a day. His weekends are free, unless they work overtime. The pay is $8.25 an hour. It's not much. But it's a start."

"He's changed, Rosemary. I didn't know him before, but I'd venture to say that he's got some very precise plans."

"We've all changed." Rosemary rolled her eyes toward the exercise bike.

"You know, Rosemary, it's strange that you think that you should be the one to save Isaac. You can't convert a man overnight. Only God can."

"I realize that, Jesse. But I can pray." She shook a finger at him. "And he needs prayer."

Rosemary took pride in the fact that she was doing something to help men and women like Isaac, who were in transition from drugs, prostitution, and other social problems. She'd been a member of Mother Bethel AME Church for thirty years, and held positions on several boards. Presently she was working on Project Hope, an organization that would house, feed, counsel, and help those individuals find jobs so that they could become positive forces in the community. She worked with another longtime Mother Bethel member, Gary Reynolds, and with Henry Miller and six other church members. Their federal grant to remodel twenty vacant homes that were owned by the church and rent them out to low-income families had just been approved. Neither Jesse nor Isaac knew the extent of the long-term goals that she and her partners planned to put into operation in the city of Detroit.

She pushed the potatoes aside and stuffed a carrot in her mouth, savoring the sweet taste. "You mark my words. The only way Isaac Coleman is going to be rehabilitated is when he takes off those blinders and admits that times have changed since he left, and therefore his dreams must change."

Our dreams must change—what a wonderful subject for a sermon.

Rosemary understood that she was fifty-five years old and had old-fashioned values. But she had always been young in spirit, young in heart; and in that light, she was thirteen years old, ready to experience life's joys and wonders. This is how she felt about her ministry. It was a spiritual journey. A journey she had longed to travel. Her dream of becoming a pastor of a large, prestigious church was about to be realized.

Rebel Without a Cause

Early Monday morning, when Isaac took the bus downtown to his first visit with his parole officer, he still hadn't been able to release the tension. He hated admitting to the parole officer that he was unsuccessful in finding a job because of his record. But having to tell Kennedy why he couldn't give her money to help support Peyton was a greater fear.

In the meantime, he took action to begin doing something positive that would make him feel good—trying to find a gig playing his saxophone at a nightclub.

One by one he was turned down—most of the time without anyone hearing him play. The minute he admitted that he'd just returned home from prison, the club owners didn't want to hear his music. Sure, they gave him an interview, just like the employment offices, but no one really gave him the time of day. Their eyes said, Why wasn't he looking for a *real* job. They all questioned his sincerity.

Pretty soon, he stopped asking the club owners for a job and frequented the bars for a few drinks and conversation. The women were all over him like the heat in Death Valley. He reluctantly took their phone numbers, but knew he'd never call. Kennedy was the only woman he'd wanted in years.

He left the establishment after imbibing two pitchers of Miller beer. But instead of feeling the numbness that he had tried to achieve, he felt as sober as an ice cream soda on New Year's Eve when his face hit the pillow. And he knew there was nothing that he could do to ward off the daily dreams about a woman who represented his past and his future.

A call from Kennedy came the following day. "Isaac, Peyton's been kicked out of school." Her voice was filled with sarcasm. "If you're not too busy, meet me at the principal's office at Pershing High School in thirty minutes." She hung up without waiting for an answer.

An hour later, Isaac learned why Peyton had been expelled—for striking a teacher. It was Wednesday, May thirteenth. School would be out for the year on the twenty-ninth. Isaac pleaded with the principal not to expel Peyton.

"Mr. Coleman," the principal began, "I realize the situation between you and your son."

Isaac cleared his throat. "And you also know I've just been released from prison. Go on."

"Your wife may not have told you, but we've had problems with Peyton for some time now. He hangs around with the wrong crowd. Some people call them thugs."

"Thugs?" Isaac was surprised by the principal's crassness.

"Yes, students who have been kicked out of school repeatedly for smoking cigarettes and marijuana on school premises, assaulting our female students on the way to school in the morning, threatening our teachers; the list goes on and on. In my eyesight those types of young men are thugs. I'm sorry, Mr. and Mrs. Coleman, your son has a lot of potential. However, if you don't get a handle on this young man right now"—he pointed out the window to three young men who were being escorted off school property by security officers—"he'll end up just like them."

Isaac stared at the young men whose half-exposed underwear was proudly displayed beneath their baggy jeans. He wouldn't be able to stand it if Peyton turned out like that—with virtually no respect for himself.

The principal continued. "Presently, Peyton has absolutely no respect for teachers. I'm sorry. Striking a member of our staff is unacceptable."

Kennedy began to cry. Still in her police uniform, she looked like she was on the wrong side of the desk. Isaac wrapped his arms around her, surprised that she didn't pull away. "I understand, sir."

The principal handed Isaac a sheet of paper with a list of schools that Peyton could attend over the summer, along with a list of schools to enroll him in in the fall.

"As you can see," the principal said, handing Isaac a copy of Peyton's report card, "your son will be six credits short of entering the tenth grade if he doesn't attend and pass all his classes in summer school."

"Excuse me, but what exactly are the MEAP scores here? I've done some research and discovered that the students are performing way below average. The graduation rate is lower than it has been in thirteen years. Especially for black males. There are no social workers in this place, nor are there counselors to listen to my black child should he have problems dealing with his personal problems at home. Problems that might affect his scholastic achievements in school. Can you tell me why these programs are in place in Bloomfield, but are not available in the city schools, where the students are predominantly black?"

"Hrrmmmph."

Isaac had heard that answer before. When he looked at Kennedy, she sank down in her chair, openly embarrassed. Isaac didn't care. If the system hadn't helped him, and wouldn't help his son, what chance did either one of them have?

Afterward, he and Kennedy said very little to each other, but her eyes castrated him. It was clear that she blamed Isaac for some of Peyton's problems. And at that moment, he felt she was probably right. Peyton was doing the same stupid things that Isaac and his old friend Eli had done when they were in their teens. Back then, he and Eli had sworn their lifelong friendship by becoming blood brothers. Both had to attend night school to graduate. Immature, and angry at the world for the lack of well-paying jobs for black men, they both ended up doing time in prison—Eli, eight years less than Isaac. Isaac could see that Peyton was heading down the same path. Maybe, Isaac thought, if he'd had a father to talk to, he might not have gotten into trouble. Somehow he had to try and derail the steam engine he could see building up in Peyton.

Back home, Isaac found it hard to shake that memory and imagine that his son's attitude should have been any different from his when he was a troubled teen. If he'd been home and been a father to him, that situation, he was certain, would never have happened. For the next half hour he tried releasing his frustrations on his instrument. It didn't work. Removing the mouthpiece from the neck, then the neck from the base, he stored the sax back in its case and placed it beneath his bed. He left the house and headed for the closest bar.

Two hours later, when he couldn't differentiate the men from the women, he realized that he'd had one too many beers. After relieving himself in the bathroom, he had the good sense to ask the bartender to call a taxi for him. He wasn't sure if he could walk the half-mile back home.

Fumbling in his pockets for his keys, he was grateful when the door opened and Jesse helped him inside.

"Where's my sister?" he slurred.

Jesse's hooked right arm held Isaac's two hundred pounds firmly around his waist, and led him downstairs.

"You hungry, Isaac? Rosemary cooked some red beans and rice for dinner tonight. I can fix you a plate if you like."

"Naw, Jesse. I 'preciate it, but I ain't hungry. I need something that Sis didn't cook."

He didn't see Jesse's smile.

Once inside the small basement bedroom, Jesse helped Isaac remove his shoes and then helped him into bed.

"You got a lot on your mind, Isaac. I'm good at listening, if you want to talk for a few minutes."

Isaac had to admire his brother-in-law. When Rosemary said she was marrying a man twenty years younger than she was, Isaac was totally against it. He wanted to tell her that he thought she was a stupid fool. Certainly, she had always been generous by nature—but marrying a diabetic and a cripple? That was going too far. But after he got to know Jesse, he knew that Rosemary had made the best decision in her life. Jesse loved her. Hands down. They didn't have the church in common, but from the sounds he heard from the ceiling above him, Jesse was taking care of other business in good fashion.

Isaac's mind was never too far from Kennedy. But even though he cared for Jesse, he couldn't tell him how he felt about her.

"I've sent my résumé to every newspaper in the city. It's been a week and I haven't gotten one response. I can't even get an interview—even when there's a job posted. It's discrimination, man. If I had some money, I'd sue the hell out of 'em."

"Calm down, Isaac. You'll get a job eventually. It's still early."

"Naw. I'm not too sure, man. I can't even get a gig playing my horn. Won't nobody even listen to my stuff."

Isaac eased out of his pants and began unbuttoning his shirt. "I'm serious. I expected that the newspaper position would take a while. I really don't have any experience. So that's understandable. But not my music, man. Not that. I knew things had changed since I went away, but I was always able to get a little weekend gig, Jesse. Now all I manage to get is a good kick in the ass. What happened? I know I still got what it takes, and damn if I can't gyrate like any of those video hoes I've seen on TV." He ignored Jesse's laughter. "I don't stand a chance, man."

He didn't hear Jesse mumble, "Rosemary's already taken care of that."

After Jesse had left and Isaac was certain that he was asleep, he picked up his saxophone. Standing beside the basement windows, he felt the soft moonlight flowing in—a welcome warmth that he felt in his soul as well.

Softly, ever so softly, a tune emanated from his mouth and heart. Isaac launched into a sassy yet sensual rendition of "Forever and Ever, Amen."

Where was the man who was so adventurous so many years ago? Had he vanished? These thoughts poured into his psyche while he played. His heart raced like that of a madman. Exhausted, he dropped the sax to his side. He felt tears trembling down his sweat-stained face, and whispered the words softly to himself: "Things got to get better."

One Desire

The following evening, the regular monthly meeting of the Zeyta Sigma Theta sorority sisters was held. Rosemary glanced at her watch. It was approximately 10:10 P.M. and the meeting was coming to a close. Rosemary, as well as sixteen other dedicated women, were at Dawn Cullors's palatial home in Birmingham, Michigan.

Ten minutes earlier, the meeting had been temporarily interrupted when Dawn, who was the general manager of the Mall of Detroit, received an unexpected call from the security supervisor.

Sitting patiently in the family room, Rosemary's Bible was open to Matt. 23:1–12. Before she left home this evening she had prayed that this meeting would end early. Exhaling, she continued to read and took comfort in the words "He who humbles himself with be exalted."

Ever since she had arrived at seven, Isaac was always on the forefront of her mind. Unconsciously, Isaac was making the same mistakes with his music career that he'd made twelve years earlier. He couldn't seem to understand how hard it was for a saxophone player to make a living playing small bars in the city.

Earlier today, she'd been at Mother Bethel AME conducting the weekly members' meeting for men and women who wanted to join the church. Typically, the attendees had averaged fifteen per week, now the number had jumped to forty. She was afraid to voice her fears to the pastor that the church was growing too rapidly. It pleased her that so many souls strived to be saved, but it bothered her that her brother hadn't even set a foot inside the church.

When Dawn returned, Rosemary would be called to conduct the closing prayer. Removing her reading glasses, she rubbed her tired eyes. Surprisingly, she felt herself getting sleepy as the relaxing tunes of classical music played softly on the stereo system.

One member was saying, "Yeah, I heard that, too. Can you imagine having plastic surgery done over the weekend and returning to work on Monday morning?"

"It's hard to believe," an older woman intoned, "but I'm reserving my opinion until I see the results up close and personal."

"So, that's why Tempest wasn't here for the last meeting," a woman named Delilah said in a loud whisper. "Tempest claims to be forty-five, but I believe she's more like fifty-five."

"Be careful, Delilah. Let's not diss the mayor's wife too tough. Especially when she's not here to defend herself."

"Excuse me, girls," Rosemary interrupted. "What church do you belong to?"

They eyed one another suspiciously. "Greater Grace," Delilah offered.

"That's Pastor Cureton's church." Rosemary smiled. "I'm told he's a great speaker. A true man of God."

Another woman spoke up. "Bishop Bowles is my pastor, you know. He founded that new church on Joy Road."

Rosemary tapped her finger on her chin and looked toward Delilah. "Didn't I see you in the prayer line at Pastor Cureton's revival last Friday night?" Delilah nodded and lowered her head. "That was a beautiful testimony you gave, Sister Delilah."

63

The young woman beamed, and the conversation began to change to a higher plane. Rosemary knew that most of the women who belonged to the Zeytas were very spiritual. It was the only reason that she'd agreed to take the chaplain's position in the first place.

Rosemary caught Miracall's smile of approval when she took a seat beside them.

The Zeytas had sponsored the Big Brothers, Big Sisters event since 1988. It was the highlight of the end of the spring season. This year's had not achieved the success of their previous events, so the women were eagerly planning next year's. Rosemary tried to appear interested, but in truth, she wouldn't be in attendance. The July meeting would be her final one.

Outside the wind wailed like a lost child's cry. It reminded her of the nights when she used to put Isaac to bed. When she silenced his cries with a soft kiss on his forehead. Where had all the years gone?

"Please excuse my rudeness, everyone," Dawn said, her face flushed a deep red. "Everything's under control." She tapped the table to get everyone's attention. "Rosemary?" she said, signaling her to come to the front of the room. "We're ready now."

It was hard for Rosemary to look at Dawn now, knowing how much pain her own brother had caused Dawn's family just a few short years ago. She picked up the Bible from her lap and took her place in the center of the room. As she waited for them to form a circle, she whispered to herself, "Dear God, help me to sustain my brother, so that he will know you through your generous love." She began to gather her thoughts and asked everyone to bow their heads. For some reason she still couldn't concentrate on today's meeting. Someone seemed to notice the long hesitation before she began to pray.

"Hrrmph," Miracall said, clearing her throat.

Rosemary looked up, smiled, and lowered her head once more. She began with the usual prayer of carrying on the tradition of the Zeytas and asking the Lord to continue to bless their efforts to help those in need of a good education receive one. She ended with the words "Let us lay aside every weight and the sin that clings so closely"—she slowed, concentrating—"and let us run with perseverance the race that is set before us, looking to Jesus the pioneer and perfector of our faith—Amen."

"Amen," the group finished.

"Amen," said Rosemary, concluding her duties as the chaplain of Zeyta Sigma Theta. It signified the end of their meeting.

Without even realizing it, Rosemary envied the friendship of the top three members, Dawn Cullors, Miracall Lake, and Tempest Prescott. The three of them had met twenty-five years ago at the University of Michigan, pledged with Zeyta, and remained friends ever since.

For the past three months Rosemary had filled in temporarily for Zeyta's regular chaplain, who was on maternity leave. They'd made her an honorary Zeyta after her second meeting. Performing this service was Rosemary's first official assignment since graduating from Wayne State's Theology School. Although she was flattered when Miracall asked her to substitute, Rosemary disliked meeting at Dawn's house. She preferred the sorority house on Livernois Avenue, just four miles from her house.

Last month Rosemary had expressed the idea of resigning once Isaac was released from prison. She felt Dawn might be offended by her presence. But Miracall convinced her that Dawn wasn't that shallow. Isaac was her brother, and Miracall's ex-husband, Loren Lake, was the hypocrite.

"Amen," Miracall repeated, briefly touching Rosemary's hand.

The women chatted as they gathered the chairs and began placing them back in the dining room. When the room was in order, they gathered their purses and began saying their good-byes.

"Good night, guys," Dawn said.

Rosemary immediately felt uncomfortable. She wanted to leave, but she always helped the girls clean up in the kitchen afterward.

Miracall added, "Yeah, see you next month."

The selection of music coming from the entertainment center on the far end of the room changed. A mellow Nat King Cole ballad flowed through the house like an old tune through a dream. It was so ironic, Rosemary thought, Nat King Cole was one of Isaac's favorites. From the look of the abundance of rows of neatly stacked disks, she suspected that Dawn owned every CD the man ever recorded. "Mona Lisa" had just begun.

At this moment, Rosemary thought, tomorrow seemed like Armageddon between the Lakes and the Colemans. In ten minutes, she'd be out of there. She had no idea how she would react if someone mentioned Isaac's name.

Keeping her mind on her present task, Rosemary balanced an empty platter in one hand and a coffeepot in the other. Breathing a sigh of relief, she backed her buttocks against the swinging doors that led to the kitchen. As she placed the objects on the counter, she could hear the *beep-beep* of pagers going off, then the starting of automobile engines.

She glanced back at the door when the telephone rang. Looking around, she couldn't remember where the phone was in the huge, ultramodern stainless-steel-and-white kitchen. By the fourth ring she found the acrylic wall telephone and picked up.

"Hello."

"Dawn? Who's this?" the man asked.

"Rosemary Jones." Instantly, she recognized his voice from numerous press conferences over the past eight years. Yet, she was positive that Loren Lake, the governor of Michigan, still didn't recognize her name as that of the sister of the man convicted of killing his niece. Possibly he'd forgotten. It was also possible that he didn't care.

"Dawn's in the living room. We're just concluding our Zeyta meeting. Hold on. I'll get her."

"No. I'll see her in a few minutes. I'm in the city. Is Miracall there?"

Rosemary felt a cold chill. Miracall had been divorced from Loren for more than ten years, but Rosemary knew that her heart still bypassed a beat or two whenever he called. She also suspected that Miracall was still in love with him.

"Yes, should I call *her*, then?"

"No. I'm nearby. Tell them I'll be there in a few minutes."

He said good-bye, but Rosemary knew that he'd already forgotten her name. The man irritated her so that she had to stop and pray. *Oh, God, help me. How could so many Michigan voters be duped by this hypocrite?*

Rosemary was still holding the receiver in her hand when Dawn plunged into the room.

"Is that Tempest? She's got a lot of nerve. Everyone's gone already."

"No." Rosemary hung up the phone, still holding the empty platter in one hand. "It was your brother," she said awkwardly.

"That's odd," Dawn said, moving to the sink. She filled a teakettle with water and placed it on the stove. While Rosemary stacked the dishwasher, Dawn left to retrieve a box of tea and a package of Fig Newtons from the walk-in pantry.

When she placed the cookies on the counter next to the half-empty Ritz cracker box and cheese spread, Rosemary's eyes watered. Just a few inches from her elbow was Friday's paper. The edition was as wrinkled as if someone had tried to crush the life out of it.

Rosemary had read the short article in yesterday's *Detroit News*, which reported that the ex-convict who served twelve years in prison for killing the governor's niece had finally been released. "Yesterday" had condemned her brother's life for over a decade. If only they could take it all back. But she realized that it was foolish to worry about yesterday or tomorrow. Life began today. No one ever served God well by doing things tomorrow, for those who honored Christ were blessed by the things that they did today. Every day for Isaac, Rosemary acknowledged, would be a new day.

Miracall subsequently entered with a twisted frown on her face. "You're acting peculiar, Dawn. What's wrong?"

"Loren's coming over." Dawn's voice was cool. "He'll be here soon." While she placed the cups on the table, she shot Miracall a warning glance that said more than words ever could.

Rosemary didn't miss Miracall's sharp intake of breath. It was very clear that neither wanted to discuss the real reason why Dawn was so upset in front of her.

The teakettle whistled. Rosemary eyed the crackers once more. She was tempted, but her cravings went numb. She knew that she didn't want to be there when Loren arrived.

"Sorry, girls," she said, looking up at the wall clock. "It's five to eleven. The late news will be on in five minutes. It's a special time at the end of the day that I enjoy sharing with my husband." Usually their meetings were over by nine. Nearly an hour was wasted waiting for Tempest. She slammed the dishwasher door shut. "I won't be able to stay for tea tonight."

Less than a week later, Rosemary couldn't contain her jubilance when Isaac told her that he'd gotten a job at Remmey's. He didn't appear too happy about it, but he would start at five A.M. on Monday.

Later that day, she presided over a funeral and went to pray for several church members at Henry Ford and Botsford Hospital. Just after one o'clock she stopped by Jones Funeral Home on Puritan and Schaeffer and gave Jesse his insulin shot.

Next, she spent an uncomfortable two hours with the staff at the church. Would she select a new administration when she took over in a few months? Was she working on new ideas to get the church debt-free? What new programs for the young people did she plan on implementing? With the increasing use of drugs in their community, the members were complaining that there weren't enough youth activities in place to keep their children busy. Would she consider starting a basketball league, youth Bible-study classes, or organizing another youth choir?

She'd been so busy with her church duties, she'd almost forgotten about Miracall, her young friend, who was also probably feeling a little down today.

Before she left for home, she tried Miracall's office number. The voice mail came on and Rosemary left a message for Miracall to contact her on her car phone. Thirty minutes later, Rosemary was in her kitchen and checking her messages. There still wasn't one from Miracall.

Next, she checked the stock in the refrigerator and cabinets for the necessary ingredients for dinner. Luckily, she had nearly everything that she needed. While removing the ham from the refrigerator, she put in a quick call to Jesse, who was momentarily unavailable. She left him a message to stop by the store and pick up a bunch of rhubarb, a pound of hot pepper cheese, bacon bits, and a twelve-pack of assorted sodas on his way home from work.

With a heaviness in her heart, she decided to give Miracall another call.

"Hello, may I speak to Ms. Lake, please."

"This is she. My secretary's taking a break, Rosemary. How are you?"

"Okay. But a little worried about you, though. Think you can come over tonight for dinner?"

It was fifteen minutes to four. Checking the timer on the stove, she knew she would be finished with everything by six.

"I'd love to, Rosemary."

"Around six?"

"Sure. I'll be there."

Jesse dropped off the items on her list, along with a box of cloves that she'd forgotten to mention.

And now, opening the oven, the heat warmed her cheeks. She inhaled the scent of the cloves that dotted the eight-pound honey-baked ham as she peeled back the foil. Dozens of pineapple chunks and maraschino cherries canopied the surface. She bent down and spooned the honey-and-mustard glaze over the ham one last time. When she withdrew the spoon, her restraint faltered. Nothing could keep her from licking it.

She had to admit that she was looking forward to the rare treat for dinner tonight. Real food. The turnip greens and smoked turkey had simmered down to perfect tenderness, and resembled a Marie Calender glossy cookbook entrée. The creamy au grautin potatoes and bacon corn bread made her hate the thought of chocolate Slim-Fast for breakfast in the morning. She had nine more pounds to lose, and she had to face the fact that she couldn't eat this type of food on a regular basis. However, the tangy aroma of rhubarb and strawberry pie seemed to fill her soul temporarily.

For the second time that afternoon, Jesse came rushing in with two more bags of groceries, worrying about being late for an almost-forgotten doctor's appointment.

"I'll try and be back by seven," Jesse said, giving his wife a kiss and heading back out the door.

Just as she had nearly finished preparing the table, she heard the doorbell. "It's always good to see you, Miracall." She greeted her friend with a big bear hug. The floorboards squeaked on the screened-in porch as she said, "Come on in."

"Okay, Rosemary. You just saw me last week. Why all the fuss on a weekday? I could have stopped by on Saturday."

Rosemary fanned her face with her apron as she headed toward the living room and motioned for Miracall to take a seat on the sofa. After she was seated, Rosemary looked at her in disbelief. "Don't you realize what day it is today?" When Miracall didn't answer, Rosemary continued. "It's the third anniversary of Sadie's death."

Suddenly Rosemary chastised herself for not using more tact. She watched Miracall crumble like bread crumbs.

"Can I please have some water, Rosemary?"

"Sure. I need a glass myself." She was having another hot flash, and prayed it wouldn't last long. "I'll be right back."

When Rosemary returned, Miracall had left the yellow chintz couch and was standing in front of the fireplace. The room, cheerily decorated in buttercup-yellow and violet, seemed to soak all the life out of Miracall's body.

"Thanks." Miracall sipped on the water and looked at the pictures that spanned forty years of memories.

Rosemary took a seat and waited. It was odd, the history that had developed between this young woman and herself. Very little had changed since she first met Miracall in the chapel at Wayne State University eleven years ago, when Rosemary had begun theology school.

During those early years, her faith was tested. She was feeling guilty about divorcing her mate. She felt unfulfilled as a woman, knowing that her childbearing days were behind her. And to make matters even worse, Isaac had had a suicide attempt that she knew she would never mention to him face-to-face. It was a difficult time, and she quit school three times before she finally made the choice to commit herself to finish.

Back when Rosemary was in her first semester of theology school for the third time, she and Miracall had been praying: Miracall for her mother, who had just been diagnosed with cancer, and Rosemary for her brother, Isaac. Because Rosemary's and Isaac's surnames were different, Miracall didn't make the connection. Rosemary hadn't said why her brother was in prison, and Miracall had been too respectful to ask why.

And now she caught Miracall pausing at the picture of Isaac playing a harmonica while he sat on the coffee table. He was ten years old.

When she turned her head away, her eyes caught the sparkle of the little crystal statues scattered all over the room that Sadie had given Rosemary just before she became bedridden. There weren't pictures of anyone else but Isaac on the mantel because Rosemary didn't have any children. Just a few feet away, though, on an old drum table, was a familiar picture of Rosemary and Sadie at Mother Theresa AME Church—Sadie was being baptized that day. Sadie had given her life to God, but she felt that her salvation could not be complete until she was baptized in water. Sadie was dressed in white, and she even wore a crest of white chrysanthemums in her hair. That picture always reminded Rosemary of how Miracall cried like a baby when they dunked her mom in the water. The flowers floated to the surface before her mother was brought back up.

"She looks just like an angel," Miracall said to Rosemary.

That was eleven years ago. Sadie had been a dear friend, especially when she was debating whether to marry Jesse. Everyone thought she was silly, especially Isaac. Near the end of Sadie's life, Rosemary felt relieved and helped to console Miracall on the days her mother was experiencing so much pain. Rosemary remembered the last words that Sadie had said to her: "You keep a watchful eye on my daughter. The man she divorced and is still in love with has proven that he's not the man for her. She thinks I'm too sick to notice the pain in her eyes. You take care of my miracle baby, Rosemary. Please."

It still bothered Rosemary that Miracall had eventually turned her back on God while she watched her mother lose the battle with breast cancer. Little by little the cancer ate up her mother's body. Rosemary had seen the dedication as Miracall prayed and prayed. Rosemary couldn't imagine how much it hurt her to see her mother in so much pain.

This young woman washed her mother daily. She took care of her for the two and a half years it took for her to die. The last three months before she died, Miracall took a leave of absence from work. Though she never said so, Rosemary knew that for Miracall those were the hardest days of all.

Sadie Petrucci weighed less than eighty pounds when she died. And when she did, all of Miracall's faith in God seemed to leave with her. God had taken the only thing that she had left in this world. She had no father, children, or husband. She was alone, but Rosemary insisted that a child of God was never alone.

And now, since Sadie's death, Rosemary treasured being more of a maternal friend to Miracall.

When she heard Miracall sniffing back tears, Rosemary touched her shoulder affectionately. They both turned toward the doorway when they heard the sad wail of music so bleak and naked in nature. *Was that Isaac?* Odd, she hadn't heard him come in.

Concentrating further, she realized that the sound had been there all the time, and that she'd been so preoccupied with her thoughts, she hadn't noticed it before.

"That's Isaac," Rosemary said, moving to the doorway. The music stopped. Miracall cringed. "He's living here? You could have warned me, Rosemary." She drained the glass of water and gathered her purse to leave. "I think I'd better go."

Rosemary felt slighted. It was as if an eclipse had occurred; everything went black for a moment. Although they'd never discussed Isaac's homecoming, Rosemary assumed that Miracall knew that they would eventually run into each other.

Isaac caught up with them before Miracall made it out the front door.

"Hey, Sis. Sorry for the noise. I didn't know you had company."

Miracall turned around and glared at Isaac as if she were gazing upon the devil himself. "Why don't you go somewhere where no one knows what kind of monster you are!" Miracall seethed, stepping away from him. Her voice was as harsh as death. Her wild eyes dismissed Isaac as if he were rubbish.

Isaac turned to his sister. "Sorry." He excused himself and went out the front door.

Rosemary felt betrayed. It was unfair for Miracall to judge Isaac. She didn't even know him. However, she was humble enough not to voice her feelings.

Miracall remained by the door, as still and cold as an icicle. She wore an expression on her face that Rosemary hadn't seen since her mother died. It was the time that Rosemary had counseled her about her anger toward God.

"What exactly did you expect me to say to him, Rosemary? After all, he murdered my niece."

Rosemary held her temper. It was a side of her she rarely used but the Lord knew it was there. "Isaac's paid for that, Miracall. And even though you've never spoken to him, I know he's sorry. He's told me so, many, many times."

"I don't ever want to hear nothing he has to say again. I heard how sorry he was at the trial. Anyway, it doesn't matter. My niece is dead."

Rosemary's chest heaved up and down as she stuffed her large hands in her apron. Her eyes began to fill with tears while she battled to stay calm.

"I hope this doesn't come between our friendship, Rosemary," Miracall said stiffly, and opened the door to leave.

Friendship? What kind of friend can't forgive? Her temples began to pound and she could feel a spot under her right eye begin to jump. *If your niece had been black instead of white, my brother would have been home two years ago.* "Isaac's paid the maximum sentence for his crime. And I'm not talking about prison time. The Lord seen to that." The tears fell, and Rosemary's lips were trembling. "My brother didn't mean to harm her. It was an accident. But because of your husband's influence, Isaac didn't stand a chance."

"I feel sorry for you, Rosemary. You're always telling me about forgiveness. About God's will. Maybe God didn't only save your brother's soul; he may have saved his life by keeping him in prison for so long." Miracall walked down the front steps. "You think about that, Rosemary, the next time you say your prayers. Pray for your brother's soul, not for my forgiveness."

Gone with the Wind

Isaac managed to avoid Rosemary all weekend. He hated working at the Remmey Grease Company. His job as a can capper seemed ridiculous. They kept telling him that there was an art form to it when he kept dropping the caps. He'd been told to get about thirty-five to forty caps out of the box and stack them against his stomach. With his right arm extended and that hand around a cap, he was supposed to hold a can with his left hand, and proceed to press the cap on top of the grease can. It was like dealing cards, he was told. He had to do at least thirty cans per minute. The entire line put out twenty-two thousand to twenty-three thousand cans daily between 7:00 A.M. and 5:25 P.M.

Isaac couldn't understand why they didn't have a machine that performed this task. *We had more innovative machines than this at Jefferson.*

It was unbelievable how many orders Remmey's received. The demand was exceptionally high. Besides the United States, they shipped grease to Holland, Africa, Europe, and Australia.

Holland ordered every item they produced—which included regular Remmey's, Super-Lite, Hair Glo, and black Beeswax for mustaches, dreadlocks, and cornrows. They also manufactured a regular Beeswax.

The employees were allowed to take home Remmey products if the cans were dented or improperly labeled.

Each night Isaac's hands were so sore, he had to soak them in Epsom salts.

73

On his days off, he caught the bus and continued to pursue the newspapers, more determined now than ever to become a journalist.

During that time, he hadn't been able to get Miracall out of his mind. He guessed that Rosemary hadn't either. He knew that sooner or later they would discuss the situation. Sure, he knew who the woman was before he came upstairs. The personalized license plates on her black Benz said: MIRACL. Over the years, Rosemary had spoken of her so highly, Isaac thought she was the same type of decent and forgiving woman that his sister was. It was a mistake on his part.

It was incredible to him that even though his sister was retired, her schedule was busier than when she worked for the city. She usually left by six-thirty in the morning and didn't come home until four or five in the afternoon. He figured that her missionary work was occupying most of her time. At least four nights a week she conducted night service and prayer meetings at church.

Next week was the Memorial Day weekend, and Isaac planned on catching the bus to Belle Isle and doing some people-watching. He loved that. Sitting back and observing others. Watching families and their little kids play together—wondering how much different his life would be with Kennedy and Peyton if things had been different. Would they be one of the loving families, laughing, playing Frisbee, while they waited for their food to cook on their small hibachi? He thought that they'd be so happy to be together, no one would care if their holiday meal was burned or undercooked.

Those thoughts were on his mind when he heard a knock on the door. Had Rosemary came back home while he was daydreaming? When he opened the door, Jesse was standing there.

"Hey. You busy?" Jesse asked.

"No, I was just about to take a shower, but come on in, man." He opened the door wider so Jesse could pass through. "What are you doing home? I always thought business was heavy during the holidays."

"Man, dead people don't rush you," he said, smiling. Jesse told Isaac that he usually took Memorial Day and Veteran's Day off. Then he explained why. "But seriously, I was in the service for thirteen years before diabetes forced me out early. I'll always consider myself a vet." He eyed the green army jacket hanging in the closet that Isaac had bought at the army surplus store. "But enough of that stuff. I'd like to show you something." He motioned for Isaac to follow him outside to the garage.

In the west corner was a waist-high lumpy pile that was covered with mounds of padded quilts.

Isaac scratched his head absently, then said politely, "Hey, Jesse, think you can do me a favor?"

"Name it."

"Ask your wife to stop washing my clothes. I don't want to hurt her feelings."

Jesse laughed. "I told her, man. She wouldn't listen." He began lifting the heavy pads. "Don't worry, I'll take care of it."

When they finally lifted the last pad, Isaac was stunned to see motorbike handlebars.

"I can tell it's a Harley, but I can't make out what year," Isaac said, scratching his head again.

This was the first time Isaac saw so much pride in Jesse's face. His next sentence told him why.

"It's a vintage 1955 Flathead Harley. My dad gave it to me when I was seventeen years old." Jesse glanced down at his leg, then back at Isaac. "I tore the entire bike apart four years ago. Some of the components in the engine aren't any good. It was so hard for me to get around back then, I got tired of hunting down the old parts I needed to fix the motor." He sighed. "Anyway, it's a beauty."

"I'll say." Isaac picked up the rich blue gasoline tank. There were a few rusty spots on it, but you could still see the chrome Harley emblem shining through.

Jesse reached into his pocket and handed Isaac the signed title and the key. "It's yours, man."

Isaac stepped back. "No way. I can't accept something so personal, man. I appreciate the thought, but no way can I do that."

"Please, Isaac. Man to man, I'll never drive it. Lifting this wooden leg over the seat hurts more than I would care to admit. It would be an honor if a man like you would put it back together and ride it for me. And maybe give me a ride on the back every now and then. It's going to take some time to find everything you need. But think of it as if it was *you* putting the pieces of your life back together."

Isaac shook his head in disbelief. No one had ever given him anything like this before. He didn't know what to say.

"I know you don't know me that well, man. But I know you through Rosemary. She can't stop worrying about you." He paused, looking back out the open doorway. "I love her, man. I knew when I married her that we'd never have children. I would have loved to give this bike to—our son. That wasn't in God's plans. So my thoughts were, the best I can do is give it to a man who could fix it up and one day pass it on to his son."

Isaac was blown away. He'd heard over the years from Rosemary how much Jesse admired Peyton. There was no way that Isaac could admit to him at this moment that he didn't even know his son. How could he? The only thing he could say was, "Thanks, man."

Returning to his room and showering, he thought about how he could begin to form a relationship with Peyton. It occurred to him that the first thing he needed to do was to get a car. Summer school started in three weeks. He couldn't depend on Peyton to catch the bus for the entire six-week session while Kennedy was at work. His only hope was to buy a cheap car and drive Peyton to and from school.

Turning on the radio, he listened to National Public Radio while he dressed. Afterward he lay on his bed, flipping through the classified ads in the used-vehicles section.

As he did so, he was intrigued by a woman being interviewed by the renowned Bradlee Meadows. Her career was one that he wasn't familiar with.

"As general manager of the Mall of Detroit, I've held this job for the past ten years. Most people take for granted the manicured lawns, cleanliness inside and out. Clean windows, security. Appearance is everything. The general public has no idea how much manpower it takes to keep a million-square-foot complex looking good at all times. Otherwise consumers would take their business somewhere else."

"Ms. Cullors, some people may not recognize that you're a descendent of a very famous family. Your father, known as 'Big Ben,' was a navy lieutenant who was highly decorated during World War II. He retired from that career and began another one as a congressman for Michigan."

"He retired from that job the year that my brother began his campaign for governor."

"And your brother is Governor Loren Lake of Michigan. He's currently running for a third term in office. For those of you who don't follow politics, Governor Lake has just won the primary. How have these men affected your career?"

"Well, I do possess a law degree like my father and brother. And in a lot of ways the Mall of Detroit is just like a city. I have to budget it accordingly. Unlike my family, I'm not interested in politics. What attracted me to the job is the retail business. I'm a clothes freak. And don't get me wrong, I love a good bargain."

Funny, over the past years, Isaac had tried not to think about this woman. About how her life changed after the loss of her daughter. He'd been too busy thinking about how his life was ruined. He knew she had been married then. He wasn't certain that she was now because the host addressed her as Ms. instead of Mrs.

He circled a few of his car choices, and listened more intently as the interview continued.

"It's my job to know every statistic in the retail business. Current information on all of my competitors is readily at my disposal, and I track the data on a daily basis. In 1998 alone, over seven million people are expected to walk through the Mall of Detroit. My goal is to make it ten million before I retire."

"Do you think that's a realistic goal, considering the crime in the city?"

"That's a good question. For those that live in the city of Detroit, safety is my biggest issue. My security officers are exceptionally trained and certified through the Michigan State Police. They have police powers that allow them to arrest people, but only on mall property. I also oversee a staff of eighty-five people made up of office staff, administrative assistants, and my ever-important press department. Weekly newsletters go out to my tenants. Merchant meetings akin to town hall meetings are held once a month with these tenants. The public relations staff and my marketing director are responsible for placing ads on billboards, in newspapers, and on television. I have to be available for weekly interviews on channels two, four, and seven—the most-viewed stations in the city."

Isaac couldn't believe how sharp this woman was. She appeared to be very sure of herself, and not the least bit intimidated by her powerful family. Had she been this way before her daughter died?

"Retail is an industry that everyone is touched by on a daily basis. It's big business. Sears, JCPenney, The Body Shop, Lord & Taylor, Neiman Marcus, Coach, Kenneth Cole, and the Gap are just some of my tenants. I also have the responsibility for the common area, meaning everything that is totally accessible to the public: parking lots and all the main corridors of the shopping center that have to be kept clean, safe, and pleasant. Lights in the parking lot have to be on for at least twelve hours of the day, seven days a week. A separate entity from Detroit Edison, the mall controls the lights."

Isaac wasn't sure if he wanted to keep on listening. It was time to leave, but something made him stay.

"Again, without repeating myself, the biggest challenge I have is shoplifting. Some consumers even have the nerve to steal the plants in the mall's atrium. One year, someone even stole the tulips bordering the entrance to the mall. They lasted three days. Someone dug them up and took them home. Now I no longer plant them. They're probably blooming right now in someone's front yard," she said, laughing. "Now, however, I use a prickly plant, like a cactus, and put the pretty flowers in the middle."

Bradlee Meadows laughed.

He had completely forgotten about buying flowers for his mother's and father's graves. It had been so long since he'd been to the cemetery. He half listened as she continued the interview.

"In all honesty, I'm regretting the meeting with my tenants this afternoon. My sixth sense tells me that the theft they're experiencing this summer is at an all-time high. Decisions have to be made now to prevent further larceny, otherwise some of my tenants won't renew their contracts. No one has to tell me how many challenges the first urban mall in Detroit is up against."

"Especially a black-owned one," the host commented.

"Exactly."

"Why did you choose to work at the Mall of Detroit instead of a mall in the suburbs?"

"I'm not sure. It was a gut decision. Don't tell my family, but I'm a Democrat at heart. Then again"—she paused a minute—"sometimes devastating things happen in your life to make you rethink your priorities."

That stung because he knew the root of her pain.

"In any case, the other malls in the suburbs are waiting for the Mall of Detroit to fail. That's not going to happen. Not as long as I'm in charge."

Isaac turned off the radio and left the house. He didn't know how to react to a woman who could deal with her daughter's death better than he could. She had managed to go on with her life. Developed a take-charge attitude—something he was struggling to maintain.

He continued to look for a job at local nightclubs over the next few days. During that time Dawn's last words haunted him like a fevered dream. It occurred to him that he wasn't in charge. Not of his life, anyway. And no matter what excuses he made to himself or Kennedy, he was definitely not molding his son's future the way he wanted it to be.

It was time to take some type of positive action. The thought of going to Belle Isle now for the holiday seemed like a poor idea. He just wasn't in the mood to people-watch.

Although it bothered him, it didn't matter what Miracall Lake thought of him. What mattered, he thought, was earning back Kennedy's and Peyton's respect.

With half a day left on his day off, he decided to catch the bus to the secretary of state's office to renew his driver's license. Afterward, he stopped by half a dozen used-car dealerships, feeling each bump on his behind from being jostled around on the dilapidated city buses.

Most of the dealers wanted twenty-five hundred dollars down because he had no recent credit history. He finally managed to talk one dealership into accepting one thousand dollars down, but the car was twelve years old and needed too much bodywork. He was desperate, but not stupid.

One of the guys who worked there pulled Isaac to the side.

"Man, you should go down to the strip on Woodward Avenue and see Eli. He owns a string of repair shops. Try the Leaf Collision Shop first. It's between

Woodward and Nine Mile Road. Sometimes customers don't come and pick them back up. Other people say he's got something going with the insurance companies." He shrugged his shoulders. "Either way, Eli ends up getting a mechanic's title on them, and selling them for a huge profit. It's possible you can get a decent deal over there."

Same old Eli. Hustling. "Thanks, man. It's late today. I'll check it out after the holiday."

He'd completely forgotten about Eli's businesses. Over the years, while he was still in prison, he'd heard from new inmates coming into the system who previously lived in his and Eli's old neighborhood that his old buddy was doing pretty well for himself. Some believed too well.

Fatigued and starving by the time he returned home, he made a BLT and watched *In the Heat of the Night* with Jesse.

Both he and Jesse had fallen asleep by the time Rosemary came home. "Isaac? Jesse? Both of y'all get in the bed," she chastised, clicking off the set.

"Night, Isaac," Jesse said, with sleep still in his voice.

"Night, Jesse."

Rosemary began turning out the lights in the room when Isaac called out, "Wait, Rosemary." He finally got up from the chair. "I wanted to remind you about next Sunday. We should both plant the flowers on Mom's and Dad's graves. I can go on Sunday or Monday. Whichever is convenient for you."

"We'll see. Good night." Her tone was so sharp that Isaac was startled. She mumbled something else that he couldn't discern.

Back downstairs, he stripped to his underwear. He felt uneasy. He'd never seen Rosemary act this way before.

He took a seat at his small desk and picked up a pen and paper. A melody began to form in his head. It was kind of sad, but it was good. He quickly scribbled down the musical score in his own type of shorthand. Every now and then he stopped to try out the tune he'd written on his sax. Sweat began to build on his brow and on the tips of his fingers. Pausing for a moment, he reached over and turned on the small fan on his dresser. While the cool air blew over his moist face, he thought about Jesse giving him the bike and hearing that woman talk about how she was renewing her life, going against family values to fight for her own beliefs. Why couldn't he be as strong?

The cool breeze from the fan began to whistle, making music of its own. And in some ways it comforted him. It dried the moist sweat on his naked chest. He left the scattered papers on the bed, and got up to look out the window.

Outside, the moon seemed to have settled just outside his window. He couldn't remember ever experiencing a moon as celestial while he was in prison, and he felt uplifted. He began to envision the words to the music that echoed in his heart at this moment.

The heat in his body had begun to transfer from his head down farther, to his loins. He began to think about Kennedy. He wanted to feel her lips on his face, the pressure of her breasts against his chest. Instantly, he was overcome with a quiver of rapture. Reaching down inside his shorts, he stroked his sex. Slowly, he continued to stroke himself, feeling his hardness grow. Then he stopped, mad at himself. He'd done enough of this stuff in prison.

Opening the window a crack, he turned around to see that the papers had whipped off the desk and were scattered on the floor.

He was so stunned, he couldn't move. At that moment, he made a decision that if he didn't find a gig in the next two weeks, he'd quit the music business altogether.

Until this point, his music had brought him and his family nothing but grief.

Touch of Evil

"We're in trouble," Gary Reynolds said as he paced around the conference table. "We tried to warn them, but no one believed we would be successful. It saddens me that so many Christian folks have so little faith."

Rosemary was just as troubled as Gary was. She watched this small black man take charge of the meeting. He was an average-looking man, with small squinty eyes and thick eyebrows—a man who wore the same suit at least three times a week. No one would suspect that this forty-two-year-old owned the Mall of Detroit and held 19 percent interest in the new mall, Jade Falls, in Auburn Hills, as well as several other expensive commercial properties in southeast Michigan. Gary had been a member of Mother Bethel since 1980, long before he became rich. He hadn't changed a bit—she respected that. Gary was also heavily involved in politics, something that Rosemary didn't understand about him.

They were ensconced in conference room number 2 at Mother Bethel, where Rosemary, Gary, Henry, and six other members—Barry Cooper, Sylvia Scott, Mabel Berry, Gail Norman, Jerry Cook, and Ross Collins—held their monthly meetings. They'd chosen the name Project Hope for the nonprofit organization that they'd formed two years earlier.

Rosemary asked the question that no one wanted to ask. "We're swamped with applicants, right?"

"True. Of the twenty homes that we've gotten the money to renovate, we've received three hundred seventy applicants. I hadn't anticipated this would happen so soon. We haven't got a procedure in place yet to determine how we will select the chosen few. A lottery is my choice. Are there any other suggestions?"

Gail spoke up. "A lottery sounds so worldly. Like gambling. I don't know if our members would appreciate using something so secular."

"I don't agree," Barry offered. "That's the only way to be fair to this many people. It's either that or pull names from a hat!"

The homes were located on Hubbell Street between Puritan and Six Mile Road. Only members of Mother Bethel were eligible for occupancy once the homes were renovated.

"Why can't we take the first twenty applicants?" Rosemary suggested. "After all, those were the ones who believed they would get a home and applied two months ago, when we first suggested this to the congregation. The last three hundred fifty, I believe, just came in the past week or so."

Gary spoke up. "That's true, Rosemary."

"I've got an idea," said Sylvia, who was normally very quiet. "I think we should go by the seniority of the members. I think that's fair."

Rosemary's heart began pounding. She had hoped to secure one of those homes for Isaac. That would leave Isaac out in the cold. Disappointed that he hadn't joined the church yet, she at least had to be satisfied that he was still employed at Remmey's Hair Grease Company.

"I agree," Mabel said.

Henry, who was usually very outspoken, said, "Suits me fine."

"No." Rosemary hoped she wasn't being too aggressive. "Some of the applicants, if I remember correctly, have four or five children. I'm talking about our young folks. It touches my heart every time I see one join. Can we reward the old and penalize the young because it took them longer to find their faith? No. We have to evaluate the needs of each applicant."

Jerry and Ross were talking to each other when Gary began again. "The first ten of the twenty homes won't be ready until Christmas, the remainder by next June. I would like to suggest that we challenge the applicants that whoever brings in the most new members into the church by September fifth gets one. It's your first official day of duty, Rosemary, and you can announce the winners during Sunday service."

Rosemary was delighted. She felt it was a good idea, though she kept silent. She wanted to wait and see what the others would say before she voiced her opinion. Now Isaac did have a chance, although it was a small one.

To her glee, the decision was nearly unanimous. The only holdout was Sylvia Scott. All the others knew why, and the reasons why Sylvia initially joined Project Hope—her husband was Deacon Scott, the man who wanted Rosemary's job.

When she made it home that night, it was eleven-thirty. Jesse had apparently eaten dinner by himself and cleaned up the kitchen. She was too tired to eat, but forced herself to drink a glass of strawberry-kiwi V8 Splash juice.

As she did so, she could hear the television in their small den blaring from the other end of the hall. The noise was followed by bouts of Jesse's laughter.

"Hi, honey," she said to her husband as she stood in the doorway. Jesse didn't even look in her direction. Odd, she thought, and moved over to him. She planted a soft kiss on his cheek and was surprised to feel his body tense, then turn away. "I know I'm late. But that isn't why you're angry. What's wrong?"

He wore navy and green polka-dot pajamas. His small body was eased comfortably back in his navy velvet plush recliner. A copy of *The Last Supper* hung on the wall behind him. Jesse had already taken off his prosthesis for the night, something that Rosemary usually helped him with. Maybe that was it.

"I'm sorry I wasn't here to help you with your leg."

"Stop it. I'm not a child, Rosemary." His still hadn't looked at her. He was concentrating on the colorful figures moving across the screen. "I may enjoy more than my share of cartoons, but I assure you, it's a distraction from my job. Not an influence of my nature."

He knew she knew that. Why was he saying this to her now? Something else was wrong. She felt she knew him, but after three years of marriage and the difference in their ages, maybe she was picking up the wrong vibes. "I'm tired, Jesse. I'm going to bed." She turned to leave. "Are you coming?"

"Later."

His voice was so dry. It cut Rosemary to the core. She went back and knelt down beside him, blocking his view of the screen. As she looked into his eyes, she could feel the heat from the television on her back. "Tell me what's wrong, Jesse. You never acted this way with me before."

It seemed like an hour had passed when he finally spoke. "What do I mean to you?" He silenced her before she could respond. "I believe you love me, Rosemary, but how much? More than Isaac—no. But I can handle that. More than the time you spend at the prison—that's unclear. More than this ministry—I believe again, no. Tell me, Rosemary, just where do I fit in?"

"Jesse—"

"No. Listen. You promised me when you retired in January that we'd spend more time together. That hasn't happened. Isaac is capable of taking care of himself. I'm sure your missionary work is important to you. Still, you're try-ing to heal the sick, comfort the prisoners, fix all the world's problems, and mend Miracall's hatred. How much can one woman do? Especially one that has a husband who has needs, too."

She was speechless. He was right. She had been neglecting him lately. She was so caught up in the church and getting her brother's life back on track, she'd neglected the one man she'd never purposely hurt. Jesse. How could she make him understand how much she loved him without making sorry ex-cuses? And what he had said about loving Isaac more than him cut her deeper than any knife could. Though it wasn't true, she loved them both equally, but in the different ways that a woman loves a husband and a brother. "You're right, Jesse. And I'm sorry. Would cutting down my workload make you happy?"

"Indeed. You're gone seven days a week. I don't expect you to give up your church work. I'm not that selfish."

"I could let the deacons conduct the members' orientations on Saturday." Why hadn't she thought of this before?

Pastor Bell never did. But no, she had to prove to everyone that she could do everything so much more efficiently if she did this and that. But there were other ways.

She felt his hands moving up behind her shoulders as he drew her closer to him. "That's fair." He smiled, and nuzzled his cheek against hers, then softly kissed her on the mouth. "I've got to look out for my wife. I don't want you getting too exhausted. I plan on spending at least thirty more years with you, Babe. You forget, you might look my age, but your body doesn't believe it." He slapped her on the buttocks. "Now you go shower and get in the bed. I'll be there in a few minutes."

He helped her up from her knees, and as he did so she wished for the thousandth time that she weighed her old hundred forty pounds. She could tell that Jesse, with only one leg to use for leverage, was straining to help her up.

"You okay, Mr. Jones?" she teased after they stood face-to-face.

He captured her face in his hands and kissed her hard. "I'm fine, Mrs. Jones." Smiling, he began to unbutton his pajama top. "Hurry, now. I don't plan on waiting too long."

Rosemary blushed. She felt so full of herself as she rushed out the room that she belched. Faint fumes of strawberry-kiwi Splash followed her.

The next morning, Rosemary felt uplifted. She'd just given Jesse his second shot and was on her way home at a decent hour. Earlier that day she'd faxed over her official resignation to the Christian Mentoring Ministries, which she'd been affiliated with for two years. Through Christian Mentoring Ministries, several lives were being changed. Those who previously had no hope were finding hope, she was told.

That night she and Jesse made passionate love again, renewing their commitment to each other. Having toned her thighs to peak level, Rosemary felt positively primal when she straddled him. Her stomach had gone down a notch or two, or so she thought. Jesse couldn't take his hands off her.

"Mrs. Jones," Jesse said weakly, "now that Isaac is staying downstairs, I'm going to have to do something about this squeaking bed."

"You're right, Mr. Jones. But not tonight," she said, moving on top of him again. "Let's worry about that tomorrow."

She ignored the bed squeaking and the headboard banging against the wall. All the hard work was worth it when she heard Jesse's sexy grunts as she rode him like John Travolta rode the mechanical bull in *Urban Cowboy*. She would not stop until she heard his timer go off.

Later, after hearing him snore, and finally drifting off herself, she was awakened by the phone.

"Hello," she whispered, glancing at the clock. It was three o'clock in the morning.

"It's Pastor Bell, Rosemary. I hate to wake you, but I'd appreciate it if you would come down to the church. The police are on their way."

"Police? Don't tell me," she said, rubbing the sleep from her eyes. "Someone's broken into the church?"

While her suspicions were confirmed, she heard Jesse slide from beneath the sheets and begin to put on his leg. When she hung up he said, "I'll drive you, honey. It's too late for you to go out by yourself."

Twenty minutes later, both she and Jesse were shocked by what they saw when they entered the side door of Mother Bethel. Most of the handcrafted stained-glass windows had been broken beyond repair. She could tell that Pastor Bell had been crying. Others still were.

What they saw brought tears to her eyes. There were what appeared to be several wet stains on the altar. But the worst part was what they'd done to the pastor's chair. It was cut to shreds. She couldn't swear to it, but upon closer inspection it looked as if someone had had an orgasm on the velvet chair cushions. Because of the warm weather, flies were already swarming in through the broken windows.

In all her adult years, Rosemary had never seen anything so blatantly evil and disrespectful.

It appeared that at least four people had broken into the church and stolen the computers, video equipment, sound system, organ, and all of the choir's musical instruments.

Deacon Scott rolled his eyes at Rosemary. "This confirms my position to move. This is the third larceny this year. As you know, our insurance premiums are going to go up. We were warned; now we're forced to purchase high-risk insurance. If someone had lis—"

"Hmmrph," interrupted Pastor Bell as he took a seat on the front pew. His voice was harsh but calm when he spoke to Deacon Scott. "This is not the time to point fingers. We're all saddened by this turn of events. And, Lord knows I have faith, but this is truly a test. September can't come fast enough."

Rosemary felt Jesse's arm tighten around her waist. She wondered if this was the time to tell Jesse about September, or wait. With all the misunderstandings they'd had lately, her mind told her that now wasn't the time. She kept silent.

Several detectives were taking pictures and questioning the other members who'd apparently heard about the tragedy and come out tonight.

To her left, two of the female members who had been openly crying left to go to the janitor's room. They returned with a bucket of hot water, disinfectant, and sponges. Mumbling quietly to each other, they began cleaning up the messes on the altar and the pastor's chair.

"I'm sorry, Pastor Bell," Deacon Scott abruptly interrupted. "I still feel that we should reconsider buying the Edgewater Park property on Seven Mile Road. It sits on twenty acres of land. Five times as much as we have now. Can you imagine all the trouble-free parking we would have."

It was a moot point. The original owners of the property had put the land back on the market after two churches reneged on the land contract. For more than five years, the property remained unsold. Something was wrong, but no one was talking. They'd lowered the price, and, in truth, Mother Bethel could push it and work out a deal, but still, it was too much for Rosemary to think about when she was just taking over a church that was already in debt. She had to find ways to increase membership and bring more money into the church. In her estimation, that meant conserving the monies they had and not spending any more.

"We've been through this," Pastor Bell cut him off. "Mother Bethel is already two million dollars in debt. How in the world can we afford to buy property that costs a million dollars at this point?"

Deacon Jones sneered. "I'm sure Sister Jones has a few ideas. After all, no one would listen to any of my proposals."

Rosemary held her temper. She'd done her best to get along with Deacon Scott. Sure, she knew he wanted her job and would do anything to get it. The Lord was testing her faith, to get along with this man. After all, hundreds of people admired him, and he oversaw the church choirs, involving more than two hundred adults and young people. He sang like the late Reverend C. L. Franklin. The members positively adored him. It would be a mistake for Rosemary to make him her enemy.

"I have a temporary solution," Rosemary spoke up. "We could pay for one security guard to watch the building twelve hours a day—six P.M. till six A.M. Or we could have a Brinks alarm system installed and wired to the police station." The security system would cost thousands. The best option, she knew, was hiring a guard.

She felt Jesse's nudge—he knew her so well. She was thinking of Isaac. He'd already hinted to her that he disliked working at the grease company.

Before she could finish her thoughts, Pastor Bell interrupted her.

"Why, Sister Jones, hiring a security guard is the best idea I've heard all evening. Look into it, will you?" He glanced at the pulpit, then lowered his head. "I'm going home."

"Let's go," Jesse said. "We can't do anything more here, tonight."

Rosemary smiled. He had said *we*. That meant that he believed in her.

From the beginning of theology school, where her class was 65 percent female, she'd been told that the ministry of women was that of service. Traditionally, they were willing to go anywhere, undertake any cause, and make any sacrifice—she was thankful tonight that abstaining from her husband hadn't been one of them.

After they returned home and Jesse had fallen asleep, Rosemary couldn't rest. It was nearly dawn outside and she used the time to edit the sermon that she planned to deliver next Sunday. Her heart felt troubled. Isaac seemed to be avoiding her. The only time she caught a glimpse of him was when he was fast asleep. She couldn't understand what was *troubling* him. What bothered her more was that she was hurt that he didn't confide in her. Especially about washing his clothes. Rosemary hated to admit it, but she was jealous of Jesse and Isaac's easy friendship.

As she sat at the kitchen table with her Bible open to Gen. 8:6–8, she turned on News Radio 95. She felt it was her civic duty to incorporate the timely news that affected today's society into her sermon. People seemed to understand her better, listen better, if they could see how the circumstances in biblical times mirrored the problems in today's times. In short, the Scripture being fulfilled.

The news was worse than she'd heard in years. Gangs and drugs were taking over the city. Executions were occurring frequently. Rosemary thought about the record Gil Scott-Heron a former inmate of Jefferson Penitentiary, had made in 1975. It was entitled "We Almost Lost Detroit."

When she glanced up and checked the time, it was seven-thirty. She knew that Kennedy would be up. Rosemary picked up the phone. They'd remained friendly toward each other, and their conversations were always easy.

"Hey, sister-in-law. It's always good to hear from you," Kennedy said, a smile in her voice.

"Say, do you remember that fellow who wrote the song about Detroit in the seventies?"

"Gil Scott-Heron. Sure, I do. The brother was bad. Ahead of his time. He was always talking about change. Everything he did had some kind of statement. He drew national attention when he wrote about the nuclear reactor in Monroe County."

"I'd nearly forgotten."

"Yep. The reactor was going to melt down. If it did, no vegetation would grow and no life could be sustained for the next one hundred fifty-five years. The authorities knew about it—the Michigan Public Service Commission and the sheriff of Monroe County. The public was kept totally in the dark."

"Gil Scott-Heron wrote songs that stimulated your consciousness. One in particular was 'Tuskegee 626.'"

"Don't you mean the Tuskegee experiment, with dozens of black men with syphilis?"

"No. I'm talking about a study at Tuskegee when they were testing the effects of LSD on unwilling and unknowing men of color. Whenever they talked about it, 626 was the code name. In 1980 he wrote a song about angel dust. That was the drug that was popular from 1978 to 1981. He even wrote songs for Indians about how the forest is now buried beneath the highways, like the peace sign has vanished in our dreams."

"My Lord," Rosemary said. "I'd nearly forgotten about the peace signs. I remember when everybody and everyone wore one. I think I still have mine in my dresser drawer."

"I think I gave mine to the Salvation Army." She paused a moment. "Yeah, the man is still doing good deeds. I heard that Gil Scott-Heron is a professor at the City College of New York. You know, I do believe that Isaac still has some of his records. That man hoards everything."

Rosemary could tell that even though Kennedy appeared to be disappointed in Isaac, she still held high hopes that he would one day redeem himself.

No matter how far their conversation strayed, they usually got back to the main topic of conversation—Peyton.

"Are you and Peyton doing anything next Sunday, Kennedy?"

Kennedy hesitated for a second. "What time? I've got plans in the evening."

"Mother Bethel around eleven." She waited for Kennedy's answer. Then Rosemary hesitated. "Could you drop by my house and pick up Isaac first?"

Kennedy cleared her throat. "Well—just for you."

"Thanks, Kennedy. I don't want to spoil my surprise. Trust me, it's important for all of us."

"Okay. But Isaac and I—Isaac and I—"

"I'm not asking for explanations. That's between you and him."

Her voice was low and filled with conviction. "I love him, Rosemary. I haven't loved anyone since. But I can't make him into the man he should be. Could be. No matter how much I love him. Or how much you love him. I want him to become the man we both know he can be."

Rosemary felt fresh tears cloud her eyes, and she dabbed at them with a napkin. Why did true love always have to be so hard?

"I've been waiting for him to get himself together. I'm confident that he will. I don't care if he doesn't become as famous as Gill Scott-Heron. I just want him to get his priorities straight. Isaac's been in my blood since I was sixteen," Kennedy said with mock seriousness. "I became a cop because of Isaac. Strangely enough, I wanted to hear from other men like him how they felt. Understand why he did the things he did to me, and to our son. I wanted to one day feel his loving arms around me and truthfully say to him: 'Baby, I understand how you feel.' "

She couldn't help it—Rosemary broke down crying. Nothing could hold back the tears that flowed from her eyes and that she felt from her heart. She had had no idea that Kennedy still felt this strongly about Isaac.

"Since Isaac entered prison, I've heard a lot of nasty stories about the Coleman men being no good. I don't believe it."

Rosemary wondered where she'd heard that. It was true about the other Coleman men, but it was a subject that Rosemary didn't want to discuss.

"Isaac is a decent man. I don't care if his last name was Winston. I just want him to be the respectable man that I know he should be."

Again, Rosemary was speechless. No wonder he loved her. This was a woman who planned on standing by her man, even if he didn't realize it right now. Without her saying so, they both knew it would benefit Isaac more if he thought she didn't care. Because even though Isaac denied it, she always knew that Isaac loved Kennedy. And always would.

After the conversation about Isaac was finished, Rosemary wanted to touch on another issue—the Detroit Police Department. She summarized what she'd heard over the radio a few moments ago.

"What's the hush-hush about, Kennedy?" Rosemary asked. "This doesn't make sense. And the mayor, I thought he was squeaky clean."

"This is confidential, Rosemary. The city is undergoing major changes. They're experiencing catastrophic internal problems that the department doesn't necessarily want the public to know about."

"I don't understand. What does that mean?"

"Simply said—politics. Election year brings out the dog in most people. Money is power. People are being paid off—right down to the police officials. It's worse than what you see in the movies."

"That's Detroit's politics for you—downright dirty. I thought I was informed, but obviously not well enough. Regardless, the church can't live without the cooperation of the city. I can't ignore that fact."

"I've lived in Detroit all my life, Rosemary. I'm ashamed to say that the image of the city of Detroit is at an all-time low. The homicide rate is higher than it's been in ten years. Rape is up eight percent. The women are afraid to go out alone at night. Last month, five women taking night courses at Wayne State were raped right on the main campus."

Rosemary took a deep breath. She'd taken night courses at Wayne for four years to receive her theology degree. During that time, she never even thought of being raped or mugged.

"Half the residents believe that the city is going downhill. Tourists are calling Detroit 'The Murder City,' instead of 'The Motor City.' The citizens of Detroit are more concerned about how many millions the Detroit Lions paid for Barry Sanders's new contract. They want to know when the new stadium will be opening for the Lions—or exactly when the new Tiger Stadium will be completed on Woodward. And Rosemary, I won't even discuss the casino, which I believe is the biggest mistake that Mayor Prescott has ever made."

Rosemary was overwhelmed. She remembered reading the stories about Detroit in elementary school. Back then, *Life* magazine hailed Detroit as a world-class city. Renowned sociologists said the 1920s were a time when Detroit was the center of technological advance in America and abroad. All the best minds in the country were here. It had some of the best art collections in the world. And because of this, Detroit was attracting tourists from all over the world.

"I know what you're thinking, Rosemary. Detroit has changed for the worse. There are so many corrupt policemen, the public would be shocked. Gang members are better armed than we are. Some of the cops won't admit it, but they're afraid of them. Millions of dollars in drug money tempts them daily. I'm not one of them, Rosemary. I want to make some changes. I believe in this city. I'd give my life for it. It bothers me to hear that Detroit is no longer respected in the eyes of this country. No one wants to live here. Relocate here. New businesses aren't breaking down the doors to return to the city. Crime is at an all-time high. Murder remains a major concern. The jails are overcrowded. And I'd like to emphasize that the *gangs* and *drug dealers* are taking over the city."

Rosemary could hear the conviction in her voice. She knew Isaac was in her immediate thoughts.

"I'm proud of you, Kennedy. You're always in my prayers. And I believe in my heart that one day you, Peyton, and Isaac will be reunited as a family."

"Thanks. You know, this will be the first time the three of us have been in church together since Peyton was christened."

"Yes, I do know. And I pray that it won't be the last."

Beware of Pity

That same night Isaac was extremely nervous. He wasn't looking forward to being forced into going to church. Apparently, Rosemary had talked to Kennedy, who managed to contact him at work. She asked if he would attend church with her and Peyton next Sunday.

Isaac hoped that a gathering such as this could be the key that would remove the barriers between him and Peyton. If it took going to church every Sunday, he was willing to do it to get his family back together. He would do whatever it took to open a channel of communication between them.

Looking in the mirror, he changed into another outfit. Several discarded shirts and slacks were laid across his bed. He reached up to the top shelf of his closet and removed a black leather hat. Adjusting the hat on his head until it rested an inch above his left brow, he checked the mirror once more.

"No, that won't work," he said, tossing the hat on the bed. "I look like a jitterbug."

He changed his clothes six more times, checking in the mirror from every possible direction. Disliking the look even less, he decided that nothing worked and he would not be attending church, or any place other than work, until he could buy some decent clothes.

The four-day, ten-hour workweek at Remmey's fit in great with his schedule. He had long weekends to hunt for a gig at a club and was able to practice for at least four to six hours a day. But on his second week of work, he was told that in two weeks the plant would be put on a six-day, ten-hour shift.

That Friday, as he usually did, he pounded the pavement in the only suit he owned. He even traveled as far as Toledo, Ohio, to submit applications to the local newspapers. To his dismay, the outcome was the same.

"Sorry, Mr. Coleman, the position you're applying for requires at least a year of experience. The *Toledo Free Press* is interested in hiring minorities—even ex-convicts. We have an Outreach Program that works with parole officers. However, those jobs are in the printing department. Would you be interested in working in that capacity?"

Isaac's eyes were steady and shielded. "No. I have a degree, sir. I intend to utilize it."

He thought about his number-one idol, the deceased journalist and anchorman Max Robinson, who died a few years before Isaac went to prison.

Now more determined than ever to use the degree that he had worked so hard for, he prayed for patience. During those trying periods he felt angry, like most ex-convicts, and believed that life just wasn't fair. Yet deep down he knew he had made his own bed and it was up to him, not Rosemary, to set things right.

The only good thing at this moment was that he'd been able to give Kennedy some money. Yet, working in a factory made him feel like a failure, like he was giving up on his dream to be a journalist. God had blessed him to earn a degree, and by giving him the talent to play music. He felt that if he didn't exhaust all of his energies to make at least one of those dreams possible, he wouldn't be able to look at himself in a mirror ten years from now—knowing he wasn't successful because he didn't try hard enough.

Another good thing that came out of the job was meeting a young man named Bernie on his second day of employment. Isaac guessed that Bernie was about twenty-three or so. Presently, he played the trumpet with a six-piece bebop jazz band that he believed would soon dwindle down to four.

"We could use a good tenor sax, Isaac," Bernie had told him after work. "The one we have now is a genius. But he can't stay off that crack, man."

Bernie scribbled down the name and address of the residence where they rehearsed every night. "I'm not sure, Bernie. I'll think about it. Maybe I'll stop by near the end of the week."

"It's tough to get work in the city. Sometimes we go as far as Grand Rapids. Luckily, we were able to secure two big weddings next month. You know how those women feel about those June weddings, man."

Isaac smiled. He and Kennedy were married in June, but it hadn't been a happy affair. Kennedy was three months' pregnant, and as evil as a hungry wolverine. And though a shotgun wasn't present, he felt that one was aimed at his back just the same.

The parking lot was small. It held fifteen cars. Before Bernie approached his, Isaac knew which one it was. A little cocky, but nice, Bernie stopped beside a 1997 silver Firebird and removed his keys. "With all the new casinos scheduled to be built next year, and all the entertainment that's booked year-round, we're going to get all kinds of work. You got to get your name out there now, man."

"I don't know, Bernie," Isaac said. "I've always worked solo." He could see the disappointment in the young man's face, and he wasn't sure why it bothered him so much. "Tell you what, I'll stop by one night this week and check y'all out."

He turned and left for the bus station. He checked out Bernie's car as he passed by and waved, turning down the ride Bernie offered. The Firebird positively glittered in the afternoon sun. Obviously, Bernie wasn't doing too bad for himself.

Isaac still hadn't made it to Eli's. But the thought of driving a fairly new car was putting bad vibes in his head. It was still too early to think about buying a car. And even though the Harley was a gift, it would cost him more money at this point than he'd previously decided to spend.

It turned out that Bernie was right—a majority of the club owners didn't want solo acts, they wanted bands. That prompted him to stop by to see Bernie.

His first impression was how good the group was. They played all kinds of music—jazz, cool jazz, pop, classical music, funk, and free-form improvisation. This was a turning point for Isaac. He hadn't realized how far today's musicians had advanced. He was even surprised to see the high-tech equipment they had. Even though he knew he had talent, his act wasn't this versatile. From that day forward he began revamping his style.

Less than a week later, when he auditioned for a new restaurant on Woodward Avenue, he played African music, then added some reggae, Kenny G, Wynton Marsalis, and even some Benny Goodman tunes. Because of the mixed crowd—young and old, white and black—that frequented the establishment, he was able to impress the Motor City Grille. He tried to contain his excitement when he was given a probationary job for the holiday weekend. If the audience liked him, they would then discuss a permanent contract.

On Saturday morning, he shopped at Hot Sam's on Gratiot Avenue and bought a pair of fluid charcoal-gray slacks and a loose white shirt trimmed with gray and black fabric on the lapels and cuffs. The outfit wasn't very expensive, but it did hang well on his body. Back at home, he showered and trimmed his close-cut beard and sideburns. Even though the clothes were new, he took the time to starch and iron them. After slapping some Cool Water on his face and chest he unplugged the iron, put the board back in its place, and left his cozy room almost as excited as the day he'd been released from prison.

When he left home at seven-thirty that evening, it was pitch-dark outside. He splurged and hailed a taxi to take him downtown. Thirty minutes later, when the taxi pulled up on Woodward Avenue, it seemed like eight o'clock in the morning, the area was so alive and brilliant.

Even the people seemed to emit some form of light. Whether it was a woman's shiny lips or a man's gold watch, everywhere he looked, someone or something glistened. After paying the driver, he eased his sax case over his shoulder and breathed in the night air. He was so nervous, he thought he'd forget every song that he'd memorized for tonight's performance.

Housed in the Fisher Building, where the Motor City Grille was located, was the Fisher Theater. *The Devil Is a Woman* was playing, and most of the crowd was already moving toward the restaurant where he would be performing. He felt energized by all the excitement.

After he entered the restaurant, he was taken to a small room where he could practice until it was time for him to perform. Even though the Motor City Grille wasn't an exceptionally highbrow restaurant, it was usually packed every night.

The gold-painted, hand-carved vaulted ceiling was a stark contrast to the automobile engine next to the hostess's stand. A huge saltwater aquarium would hold your attention for a while, but only reminded you of an expensive seafood restaurant. The brightly colored car motifs on the walls seemed quite innovative at first glance, but were too trendy to be deemed elegant. But Isaac had done his homework. The Grille was in an excellent location and did a ton of business.

An hour later, Isaac was all about business. The knock on his dressing-room door meant it was showtime.

Having gone over the stage lights with the manager beforehand, he waited until the disco ball began to glow. A small applause from the audience followed before Isaac placed the mouthpiece against his tongue and began a slow introduction to "Soul Serenade." He didn't appear onstage right away.

He wanted to delay his entrance as long as possible, until all heads turned to see where the music was coming from. It took only thirty seconds for the crowd to quiet down and move toward the stage. People began to snap their fingers and clap to the beat. It was then that Isaac picked up the tempo and stepped out from behind the curtain. He began working his shoulders up and down, using his sax as his dance partner as he moved toward the center.

Sweat began to coat his forehead and armpits, but it wasn't nervousness. No, glancing at the crowd enjoying his performance made him feel excited. This was the best time he'd had in a long time, and he wanted to capture the moment.

He continued to move across the stage like a whisper in a dream. The loose white tunic and slacks he wore didn't hide the muscular body underneath. And the way he swayed his hips let you know the muscles didn't end there.

By the third song, the women were grabbing at him. By the fourth, people were standing outside the restaurant looking in and, he was sure, wondering what all the excitement was about.

Just before the intermission, he noticed three particular women who had been eyeing him all evening. One was Caucasian and had on a tight white tank dress. The second, who was particularly sexy but certainly not the best-looking, wore a black lace dress. And the third he thought he recognized. And then he knew—it was Miracall. She wore a simple pale-gold raw-silk minidress with a matching wrap that had slipped down around a pair of perfect shoulders.

Someone shouted to him, "You sound just like Everette Harp!"

Another said, "He sounds better than that. Can you play 'What's Going On?' We want to dance."

Isaac was too overwhelmed to speak. He had no idea who Everette Harp was.

Gathering his thoughts and his voice, he began the intro music to his next number, then paused, letting the sax fall to his side. He picked up the microphone and said in husky whisper, "Wow!" The crowd settled down, knowing what the next song would be.

Isaac began softly whispering the words to his favorite version of "Fire and Desire," by Rick James and Tina Marie. He noticed that someone was singing the words with him, a woman who had the voice to do Tina's part. The audience turned, hearing the sensual resonance of her voice. Isaac made a motion with his hand for her to come onstage. The young woman began to sing the words with so much soul that it would have made Tina Marie jealous.

Everyone was shouting and screaming. The duo was fabulous, and he'd gotten the crowd involved. He looked toward the back and saw a wide grin on the owner's face. The first set was nearly over—and his confidence in himself was overflowing. He anticipated that the second would be twice as good.

As he turned to leave the stage, he noticed that the three foxy ladies were gathering their things to leave also. And as he left to freshen up and prepare for the next set, he couldn't figure out why he couldn't get the look on Miracall's face off his mind.

Although it had been known among the staff at Mother Bethel AME, the congregation hadn't been apprised of Rosemary's appointment that transpired on May 1.

She'd worried herself nearly to death over how the church would receive her. What if they rejected her? What if they demanded another male minister for their pastor instead of a female one? What if they walked out? Then what would she do? All night she'd prayed for the answers to these questions. She kept hearing the word *family* being repeated in her mind. And then she knew—it was important for her family to be there tomorrow, to show their support.

Isaac didn't come home until four in the morning. She prayed that he wouldn't come up with a pitiful excuse why he couldn't come today. Before she'd gone to bed last night, Kennedy had called her and said that she and Peyton would be at her house around ten A.M.

Rosemary had invited Miracall as well, but hadn't heard back from her. She assumed that Miracall was debating whether she wanted to face Isaac again. Rosemary was honest and told her that he would be there, along with his ex-wife and child. But she told Miracall that it would especially please her if she would attend today.

It was fifteen minutes before ten, and Rosemary felt nervous as she stood before the mirror in the front hallway. Jesse had already left; he taught Sunday school each week to thirty vociferous teenagers. As she lifted the small corsage of pink roses from the plastic container and pinned it to the lapel of her size twelve navy linen suit, she heard the hesitant dragging of her brother's footsteps coming up behind her. As a child, Isaac always walked this way after he had done something wrong. The familiar pattern made her smile to herself, but since she had already anticipated Isaac's excuse, she was prepared for him.

"I can't go, Rosemary. My suit is at the cleaners," Isaac said, yawning. "And you know Jesse's clothes are way too small."

You'll soon have enough money to buy two or three, she thought, thinking about his job at the hair-grease company that was working out just fine. "Times have indeed changed, Isaac," Rosemary reminded her brother as she secured her white straw hat with a pearl-tipped hat pin. "The Lord will accept you wearing a pair of jeans and a clean shirt. I've already washed and starched them and they're hanging on the clothesline downstairs."

So, without any further excuses, Kennedy and Peyton picked up Isaac at ten A.M. and together they followed Rosemary to church.

Dinner was already prepared. Rosemary had risen at five A.M. and was proud of herself for sticking to the strict regimen of her diet. She hadn't cheated, not once, by dipping into the pots of smoked turkey and greens or sampling her three-cheese macaroni-cheese casserole oozing with sweet butter, or making sure her butter frosting for her famous coconut cake was sweet enough.

When they entered the church, Rosemary was so proud of her brother and his son and wife. People greeted them so kindly, as if they had been regular members for years.

Rosemary had never seen Kennedy look so pretty, except on the day that she and Isaac were married. Today, she wore a two-piece white suit with black-and-white spectator pumps and a matching purse. Rosemary was certain that Isaac had had something to do with her choice of clothing; and he hadn't taken his eyes off her since they got out of the car. Peyton was equally handsome in black Polo jeans, shirt, and matching gym shoes.

All four took a seat in the middle section. The choir entered shortly afterward from the rear, followed by the pastor, and began the first selection.

Rosemary stood, along with the rest of the congregation, and began singing the words to the song "I Love You with My Whole Heart, Body and Soul."

After the second song, everyone bowed their heads as the assistant pastor lead the morning prayer. Reading the Scriptures, the announcements, the invitation to join the congregation, went by quicker than Rosemary had imagined it would. When the door opened on the side of the pulpit, the bishop entered.

This is it, Rosemary thought. She felt the tranquillity of a single white rose. The feeling soothed her spirits and made her feel melancholy, all at the same time. And it was all she could do to hold back tears of joy. She knew that other Christians, like her, also had the potential of a rose—to grow, to bloom, to release their sweet fragrance and give beauty to all who came near them.

She heard the doors swing open, and when she turned around, as several other women had, she saw Miracall taking a seat in the back pew. She swallowed back tears. God had answered her prayers.

Just in time, she thought as the bishop stepped up to the microphone.

"As you may know, Pastor Bell is ill. He'll be leaving us in September. We have a wonderful replacement for him who we're happy to announce has accepted the position. We are asking for your blessings."

He then looked over toward the assistant pastor, who nodded and then stood. Pastor Bell stood next, raised his arm, and lifted his opened palms toward Rosemary. "Won't you stand, Sister Jones."

Rosemary clutched her hands against her Bible and watched from the corner of her eye as the entire congregation turned to the area where she and her family were sitting. When she stood, she could hear Isaac and Kennedy whispering beside her.

"I'd like everyone to give a hearty hand-clap to the new pastor of Mother Bethel AME." Pastor Bell motioned for Rosemary to join them onstage.

She measured each step carefully until she reached the pulpit. Smiling, she held her head high. Even though she held a written copy of her sermon in hand, she had tried to memorize as much of her message as possible.

After adjusting the microphone she said nervously, "Thank you, Bishop, Pastor Bell, Assistant Pastor Nixon. I'd like to give honor to Pastor Bell today and hope that God will grant him better health in the future." Carefully realigning her thoughts, she swallowed hard. She wanted to say that even though Pastor Bell was ill, she didn't want to overstep her position until she was the official pastor in September. Instead she said, "My message today, ladies and gentleman, is Trying to Find Hope in Difficult Times."

Within seconds, the choir began to hum "How Firm a Foundation," with a female soprano softly singing the lead. The melody was lighter than air—full of musical striving and stretching that made one's spirit feel as if it were being elongated. Rosemary hummed along with them, feeling as if she were being massaged from the inside. Even without the accompaniment of instruments, there was no better thrill for her than emotional messages underscored by emotional music.

Her eyes focused on the upper balcony, filled mostly with teenagers. "We must pray for the souls who broke into our church." She noticed that some of the young folks began to ease back in their seats. "We don't know their circumstances. We don't know what drove them to feel such animosity toward the church. Who are we, then, to judge them?"

Pastor Bell began to rock.

"Amen," the bishop shouted.

"I'm afraid there are a good many of us who are tempted daily, and I believe a great many of us here today that indulge in the practice of calumny; folks who go around speaking evil of our neighbors, our friends. Even speaking evil of the church. I'll admit, and I believe many of you will as well, that calumny is one of the crying sins of today's society, and one which, though it is of the most pernicious consequence to the public and private peace and virtue, is one of our hardest vices to repress or control."

She thought about Isaac, Paps, and the problems that Peyton was experiencing in school, and her voice deepened. She remembered the hatred that registered on Miracall's face when she saw Isaac. It was evil. It was the devil.

"The evil in some degree can be neutralized, but the slander that is transmitted over telephones, cell phones, beepers, and via email, that is hinted at by one and magnified by another, is impossible to counteract."

She hadn't meant for the words to carry such a sarcastic edge. To some they did. Then she heard Pastor Bell say, "Amen," followed by several others in the congregation. It was like a bell ringing and reverberating: "Amen, Amen, Amen." She reared her shoulders back, holding her head even higher when she spotted Jesse's somber face near the rear doors.

"When people speak evil of you, let it be a warning to put a halt to those vices of which you are accused," she began, speaking out of her own intuition. "Surely, we have more temptations in these times than did our ancestors. But I'd like to remind you of one great man, Plato, who was told that his enemies traduced him. His reply was, 'It's no matter. I will live so that nobody shall believe them.' "

Removing the microphone from its stand and walking down the steps of the pulpit, she paused on the bottom step. She emphatically repeated the phrase " 'I will live so that nobody shall believe them!' Hallelujah!"

She could feel the perspiration coating her forehead, and took a moment to mop off the moisture with a handkerchief, then quickly scanned the congregation, gauging the reactions on their faces.

When the choir had finished their selection, a woman sitting in front of Miracall began to sing, "Amazing grace, how sweet the sound."

Moving down the aisle, Rosemary spotted a weeping mother rocking her crying infant. Extending her arms, she said, "May I?" The woman, relieved and still crying, handed Rosemary the child. The wailing baby felt so good against her bosom as she rocked him.

"What a beautiful baby." Picking up the infant's hand, she stroked the inside of it, felt his little fingers clutching around hers. His cries became slumberous and Rosemary felt encouraged.

She smiled, stroking the child's moistened cheeks.

"Just days ago, many of the mothers here today probably received gift-wrapped boxes of chocolates for Mother's Day. There might have been a single piece missing in some. We probably could even guess which one of our children took it." Swirling around, she studied the mothers' faces, smiling and nodding back at her. "I believe that none of the mothers here today would believe that their sweet child was capable of anything as serious as breaking into a church and stealing their treasures."

When Rosemary noticed that the child had fallen asleep, she walked back to the mother. "There is good in all of God's children," she said, and handed the baby back to the woman.

"There is good in all of God's children," she continued, moving down another aisle. "We are already His created children. But, church, we know that when you're saved, you become a child of God on a different level."

"Amen, preach, Pastor Jones," someone shouted.

"Some of you here today may wonder, how do I become saved?" Her voice was as calm as a saint in Paradise. "All you have to do is believe that Jesus died for our sins. Once you do, you've got a new spirit. You've got a re-created spirit. The things you used to do, you won't have the desire to do anymore. You won't even understand it. God said, 'You aren't here because you chose me' . . . Oh, no . . . God said . . . I chose you. God said, 'You are my child and you will be saved.' "

People stood up clapping and shouting: "Preach! Preach!" Rosemary wiped her forehead and felt more relaxed than she had before.

Standing before the middle row, she noticed a young man openly crying. She moved to a spot in front of him and touched his shoulder. "This youth is struggling with something today. God said you got to turn it loose." Releasing him, she backed up, placing her hands on the youth beside him. "God might tell another, 'Hold on.' About time everyone gets through turning loose and holding on, folks in here are going to get saved. Lives are going to be changed."

She smiled at the young man, who was whispering "Thank you, Jesus" as she headed back toward the pulpit.

"When you were born God cast a vote for you in heaven. The Devil said, 'Oh, no,' and cast a vote for you in hell. There's a tie going on and it's up to you to break it.

"These youths that stole from us was nothing but the work of the devil. They know not what they do. These are not *saved* children. Many of our young people today are influenced by gangsta rap music, high-salary athletes, and violent films that tend to sway the children to vie for the bad guy's success over the heroes. We need not put our faith in these worldly devices, and urge our children not to as well. We have to focus on what's really important to us as Christians, which are the needs of the poor and introducing hope in the face of monumental cynicism." She gathered her papers, and somehow found herself staring directly into Isaac's somber eyes. "I ask you today for grace. Grace is what we seek for every situation and every need in these difficult times. Pray for our young people today, church, so that they will live in a manner that we will always trust and believe in them." She paused. "All heads bowed, every eye closed—let us pray."

Though Miracall refused to come to dinner, Rosemary was proud that she had accepted her invitation to come to church today. She couldn't shake the strained look on Miracall's face after she hugged and kissed her, then left. It was obvious that Miracall didn't know what to say to Isaac and his family. But with prayer, Rosemary knew, all would be well soon enough.

Later, when she returned home, she noticed Kennedy's car parked in front of their house. Once inside, she saw Jesse sitting at the dining room table, wearing an angry expression on his face. Up to this point, she hadn't realized that Jesse hadn't congratulated her on her sermon or her position as the new pastor. Rosemary was genuinely hurt by Jesse's attitude. Totally out of character, he looked like he was ready to explode.

"I don't like it, Rosemary," Jesse mumbled as he removed his tie and laid it on the table. Rosemary, standing behind him, quickly picked it up.

Rosemary rolled her eyes at Jesse, ignoring him. He knew that she didn't allow anyone to sit at her mother's table. Removing her hat, she placed her purse, Bible, and Jesse's tie on the chair in the hall and noticed that Isaac and Kennedy were sitting side by side on the living room sofa, having what appeared to be a very private conversation.

Rosemary smiled. Even though her brother denied it, she knew how much he still loved Kennedy. It was only a matter of time, she thought, before they would be back together. She hoped Isaac realized that things like this took time. They had to get to know each other all over again if they were ever going to have a lasting relationship.

"Where's Peyton?" she asked Jesse as she passed by him on her way to the kitchen.

"Downstairs," Jesse answered. "He mumbled something about checking out Isaac's record collection he'd been bragging about ever since he came home."

She heard him strumming his fingers noisily against the table, and imagined ugly hand marks all over the beautiful cherry wood. "Jesse?"

"Are my khakis washed?"

Moving over to the shelf that was lined with six elegant cake stands, she removed one. "Yes, they're in the third dresser drawer."

She flipped the switch to the ceiling fan on, then turned on all four burners to heat up the food. Not an exceptional singer, Rosemary loved to sing while she cooked. She began with "Precious Lord, Take My Hand" as she placed the yellow cake on the platter and began applying the cream-cheese icing.

Her well-equipped kitchen would be the envy of many professionals, with four mixers, a giant food processor, and other machines for making culinary magic. The kitchen was the largest on her block, and she loved for a neighbor to drop by on a Saturday morning for a cup of coffee and a croissant and admire a new gadget or wall hanging that Rosemary had recently purchased.

By the time she placed a pretty peach linen tablecloth on the table, Rosemary had begun singing "What a Friend We Have in Jesus." She set the table with peach and white floral china and gold flatware, and placed a small vase with fresh wildflowers in the center. Standing back to admire her work, she smiled. "Perfect."

Her hands were resting on the back of the chair when she felt the floor beneath her feet vibrate. Peyton had turned up the music full blast, and the poor old house was voicing its objection. Curtis Mayfield's "Keep on Pushing" was obviously a song that Peyton could identify with. Not too bad, she thought. It talked about reaching higher goals, realizing that one had strength. She loved hearing "Hallelujah. Hallelujah."

Without realizing it, she found herself fanning her face. She hadn't noticed before how hot the house was, and turned the air conditioner down to 66 degrees. Isaac and Kennedy must have felt stifled by the oven, because when she checked on them they were already sitting on the front porch.

It was 85 degrees outside. The fresh fragrance from the gladiolas in her flower garden seeped into the screened-in porch. Purple hydrangeas and petunias from a neighbor's yard across the street danced to the rhythm of the wind, adding to the balmy atmosphere. She admired all the beauty she saw here today, and wondered how long it had been since she'd associated this same fineness with her mother. It had been years since she planted flowers on her grave. The last time she went, the lifeless stems, fallen leaves, and colorless weeds reminded her of . . .

"Rosemary? Are you okay?" Isaac asked.

She hadn't realized how long she'd been standing in the doorway. "Sure. The oven's turned off now. I turned the air-conditioning up. You two can come back inside in ten minutes. The house should be cooled down by then."

As she passed back through the dinning room, she hollered down the hall, loud enough so that Jesse could hear her in their bedroom, "Come on in here, Mr. Jones. Help me get this supper served."

By the time Rosemary called them to the kitchen for dinner, she and Jesse had called a truce, which Rosemary knew was certainly just temporary. Peyton was already seated when Isaac and Kennedy came in from the porch and took their seats.

"Tell me. How is your job working out, Kennedy?" Jesse asked.

Just as Rosemary knew she would, Kennedy elaborated on how some of the male officers at work treated her. Rosemary had heard Kennedy's complaints before. They began four years ago, shortly after Kennedy took the recruitment test. She mentioned how difficult the firearms training was, and how each year she had to qualify at the marksmanship level at the pistol range—this was the only part of her job that she hated. Ironically, it was the one that would probably save her life. Kennedy told everyone at the table about the problems she was having getting respect on her job.

"With so many women joining the police force now," Jesse began, "does the department pair them off with other female officers first?"

"No. Seniority has a little to do with being able to pick your partner. The sergeants do try to be fair. They realize that some men don't want to work with female officers, even though most of the female cops are as good or better qualified. Most are better educated."

"How about the pay scale? Male verses female?" Jesse asked Kennedy.

"It's the same everywhere. Men always seem to make more than females no matter what the classification. In most cases, twenty to thirty percent more."

Rosemary said a silent prayer. She and Jesse never discussed money. Both were tightwads and enjoyed living a simple life. He knew her salary when she worked for the city, and he showed her his income tax statements for the ten years before they were married. They'd budgeted their bills accordingly, and both seemed to be satisfied. Her income as pastor would be substantially more than his, and she wasn't sure how he'd handle it.

They made it through the main course—corned beef and cabbage, macaroni and cheese, and pickled beets—peaceably, and were about to dig into dessert—a triple-layered coconut cake with lemon filling and vanilla ice cream—when Jesse pushed aside his dessert and turned to Isaac. "Tell me what you think, Isaac," Jesse inquired, "about your sister becoming a pastor. C'mon, speak up. I respect your opinion, man."

Rosemary felt herself getting angry and it wasn't about his stupid statement.

"You have to excuse me, Jesse. I've been out of touch with things." He turned toward Kennedy. "I would have never expected that Kennedy was the type of woman who would want to become a cop. All that tough training she went through. Whew! And now, risking her life on the streets with these gangs out there. Hey, she ain't the same woman I left twelve years ago. But I have to admit. I'm proud of both of these women, man."

Rosemary beamed. But one look on Jesse's face and she knew he hadn't absorbed a word Isaac said. Anger was building up in his body like Old Faithful at Yellowstone National Park.

"I don't believe no woman should accept any position when it's going to keep her away from home and her wifely duties," Jesse said. "Call me a chauvinist pig. I don't care. It ain't right."

Rosemary spoke up just as Isaac was about to comment. "You're such a hypocrite. All the time I was going to school, you never said anything. What did you think I was going to do with that theology degree, eat it?" She glanced at his cake and began to pray silently. *Lord, I'm putting this matter in your hands. Please help my husband understand that I'm merely doing your work.*

With Kennedy's power over Isaac right now, Rosemary knew he wasn't about to go against a female's desire to do a man's job at this point. He would be making two enemies, Rosemary and Kennedy.

"Like I said, brother-in-law, I've been out of touch lately. I'm afraid my opinion wouldn't mean much," Isaac said. He touched a bud from the vase and lifted it slightly. "I'm planning on picking up a couple of trays of flowers from the corner stand tomorrow." He turned to Rosemary. "You haven't forgotten about going to the cemetery tomorrow, have you?"

Rosemary recoiled as if she had been face-to-face with an apparition. While Isaac was in prison, she hadn't been to the cemetery. Not once. Even though she'd forgiven her mother, she still hadn't forgotten what she'd done to her and Isaac. She could still hear Isaac screaming for his mother that night, and running in to comfort him. When she looked at Isaac, her eyes filled with tears. Would they ever be free from their past?

"Rosemary?" Isaac said, moving beside her. "What's wrong?"

"Nothing," she sniffed, getting herself together. "It's all this hot weather getting to me, I guess." This just wouldn't do. She was a stronger woman than this.

"Can I have another piece of cake, Aunt Rosemary?" Peyton asked.

"Peyton!" Kennedy snapped. "Do you have to be so rude?"

Jesse had scooted out of his chair and was at Rosemary's side. "Maybe you should lie down, darlin'."

Rosemary had to smile—Peyton hadn't heard a word they had said. "I'm fine." She got up and gave him a quick hug. "Today's been a busy day. And to be honest, my girdle is killing me!"

When Kennedy rose to collect the dirty dishes, Rosemary stopped her. "Company doesn't clean up. Especially family. I appreciate the gesture. The dishes can wait."

Isaac and Jesse had left out the back door, heading for the garage. Rosemary said to herself, *One day I'm going to let that man know that I know exactly what he's doing out there.*

"Put some aluminum foil around that cake, Peyton," Kennedy scolded. "It's time for us to go." She turned to Rosemary and whispered conspiratorially, "Things are okay between you and Jesse, aren't they?" Rosemary nodded yes. "Because I was thinking about asking Isaac to come over for a few hours."

Rosemary winked at her. "Y'all have my blessings. Jesse and I'll be fine. Don't worry. But thanks for asking."

Kennedy ignored the gentle hand touching her shoulder and began humming the tune "Keep on Pushing."

Isaac was grateful for the opportunity to get out of the house. It was the first time he'd heard Jesse and Rosemary argue and he figured they needed some space. All through dinner, it was hard for him to contain his laughter. He had never witnessed Rosemary stand up to Jesse before. Certainly they'd had an argument or two, he assumed. All married people did. But never when he was around. Rosemary weighed over 150 pounds. Jesse was three inches shorter and ten pounds lighter. The sight of the two of them facing off was so funny, Isaac had to smile.

Since he began paying Kennedy decent child support, he wasn't the least bit surprised when she asked him to stop by this evening.

He changed out of his starched clothes and put on his old jeans and T-shirt. By the time he walked over to Kennedy's house, it was just past five.

Looking up at the sky, Isaac found himself thanking God for the beautiful day it had turned out to be. The Lord certainly did work in mysterious ways, just like Rosemary always said.

When he reached the house, Kennedy hadn't made it home yet. He decided he might as well make use of his time. Opening the gate that led to the backyard, he picked up the hose that was in a neat coil on the back patio. An old metal bucket and a weather-worn broom were on the ground beside it.

Knowing that the way to impress a woman was through good deeds, he lifted up the door to the mailbox and felt inside for the keys Kennedy had always managed to keep taped to the top of the inside of the box in case he lost his. He knew she probably continued to do this for Peyton. Bingo! He removed them, unlocked the back door that led to the garage, and started to work. In five minutes he was sweating like a pitcher with ice water in it on a hot summer day. Damn, it felt good. He removed his shirt and built a makeshift shelf in the center of the garage roof rafters. Two at a time, he began to store on it most of the objects that had been cluttering up the floor space. With each drip of sweat he felt closer to coming back home.

Isaac looked up when he heard Kennedy's 1996 black Mustang pull into the driveway. He could smell her as she walked toward him. She no longer wore the freesia perfume he remembered. Even so, he could smell the natural scent of her. The memory of her was so fresh in his mind, he could pick her out of a crowd blindfolded.

"Well, now," Kennedy said with both hands on her hips. "I hadn't expected that you would do such a thorough job. Now that you've shown me how much junk I had in here, do you plan on mopping the floor, too?"

Isaac's shirt was off and sweat glistened across his muscled chest and arms. "Got some cleaning stuff? I've got plenty of experience."

"I'll be right back with Pine Sol and Ajax. You might as well do it right."

When he sprinkled the Ajax on the floor, he sneezed. He heard her laugh and it brought back old memories. He felt her relax. "I expect a tip when I'm through." This time Kennedy's laugh was more subdued.

Isaac hadn't realized at first that those were the same words he used to say to her during their lovemaking. "I'm working real hard, baby. I expect a tip when I'm through."

"Say," Kennedy asked, "how'd you like a T-bone and smothered potatoes and onions? Personally, I'm starved. I think Peyton was the only one with an appetite at Rosemary's."

Isaac couldn't help but stare as he gazed at Kennedy's beautiful shiny brown eyes. It was just like old times. Even better. She looked more handsome than he remembered. Excited by the promise of a good meal cooked by the woman he had never stopped loving made him work faster and harder. Just the sight of her in her policeman's uniform, with a 9-mm Glock 22 semiautomatic pistol resting against her hip, created an image of a sexual masquerade in which he became the audience as well as the participant, and it aroused him no end.

In no time at all he had completed the dirty task. He could hear the echo of a train whistle in the background as he headed for the back door.

Night fell.

It was eight o'clock by then and still humid and hot outside. It hadn't rained in weeks. Looking up, he noticed that even the dazzling stars looked pale tonight.

While he washed himself in the laundry room, he hollered over his shoulder at Kennedy in the kitchen, "If you still have a set of tools handy, I can fix that garage door. I found some bolts and nuts lying on the floor. It looks like Peyton was trying to fix the hinges, but flubbed."

"That's Peyton, all right. He's no fix-it man."

Isaac guessed that their typical teenage son had knocked the door offtrack. He messed up the hinges so bad trying to fix the door, Kennedy said she had told him to leave it alone.

"I thought he came home with you. Where is he?" Isaac tried to mask his disappointment and sound upbeat. "I was hoping that the three of us could have a little sit-down." Maybe they could begin to iron out some of the questions that his son had about him, because it was obvious that Peyton didn't want to talk to him man-to-man yet.

"He's playing video games at a friend's house." Kennedy came through the doorway and handed Isaac a sixteen-ounce Budweiser.

"Thanks." Isaac put his shirt back on and then stepped into the kitchen and took a seat. He admired Kennedy's athletic frame as she made her way around the kitchen. While she set the table, Isaac picked up the newspaper and began to read. He'd done as Jesse suggested and was keeping up on the news in the city. A picture of a familiar woman caught his eye.

Kennedy turned the T-bone over inside the broiler and looked over his shoulder and asked, "Pretty, isn't she?"

It was a picture of Tempest Prescott posed at the front of the law firm Harris, King & Harris, in which she was a senior partner. The renowned practice was moving to a larger office three doors down. He remembered her—she was the woman wearing the black lace dress that night.

Tempest was sitting on the brick ledge outside the new building in downtown Detroit; her three white male partners were standing behind her. "Not exactly my type. She looks too high-maintenance for my taste." Isaac wanted to tell Kennedy that Tempest couldn't compare to the natural beauty he saw in her, and remind her that light-skinned women never turned him on. But it was too soon for that. In time, he'd let her know exactly how he still felt about her.

There had been two other women with her. It was so clear to him now. The white woman was Dawn—the mother of the child whom he'd hit. That night she looked so sad, unlike the spunky woman he'd heard over the radio.

And finally there was Miracall. He'd dreamed about her last night. Most would consider her pretty, but that wasn't what had drawn him to her. It was something that he couldn't define.

"Is the steak too well done?" Kennedy asked, closing the blinds in the kitchen. She'd removed her gun holster and unbuttoned her blouse to the breastbone.

"No," he said, trying hard not to stare. "Perfect."

While they ate, Isaac was beginning to feel more and more at home. He and Kennedy seemed more relaxed with one another than they were when they were married. They shared a couple more beers after dinner, and it felt so natural when she reached over and undid his ponytail.

"I love your hair this way." Her voice was more lighthearted than usual.

He felt her eyes on his lips, and turned her chin to his and kissed her. Kennedy slid down in the chair, settling comfortably on his lap. When she kissed him back in her special way, just the way she used to, Isaac began to sweat. He hadn't realized that the chair was tipping backward. They fell onto the floor, laughing like a couple of hyenas. When he kissed her again, he wasn't laughing, and neither was Kennedy.

"It's too soon, Isaac," Kennedy said, turning away from him.

Even though Isaac hated to admit it, he knew she was right. He remained on the floor, taking in all the familiar surroundings that had been home too many years earlier. Even though a lot of remodeling had been done on the outside—a new cement driveway, new vinyl-clad wood windows and doors— the inside remained the way he remembered it. Their old yellow curtains were replaced by new ones, but the same yellow-and-white Congoleum tile that needed replacing looked fine with a fresh coat of wax. Even the cabinets that were wide open and empty the night he left looked exactly the same.

"Excuse me a minute, Isaac."

While Kennedy was in the bathroom, he hollered through the closed door, "What time is Peyton coming home tonight?"

"He should be home around ten."

That wasn't what he wanted to ask. He wanted to ask her why she hadn't let Peyton come to see him while he was in prison. If he wasn't tactful, he might alienate her altogether. She was a different woman now. Stronger. This wasn't the woman whom he'd fallen in love with. *Did that woman even exist anymore?* He had to find out.

Taking a deep breath, he found the courage to ask, "Kennedy, I'd like to sleep here tonight, if it's okay. On the couch, of course. . . ."

The phone interrupted him. Kennedy still hadn't come out of the bathroom, and he didn't feel right answering her phone. When the machine turned on, he heard a familiar male voice.

"Hey, it's me. When you get in, give me a call."

He recognized the voice immediately.

Isaac was furious. *"Hey, it's me!"* He didn't even leave a name. Apparently this wasn't the first time he had called.

When Kennedy finally came out the bathroom, Isaac had a scowl on his face.

"Who called? Was that Peyton?"

"No," he said, then pushed the play button on the answering machine. He listened as she did. "Is this something I should know about?" When Kennedy erased the message and yawned, it irritated Isaac even more.

He waited for an explanation that didn't come, his anger increasing as each second passed.

"What in the hell is my best friend doing calling here?"

"You and Eli haven't been close in years." She turned her back to him and began cleaning off the table. "In all fairness, I think I should tell you something, Isaac. We're legally separated—not divorced. I never went through with it. When I heard you were enrolled in school, I was so proud of you. I wanted to give you a chance—to see if you could finally get your priorities in order—putting your family's welfare first."

He paused to light a Kool cigarette that he swore would be his last. *Still married—why hadn't she told me before now?* "What in the hell are you talking about, woman? I'm not some kind of test case that needs to be studied and tested. I deserved to know the truth, Kennedy. I deserved to see my son." He ignored the glistening mist in her eyes. "Has becoming a policeman hardened you that much?"

"No. You did. For seven years, I worked two eight-hour jobs. I didn't want my son to feel he was missing anything that both of us could have provided for him together."

"You didn't answer my question," he snapped.

Kennedy hesitated. "I told him that you left. That you'd gone away."

"What! You made my son think that I'd abandoned him!" He looked into her hardened eyes, then dropped his head in his hands. Disbelief and anger were written all over his face. "How could you?"

"I did it out of respect for you." She spoke fast, as if she were trying to convince herself that she'd done the right thing. "I knew deep down that you wouldn't want him to see you there. As he got older, he accepted what I said, and never questioned me."

And Rosemary? Did she keep up the lie, too? It was all too much. Cigarette ashes fell to the floor. Its deathlike grayness reminded him of how much of his life he'd lost. Crushing the butt in the ashtray, he gulped back harsh words. "I'd better go. I'm really upset and very confused. I'd better go and try to work things out in my own head."

113

Kennedy emptied the plates into the sink, then flipped on the garbage disposal. "Maybe so. Sometimes the truth is as wicked as we are." She stared at him, forcing him to look her in the eye. "But you've always been afraid of the truth, haven't you, Isaac."

Isaac got up from the table and lit another cigarette. With the Kool dangling in the corner of his lips, he took a long drag and blew out the smoke. His eyes began to burn so feverishly, he wasn't sure if it was the smoke or his anger causing it. He moved so close to her that he could smell the Suave shampoo she still used to wash her hair—so close that he noticed that her hands were trembling. "No," he said finally, stubbing the cigarette out in the stainless-steel sink after two drags, "you're the one who's afraid."

Leave Her to Heaven

The air was as still as a marble tombstone. Isaac squinted his eyes against the blinding sun rays as he hauled the trays of pink and white begonias to his father's gravesite and placed them on the ground. A swarm of gnats circled in his face and he fanned them away.

It was late afternoon, and the cemetery was more crowded on this Memorial Day Monday than he ever remembered it to be. Determined to complete his task alone, he had purchased two trays of flowers across the street from the cemetery. He walked the distance to his father's grave, sweating profusely, feeling stupid and ornery. He should have taken the ride that Jesse had offered him.

Of his earliest memories as a child, when he learned that Rosemary was his sister and not his mother, he couldn't remember a single occasion when he felt she had lied to him. But he had felt that way this morning when she told him that she couldn't go with him, her excuse being that she wasn't feeling well.

Isaac wondered what could be worse—having Rosemary lie to him, or having an adulterous wife. Then again, without realizing that he was still married, he'd had an affair. Did it still count?

Damn!

It was 90 degrees today, and he could feel waves of sweat staining the armpits of the sleeveless white shirt he wore. And the begonias looked as wilted as he felt.

As a troubled teenager, he remembered hitching a ride to the cemetery and sitting on his mother's and father's graves. He would begin a conversation about nothing in particular. Later on, the talks were about girls, dating, and marriage. He never experienced any kind of epiphany while he sat there—he hadn't expected any. One sunny day, he met the caretaker, who took him all around the cemetery, pointing out all the famous people who were buried there. Until the year before he went to prison, he had still taken comfort in frequenting the cemetery. He never told anyone. Not even Rosemary.

When he saw the landmark that designated where his father was buried, he breathed a sigh of relief. Exhaling, he placed the flowers on the ground beside it and removed the trowel from his back pocket. A few yards away he noticed an empty milk jug and filled it with water. Before planting the flowers, he rested on his knees for a moment, observing all the families bending over to read the headstones. One group was visibly crying out loud as they knelt beside the fresh mound of dirt from a recent burial.

He looked away and began pulling out the dead weeds. Instantly, he was angered. The grass on the grave was a dead green, an ugly color of rotting and decay. It looked as if no one had touched the grave in years. He could barely make out his father's name: JAMES COLEMAN 1923–1961.

Working as fast as he could, he cleaned the small space and planted the begonias. Before he left, he said a small prayer. It took him a while to find the right words, because he couldn't remember his dad; he'd only seen pictures. It was hard to love without a memory. No matter what, he felt certain that he would do his best to become more than a picture in Peyton's life.

His mother was buried a half-acre away, just a few yards from where Michigan's members of the Iron Brigade were buried. The remains of 205 officers and men who fought in the Civil War as well as soldiers and sailors from the War of the Rebellion were interred there. A flag was flown day and night as a memorial to those patriots.

Looking up, he noticed that the flag was as lifeless as the graves. He removed his sweat-stained shirt and tucked it into the back of his waistband. Disappointed when he witnessed another overgrown, weed-infested grave, he had to sit down, not from the heat but from all the questions that were swarming around in his head. What had Rosemary been doing? Pushing the negative thoughts from his mind, he cleaned off the grave, then went to refill the jug.

Clouds of dust from the road signaled the additional cars coming and going. With very few trees providing shade on the cemetery's grounds, Isaac couldn't blame them for leaving quickly.

Looking to his right, he noticed a familiar face among several others. It was Miracall. He recognized the license plate on the Benz that she had just exited. She wore a tan T-shirt and frayed blue jean shorts. A wide, floppy straw hat provided shelter from the sun.

His first instinct was to say something, but he changed his mind. He had enough problems. Besides, she was Rosemary's friend, not his.

After planting the flowers, he found that he had a few left. He thought of Becky and wondered if she was buried here. For twenty minutes he walked around the grounds looking for a headstone that said BECKY CULLORS.

When he found it, he wasn't surprised that this grave was perfectly tended. There was barely any room for his small addition of flowers, but he put them in just the same and said a short prayer.

Removing the empty trays, he placed them on the curb, where dozens of others were dumped. The groundskeeper would discard them later.

Just ahead, barely forty feet from the road, he saw Miracall again. He saw her move toward a water faucet. He watched her stand there for a moment, then angrily stomp her feet. Anyone could guess what the problem was—all the empty milk cartons were in use, and she hadn't brought one with her.

He took a seat on the side of the road and continued to watch her. She walked a little farther, apparently looking for an empty container. Instinctively, he began to follow her. Fifteen hot minutes passed. Every so often, he saw her checking back over her shoulder, obviously to get her bearings. Still no luck. She navigated a little farther, wiping the sweat from her eyes as she did so. By then, she looked faint. Turning around in a circle, then another, she stopped. He stifled a laugh, knowing that she was lost.

Miracall hadn't realized it, but she'd gone in a circle and they were close to the historical chapel. The chapel was built from quarried limestone in the Norman Gothic design in 1855. It fell to disuse in the late 1940s and was restored in 1957. To their right, he noticed the flag fluttering. It was the first

116

flow of cool air that he'd felt all day. The breeze tipped her hat slightly, revealing more of her face.

From where he sat, he sensed that she was about to cry. By the time he approached her, she was sitting on the ground, fanning herself with her hat.

"Hi," he said, tapping her on the back of her shoulder. "I hope I'm not intruding. But you look like you're lost."

"What are you doing here?" she snapped.

"My parents are buried here. And you?"

She started to get up. "None of your business."

At that moment, Isaac felt supremely foolish. From the corner of his eye he could see that Becky's grave wasn't too far from their view. Of course she was here for that reason.

"My niece's grave is around here somewhere."

He'd come too far to back out now, he thought. "Follow me, you're just a few yards away." Isaac turned and felt her following close behind him.

"There! See the blue and purple pansies. Dawn and I planted them three weeks ago." Each word after *Dawn* seemed to lose strength as she became more aware of whom she was talking to.

"It's a beautiful grave," Isaac said, not knowing what else to say.

He watched her bend down in front of the grave, fingering the flowers. She stopped, noticing the newly planted white begonias. "Who put these things here!" she said in an irritating tone.

"I did."

She looked startled. "It's a little late for that."

"I disagree. It's never too late to try and right wrongs. I thought that today was the right day to honor Becky for the life that she lost." He lowered his head respectfully before he spoke again. "I know I was wrong for drinking and driving—it's still hard for me to believe. I'd never done anything that stupid before. And I'm truly sorry." Looking toward Becky's grave, he spoke as intimately as if he were talking to himself. "I'm sure you loved Becky a lot."

"Yes, I did. She was a lovable child."

There was a short silence as Miracall stared at Becky's grave, then, turning back, her tear-stained eyes met his.

"Look, Miracall, we need to get over this. Put the past in the past. If not for sanity's sake, for Rosemary's sake. Since I've been home, I've noticed how much Rosemary talks about you. She seems to love you a lot. The same way, I think, that you loved Becky." He took a small step toward her.

She took a step back and wiped her eyes with the back of her hand. "Rosemary's been a dear friend. Especially since my mother died."

"Frankly, I'm a little jealous," Isaac said, smiling. "I've always been the center of Rosemary's life."

Miracall blushed. "Now it's my turn to say I'm sorry," she said, managing a small smile.

Isaac extended his hand and Miracall took it. "Truce?"

"Truce." Still, he could tell that Miracall was skeptical of him. By that time, the crowd was beginning to thin out around them. A few people waved goodbye to each other as they made their way back to their cars. Isaac checked his watch.

"What time is it?" she asked.

"Three."

"Shoot! Half the day has gone by and I still haven't finished planting my mother's grave."

He watched her eye the carton half-filled with water sitting beside Becky's grave.

"Do you need that water?" Isaac asked. She didn't have to answer. He went and retrieved it, handed it to her, then turned to go. It was fruitless, he thought, to help her any further. Someone else less involved could help her just as easily.

He heard the hesitation in her voice when she asked, "Do you happen to know which way is the south section? My mother is buried in lot three, fourth plot, six rows from the edge of the road."

Isaac knew that none of the roads were named. To anyone unfamiliar with the cemetery, it appeared like a maze.

Isaac laughed. "You're still lost?"

Miracall was silent.

"You said the south section, right?" She nodded. "I know this place like the back of my hand. I worked summers here for extra spending money when I was a kid." It wasn't the truth, but it sounded believable at least.

After Miracall told him as much as she knew, Isaac took the carton and led the way. There was a lot he could have said—told her again how sorry he was about Becky. But how many times could he apologize? Instead, he decided to give her a history of the graveyard as they headed south.

"All the men who met with Fredrick Douglass are buried here." He pointed out the graves of some of the wealthy abolitionists who helped to build the city of Detroit, as well as the previous mayors of the city, even the Honorable Coleman Alexander Young.

Isaac told her that George D. Baptiste, prior to residing in Detroit, was the White House steward and a close personal friend of President Harrison. He became a successful merchant and used his ships to transport runaway slaves to Canada. Dr. Joseph Ferguson, the first black physician in Michigan, was a practicing licensed physician in Richmond, Virginia, before coming to Detroit. It was amazing, all the important people he knew about. It was equally amazing that he knew all about Elmwood Cemetery. Elmwood, the first black cemetery in Detroit, opened in 1846, two years after Mount Elliott, the cemetery that bordered it. In 1949 Elmwood was incorporated with a board of trustees.

He briefly mentioned where his mother was buried, and pointed to the flag. She really seemed interested when he told her about the Civil War and the war heroes who were buried nearby. He had no way of knowing then how much Detroit's history played a part in her job.

"I didn't know that my mother was in such good company," Miracall said after she and Isaac completed the arrangement on her mother's grave.

He spoke slowly, in a calming tone. "Look around. See all the beauty, all the life that's still felt here." He pushed his hands into his pants pockets, his eyes observing the peaceful surroundings. He envied her thoughts about her mother. There was no need to acknowledge that his mother was a woman whom he couldn't even remember. It was a kind of shallow pain that he never understood—but one that he wanted to understand. Would it make him a better man? A better father? Husband? Brother? One day he knew that he had to find out. He turned from her then, embarrassed to feel the tears well in his eyes.

He looked back in the direction of his mother's grave. "There are two lives to each of us, the life of our actions and the life of our minds and hearts. History reveals men's deeds and their outward characters, but not their real selves. There is a secret self that has its own life, unpenetrated and unguessed."

"Secret self," Miracall repeated, stooping down to eye level with the photograph of her mother. "I like that. My mother's last words to me before she died were, 'Don't worry, baby. I'm not afraid.'" She sniffed back tears. "There wasn't time for me to tell her how afraid I was of being alone. I think now of all the things I wanted to tell my mother at the last moment and was unable to. It was your sister who gave me a framed early nineteenth-century sampler that I'll always cherish. It's a quote by John Newton and hangs over my bed. I read the words every night. 'If I ever reach heaven I expect to find three wonders there; first, to meet someone I had not expected to see there; second, to miss someone I had expected to see there; and third, the greatest wonder of all, to find myself there!'" She bent down on her knees, face-to-face with her mother's oval image.

Isaac hadn't expected that he would feel so moved. He heard her let out a sigh, then fall ever so gently against the tombstone. Her shoulders began shaking. It was obvious that she was crying, and he had no idea what to do. He didn't want to take the chance of touching her again. He bent down beside her and said as gently as he could, "Miracall, are you okay?"

"I'm sorry," she said, caressing her mother's picture, then rising.

"She's in the Lord's hands, Miracall."

"I don't trust the Lord anymore," said Miracall, deadpan. "He took the one person in this world I loved more than I love myself. My mother was someone very special. Not just to me. Rosemary said that she was one of God's special prophets. Why, then, did He make her suffer so? Why did He take away her hopes? Heaven? Is that supposed to be a better place? No one knows that for sure. Just like Rosemary—it's their belief."

They started to leave and he felt her pause. She had turned back around, taking a final look over her shoulder at her mother's angelic face.

"No. I'm not ready yet, Isaac. I can't let her go. Not yet. Until I can reach that state of peace that Rosemary talks so much about, I'll never be ready to simply let heaven have her."

2

The Anger of God

Help Us

Her gates are sunk into the ground; he hath destroyed and broken her bars: her king and her princes *are* among the Gentiles: the law *is* no more; her prophets also find no vision from the Lord.

—Lam. 2:9

The Road to Yesterday

It was Saturday, the sixth of June. Storm clouds had been threatening the city for days, and now thick gray clouds staggered across the sky. Rosemary observed the mashed-potato heaps of cumulus clouds slowly darken to charcoal as she traveled west on Interstate 94 toward Jefferson Penitentiary.

She prayed that the weather would hold out until evening. Secretly, she was afraid of thunder. She never believed that all the cracking and ground shaking was God arguing with the devil. Her memories of thunder and lightning were more real than surreal.

Thirty-three more miles and she'd be there. Just as she passed Ypsilanti, the roadside was beginning to come alive, dappled with bursts of purple and gold blooms. With the Lord as her companion, she passed mounds of firework goldenrods, purple joe-pye weed, and plush blue-purple New England asters. They bowed to the wind as she sailed by.

Luckily, it worked out that Jesse was attending a weekend convention in Chicago with the Masons and wouldn't return until late Sunday night. She wouldn't have to be in a rush. Her visit today with Paps wasn't a regular visit, and she didn't feel like explaining her reasons why to Jesse.

Thraack! A clap of thunder.

She cringed inwardly and began to sing a new hymn that the choir had introduced a few weeks ago—forgetting some of the words, but still enjoying the melody.

In no time, she was approaching the prison. By then the sky had turned dull—the clouds hanging oppressively low in the heavens. The automatic headlights switched on just as heavy pellets of rain began to fall. She could scarcely make out the shapes of several buses that were ahead of her as she stopped at the gate. Moving up the line she noticed that the buses were heading for Middle Prison Block B. Her headlights shone on several saddened black faces, looking back at her. As the bus moved forward, one man waved, his handcuffs sparkling like a Cartier platinum watch in dark contrast to his obvious circumstances.

After parking, she retrieved the umbrella from the backseat and exited the car. Looking up, a sense of insufferable gloom pervaded her spirits. Though the penitentiary had been remodeled, it still remained a desolate-looking building with vacant, eyelike windows watching all that entered.

The thunder cracked, and the rain, heavy as it was, began pouring down harder and faster. She was soaked from her waist down by the time she was seated in the visitors' lobby.

"It's so good to see you, Rosemary," Paps said, looking exceptionally trim in his regulation jeans and shirt. "Tuesday is the primary election. Are you planning on voting?"

"Wouldn't miss it." Rosemary removed a handkerchief from her purse. Trying to dry her clothes seemed futile, but at least she'd give it a try. She felt chilled to the bone. "Isaac surprised me, though. He registered on his own. However, I think he plans on casting only one vote—for Clyde Miller, the Democratic candidate for governor. The only reason Lake won last time was because only twenty-two percent of blacks turned out to vote. But now, with a strong black opponent this year, that number should increase substantially."

"I read that Governor Lake—" Paps stopped. "Wait, I'll get you some paper towels." When he returned from the bathroom, he handed Rosemary the wad of towels, then continued. "The governor's popularity is declining in the polls. Can't say I'm surprised."

"Seems like all he wants to talk about is the double-digit increase in the MEAP scores," she said, bending over to dry her black pleated skirt. "But people like me ain't interested. People like me want to know why there aren't jobs available for our youths. No wonder the prisons are overcrowded." Rosemary thought about Isaac's problems landing a decent job. "Why is the state spending so much money building a youth prison when they could be spending it on reeducating and training the youths in the inner city?"

"Amen."

Rosemary took a deep breath and slowly blew out. She hadn't realized how exhausted she was. "Everybody black knows the biggest reason for crime is poverty. Why aren't there more opportunities in place for blacks to own businesses in the city? This is what Detroit should be about. Black people owning their share of businesses here. And when you own something, you hire people that look like you. Then, that will break the cycle of crime."

They talked about the problems that Jefferson Penitentiary was experiencing at the moment. She wanted to confide in Paps about Gary's plans to build a new prison. But it would be premature to speak of it until he had actually gotten the okay. Governor Lake, if he was reelected, would prove to be a snag in his plans.

"Get lost, Victor!" are inmate said to another who was sitting directly across from Rosemary and Paps. He'd been visiting with his wife when Rosemary arrived and she hadn't noticed when the other gentleman, named Victor, began to make a nuisance of himself. Victor kept touching the man on his shoulder and gently massaging it while the woman's eyes grew wide with anger.

"I know what you're thinking, Rosemary," Paps began. "I'm ninety-nine percent sure that Isaac didn't succumb to the carnal desires of the flesh, as some of these men did." He leaned closer to her, nearly whispering. "Society has no idea the amount of men in here who fall in love and undergo the surgical transformation of an extroverted body into an introverted one, or vice versa; the ultimate gesture in the quest for self-improvement." He shrugged, leaning back in his chair. "I'm so honest, I'm cruel."

"I'm sorry," she said shamefully, "but pardon me if I don't feel a bit put out about Michigan's ludicrous laws against conjugal visits. No wonder men walk around looking and speaking like fashion models."

"You might not have noticed, but there's quite a few female guards working here. They used to be welfare recipients. Now these women are making twelve and thirteen dollars an hour. Homosexuality has gone way down. The downside is that these men have so much power over these women, it's pitiful. So many of the female guards get pregnant. Because of shift rotations to prevent long-term relationships between the guards and inmates, you now have hundreds of cases of gonorrhea, because the women are having relationships with men in each block of Jefferson."

"I had no idea that was even a problem. Isaac never mentioned it before."

Paps nodded his head toward a group of well-dressed men who had just entered the area. "Even still, we will always have men like them, walking around with alligator shoes on and all the gold jewelry. They have a different agenda."

"I don't understand what you mean by that."

"They have no plans on ever leaving here. They feel life on the outside is too hard. And for others it isn't as hard as they make us believe. I know that sounds like a contradiction. It isn't. Success on the outside is a case-by-case basis. Some ask: 'Why do I have to be subjected to bread crumbs when everybody else is getting slices?' "

Though she tried, Rosemary couldn't totally understand this thinking. She figured it was a male psyche thing.

Paps nodded his head toward the other inmates who were even more elaborately dressed. "Look at them. Most people on the outside would never imagine that prisoners get paid twenty-five to forty-two cents an hour and are walking around in fifteen-hundred-dollar shoes and wearing more jewelry than a mannequin in a window at Van Cleef and Arpels. They're no longer angry. They've adjusted to prison life, and some of them wouldn't dream of living anywhere else."

She glanced at her watch. It was 1:50. When she looked up, an effeminate-looking man wearing pink alligator shoes and garish gold chains stopped a few feet in front of her. His voice sounded more feminine than hers. "Excuse me, Miss Rosemary, Paps." He reached inside his orange silk shirt and pulled out a letter and handed it to Rosemary. "Could you please give this to Isaac. I missed seeing him before he was released." He didn't wait for an answer. He just said thanks and switched off to the group of others who were dressed just like him.

"Just in case you're wondering, he's highbrow. Comes from a well-to-do family in Detroit and was straight as an arrow when he got here."

"What family? Tell me." Rosemary stopped, feeling her face flush. "Never mind. It's none of my business." She knew better than to start gossiping.

She'd preached enough about it. "Family shame goes much deeper than some folks realize. I never asked you, Paps, but are you proud of your last name?"

He took a moment to think. A proud smile registered on his handsome face when he answered, "Yes. I'm the third generation. My family is from Omaha. We own a brewery there. Two of my brothers run it. My eldest sister sits on the board, and one of my nephews is being groomed to take over as vice-president when he graduates from law school next year."

"You never mentioned this before," Rosemary said, surprised.

"You never asked." His eyes darkened when he spoke. "One of my brothers writes me and even sends pictures of my nieces and nephews. The other pretends that I don't exist." Paps stared out the window, watching the sky being lit up by sheets of lightning. "And the Joneses?" he asked finally.

"I'm not a Jones. I'm a Coleman, Paps." *We both know that,* she thought. "Anyway, the Coleman name is not held in high esteem in Little Rock, Arkansas, or in Michigan." She asked him what his thoughts were about why people didn't care about their names anymore. Paps couldn't come up with a good answer. "Certainly black people should be proud to be called Miller, Hunt, Campbell, Noble—just like the Rockefellers and the Kennedys. Have you ever seen a Vanderbilt that isn't proud to be one?"

"No."

Rosemary checked her watch again—it was nearly three. The storm wasn't letting up, and if she didn't leave soon, she'd have to stay at a motel. Jesse would have a fit if he found out.

"I know it's not our usual visitation, Paps. But I wanted to talk to you."

Paps placed her hands in his. "We've known each other too long for you to preface your visit. Now, come on and tell me what's the matter. Is it Isaac?" He looked into her misty eyes, shaking his head no. "I see. It's deeper."

"Paps?" Rosemary reached into her skirt pocket to get her handkerchief. She couldn't stop the tears from falling. "I've never spoken to you about Jesse before." She dried her eyes. Afterward, she removed a typed piece of paper from the pocket. "Here," she said, handing the paper to Paps, "read this."

Paps read the words out loud: " 'The true social reformer is the faithful preacher of Christianity. Changes are needed in the ministry. Some believe that it is women who have the opportunity to either validate the ministry outside of the old concepts of office or to renew the office so that it becomes what it was meant to be—service, acceptance of the community and accountability to it. Women should be more responsive to needs and open to individuality and diversity. The tradition of women in the ministry points to works that are consistent with these principles of ministry. In the past, the ministry of women has been that of service. Women have been willing to go anywhere, undertake any cause, and make whatever sacrifice is necessary.' " He paused and then smiled. "It's you, Rosemary."

"Thank you, Paps." She kissed him on his cheek. "I knew you'd understand. Jesse didn't."

Rubbing his fingers through his long salt-and-pepper hair, he said, "He's against your ambitions of becoming a pastor?"

"Yes."

"Will you give it up?"

Rosemary knew he was testing her faith. Just as she had tested his Jewish faith throughout the years they had known each other. "No."

"Will your marriage survive it?"

Survive? That's what Isaac was trying to do. "I believe, Paps, that my becoming a pastor is more of a calling from the Lord than asking for something from the Lord."

Paps crossed his legs, pondering her last words.

"Jesse feels that I've misled him. I told him that I would be more involved in the church in the future. He knew I was preaching once a month. However, I saved my real appointment for a surprise. I'd hoped he'd be pleased."

"No?"

"No. He won't listen to me. Doesn't believe it's a calling. Says I'm looking at all the money the politicians are offering me for the church's support. He believes that they're just like vultures preying on me. The church is big business, Paps. And I can't say I'm not happy with the salary that I'm receiving. I've never made this much money annually in my life. I hadn't expected this." She folded her hands like a steeple on her lap. "I'm not sure if he's coming to church next Sunday. He's hinted to me that he might be looking for a new church home."

"Would that affect your sermon?"

"Temporarily. But it would give me a feeling that the support I needed wasn't there. People will look at me and ask, 'Where is your husband?' And begin to question my appointment. They'll wonder—why isn't he here? That's the way the naysayer can come against my ministry."

"So Jesse doesn't believe that the Lord called you. He believes that women should be silent in the church." Paps quoted 1 Cor. 14:34: " 'Let your women keep silence in the churches: for it is not permitted unto them to speak; but they are commanded to be under obedience, as also saith the law.' "

They looked up when they heard the guards rushing in. They cuffed a skinhead and led him out of the room. Everyone was looking at the scene. It seemed an appropriate time to go, and some visitors gathered their things in preparation to leave.

"You're right, Paps." It was silent now, except for the building thunder outside. You could feel the tension in the air.

"A woman such as yourself, so attentive to others, will always find the courage to live right. I believe that you will not be deterred by their present anxiety, but will look to a future rich with hope."

"Because the Lord loves the listening heart." Rosemary blushed. "If the Lord knew what was on my heart last night, I'd be thrown out of the church. I had to do some serious praying."

"If you're human, Rosemary, like the rest of us, it's only natural that you have some weakness for the flesh."

He's right, she thought. She realized that she had to do the will of the Lord in the spiritual sense, but her body in the flesh needed to be fulfilled in the natural sense. So, there was a war going on—a continuous war with no end. Because the flesh was the flesh and the spirit was the spirit. It was an ongoing struggle to overcome the battle of the flesh.

"Being married doesn't necessarily mean that a woman is fulfilled. Jesse doesn't satisfy all my needs. Something's missing."

Paps suggested, "It's like spiritual foreplay."

"Yes. But it's more. I know what it means to be satisfied spiritually. But not naturally so."

"I'll pray for you, Rosemary."

He stood, and extended a hand to help her up. "And I'll pray for you," she said. Rosemary hugged Paps, "You know, I've been thinking lately about how much today's religion differs from that old-time religion. Too many people no longer believe in the power of prayer."

"Yeah." Paps pondered. "You're right. In my day we prayed so hard and so long our knees ached."

Leaving Jefferson, she headed back down I-94.

Rosemary wasn't in any hurry on her return trip, so she stopped by the Bob Evans Restaurant a few miles out of Jackson and ordered fish and chips for dinner.

She noticed a few familiar faces during her meal that she'd remembered from Jefferson. It was the first time that she'd taken the time to stop and eat, and she secretly thanked Jesse for being away.

"Will you be ordering dessert, ma'am?" the waiter asked.

She couldn't get the chocolate brownie delight with hot fudge out of her mind. Her mind said no, but her mouth said, "Yes, the brownie delight, please."

Every second she waited for the dessert to arrive seemed longer than the one before it. While she waited, she removed the cell phone from her purse and called home to check her messages.

There was a message from Gary Reynolds, one from Pastor Scott, and, finally, one from Jesse. Her heart leaped as she listened to him tell her how much he missed her. People running out of the restaurant interrupted her bliss.

It was still raining profusely outside, but the thunder and lightning had ceased.

"What's wrong?" Rosemary asked when the waiter placed an art piece of walnut brownies, whipped cream, and dark hot chocolate syrup poured lazily over the top that made her nostrils flare open. She reached for the cherry, barely paying attention to what the waiter was saying until she heard the word *escape.*

Next she heard the whirl of helicopters hovering above.

"The state police are on their way," the waiter told her, then left.

Rosemary dropped the cherry onto her plate. A Caucasian woman in the booth behind her was crying. Turning, Rosemary asked, "What happened? Is it something at the prison?"

"Two inmates escaped from Cement City Penitentiary this morning—a killer and an armed robber. They've just been spotted in this area. They're said to be armed and dangerous."

Cement City was approximately twenty miles south of Jefferson prison and seventy miles from Detroit. The prison in Cement City, Rosemary knew, was a private prison. What was going on?

The woman looked as if she would faint. "They're telling everyone to stay inside and lock their doors."

From not too far off, sirens could be heard coming from the east side of the freeway. One after another the sound continued to get so loud, it sounded like they were about to drive straight through the front door of the restaurant.

Someone turned on the television set. Pictures of the two men were now plastered on the screen. The reporter said that the convicts had been nearly caught while stealing food from a gas station less than two miles from the restaurant.

When she turned back to ask the woman what she planned on doing, she was gone. Rosemary immediately left the money for the meal and joined the crowd, which was now glued to the television set. A special broadcast was being televised on channel 7.

Afterward, there was nothing to do but sit around and drink coffee. After imbibing two cups past her daily limit, Rosemary went around the establishment and tried to calm some of the other folks.

By two that morning, Rosemary sounded as hoarse as a horse, but the convicts had been apprehended. Too tired to drive home, Rosemary got a room at a motel across the street from Bob Evans.

She fell into bed with all her clothes on, knowing no one would be there to judge her or smell her unfavorable scents.

With less than three hours of sleep, Rosemary finally made it home by seven Sunday morning. She had left a message on the assistant pastor's answering machine the night before and asked him to preside over the first service. She'd be at Mother Bethel for the eleven o'clock service.

Not bothering to park the car in the garage, she lifted her weary body out of the car. To her right she could see her neighbors parking their car in the drive-

131

way. The glare from the early morning sun radiated off their glasses. Rose-mary waved. The entire family of five was wearing glasses, down to the eight-month-old baby girl.

Laboring up the front steps, she was shocked to see Isaac sitting in one of the patio chairs. He didn't even wait until the door was closed before he started.

"What do you think you're doing, woman?" *Woman?* He'd never used that tone on her before. She opened her mouth to speak and he cut her off. "You haven't been home all night. I've been worried crazy."

"I stayed at a motel. Didn't you hear about the escape?" She took a seat, re-moving the shoes from her swollen feet.

"Yeah. I heard all about it," he stated candidly, and moved in front of her. "What were you doing in that vicinity anyway?"

"Visiting Paps."

"Why? I don't understand you. Even though you're a pastor, you're still a married woman. You're not God."

"Calm down, Isaac, you don't understand. Paps—"

"Is a man. Just how much does his friendship mean?" He talked as if his mouth were bone-dry. "And let's not forget your lopsided friendship with Miracall."

"You don't know her, Isaac. I first met Miracall eleven years ago when I entered theology school at Wayne. We'd run into each other every now and then in the cafeteria. But then I quit. A few years later I went back and she still remembered me. Her mother, Sadie, had mentioned to Miracall that she and I attended the same church.

"Anyway, during that time, Sadie became ill. She was diagnosed with ter-minal cancer. Since she was unable to go to church, I'd visit Sadie and pray with her. That was when Miracall and I became good friends. When Sadie died almost two years later, I'm proud to say that Miracall trusted me then to pray for her mother's passage to glory."

When Isaac looked away, she wasn't sure if he was listening to her or not, but she went on.

"I wasn't licensed back then, but Miracall still wanted me to conduct the eulogy at her mother's funeral when it was time." She bent down and mas-saged her swollen feet, sighing. "After Sadie's death, I brought Miracall

132

through the many stages of grief while she searched her feelings of guilt and despair to the point of finding God. Even after reconciling and accepting God's mercy and love, Miracall was still not convinced and became a bitter young woman."

"That was very nice of you, Rosemary," he said, taking his seat, "but I don't feel all that was necessary."

"I wasn't married back then. I didn't have any children, and chances were I never would. Miracall was like the daughter I never had. I felt so much compassion for this young woman, I couldn't understand it myself."

Isaac didn't bother to respond. He just sat there, as though for a prolonged discussion, his legs spread wide apart with all the pageantry of a concerned brother.

"You were too young to remember, but when I experienced the death of our mother and father, I had no one. I identified with Miracall because of that fact. I learned through my journey toward becoming sanctified that while every circumstance of life is a challenge, we must learn there must come a change, and sometimes that change involves death. And at some stage in the process we go through denial. We pretend. We must recognize change in death and confront it without fear. Accept it more casually, as a final step in the process of growth. We must confront the changes outside to hear more clearly the change left internal. Then we can experience, along with sorrow and grief in the separation from loved ones, some small joy that they can at last experience eternal rest."

His tone was sharp. "Is that why you haven't been to our parents' graves? Because you're still so overcome with sorrow and grief? Or is it that you cannot accept death as a change yourself?"

Now Rosemary was silent. She had no defense.

Every muscle in his face appeared strained. "When you're ready to talk about it, I'm listening." He knotted his fingers and the knuckle joints cracked in annoyance. "You have a gift to put together beautiful words. And I respect you. But, woman, you've got a lot to learn. You're fifteen years older than I am, but you're acting like you're fifteen years younger. Where are your priorities? Where is your loyalty to your family? You make young friends, marry a young man, retire, become a minister, and now you think you can take on the role as the almighty savior, too?"

133

"It's my life, Isaac."

"No, you're choosing a cause that's different from anything that we've ever discussed. And now Jesse and I have become secondary priorities. You're wrong. You've got a family. There's no need for you to adopt one."

Rosemary's eyes began to swell. She felt that Isaac was being selfish, but she couldn't blame anyone but herself, because she had spoiled him by giving him every ounce of her love that she could spare. Who could she blame now for his feelings but herself?

"Look, I understand that you and Paps were *friendly* toward each other, but I would hardly call the two of you friends. It's time for you to back off. I am here now, not at Jefferson prison. And may I remind you that your husband doesn't like it either."

"But Paps looks forward to the B'nai B'rith magazines."

"I'll mail them for you." These simple words fell from his lips slowly. He eyed her, waiting.

"But—"

"Rosemary," he said, cutting her short, "is there another reason—"

She hesitated, trying to gather the right words. "What if I told you that I see him in the capacity of a minister, not as a friend, Isaac."

"You can pray for him at home." Isaac stood to leave with a frustrated look plainly registered on his face. "It's time that I move on, Rosemary. I'll be back for my things tomorrow."

"Don't go, Isaac. Please. You don't understand. You see . . . I spend time with Paps . . . well . . . because he's just like Miracall. A lost soul."

The look on his face was as cold as a skeleton. "What does that have to do with you?"

She lifted her heavy body and looked at Isaac. Her cheeks and chin were pulled down by an invisible weight, all of which added a look of sadness to the trembling corners of her mouth.

"What's the matter with you? Did I get you that upset? I'm sorry, but I'm not sorry. I meant what I said."

She said nothing. Even when he grabbed her shoulder as she moved toward the door, her lips were as still as a tombstone.

"Rosemary!"

She pulled away from him and went inside, shutting the door behind her.

Shake Hands with
the Devil

At a quarter to seven in the morning, Isaac was waiting in the driveway of Kennedy's house for Peyton to come outside. Isaac had dropped Jesse off at work at six, promising to return his car by the evening. It was Peyton's first day of summer school. Five minutes later, Peyton came out, ignoring him.

He wasn't in the mood for this bullcrap today, Isaac thought. Then he heard a loud noise coming from down the street and looked in the rearview mirror. He spotted a young Caucasian girl driving a brand-new black convertible BMW, which was just now pulling up behind him. Music was blaring loud enough to wake the dead. The girl looked to be about seventeen. Two male black teenagers sat in the back, with the empty space in the front obviously reserved for Peyton.

"Hey," Isaac yelled to Peyton.

Peyton walked back to the car. "What!"

"I don't know what you take me for. I told you last week that I'd be here by six forty-five."

Peyton's expression said, *Like you thought I believed you.* Isaac was furious. He wanted to crush this skinny boy with one stomp of his size 9 loafers. Anything to make him pay attention.

"Look," Peyton said, resting his elbows just inside the window ledge. "I appreciate what you're trying to do. But look, I can handle this gig."

When Peyton started to leave, Isaac said coldly, "What kind of fool you take me for, Peyton." This wasn't the way he wanted to start with his son, but there was no way to avoid it. Without respect, he would never gain his son's love.

Peyton shrugged his shoulders noncommittally. The perky girl in the BMW was applying an unnecessary coat of loud black lipstick. He could see that she was getting impatient.

One of the guys in the back leaned over the front seat and beeped the horn, then yelled, "C'mon, man, we're gonna be late."

Before Peyton moved another foot, Isaac said, "I'll be back, tomorrow."

After they left, he walked up the steps and knocked on the front door. When he'd told Rosemary that he was moving, it was a lie. Now he had to act on it. Yesterday had been a turning point between him and Rosemary. Too much had happened. There was nothing left to do but move.

Even though he had his spiel already worked out in his mind, he hadn't considered that Kennedy might reject his offer. He kept reminding himself that they were man and wife. How could she tell her husband no? A shiver ran down his spine as he rang the doorbell. He had exactly ten minutes to plead his case before Kennedy left for work.

When she opened the door, she eyed him quizzically. "Good morning." Looking past him she asked, "Have you taken Peyton to school already?"

"No. He went with his friends. We'll discuss that later." He pushed open the door and stepped inside. "I'm moving back home. I'll sleep in the spare bedroom upstairs."

He heard her marching behind him. "Oh, no, you won't. Just like before, honey, you ain't paying the rent."

"Look, woman, I ain't your honey. I'm your husband—remember?" he said. "I went to one of those twenty-five-dollar attorney offices. He told me that if I hadn't harmed you, you can't prevent me from living in this house. It still has my name on the deed."

In the end, Isaac settled for the studio apartment above the garage. There was a staircase around the back that led upstairs. Once there, she turned on the lights. "It hasn't been used for a while. I rented it out for extra spending money when I was in the police academy. Still, it's plenty of space." She shook her head in disbelief as she handed him the key. "I don't expect you to pay rent, but the utilities are on a separate bill. I *do* expect you to pay that."

He could see the unsettledness in her eyes. "That's only fair." He scanned the room. Years of dust coated the walls and floor. The tenant had left one wicker chair and a large suitcase. Moving to the sink, he turned on the water. He wasn't surprised when it rattled, spit, and spurted brown water. He let it run. "I plan on moving in today." He ignored the surprised look on her face. Any other time he would have taken a few days to clean the place up, but now he didn't have the time. Besides, he'd lived under worse conditions in prison.

After Kennedy left, he sat down and made a list of the things he needed.

Lifting the large suitcase and moving it toward the window, he thought about using it as a cocktail table.

As an afterthought, he locked the door on his way out. When he was back in the car, he had to laugh. Anyone with a pair of vise grips could break into the place in less than thirty seconds.

He laughed again. It didn't matter. Nothing did. He was home.

When he finally came to his senses, he realized that he needed a telephone. With that in mind, he headed down Greenfield Avenue. To his dismay, Ameritech still had an unpaid bill of $663 in their records from 1984. Even though it was considered a charged-off (the monies were never collected) Isaac would have to leave a $500 deposit if he wanted his phone turned on. *No, thank you.*

Instead, he bought a cell phone for a dollar and had it turned on without a credit check. The thirty-nine-dollar deposit seemed minuscule in comparison to what the telephone company was demanding for a security deposit.

Before Isaac returned Jesse's car, he plunked down another three hundred dollars to a car-rental agency.

They delivered the 1995 Jetta to his apartment by six. An hour later, Isaac found himself going through the checkout at Meijer with buckets, cleaning products, a sleeping bag, toiletries, and an alarm clock. It took him all afternoon to mop and clean the place. He spotted Peyton a few times, and waved. Peyton didn't wave back. When he finally fell asleep on the floor that night, he ignored the mice gnawing at the woodwork and the water dripping angrily in the sink.

He was home.

It wouldn't be long before he'd be back sleeping in his master bedroom.

The conversation Peyton had had with his mother was still fresh in his mind. He could still hear her saying: "Peyton, do you remember the conversation we had when you were five years old? You asked me where was your father and I told you he had gone away."

"Yes, Mom. I remember."

"Well, as you now know, he was locked up at Jefferson prison for killing a young girl. It was an accident, but your father was driving drunk. I told you the truth that he was gone away, but I didn't tell you I knew where he was.

"At the time you were going through some difficulties. I planned to divorce

Isaac. I thought it would be better to cut him out of our lives. I also knew he was a proud a man, but he was also very ashamed and bitter. I know he loved both of us but couldn't do anything to help. I decided it would be better for all of us if we severed all ties. I always intended to tell you about your father. I just couldn't seem to find the right time. And now, he's going to be living over the garage for a while."

He'd stared at his mother in disbelief. Her eyes were soft, but her tone was brusque.

"Peyton, nothing would make me happier than if you and Isaac could establish a good relationship. I know he can teach you a lot."

"Mom, I always felt my father was still alive, but I also could see you didn't want to discuss him, so I accepted it. I'll tell you this—it's going to take some time on my part to feel something for him. For some reason I dislike him, but I can't for the life of me figure out the reasons why."

The next morning, every muscle in Isaac's body ached when he walked down the back steps. He hoped that he wouldn't have to put up with any of Peyton's bull.

Just like Friday, Peyton came out at 6:50. The car with the young, boisterous girl and two guys arrived less than a minute later. This time, Isaac walked behind Peyton and politely told the girl to leave.

"Are you crazy, man!" Peyton yelled. "That's Windy and my boys—"

Isaac reeled back and slapped him in the mouth. "Don't you ever let me hear you raise your voice like that again—to me or your mama."

Blood trickled from the side of Peyton's mouth. He had finally managed to get his son's attention. Peyton rolled his eyes at him. It had hurt him to hit him, but Isaac knew that in order to gain his son's respect, he had had no choice. His lack of respect for adults was the reason he'd gotten kicked out of school in the first place. He had to push forward.

"And if you have friends that behave like that, get rid of them." He pointed to the Jetta. "That's my car on the street."

Peyton didn't say a word. Waving his friends off, he followed Isaac, then opened the door to the passenger side and got in.

.   .   .

After work that week, Isaac casually drove down Woodward and checked out Eli's collision shops. There was so much activity going on, Isaac felt intrusive stopping by. He caught a glimpse of Eli, though. Still skinny, and still an inveterate wearer of black leather caps. He hadn't changed much.

Meanwhile, Isaac used his cell phone to call around the inner city and check on any available parts for the Harley. If all else failed, he might be driving it until mid-November. Jesse had said a year. Ha! Isaac loved a challenge. He'd already found the carburetor. He had to laugh when he thought about acquiring a motorcycle license.

Within days, he had transported all of his personal belongings from Rosemary's. Shopping for groceries, finding cheap pieces of furniture, and working occupied most of his time. Neither he nor Peyton mentioned the fact that Isaac was back home. Isaac was certain that Kennedy had told him that they were still married. Isaac wasn't sure how the boy felt about it, but it was too soon to discuss it. He needed time for Peyton to adjust to seeing him around first.

In the evenings, after cooking his meal, he read the cycle manual. It was harder than he'd imagined.

All his studying didn't matter. He flunked the first written test. Two days later he passed it. Then he borrowed a 750 Honda from one of Jesse's Mason friends to take the road test. He flunked it twice before actually receiving his motorcycle endorsement. By that time, he'd gotten feedback from the Internet. All the parts he needed to assemble the bike were available from a senior citizen residing in Los Angeles, California.

He and Kennedy talked very little during that time, but he could tell that she noticed that he'd taken the time to take Peyton to and from school every day.

Still, he wanted her. He needed to know that she was considering making a go of their marriage again.

It was getting near time to let the the gods deal with his fate, whether it was the Lord's will or the devil's. At this point, Isaac didn't care. If Kennedy was the flesh of the devil, he welcomed the heat. For some, hell might be the fire of pain, but for Isaac, it was the fire of delight when he thought of making love to Kennedy. He wanted a free-floating romantic life. When he was drunk he'd sing to her, then they'd make love. When he felt wild he'd dance with her, then they'd make love. When he was sober he would stop, and slowly, so tenderly, make passionate love to her once more. Whoever wanted to criticize, let them. For he knew that his and Kennedy's life would be an absolutely carnal affair.

By the end of June, Isaac had put his Harley together, had it running well, then put it in the body shop to get repainted. From start to finish the entire ordeal took only three weeks. In the meantime he'd depleted all of his savings, and was living week-to-week on his earnings from Remmey's. The support money that he paid Kennedy weekly always managed to bring a smile to her face whenever he saw her.

Then, one night, with a sixty-hour check from Remmey's and a fat check from the Motor City Grille in his pocket, he felt like the *pop* in *snap, crackle, pop.* It was then that Isaac decided it was time to drop in on Kennedy.

He wondered if Kennedy had read the reviews about his performance at the Grille. Some critics had crucified him for trying to imitate Everette Harp. Isaac still didn't know who the man was. Others had said he was talented, but needed to find his own style. He seemed to be trying to imitate too many other artists. Putting his ego aside, he rationalized each comment, positive or negative, and worked to transform himself into the quintessential professional that he knew he could be. The outfits were costing a fortune, and Bernie had suggested that he hire a seamstress to design and sew his costumes. It would cut his costs in half.

It would be nice, he thought, if he could bring Kennedy to his place, away from the eyes of his son. But it was impossible at this point. Refusing to take Rosemary's offer for furniture, he still didn't own a sofa. He sat on milk crates, but was happy to have a bed and a dresser. Even with so little, he felt that the most important furniture he would ever own was his stereo equipment and his recordings. One of his favorites, "Doggin' Around," by the late Jackie Wilson, was on: "You'd Better Stop Doggin' Me Around." Followed by Jackie's words that mirrored his now: "Or I'm going to have to put you down."

Isaac wondered how long Kennedy thought he would wait. He was trying to be true in that area. Sure, he could have had another woman by now. Even prostitutes had begun to look good. But why? He and Kennedy were married.

Knocking on the door at Kennedy's house on Friday night, Isaac felt lucky. He felt so lucky, he had decided not to call first. He was dressed in one of his newest Grille outfits. He'd even splurged, spending more than a hundred bucks on a bottle of men's French perfume: Burchoern.

Peyton answered the door. "Hi, I—, sir," he said, then stepped aside, sniffing.

"Is your mom home?" Isaac tried not to look like the desperate man he felt like. He'd made it this far to earn his son's respect; he could not go backward.

Peyton let him in, rubbing his nose like it was itching. "She's changing her clothes. You can wait in the family room," he offered awkwardly. "She should be ready soon."

Apparently Peyton thought that Kennedy was getting dressed for him. Less than a minute later, the doorbell rang. His son was still sniffing and Isaac began to feel uncomfortable. Maybe he'd put too much perfume on.

For the first time in twelve years, Isaac heard Eli's voice in person. "Where's Kennedy? She was supposed to be ready by seven."

Every ounce of blood in his body began to burn in his soul like a curse. He tried to decide whether to face the music now or later. With that in mind, he left the room and went into the kitchen, where Eli sat like he was waiting to be served. Trying to rationalize the whole thing, he thought, maybe he and Kennedy were just friends. It was too early to jump to conclusions.

Isaac and Peyton avoided eye contact when they passed each other.

"Eli! Is that you, man?" Isaac extended his hand, and hugged Eli when he rose from his seat.

"I didn't know you were out," Eli lied. "Why didn't you call me? I missed you, man."

Why didn't you call me? Isaac cringed. "It's been a while." They both looked at each other before making any further comments. "You look good, Eli." Isaac thought that his old friend looked fifty. Still his high school weight of 160 pounds, he looked worn. Used. His skin was darker than Isaac remembered. And dressed in all black, with the signature black leather cap, he looked dated. Didn't he know, Isaac thought, that all black went out of style with Michael Jackson?

"And you." He casually tapped Isaac's muscled arms. "You were a size thirty-eight the last time I saw you. What are you now, forty-two?"

"Forty-four," Isaac said flatly. That was it. Any further conversation would have brought everything out in the open. It seemed like eons before the sound of clinking jewelry was heard, coming from down the hall. The time had come for both men to state their purposes. "You here to see Kennedy?" Isaac started.

"Yeah, we've got tickets to see *Miss Saigon* at the Masonic Temple."

That was it. No explanation—no mention of a previous relationship. Isaac couldn't stop rewinding the recording: *"Hey, it's me. When you get in, give me a call."* But what could he say? Still, why his best friend?

Kennedy entered the kitchen with titillating tinkles from myriad gold bangle bracelets that she wore on both wrists. He'd never seen her look this way before. She looked like a gypsy, dressed in several layers of chocolate-on-chocolate breathy silk. It blended so closely to her skin color, she looked naked. The only thing that distracted the eye from her svelte body was the hot fuchsia lipstick painted so perfectly on her mouth.

She sounded so casual when she spoke. "Hey. Isaac. Eli. I hadn't expected both of you."

Isaac knew all of her looks. She was nervous. He said, "I'd better go. I came to see Peyton. I didn't know you were going out. I'll come back some other time." He felt like a fool when he passed his son, whom had obviously heard his lie, in the hallway. "I'll see you on Monday, Peyton."

Once he made it back upstairs and was finally able to breathe, he let out a burst of air. Turning on the stereo, he placed an old Marvin Gaye tape in the tape deck. The hum of a car engine brought him to the window. The music temporarily soothed him until he spotted Eli opening the door of his gold Benz for Kennedy.

Marvin Gaye's "Ain't Nothing Like the Real Thing," was playing when the car backed out of the driveway. Isaac was temporarily transported back in time to when things were good between Kennedy and himself. When things were candy-sweet.

She must have forgotten, he thought when he finally stopped looking out the window and took a seat on one of the milk crates.

He thought about the song he sang the first night at the Grille—"Fire and Desire." It was the way he would always feel about Kennedy.

Undeniably, he was the fire. And Kennedy, well . . . she was *still* his desire.

Isaac gunned the motor on the Harley for the zillionth time. It was like the sound of Geronimo's war drums. It was as smooth as the flight of a dream. The Harley was ready.

He had less than two hundred dollars stuffed beneath his mattress. In the seven short weeks he'd been home, he'd become nearly broke, but his spirits were high.

No doubt, the Harley was a beauty. He had put more than six hundred miles on it over the weekend. It took all those miles for him to realize that winter would set in soon and he had to be practical—he would need a car. He thought about Eli's shop. This would be a good time to feel Eli out.

He felt rejuvenated when he drove up to Curry's Collision on Woodward Avenue on Saturday morning.

Since he'd last been there, a new gate had been installed. There was even a guard posted nearby who he was certain was armed. He didn't know what to think when he said hesitantly to the receptionist, "I'm a friend of Eli's. Is he in?"

"I'll see," she said, pushing a button. "Pull over to your right and wait there."

Eight minutes later, Eli appeared, driving a golf cart. "What's up, man? Come on in."

Isaac revved up the motor and said, "I'll follow you." He knew most of the men were looking at his clean machine. He couldn't thank Jesse enough. The bike had brought more attention to his person that he had ever needed.

After they parked and shook hands, Isaac said, "I heard you had some nice used cars for sale. I'm looking for a good deal. I hope I came to the right place."

He couldn't be sure, but when Eli said, "Follow me, friend," it sounded genuine.

Isaac could tell as they walked around the ten-acre lot that this wasn't Eli's usual function. The other employees eyed Eli speculatively for the ninety minutes that he toured the lot. And boy, were there some babies. A 1996 champagne Pontiac Firebird in particular. Isaac could see himself driving it.

They made small talk to fill the time while Isaac filled out the necessary papers in Eli's office, which was elegantly decorated in delicate shades of cream, gold, and white. Isaac was positive that Eli had hired someone to decorate it because his friend didn't have an ounce of class in his entire body. There were several pieces of artwork, but no pictures of family, friends, children. And none of Kennedy.

The creaking sound of Eli rocking in his chair brought Isaac's attention back to the present. Eli was currently reviewing his application and talking more to himself than he was to Isaac.

"That's a start," Eli said, "working at Remmey's. I know the owner's brother. Matter-of-fact, I use the products." Isaac stifled a laugh. Although he didn't remove his cap, Isaac could see the thin strands around the edges. He guessed that Eli had about as much hair as a dead roach.

"They send me the burgundy-colored pomade by the case. They're good people, man."

"It's paying the bills at this point." There was no need to mention child support. Isaac didn't know how much of their personal business Kennedy had repeated to Eli. "I do have a gig downtown playing my music—a dream come true. It's going good."

"Dreams are good, man. It's something that the white man can't take away from you."

Isaac noticed that Eli wore garish gold rings on eight fingers. "You married, man? Any kids?"

"Naw." He blew on the four-carat stone weighing down his bony ring finger.

"Just in case you didn't know it, Kennedy and I are still married."

"I heard." His eyes rolled in amazement. "We're just friends, Isaac. It's like old times, when the four of us were together."

Bullshit. "Yeah." He managed to smile. "Whatever happened to Arlyn?" The last time he saw Arlyn was the week before he went to prison. He could tell she was using drugs.

"That ho overdosed, man."

Sometimes Isaac couldn't believe how cold Eli was. But for whatever reasons, he never treated Isaac with anything but love and respect. Isaac had to compose himself. He wanted to punch Eli. *So that's what you think about the woman who aborted three of your kids and whom you started on heroin in the first place.* Isaac had heard the gossip. The same stories went on in prison, just like it did on the outside. "I'm sorry to hear that."

"I told that girl, 'Be strong like Kennedy. You can kick this shit.' "

Isaac knew that Eli had always had a crush on Kennedy. But back in those days, it wasn't cool if your best friend didn't desire your woman. It was a known fact. It made you the man. But now, every time Eli looked at him, guilt was written in his eyes.

144

"Minnie," Eli said, pushing down the intercom button, "I'm faxing you a copy of this application. Do a credit check ASAP, please."

The subject of Eli and Arlyn had disappeared so fast, Isaac wondered if they'd ever discussed it. Now Eli was moving around the office in a fastidious manner. He was all about money, feeling inside his pocket, touching the bulge of cash protruding in an obviously vulgar manner.

"How much of a down payment are we talking about, Eli?"

Eli hurriedly took a seat at his desk. His eyes were on the buttons that lit up the twenty-four–line telephone. "Man, if your credit checks out, zero. I accept bimonthly or monthly payments."

"I don't need the car today. I wanted to see what I could afford first before I made a decision."

The phone rang. Eli talked for a short while, then hung up. "Don't get beauties like that Firebird often. You better get it while you can. It may be January . . ."

Isaac tuned him out. Eli resembled a salesman from back in their ghetto days. He was selling too hard. Something didn't feel right. He listened to Eli continue on with his spiel.

There was a knock at the door and the young girl named Minnie came in. "Credit checks out, boss. We're good to go on that Pontiac Firebird."

Eli extended his hand.

Instincts told Isaac this stint was all wrong. He was being set up, but he couldn't say how. "I've got to think about this, man." He stuffed his hands in his pants pockets and rose to leave. "I'll check with you in a few days."

It was like shaking hands with the devil, and Isaac could feel the heat.

Public Enemy

"I never thought you'd lie to me," Peyton said to his aunt.

"I didn't, baby," Rosemary replied.

"You never told me where my dad was."

"If you had only asked me, I would have told you. You never asked."

"Was I supposed to believe that my mom was a liar?"

"No. You were supposed to trust that she loved you."

"But what about you, Auntee? You took me to all my baseball games. Came to my parent-teacher conferences when my mom couldn't. You even drove me to day camp every summer at the YMCA. We were so close. Yet it seems years ago. I realize that I'm a teenager, Auntee Rosemary, but I ain't stupid. Somebody should have told me where my father was. I needed to see him. I needed to know that he cared about me."

Peyton had wanted to tell his aunt that for the longest time he figured his father was alive and he'd get a chance to see him someday. He was nine years old when the inevitable happened—when he began to lose all hope that his father would come back.

If he lived to be a hundred he would never forget the early summer of 1994. Peyton had taken first place in the first round of a triathlon. It was his first year in the Junior Olympics. His coach told him that if he placed in the final round of competition, he would go on to the finals in Lansing, Michigan, to compete for a medal. He was scared. Already two inches taller than most of the other guys, he felt good. Watching their parents cheering them on was overwhelming. Just seeing the expressions on their faces reduced Peyton to a mere shadow. Panning the crowd, he wondered what it would feel like to have his father cheering him on. He understood that his mother was extremely busy. She'd had been hired by the Detroit Police Department. His aunt Rosemary was enrolled in seminary school. There was no one to cheer him on. He knew that he had the talent and the drive—he overexcelled in that department. But he needed someone to believe in him. Without voicing his thoughts to anyone, he knew that he was beaten before the final competition began.

Now, Peyton lowered his eyes and his voice. "I love my mom. And I know she thought she was doing what was best for me by not telling me about my father. Somehow I feel she made a mistake."

No matter how cool his mother was, man-to-mom talk wasn't like man-to-man no matter how hard she tried. Maybe, he thought, that's why he found himself hanging around with J-Rock more and more.

J-Rock told him that adults were nothing but liars. All they cared about was making money. Even though Peyton secretly believed that the Prophets had initially recruited him because he was a cop's son, he had to believe that through the years they'd learned to trust him, respect him. It seemed that all of the members had problems. Some openly discussed them. Others kept their secrets hidden. No matter, frustration and unhappiness were written all over their faces.

And right now he could see the same agony in his aunt's face. It hurt him, but how did she expect him to feel? He couldn't trust his mom, his dad, or her. Where did that leave him? There was no one to turn to other than . . .

Heat and Dust

"I wouldn't have believed it if I hadn't seen it with my own eyes," Jesse said to Isaac. Jesse walked around the Harley inspecting every piece. "It's pretty, real pretty."

Parked midway in the driveway, Isaac kept glancing back at the house, hoping that Rosemary would come out. He remembered her schedule fairly well, and she usually left home for Friday night service at Mother Bethel around six-thirty. It was five minutes past that now.

"Thanks, Jesse." He told his brother-in-law about the offers he'd received lately to sell it. The latest was eighteen thousand dollars. The same guy even told Isaac that he'd trade him the title to his 1993 Corvette for the bike.

Jesse whistled. "I'm not surprised, Isaac. It's a beauty."

Just then Rosemary stepped down the front steps. Isaac did a double take. His sister looked like a model on the Ebony Fashion Fair runway at Ford Auditorium. The black suit she wore with a cream lace blouse pecking out at the neck and sleeves looked striking. Three strands of pearls, a beige summer hat, and gloves completed her ensemble. Even wearing black, he could tell that she had to have lost at least ten pounds. "Hey, sis. You look great. On your way to church?"

Rosemary was short with him. "Apparently so." She came over to kiss Jesse, stared at Isaac, then said, "You ain't been back to church. I've seen Kennedy and Peyton, but not you." He heard a chilly "Good evening" to Jesse as she opened the door to her car, then left.

"Who was that?" Isaac exclaimed.

"Don't take her seriously, Isaac. She's going through some menopause thing—"

"And it's affecting her brain." They both laughed. "No, seriously, Jesse. We've never been this cold toward each other. We've barely spoken in nearly a month."

Jesse snapped his leg back in place, unaware that Isaac had noticed the visible pain on his face. "She's fine." Jesse winced, and Isaac asked if he was okay. Jesse looked embarrassed, and Isaac scolded himself. He'd never once heard Jesse complain about his leg or his diabetes. It was the kind of inner strength that one day Isaac aspired to achieve. "I've got a Mason's meeting tomorrow, Isaac. Why don't you come along with me? Meet some of the guys—"

Isaac climbed onto the bike and started the motor. It was just beginning to get dark. "I don't do well with strange people, Jesse. My main friend will always be my woman. After that, Rosemary, then you." He walked the bike backward, steering the polished machine to the edge of the driveway. "Three good friends are more than an honest man deserves." He waved good-bye and headed back home.

When he arrived it was refreshingly warm out. He'd planned on surprising Peyton and taking him for a ride on the bike.

Peyton's upstairs bedroom faced the driveway. Kennedy had given him carte blanche on the entire second floor. One room was for his computer and video games, the other for a waterbed and dressers. A half-bath completed the eight-hundred-square-foot area. The first thing Isaac noticed was the black BMW in the driveway. He gunned the motor, wondering if Kennedy was home. The curtains to Peyton's bedroom moved back and he saw Peyton wave.

Just then, Kennedy opened the front door, yelling, "Hey, quiet down." She waited for him to sprint up to the front door. "My neighbors are old. Any loud noises and they freak out." She laughed when she said, "They can't call the cops because I'm a cop."

Isaac barely heard her. "Does Peyton have company?"

"Yeah. Windy's upstairs. They're playing video games—"

"Woman, are you crazy! Playing games at fifteen?" Isaac went inside and stopped at the bottom of the steps. He yelled Peyton's name.

Times hadn't changed that much, Isaac thought. He was screwing before he had turned fifteen. If anything, these young folks were experiencing things much earlier. He turned back to Kennedy, frowning. "Why would you let your son take a girl into his bedroom?"

"Windy's cool. I know her people."

Isaac shook his head, mumbling to himself, "Have you lost your mind, woman?" Peyton appeared, skipping down the steps and smiling broadly, like he was running for office. Windy followed him.

"Hi, Mr. Coleman," she said.

Isaac grunted hello. "Peyton, I wanted to take you for a ride, but if you're busy I'll come back at another time."

Windy and Peyton exchanged glances. "No, sir. I was just leaving." Windy said good night to Kennedy and Peyton ran upstairs.

The telephone rang in Peyton's room, and Isaac could hear him whispering into the receiver. Kennedy offered him a glass of lemonade while they waited for Peyton to get off the phone.

They sat at the table barely saying a word to one another, until Isaac checked his watch. "That boy should have been down here by now." Kennedy said she'd check on him and headed up the stairs. She came back a few seconds later.

"Peyton's gone. Apparently he sneaked out his bedroom window."

"Where do you think he went?" Isaac asked irritably. It killed him not to tell her that she didn't have a clue about how to raise and discipline their son. It didn't make a bit of difference that she was a paid disciplinarian. Kids were different. His conscience said: *What makes you think you could have done a better job with him?*

"He's got so many friends, I don't know. Peyton's had some problems in school this year, but other than that he hasn't given me any problems. He's a good kid—just a little confused about our situation."

"We need to talk, Kennedy. All three of us. I've mentioned this before. I'd like to stay here until he comes home. I don't care what time it is." She nodded her head okay and went into her room.

By twelve o'clock Peyton still hadn't made it back home. Isaac had gone upstairs and locked his window so that he couldn't sneak back in without them knowing.

Later that night, after he'd fallen asleep watching the History Channel, he felt a tap on his shoulder, awakening him. "Why don't you stay here tonight, Isaac," Kennedy volunteered.

"Are the blankets still in the same place?" he asked her.

Kennedy helped him spread out the blankets on the sofa, then said good night. Isaac stripped and flicked on the television set again. He scanned the cable channels, getting madder by the minute. And Kennedy, a cop, didn't she keep track of her own child?

He went down the hall to use the bathroom, and when he returned, Kennedy was sitting on the couch.

"I can't sleep either." Her robe was tied loosely around her waist, but Isaac could still make out all the curves. "Like I said, Peyton's a good kid, Isaac. He hangs around with a few friends that I don't like. But I can't watch him every minute. It's not easy raising a male child these days. Especially when he doesn't have a positive role model to look up to."

Isaac was fuming. "You got any beer? I could use a liter." She'd turned him on and turned him off within seconds. At this moment, he wanted to go home to his little place, where his only problem was balancing four loads of laundry up and down the back stairs after spending two exhausting hours at the Laundromat.

When he took a seat back on the sofa, Kennedy handed him the beer, then scooted closer to him. "I'm sorry. That wasn't fair." He ignored her. "Isaac—"

"What," he said irritably.

"I'm sorry." Her eyes locked on his. "We should start over. Really. It's all my fault. I didn't want it to be this way." Her damp fingers closed over his—opened and closed, opened and closed.

He froze.

"I love you, Isaac. You know I do. I want you back, but not until you show me that you can secure a good job as a journalist first."

Is that all? He heard her say that he would have to put his music career on the back burner until he proved to her and Peyton that they came first. The music business wasn't stable, she went on. It was obvious that Peyton needed a strong male figure in his life. He needed a family that embodied strength, courage, and stability to secure his future. Being a musician would jeopardize that by constantly moving, changing schools, and being around people whom he wouldn't consider as role models.

"You're right," he whispered, then kissed her ever so lightly. "Whatever it takes, Kennedy. I'll do whatever it takes to get my family back together."

Kennedy took the beer from his hand and led him back to her room. She didn't say a word. But they both knew the best sex they ever had was during heated argument. It never mattered who was right or wrong. The sex was always right.

Minutes later, as they began removing their clothes, he hungrily watched her watch him. Admiring her naked body, lit by a corner night-light, gleaming in the semidarkness, he felt dizzy with anticipation. He'd dreamed of this moment so often, it was hard to believe that the time had finally arrived. And now he wanted to take the dream past the outer limits of his mind.

For Isaac, his love for Kennedy was as pure as angel worship. It was born from the eyes and heart. Her eyes made it blossom and his heart matured it.

When Kennedy turned toward him, he was pleased to see a sweet smile tugging at her sensual lips. When she stood before him, he wrapped his arms around her, cradling her against his body, burying his head in the hollow curve of her shoulder and neck. "You sure you want this, baby?" he whispered.

An intoxicated yes fell from her lips. She circled him in her arms, running her hands up and down his back in soothing, comforting motions. A feeling of peace settled over his heart like a rainbow rests upon the earth, but its arch is lost in heaven. For a moment, he didn't want to move—he just wanted to hold her.

Balling one hand into a fist and placing it beneath her chin, he tilted her face up to him, then kissed her mouth. Her tongue felt unbearably alive in his mouth. He breathed her breath and tasted the sweet moisture before combining it with his own.

Eventually, his lips left her mouth to feast on her chin, her jawline, and linger on the throbbing pulse at the center of her neck. As he did so, his hands slipped to her waist and gentled guided her down onto the bed, and he straightened his lean body against the length of hers. His lips covered hers once more and he felt her cashmere breasts brush against his hardened nipples. Reaching

151

down, he touched, then stroked, the thick mound of pubic hair. It was much thicker and coarser than he remembered as he felt her press herself against his knee.

"I want you so badly," Kennedy whispered in a husky voice.

When he felt her hips hinge up to him, he pulled her hands harshly above her head and brushed his hot lips down her throat, across her collarbone— back and forth in whisper-soft movements that teased and tormented.

Kennedy arched and wrapped her legs around his thighs, pulling him tighter against her. With his hands on either side of her head, his forehead pressed against hers, he eased easily inside her, pushing himself, deeper, until he was all the way inside her.

The power with which she ground her hips against him was shocking, and he couldn't concentrate on anything further. Within seconds his entire body went rigid with the tension of his approaching orgasm. Stronger and stronger he felt the need for release build within him like black steam. His first orgasm came in seconds. He recovered so quickly, he was certain that she hadn't noticed.

Determined to give her the same pleasure, he began his own eager assault, as his hips quickened to a steady but demanding pace. His rhythms quickened and he felt her body moving with such incredible sweetness beneath him, he wanted to scream. Before he did so, she screamed. When his eyes caught hers, their bodies were fluttering.

Hot sweat rolled into his eyes so sublimely, he thought it was tears. Their short pause for breath slowed down their movements. They turned slowly, tilting their wet bodies over the narrow edge of the mattress like a clock with one arm. The threat of falling out of the bed seemed to entice them even more.

Entering her from behind, and cupping his hands beneath her heavy breasts, he felt her rear back, pushing her buttocks against his abdomen to suck in every inch of him. Every gesture was filled with meaning.

He could feel his own orgasm moving within him, then suddenly dart in a new direction, like a flashing flame changing temperatures by revealing the colors blue, gold, red, and orange.

At this moment he felt the hottest ecstasy he'd ever imagined—a cool, cruel blue. His body stiffened. He felt the explosion in his mind first, then in his body. Together, their bodies communicated a mild, slow-burning rapture that he believed transcended ecstasy to another level. He fell back and felt his organ soften and slowly ease out of her. A part of him wanted to stop and absorb the moment, but his excitement was still too new, too raw.

He recovered quickly, feeling the pressure increasing in equal measures to his heart and manhood. Still, he knew this moment was far from over. Turning her onto her back, he slid deliciously back inside her.

Kennedy winced as he entered her.

"Baby, did I hurt you?" He raised up on his elbows, his eyes touching every inch of her upturned face, making sure she was okay.

She answered him by clutching the backs of his thighs tighter. He felt her face turn to the side and press against his shoulder, her teeth softly biting into his burning flesh, her fingers digging into his taut buttocks. He felt her shudder, then scream his name. For a moment she held her frozen pose, then collapsed back on the bed. "I've missed you so much, Isaac."

The room throbbed with her words.

He stroked her cheek, then took his time outlining the moist interior of her lips with his tongue before kissing her. He was in no hurry. Time, like the chrysalis of eternity, had ceased to exist.

Reaching down, he fondled the treasure nestled between her shapely thighs. In the darkness it looked like a flower made of flesh, its petals all shiny and twinkling with dew. For him divine love was like a sacred flower, which in its early bud was happiness, and in its full bloom, heaven.

At this moment, Isaac felt closer to her than he ever had. Because he realized that the love of a man like himself, in his mature years, was so much stronger by giving love than by being loved.

"I love you, Kennedy." He pulled her close to his chest and held her, feeling her heart beating blindly against his. She clung to him as flesh holds flesh, and the soul holds another soul.

Releasing her, he watched the knowing smile slide across her face as she stared at his hardness with greedy desire.

As swift as a fleeting shadow, he began to gyrate his hips slowly at first, gauging her response until he knew that it was time to increase the tempo.

She lifted her hips to meet and greet his every beat. They were so close, their bodies slapped together like hands in a hollow, wet clap. Timing her movements to suck him down deeper, he pulled back, lifting her buttocks higher in the air and back down again, like a game of tug-of-war, rebuffed by love.

Isaac admired her small, deep-naveled belly sucked so thin from breathing that it formed a curve like that of an ancient bow.

A violent tremor shook them, and still they clung to each other, their arms and legs tangled together, as if they loosened their hold, they might slip away from each other forever.

Eventually, they collapsed on their backs, catching their breaths.

But the fire of their passion singed their souls even at a distance, propelling Isaac to move in spite of himself.

Pushing himself up on his side, he twisted his head, swinging his hair so that it hung down his back. His passionate eyes bored into hers before he spoke. "Do you remember when you were pregnant and we had to invent different ways to have sex because you'd gotten so big so fast?" he asked in a low voice broken by passion. "Your body was like a furnace then."

She placed his hand between her legs. "Especially here." Her hands, her lips, spoke to him of her wants and needs. They told of her pleasure in touching and loving him. Placing both palms on his hairy chest, she gently shoved him onto his back.

Kennedy leaned over him, her lips touching his face, brushing kisses over his forehead, eyes, nose, and lips. They blazed a torrid trail along his throat and across his broad shoulders. She balanced herself expertly above him, rocking back and forth on her knees. She rolled her buttocks in a circular motion, pulling him deeper inside her, then releasing him. Reaching behind her, he felt her fondling his delicate sacks that grew taut and tight with each caress.

"I've wanted you so bad," she whispered. There was something wild and a little cruel in her voice, like a wanted criminal asking directions to the freeway.

Her hunger terrified him.

The power with which she pressed herself against him was overwhelming. He could envision the division in her genitals, the rhythmic thrust of her sex sucking him deeper inside her, yet he could feel himself inside her striving to become numb.

To balance herself, Kennedy planted the heels of her hands on his shoulders. While she worked her lower extremities to suit her needs, he was vaguely aware of their shadows against the wall, the creaking of the box spring, the tiny lint balls from the blanket scraping against his buttocks. Then, like a mirage, the pleasure overtook his senses, and he was lost and back with her again.

Covered in sweat, his muscles ached as if knotted with fever. Before he could recuperate, Kennedy had slipped a hand down and inserted a finger on her clitoris. He was entranced as he watched her stroke herself with rapid, circular motions while she raised and lowered herself on top of him. Her up-and-down motions were timed perfectly with the penetration of her finger.

She gasped and fixed her eyes on him for a quick second, gauging his reactions. Almost instantly, she closed her eyes and bent down to touch her lips with his.

Isaac wasn't sure how to feel. She'd never acted this way before. Though he was still aroused, he'd lost something in the process. Without wanting to, or understanding why, he felt his own orgasm creeping down lower and lower to the tip of his manhood, until he couldn't sustain the pressure a second longer.

When she climaxed, her body quivered as if she were a lone leaf in the wind. Instantly, he was with her, feeling the rush of his semen race through him like wild surfs on the sea. He grabbed ahold of her back, instinctively afraid that this might be their last moment together, and arched himself toward her as he came until his insides felt raw with release.

Whatever semen he had excreted at that moment had left a mammoth storehouse behind. His scrotum shriveled up like a dried-up prune. His feet, hands, and mouth went icy cold. His mouth, moments before wet with hot desire, was dry as desert dust. His muscles caved in, his lungs shriveled like an ancient scroll, but he continued to come.

Afterward, he was so sore, he could barely move. He lay in bed for what seemed like an eternity listening to Kennedy's soft breathing, admiring her love-stained body still inflamed, like a sheet of molten gold.

Still reeling from the elation of being satisfied, his instincts kept reminding him that something was wrong. Even though they hadn't been intimate in years, he was astounded by Kennedy's belligerence. In the final analysis, Kennedy had taken control, making love to him, instead of it being the other way around. Isaac attributed her behavior to her job as a police officer.

Turning over, he gazed at the woman who mirrored his spirit in mind, heart, and soul. Their union tonight was the sacrament that confirmed his thoughts. It was the spiritual impact of eternal love, one that he knew he'd never experience again.

Isaac wearily lifted his nude body from the bed and headed for the shower. Afterward, not knowing whether to go home or stay until the morning, he slipped back between the sheets, once again watching her sleep. Tonight she'd been more aggressive than he remembered. Had it been that long? He wasn't sure if he enjoyed it or not. The strongest emotion he had right now was relief. He turned on his side, watching her sleep, pulling the sheets back to admire her shapely body. He watched the clock tick for nearly an hour. And he sat there quietly thinking how much this woman, like his sister, had changed.

Maybe she'd changed since she became a cop. He couldn't be sure. He lit a cigarette while she slept. It could be that she was different because of the kind of company she was keeping—Eli. As a cop, she had to know that he was still dealing drugs. And why have a man like that around their son? he thought as he changed into his clothes. It didn't make sense.

Still, he thought, glancing back at her as he turned to leave, *nothing made sense.*

The next morning his head was clear and he recalled the loved night he had shared with Kennedy, but something still wasn't right.

Foremost in his mind was how to get a handle on Peyton without causing too much disturbance. The first thing he did was to ground his son from leaving the house for two weeks. When Peyton started to object, Isaac stopped him. "I'm still your father, and if I have to, boy, I'll whip your ass."

Peyton rolled his eyes, but didn't say one word.

Just over a week later Kennedy called him on his cell phone. Was he avoiding her, she wanted to know. She had seen neither hide nor hair of him for days. He told her that he was working twelve-hour shifts at Remmey's. Even though he was madly in love with her, a man still had to have his rest.

Isaac had no idea that a three-year FBI investigation of a lower East side Detroit drug operation was in progress and that Kennedy was part of the undercover team. The investigation culminated Monday night with the arrests of nineteen suspects, all members of a street gang, and the possible seizure of more than three million dollars in property bought with drug money.

The West Side Trojans, allegedly headed by Reuben "Mayor of Woodward" Conley, was a well-organized drug-trafficking and money-laundering gang.

All types of questions ran through his mind as he drove his bike toward the Detroit Receiving Hospital. Someone named Doris Gilbert had called and told him to get there as soon as he could. Kennedy was hurt.

"Miss," he yelled as softly as he could at the woman at the front desk, "could you tell me what room Sergeant Kennedy Coleman is in, please? I'm her husband." They didn't give him any additional information concerning her condition, even though they knew that he was her husband.

Three hours earlier, Isaac had been hauling a nineteen-inch television set up the stairs of his apartment. Art Van Furniture had delivered a green floral couch and love seat earlier that afternoon. With his continued success playing at the downtown bistro, he had been able to secure a small contract with the management. They signed him for a three-month stint and advanced him one thousand dollars, after a lot of haggling.

With extra cash in hand for the first time in months, Isaac did what any single male would—he got drunk on two bottles of champagne.

He was fast asleep when the call came in on his cell phone. The continuous ringing agitated him, finally awakening him from a deep sleep.

Kennedy was asleep when Isaac entered the sterile room. Her eyes were closed. The incandescent light in the room cast an odd stream of light across Kennedy's swollen face. There were several tubes leading into her arms from the respirator and another up her nose. More tubes looped down from the bottles and bags that hung above the bed and they met in a tangled fury at her neck, as if fighting to be first into the valve slotted into her jugular. The valves were masked by flesh-colored tape, as were the electrodes on her temples and upper chest, and the hole they had cut above her breastbone to insert a fiber-optic tube into her heart.

"Baby," Isaac said, gently waking her, "what happened?"

Her smooth face was covered with purple bruises. She barely even recognized who he was. Her voice was groggy from the medication. "Hi. I knew you'd come."

In the background, the eleven o'clock news was replaying the drug busts, showing the crack house where the whole affair had transpired.

"We were outmanned," she said weakly. "Usually our department is equipped with nine millimeters with a nine- to ten-pound pull or fifteen-round Glocks. New York uses a twelve-pound pull on their Glocks." She stopped to take a break. "Anyway, in the end, it didn't matter. Those hoodlums had AK-47s, and double the people. They looked like they came from China. It's a miracle we survived at all."

"How many others were shot?"

"One officer was shot and killed. I think five were wounded. I'm not sure. But, Isaac, they were just kids who were shooting at us. Probably not more than seventeen years old."

"I can't understand it."

"It's not over," she said in a ghostlike voice. "Three of the gang members were killed. But not the ringleader, the Mayor of Woodward Park. He's probably back out on the streets now. He's got connections in the city that everyone in the police department wonders about."

Suddenly, Isaac didn't care about the kids, the mayor of Detroit, or the Mayor of Woodward Park. All he cared about was his wife lying in the bed, hurt. "Damn! Why weren't you wearing your vest?" Isaac, hunched over her prone body, assessed every inch of her as though he were her doctor.

Kennedy forced a smile. "The bullet hit above the vest and shattered my collarbone."

"I don't like it, Kennedy. This ain't no type of job for a woman. You could have been killed!" More and more he didn't understand this woman he'd loved forever. Why would she risk her life like this? He wanted his old wife back. He wanted to take care of her, and wanted her to rely on him to take care of all her needs.

"Don't, Isaac. I worked hard to get this job. I won't say I love it, baby. I don't. Think of my job as that of a sanitation worker—they don't like their job either. But someone's got to do it. After a while, you get used to it."

"Still, can't you get a desk job? I've seen female cops walking all around the office—"

"Stop it. I'm a street cop. Period. Accept it, Isaac. I have." She winced, and he could tell that even with all the IVs and medication dripping down the tubes, they still didn't numb all the pain. "Turn the volume on the television set up a notch, will you, Isaac? I want to hear this part."

Turning up the volume, he knew he would never accept it. As soon as they got together, he would convince her to change her mind. Now wasn't the time to argue with her. "Did you know the officer very well who was killed?"

"Not really. He was a rookie—twenty years old. Hadn't been out of the academy but five months. And those hoodlums shot him down like his life wasn't worth a second thought."

He smiled ironically, thinking about her aggressiveness in the bedroom. "Aren't you afraid of guns?" They both stopped and listened when the reporter showed the covered-up body of the dead policeman that was being put into an ambulance. There was talk about contacting his family first before releasing his name.

"No. I've been trained to control my fears." Isaac could see that she was straining to watch the news, so he went and lifted the set at the end of the bed higher so that she could see. "Thanks. What I am afraid of are these gang members high on drugs shooting and killing people for no reason. There's so much corruption going on in the department, everyone is looking at everyone else cross-eyed."

Isaac couldn't digest the fact that this woman appeared fearless—even cold at times. She had more guts than he did. The camera panned to a gentleman who was instantly recognizable. "What the hell has he got to say!"

"Shhh," Kennedy scolded.

Flashbulbs went off, and dozens of microphones were pushed in the mayor's face. A press conference was about to begin, and none of the reporters looked pleased. They'd heard the mayor's excuses before. When cops were shot and killed, it was time to act, not make promises.

Though he appeared haggard, as if he hadn't slept in days, the reporters hounded him just the same.

"Six months ago, I went to Governor Lake for help. The gangs and drugs in the city of Detroit were getting out of hand. I asked for state police assistance. The governor insisted that the situation in Detroit wasn't as bad as I was making it out to be. He kept putting me off. Now look at what's happened." He pointed to the ambulance that was whisking the deceased policeman away. "Last time I came back empty-handed. But I won't leave this time without a commitment from Governor Lake."

159

"Too little too late," Kennedy said. Her voice was hoarse. "The police department is a joke. I don't know if the mayor knows what's going on or if he's just ignorant."

"Are things really that bad on the force?" Isaac asked, moving to take a pitcher from the side tray and filling a glass with ice water.

"Most people have no idea." She caught the tip of the straw and took a long drag. After licking her parched lips, she exhaled. "The executive deputy chief, Calvin Hicks, has a plan that he feels will cut down on some of the drug crime. It calls for shutting down the Third Precinct, just southwest of downtown. It requires approval from the board of police commissioners and Mayor Prescott. They're expected to act on the plan soon."

"What good will it do to close down a precinct?"

Kennedy explained that the Third Precinct was the second quietest precinct in the city. Those officers would be redeployed to the new precinct after it was built.

"We should not have to find out from our citizenry that they've had a dope house next door to them for three months," said Deputy Chief Hicks. "Our response to their complaints should be no more than forty-eight hours. The Narcotics Division will be beefed by merging it with the Special Crimes Section, known as the Gang Squad."

This was all too much for Isaac to absorb. She was talking about arresting and killing kids. He heard her talking about dividing the city into eight parts, each with investigators focusing on three areas—conspiracy, street enforcement, and youth drug crimes. *What did all this mean?* he thought. "Wouldn't it bother you to kill a teenager no older than our son?"

He should have anticipated her answer. "No. Not if they were trying to kill me. In 1998 there were more than ninety-seven hundred drug arrests in Detroit. At least seventy percent of them were kids under the age of twenty. I suspect that the kid that shot me was between the ages of seventeen and nineteen. I'll never forget his face. He winked at me before he shot me." He could see her toes curling up beneath the white spread. She was obviously experiencing more pain.

"I can get the doctor, baby. I'm sure he's right outside."

She reached an arm out to stop him. "No. Listen to me. I'll be laid up for six weeks. Isaac . . ."

He knew that tone. "Damn"—he popped himself in the forehead—"where's Peyton? Is he at Rosemary's? And who's the woman who called me?"

Isaac watched Kennedy purse, then unpurse, her lips. "Sorry. I'm fine. Doris is my neighbor. She's always had a key to my house. I had the nurse call her when I was in the emergency room. She managed to locate Peyton at the arcade. He should be back home by now." Her words were very slow now, her eyes closing in exhaustion. "But, Isaac, I want you to get him. You two have to get to know each other."

Isaac nodded his head, thinking that Peyton had disobeyed him and gone out anyway. He'd deal with him soon enough. "Sure. Don't you worry, baby."

"I don't mean just tonight, Isaac. I mean for good." She took a deep breath. "Listen to me. You don't even know your son. He doesn't know you. I can't fix it right for either of you. Y'all act like you hate each other."

"Naw. It ain't like that, Kennedy. Give us time."

"I'm serious, Isaac." Her eyes began to moisten. "I want you to take Peyton home. Raise him the way we were raised." She smiled. "You know, to be a tax-payer." More serious, she added, "It's your turn now." She sniffed tears. "I've done the best I could, and I see now, my best ain't been good enough. I can't do it anymore." Isaac wiped away her tears. "He's got so much hatred built up in-side of him, it scares me." She grabbed his hand, and looked deeply into his eyes. "Isaac, one of the gang boys who was killed was Peyton's best friend. I recognized him."

People Will Talk

"Be still, Jesse," Rosemary scolded, inserting the needle. *He's just like a baby,* she thought, *tossing and turning, squirming to avoid the inevitable.* "When are you going to get used to this?"

Jesse angrily rolled down his sleeves. "Never. I don't like it. Do you want me to pretend I do?" He went to the desk and slipped his tan linen sports jacket back on. In the background the organ music to "Precious Lord, Take My

Hand" was softly playing. He had a one o'clock funeral in the west wing, and another beginning in the south wing at two.

Through the bare window she could see the beginning signs of fall: the leaves falling as soft as snow on snow, the few mosquitoes that flew slowly here and there looking feeble and pathetic. She felt a pang of loneliness. It was mid-September and Rosemary had been ensconced as pastor at Mother Bethel for two weeks. At this point she couldn't say she was enjoying it. There was more pressure involved in running the church without Pastor Bell's help than she had ever imagined.

Mother Bethel was a growing church, with just over three thousand members. They held two services each Sunday—at eight A.M. and at eleven A.M. The eleven o'clock service was telecast locally every Monday and Thursday evening. Cassette tapes of Sunday's services were sold in the church store-library.

When she looked up, Jesse was staring at her. No, glaring at her. "Jesse, what's wrong? I know I've been extremely busy. I'm sorry."

"Our fourth anniversary was two weeks ago. I was waiting for you to mention it."

She felt like the biggest hypocrite alive. All the "I'm sorry's" wouldn't do. How could she rectify this situation? "Jesse—"

"Stop. That's not what's really on my mind." He walked across the room and closed the door. "Just in case you didn't know, most of my customers are members of Mother Bethel. I hear a lot of talk. Gossip. People get nasty when someone they care about dies, or gets killed."

Rosemary was defensive. "What's that have to do with me?"

"Jefferson Penitentiary. Word is you've got a man up there." He raised a hand to silence her. "I never told you this before, but our next-door neighbors on our left, the Scotts, heard the argument this summer between you and Isaac. Just in case you didn't know, they're the worst gossips on the block."

"What did they say?" Rosemary was struggling to remember back that far. So much had happened, the scene was sketchy.

"You'd come home from the prison early the next morning, after being out all night. I was in Chicago. Remember? Isaac told you that Paps wasn't your friend. He encouraged you to stop the visits."

My God, they'd heard every word.

"Yet, you didn't heed his advice. You didn't even tell me that you didn't come home that night. Nor did you stop your visits twice a month. You won't listen to your brother's advice. Will you listen to me? I don't want you to go back up there."

"Gossip! You're listening to idle gossip!" she screamed.

Jesse raised his finger to his lips. "Shhh."

"What! We'll wake the dead." Rosemary let out a shrewd laugh. "Who's going to hear us? Who's going to care?"

"We owe the family some respect. Being silent always shows respect."

Gathering her purse and shawl, she made preparations to leave. "I'm your wife, Jesse. I don't care how many people talk. If you believe them over me, our marriage doesn't stand a chance."

Jesse looked absolutely shocked.

Her feet hurt and she groaned at the thought of another ingrown toenail. "The next time you want to talk about gossip, please allow me to remove my shoes first."

She slammed the door when she left. If the dead were asleep, they were certainly awake and listening now. It was probably the newest bit of gossip they'd heard all day.

Dozens of pounding footsteps synchronized in an irregular harmony, and the zealous vigor of bated breaths of air was pushed beyond the surrounding glass walls of the quarter-mile indoor track at the Rivercrest Country Club. Multicolored blurs of scantily dressed weight-conscious middle-aged men and women switched positions. First, one gained the lead, then another ran ahead, creating a faster pace for the healthier, more fit, to follow. Today, Rosemary could feel the adrenaline in her body surging as she hustled up the small flight of stairs leading to the athletic club that was located on the second level.

Rosemary couldn't say the last time she'd felt so fabulous. The Zeytas had treated her to a spa day. She luxuriated in every minute of it.

Carrying her DKNY sports bag, Rosemary joined Dawn, Miracall, and Tempest at the snack bar. The eldest and heaviest, she was the last to get dressed after they'd completed twenty laps in the pool. She had completed only fifteen.

"Whew!" Rosemary exclaimed, sipping on a bottle of fresh mountain spring water. "I hope I didn't hold you girls up. This is more exercise than I'd ever imagined."

She watched Tempest check the time on her Cartier gold tank bracelet watch, one of many gifts her husband gave her. "It's okay, Rosemary. You're a great reminder of how we'll look in twenty years if we slack up on our regime." She smiled. "No disrespect intended."

Rosemary held her temper. She knew that she couldn't be more than ten years older than Tempest. And truth be known, her skin looked just as tight and taut as any of theirs.

Even though she was heavier and older, Rosemary knew that she looked good in her charcoal gray and silver jogging suit. She had even managed to find a pair of silver sneakers at the Designer Shoe Warehouse at the Tel-Twelve Mall in Southfield.

Both Tempest and Miracall were dressed impressively in bright white and navy gold-buttoned St. John's cardigans. Tempest chose to wear white capri pants with her cardigan. Miracall looked even more chic, Rosemary thought, in matching navy wool crepe slacks.

Dawn's simple attire was completely opposite. She had on a light pink Reebok sweat suit that Rosemary was positive she remembered seeing on a sale rack three years ago at JCPenney. So, the two of them did have something in common, she mused.

It was just after three, the time of day when attendance at the exclusive club was at its peak, and this afternoon was no different. Rosemary noticed that of the four of them, Tempest loved every crowded minute of it. She excused herself when a familiar face appeared, and Rosemary knew why. Everyone who was anyone was here.

"You didn't have to rush, Rosemary," Miracall said, reaching over to straighten the lapel on her jacket. "We weren't going to order without you."

"Hmm, what's that new scent? It's coming from you, Dawn." Tempest leaned over closer to Dawn and sniffed.

"A little sweet, but I like it," Dawn said, blushing. "It's Strawberries and Champagne cologne from Victoria's Secret."

Rosemary felt out of place. She hadn't played these catty girlfriend games since she was twenty-two. But she felt obligated to be silent. After all, this spa day they were treating her to must have cost a small fortune.

Tempest snarled, "Gracious, Dawn. When are you going to stop shopping at the mall? It's bad enough you run the damn thing, but do you feel the necessity to shop at the quaint little shops there as well?" Tempest made a *tsk tsk* sound with her teeth. "You're so cheap," she mumbled.

Dawn didn't bother to answer her, electing to read the menu instead.

Rosemary had heard snippets of gossip about Rivercrest Country Club. The one-time initiation fee was $12,000, and the monthly fee was $490. It didn't make a difference that the three of them were rich. Rosemary felt that they all were crazy to pay these exorbitant prices.

"Let's eat," Miracall suggested, picking up the menu.

"I'm starved," Dawn agreed. "I'm going to order a huge salad with eggs, cheese, nuts, cranberries, and maybe a few onions, since I won't be kissing my man tonight."

Turning up her nose, Tempest spoke in an uppity tone, enunciating clearly and accenting every point with the slightest neck roll. "It must be nice not to have to worry about calories and kisses. What do you think, Rosemary?"

It was the first time that Tempest had asked Rosemary her opinion. Tempest had missed three of the four meetings that Rosemary had presided over. And at the last one, Rosemary hadn't felt obligated to attempt to cultivate a friendship.

"I'm nearly too old to comment. As for the kisses, Jesse—that's my husband—he wouldn't care if my breath smelled like onions or Altoids."

"For those of you who don't know, my friend Rosemary has just been appointed the new pastor of Mother Bethel AME Church," Miracall said, then toasted Rosemary with her water glass. "I think I'll have onions on my salad, too." She signaled for the waiter.

During lunch, Tempest's mood began to soften. She admitted to Rosemary that she'd been a little catty. "It's Edwin. He's been in a sour mood lately. The drugs, gangs. Police officers being shot. The entire ordeal was an embarrassment to Edwin's administration. The press wasn't being fair to him at all."

Rosemary cringed. She did her best not to be prejudiced against the mayor. But he did appear to be losing control lately.

"Damn!" Tempest said abruptly. "Why is everybody acting so boring lately?"

Dawn finally spoke up. "Miracall and I have been worried about you, Tempest. You haven't been yourself, lately. What's wrong?"

"Nothing." She turned again to Rosemary. "Look at my friends. Aren't they gorgeous? Anyone would be envious of them."

Dawn was petite and as pale as sugar water. She looked like a fresh-faced, freckled white kid on a box of Kellogg's Corn Flakes. Her baby-fine, strawberry-blond shoulder-length hair that was usually pulled back into a single French braid and barrette only added to her youthfulness.

And Miracall, well, she was stunning. Half-Italian and half-black, she wore her hair cropped short. With perfect cheekbones, large, slanted eyes, and luxurious Cherokee-rose coloring, she looked exotic. In fact, Rosemary thought, she looked just like the model she'd seen on television advertising a trip to the Caribbean Islands. No wonder Tempest was jealous; she paled in comparison to both of her friends.

Rosemary spoke up. "Certainly your friends believe that you're equally attractive, Tempest." This was when Rosemary took a good look at Tempest. It was true. She wasn't pretty. She had no definable cheekbones. Her shoulder-length hair wasn't baby soft but thick, with tight, angry curls that needed a super perm every three weeks. Unless she wore couture three-quarter-length blazers, you would notice how narrow her hips were in proportion to her broad back and flat buttocks. Even her skin was a dingy grayish-brown hue that Prescriptives cosmetics couldn't even custom-color match. But Tempest had one exceptional feature—her hypnotic smile, which looked like the smiley face that was popular in the sixties. No one could argue that she exuded class. And class, Rosemary knew, would win out over beauty every time—unlike withering physical beauty, which faded with time. Gary had told her time and time again that Tempest's father, the Honorable Judge Beauford Tillman, had taught her that at an early age. Money. Power. Education. Culture. Class. The judge had made sure that his only child had it all.

Tempest decided to address Dawn's question of "What's wrong?"

"It's Edwin," Tempest lied.

"Is it another woman?" Miracall kidded.

"I wish." Tempest leaned across the table and covered her mouth and nose with her hand. "Have y'all ever seen a mosquito die of shock?" She took a breath. "Honey, after Edwin's had a pound of pistachios, every insect in the house is dead. Sometimes I catch him sneaking a bag out of the nightstand. I don't say a word. I politely get up and sleep in the guest room. It pisses me off when I see pink fingerprints all over my Ralph Lauren sheets. That bastard has nuts hidden all over the house." She whipped back around to where Rosemary was sitting. "Sorry. Please excuse my language."

Miracall and Dawn fell out of their chairs, laughing.

Rosemary merely smiled. She hoped that these sophisticated women had the decency to know that she had had enough entertainment today and was ready to go home. All three had been extremely polite in extending their thanks for her short tenure as the chaplain of the Zeytas last summer. It was over now. A new season had begun and it was time to move on.

Rosemary relaxed and turned to see Tempest waving at a young couple who had just arrived and were being seated at the table opposite theirs. It seemed she knew everybody. Being the mayor's wife kept her in the limelight at all hours of the day.

"Haven't you girls been reading the papers lately?" Tempest opened her purse and removed her date book and began flipping through it. "The police department is headed for a lawsuit. I've been spending all my free time at the firm lately, checking out information for Edwin."

Rosemary merely smiled and thought, *Politics again.* This was another moment when she needed to appear invisible.

"Tempest?" Dawn began. "Haven't you ever considered going back to work for real? Do I have to remind you that you're a senior partner? You worked long and hard hours to get there, and we were all so proud of you when you made it to the top. Wouldn't it be nice if your colleagues saw you more than just a couple of times a month?"

"Yeah," Miracall said. "I was wondering the same thing. With Amia going to college this fall, you're going to be bored, girl."

Rosemary listened. She hadn't known about the daughter.

"You must be kidding," Tempest said, looking up, then once again consulting her date book. "I'm having lunch with Marion Solo tomorrow." Marion was the wife of Solo Pizza king Steve Solo, also owned the Detroit Tigers and had millions invested in other commercial developments and properties in the city as well. In March of this year, Marion had been selected to be one of the four owners of the new casinos designated for the downtown area. "As long as I'm married to the mayor, I'm not going back to the firm full- or even part-time. I've paid my dues," she stated matter-of-factly. "Anyway, Edwin's too dependent on me. He can't run the mayor's office without my help. He'd be lost."

"Otay," Dawn kidded. "Boy, you're getting more arrogant with age." Tempest snarled at her before Dawn added, "So, is Edwin's administration under fire?"

"Have you been talking to Loren?" Tempest turned to Miracall, but it was clear that her statement was directed to Dawn.

"That's enough, Tempest. We do have a guest, you know," Miracall scolded.

Finally, someone remembered that she was still here. Tempest turned to Rosemary. "We agreed that we would never discuss politics. Especially since some of us are Democrats and some of us are Republicans."

"We're embarrassing our guest," Miracall said, patting Rosemary's arm.

Tempest ignored Miracall's second warning and launched into an all-out brawl. "Dawn, don't take this personal, but sometimes I can't stand your brother. You'd think he'd try and help Edwin instead of constantly attacking him. After all, Detroit is still a part of the state of Michigan. When the city is performing well, they both look good." Tempest reached inside her purse for her Bobbi Brown compact mirror to check her makeup. "And what do you think, Miracall? You're a little more closed-mouthed than usual. Are you taking Loren's side too, Ms. ex–First Lady? Or is it because you're still humping him?" She clucked. "You must not be humping him that often by the way you're gobbling down the onions in your salad."

Rosemary didn't get an "I'm sorry" this time. Probably because Tempest had had the waiter replace her mineral water with vodka. Sure, she was a pastor, but she was far from dumb.

Miracall looked shocked. "Excuse us, Rosemary." Miracall glared at Tempest, reminding her that they were in the company of a pastor. "I thought we agreed to keep politics out of our conversations. We're only going to argue. And who I'm sleeping with is personal, not public, information."

Dawn reached for both their hands and held them. "Now stop it. I love you two. We've been friends before Loren or Edwin came into your lives. Let's not let either of them come between us."

"You're right." Tempest grasped Miracall's and Dawn's hands tighter. Certainly, Tempest loved her friends, Rosemary contemplated. But politics were politics. She was certain that they had heard about Edwin sponsoring a fund-raiser dinner for Clyde Miller, the Democratic candidate for governor. Even Mother Bethel had been supporting him. "Now, come on, let's discuss the details for the young men's workshop in August. Edwin has agreed to volunteer again next year." Tempest laughed. "And of course I turned him down, again."

If there was one way of pissing Edwin off, Tempest told them, it was belittling his position as mayor, and making herself appear to be more important. He was so stupid, he never realized how easily he could be set up, something she was certain that the police department had also discovered.

Rosemary couldn't wait to leave. She was wondering if they had even noticed how uncomfortable she felt. Tempest's constant disregard for her made her feel like their housekeeper. All three were members of Greater Grace Baptist Church. By the tone of their conversation today, Rosemary wondered when the last time was that they'd gotten a good dose of the Holy Ghost spirit.

"How could you, Tempest?" Dawn said in a serious tone. "You know very well that for the past three years the volunteers from our members' husbands have dwindled substantially. If this continues, we'll have to reschedule, or cancel the program altogether."

Miracall voiced her concerns as well. "I think this is one of the best things that our sorority is involved in. I've tracked some of the young men who have participated in our workshops. A large majority of them have gone on to do some great things for the community."

"Maybe you two should consider getting remarried and volunteering your own husbands!"

Miracall rolled her eyes at Tempest. "You're such a catty bitch, Tempest."
"I'm sorry, Rosemary," Miracall said to her.

"What?" Tempest looked bemused. "Did I say something wrong again?"

Dawn's voice was as dry as Tempest's side smile. "Cut it, Tempest. There's no need for this bullcrap."

Dawn's unexpected retort was interrupted by a call on Tempest's cell phone. Tempest enjoyed putting on a show for the girls, and showing them how lovey-dovey she pretended Edwin and she were. "Sure, honey. You know I will, baby. Love you, too."

When Tempest finished her call, a photographer from the *Detroit Free Press* appeared at their table. He asked their permission to take a picture. Of course, Tempest was the first to say yes, encouraging Miracall and Dawn to smile as beautifully posed as she did.

Rosemary scooted her chair back. She didn't want her picture taken. Afterward, Miracall had the decency to take the situation into her own hands. "Ladies," she started, "it's time to go. We've insulted our guest enough."

Rosemary couldn't agree more.

The following day was Sunday, the end of Rosemary's second official week as pastor. Thinking back on the conversation she had had with her husband, she decided to make gossip the topic of her sermon today.

After the choir finished their second selection, Rosemary stepped up to the pulpit. She began to speak, then stopped midway and turned to her left. She heard a voice. Lifting the microphone, she went down the steps.

She heard the voice again. "Stop here," he said. "The woman in blue needs your help."

Looking at every face in the second row, she began, "I know that you were reared in the church and you know about the Lord. But somewhere down the line you got off track. The enemy has put you in a place that you don't want to be. And the Lord is telling me today that he is going to set you free. That he is going to deliver you and set you free from this spirit of lust."

The woman in periwinkle blue hesitated a moment, then bravely lifted both hands from her lap, whispering, "Thank you, Jesus!"

"The spirit casts you out in the name of Jesus. Receive it in the name of Jesus. Believe in your heart. And tell the Lord, 'Thank you for setting me free.' "

The woman in blue began to cry. Her head fell to her lap. She raised a shaky hand slowly, as if asking for help.

Rosemary knew that this woman had reached the point where she wanted to be set free. As she lifted her hand toward her, she began to see things about her. She could see sorrow, she could see hurt.

"There's a lot of pain and sorrow—the Lord told me to tell you that the Lord is with you. You be encouraged."

Wearily the woman rose, tears rolling freely down her face. "Thank you, Jesus. Thank you, Jesus!"

Along with Rosemary, the congregation said, "Bless her, Lord. Thank you, Jesus! Thank you."

The next day, Rosemary received a call from Miracall, apologizing for her friends' actions.

"Tempest had way too much to drink. You probably noticed. Normally, she's very funny, and extremely nice. I'm ashamed for all of our actions. We sound like schoolgirls sharing our latest diary entry. But before I hang up I wanted say to one more thing."

"I never owned a diary, Miracall."

"Be quiet. I'm trying to apologize."

"You already did."

"No. It's deeper. It's about your brother. I met him a couple of months ago at the Motor City Grille. Then again at the cemetery. He was planting flowers on Becky's grave."

Rosemary was stunned. She had no idea that Isaac had come so far. He didn't tell her that that weight was also bearing heavily on his heart. Had she known, she might have understood why he wanted to move out.

"He shared his thoughts about my mother's death, you, heaven, life, and even gave me a history lesson on the cemetery—things that I hadn't considered before. He comforted me, in a sense."

What could he possibly have told her, Rosemary thought. She couldn't imagine. "So, you're feeling—?"

"Stronger."

She wouldn't have guessed that she would use that word. Especially this soon. "I don't understand you, Miracall. You feel stronger. How?"

"More independent. Loren thinks so, too. Of course I didn't tell him why, but I feel more open-minded. I seem to understand things that troubled me for years a little better now. I don't know if that's the right phrase. I tell myself that even though Loren doesn't confide in me the way he used to, he never stopped loving me."

Rosemary felt sorry for Miracall. This child acted like she still saw the same stars in her eyes that she did when she was sixteen years old. Girls that age had more sense than she did. "So you and Loren are planning to remarry?"

"He's hinted that he's going to make the announcement before his inauguration in January. I'm not holding my breath, though."

Rosemary thought about Sadie and her last words; *"Take care of my miracle baby."* Though she hadn't borne any children, her instincts told her that few women were wrong about the nature of their child. "Clyde Miller is steadily gaining ground in the polls. Just how sure are you that Loren's going to win? And how sure are you, if he loses, that he will still want you?"

It hurt Rosemary to be so direct, but it was time for Miracall to face facts. She didn't have any siblings to confide in, and Rosemary felt obligated to be blunt.

Miracall took her time discerning these thoughts. Rosemary waited. She wondered out loud: "What will people think of a white governor who has a black wife? What will people think of a woman who hasn't borne the governor a child?"

Miracall voiced what they both were thinking, "It won't matter if he wins."

Pride and Prejudice

Rosemary knew that it was foolish for her to be mad at Isaac. Kennedy had been released from the hospital at nine this morning—three short weeks since the shooting occurred. After driving Kennedy home and helping Kennedy into her bed, Rosemary stayed for a brief visit, at which time she learned that Kennedy and Isaac were still married. Rosemary was hurt that Isaac hadn't confided in her. She thought back on the last conversation she had had with him.

"I've been unfair to you lately, Isaac. I'm sorry." Rosemary took a seat on green floral love seat in his living room.

"No problem, sis. I know you've got a lot on your mind. Church, your husband, board meetings. I understand."

Even as he uttered those words, Rosemary could hear the hurt in his voice. Never had any of those things come between them before. Why now? "No. Whatever or whenever you or Peyton need me, I'll make time. Nothing's more important than my family. My Lord, I get upset just thinking about how confused Peyton must be. I'm worried about Kennedy, too. I saw her this afternoon. She didn't look too good."

"Kennedy's tougher than you think. The doctors said she should be back to work in a few weeks."

"They healed her body. Not her mind. She's tired, Isaac. Completely worn-out mentally. Don't put too much pressure on her. I guarantee you that she needs rest." She moved to the sofa and began rearranging the pillows. "Can I help you with anything, Isaac? How are you going to manage?" She didn't say the place was so small, but she knew he knew what she meant.

"We'll be fine, Rosemary. But I appreciate your asking." He took a seat on the sofa and urged her to move and sit down beside him. "I want to apologize about Paps, too. That was selfish of me to try and tell you how to run your life."

Rosemary went to her brother and hugged him tightly. "You don't have to worry, Isaac. No one will ever come between us." *You're just like my own child,* she thought.

"Not even Miracall?" Isaac kidded.

"No, Peyton's real close, though." Her smile died on her lips, and she could feel the tears pressing against her lids. "I love that child, Isaac. But he's so confused. I can't stop worrying about him."

"Peyton's trying to adjust to everything that's happened to him. In a matter of weeks he learned that he's got a father, his mother and dad are still married, and his mother's job is far more dangerous than either one of them had ever discussed before. He's trying to be a man, when he's only a child. I think he resents me coming back into his mother's life when he's always been the center of her attention. That's understandable." Isaac led her to the small kitchen table and said, "I've got some ideas—mainly being patient. We won't bond overnight. That's unrealistic. He needs a certain amount of space. After all, we barely know each other." He grinned guilelessly. "Now, you stop worrying so much and start praying a little harder, like I'm doing. We both know that nothing's stronger than blood."

She had to laugh at Isaac. He was kidding her, but she could see the serious look in his eyes even as he smiled.

"I saw this shrimp-and-crab-salad recipe in Sunday's paper and bought all the stuff to make it. It even has pecans and walnuts."

"I didn't realize you could cook." Rosemary had blushed, and she felt her stomach grumble. "I already had a salad today."

"One meal won't hurt. C'mon. Treat yourself. Nothing's better than a delicious meal that you didn't have to make yourself." He went to the freezer and removed a package of garlic bread. "Now, this is delicious with butter and Parmesan cheese melted on top."

"Okay, Isaac," she conceded, laughing, "feed me."

The following weekend Rosemary and Jesse took their nephew to Don Pablo's Mexican Restaurant on Northwestern Highway. Afterward, they stopped by Kennedy's house for a quick visit.

Rosemary looked back over her shoulder. Peyton was sitting in the backseat frowning as he glanced out the window. He'd barely said a sentence at dinner.

He blew out a bored breath, then asked, "Am I going home, Auntee Rosemary, to my dad's place? I'm tired."

They were in Rosemary's car, and she'd already turned onto Shaeffer Avenue. They were less than three miles from their house. "No, your dad called while you were in with your mother. He asked if you could stay one more night with us. They added a late show to his schedule in Cleveland, Ohio."

Peyton stomped his feet and mumbled something under his breath.

"Rosemary?" Jesse had been silent until now. "Cleveland's just a three-hour drive. We could be there in no time."

"I don't know—"

"Pull over. I'll drive."

They stopped at the gas station on Greenfield and Seven Mile Road, filled up, and bought some snacks for Peyton. Rosemary used the telephone to call the Motor City Grille for directions. Afterward, she read to Jesse the confusing instructions that she'd gotten from Isaac's friend Bernie. They headed south on Southfield Road. By the time they turned onto Interstate 75 South just nine miles away, Peyton was fast asleep. It was a quarter past seven. A tie-dyed sky of grape, melon, and pineapple lit up the horizon. The beautiful sunset that divided day from night cast a warm glow against Rosemary's face and she found herself nodding in the quiet.

The tired threesome arrived at Bicentennial Park at 10:20 that evening. They could hear the speakers, which were nested thirty feet on top of the poles when they pulled into the parking lot. The current entertainers' performance felt so alive, it was as if they were right in front of them. Life-size posters featuring Ramsey Lewis, Gladys Knight, and Terri Lynne Carrington were pasted on billboards. In smaller letters was the name ISAAC COLEMAN. Jesse managed to buy three tickets from a scalper to the nearly sold-out event.

It was the eleventh annual Jazz and Rib Festival. Mountains of smoke from hundreds of barbecue pits clouded the air above them. Rosemary was tempted to buy an entire slab, the spicy aroma was so strong. Rationalizing that she'd have heartburn in the morning from eating pork so late at night, she resisted.

Jesse learned from a security guard where Isaac would be performing. There were two stages at the park, and one floating stage on the Cuyahoga River. Rosemary was overwhelmed. Isaac was scheduled to go on the floating stage in five minutes! The thought of him performing there terrified her.

They made their way to the top of the grandstand and searched for their seats. Peyton, following as close as a shadow behind them, was unusually silent. Minutes later, a barrage of fireworks exploded in the sky, lighting up the stage. Dozens of spotlights circled the water around the stage. Rosemary noticed that Peyton was standing on his tiptoes trying to get a better view. People around them began to scream when they heard the first sounds of a drum roll.

"There's our section over there." Peyton pointed to the third row, just two rows down, where there were three empty seats.

As they made their way to their seats, Rosemary was mesmerized by the amount of energy she felt from the crowd. In a sense, it was as if some sort of spirit were moving through everyone.

The moment she heard Isaac's name being introduced, she compared it to the moment when the bishop had first introduced her as the new pastor of

Mother Bethel. It brought tears to her eyes when she saw her brother float across the stage like the deluding mist of a mirage. Jesse let out a loud whistle when Isaac finished the first number. Isaac was a gifted saxophonist, just like Jesse had told her months earlier. Why hadn't she listened?

Peyton followed Jesse's lead and let out a long whistle. Rosemary was certain that it was the first time he'd seen his father perform. Never mind the stories that he might have heard from his mother. There was nothing like the real-life drama to put things into perspective.

"I told you, Rosemary," Jesse said, clapping after Isaac had finished his third number. "He's awesome."

Rosemary stood then, proudly clapping, as the darkness engulfed them. She couldn't remember feeling so fulfilled, or so proud. Her emotions were premature, she acknowledged when she heard the sadness in Isaac's next selection. The crowd had quieted down and began paying attention to the emotion that Isaac was conveying. The song was "When You Cry," by the Winans. He began slowly, then built to a crescendo that left Rosemary perspiring. Even the crowd was standing on their feet, applauding, when he finished.

"Thanks for coming out, y'all. I hope you'll be patient with me one more time for my last song. I hadn't planned on playing this song tonight. But I feel moved to do so. It mirrors a feeling that I've been troubled with lately. Maybe some of you may be experiencing a similar pain—problem—anyway, I hope you'll enjoy this."

Every fiber in Rosemary's body tingled when Isaac began playing his rendition of the hymnal "What a Friend We Have in Jesus." He paused after the first stanza, and sang the second section: "Have we trials and temptations?/Is there trouble anywhere?/We should never be discouraged,/Take it to the Lord in prayer;/Can we find a friend so faithful . . ./Who will all our sorrows share?/Jesus knows our ev'ry weakness,/Take it to the Lord in prayer."

"What a friend we have in Jesus," Rosemary finished.

The entire audience was silent as he captured the emotions of hundreds of people. Rosemary had never heard Isaac sing before. His voice sounded like an angel's.

She felt Jesse place her hand in his. And looking to her right, she noticed the look of pride on Peyton's face. Just then, the crowd began to scream, "We want more! We want more!"

The master of ceremonies spoke loudly and said: "This is Isaac Coleman, ladies and gentleman. Remember that name. Isaac Coleman."

Peyton began clapping, whistling, and waving as they made their way out of the stadium. "Do you think we could find him, Uncle Jesse?"

"No, son, not in this crowd."

"You'll see him in the morning, son," Rosemary said, beaming. "Then you can tell him how much you liked his performance."

Peyton stayed awake all the way back home, silently humming every song that Isaac had played. He told them that he couldn't wait to tell his friends about his father. Rosemary fell back on her seat. She felt so good, she temporarily forgot about all of their familial problems. Instead, she took solace in knowing that her brother had finally made his family proud—done himself proud.

The Naked City

The autumn season impressed Isaac already as being one of melancholy. Looking back to the spring and early summer, Isaac realized that, although his first five months of freedom had meant trials and tribulations for himself, Kennedy, and Peyton, it had reinforced his commitment to sustain his family.

In the hope of ensuring a better future for his son, Isaac began putting aside money for Peyton's college education. He had no idea what career choice Peyton had selected. They'd never discussed it. Isaac made a decision that when he and Peyton went to see his probation officer together every other Wednesday, they would stop by the Detroit Public Library and then walk over to the campus of Wayne State University.

"Do we have to come here every time?" Peyton asked Isaac as they were walking up the steps to the university.

"Yes," Isaac stated matter-of-factly. "Coming here may seem boring to you at times, but one day you'll understand what I'm trying to do."

Every now and then Peyton wanted to talk about Isaac's stint in prison.

Isaac wasn't ready to disclose those details to his son yet. But when Peyton opened up about his friend who had died in the cross fire with the police a few weeks back, Isaac understood the connection.

Peyton asked, "Even though my friend was a known gang member, did that mean that I wasn't supposed to like him?"

Isaac shouldn't have been surprised at how deeply the youth's death had affected Peyton. Still, he wondered how he could be honest with his son about associating with individuals who were involved in crimes and still keeping those people as friends. People like that ended up dead or in prison. There was no way Isaac wanted to encourage his son to forge those types of friendships.

Contemplating these thoughts as they walked to the parking lot, he sensed that Peyton was somehow involved with other gang members. He could only guess to what extent. The lot was nearly empty, and Isaac took a moment to light a cigarette. "Tell me what it was like in prison." Isaac watched his son flip through the papers they'd copied at the library, then stuff them in the saddlebags.

"Going to court, standing before the man, was a humbling experience," Isaac began. "You tell yourself that you shouldn't be scared. But you are. Sitting up high on that wooden bench is a man dressed in black robes that has heard every lie a black man could possibly think of telling, because men like him taught black men how to lie in the first place. When he looks at you, you know he's not in the mood to hear yours. Then you're scared, but you don't show it. These judges hold your life in their hands. While you're awaiting sentencing, the judge is reading your file. The silence nearly kills you. You pray for justice, but when the judge looks up, his dispassionate eyes make you feel as insignificant as a wrinkle in his robe. You feel helpless. And the sad thing is, there is nothing you can do about it. No matter your guilt or innocence—justice is just a word. You know you're not going to get it." His blood was cold now, without sentiment. "By then, your fear is replaced by hate. The hate you feel knowing that this man is holding your life in his hands. By the time he sentences you to time in prison, your mind is numb."

"Was prison that bad?" Peyton prodded gently. "You know, like on the television show *Oz*?"

"I only watch *Oz* when I'm feeling sorry for myself. That show serves as a reminder of how blessed I am." He placed an arm around Peyton's shoulders. "Prison is hell. It's a world within a world. It has a violent undercurrent. It has a violent overcurrent. It's a place no one can actually put into words. To know that you would have to be there. Just take my word for it, son, you don't have to die and go to hell. Jefferson prison *is* hell. At night the lockdown is so final— it has such an intense sound that you really know it's final. It's extremely pronounced, like a locking sound when you're watching an old cowboy movie and they're trying to break open a safe." Isaac tossed the butt of his cigarette into a small puddle of water and watched it sizzle out. "It's like that, but magnified."

Peyton picked up his cycle helmet and put it on. "I don't ever want to go there."

Isaac zipped up his son's jacket, then put his helmet on and started the Harley. Balancing the bike as Peyton's slight body climbed on behind him, he had to smile. "And I'm going to make sure that you don't. Now, let's ride, boy!"

Respect between the two men was shaping up like Fisher-Price building blocks.

It was the second week of October, and the temperature had dropped from a pleasant 60 degrees to a frosty 32 overnight. The heavy smell of smoke was in the air. Dead brown leaves were scattered all over the ground like mulch.

Signs of Halloween were everywhere. Pumpkins of every size and shape were for sale at grocery stores and at several corner stands that sold flowers during the summer months. One small regret that Isaac held was that he'd never been able to carve out a pumpkin with his son. Peyton would be sixteen in two months—too late to recapture childhood activities such as that.

Competing with the children's euphoria of selecting the hottest costume for this year were the Democrats and Republicans who were determined to elect their party candidate for governor. The entire process was getting ugly, and Isaac wasn't sure if he even wanted to vote for anyone. He knew that Loren was a shoo-in to win, regardless of his single vote.

There were a few white guys at Remmey's who loved to argue about the climate of this year's election. *Why did it always have to be black against white?* Isaac thought. An argument had precipitated at work last month about Loren Lake being involved with the Ku Klux Klan. The black workers believed that his involvement was the main reason why Loren received so much support from the rich white racists living in the upper part of the state.

"He looks just like the Grand Wizard. I bet he's got the hat in his trunk," one black man shouted to the small group of white men who proudly wore their Loren Lake campaign buttons.

Isaac had helped to break up the fight, but refused to get involved any further. It was ironic, the label stuck and in no time bootleg costumes of Loren Lake wearing a Ku Klux Klan hood over his head swarmed the inner-city party stores.

Kennedy had begun to drop by after work, bringing Peyton his favorite snack, Reese's Pieces, so that he could concentrate better on his studies. Isaac figured that Peyton wasn't her only reason for stopping by—she wanted to check to see if Isaac was dating anyone. On her last visit she asked Isaac if he'd seen Governor Lake's latest campaign tactic.

"I'm told by a friend that you stop by Tas-T Donuts on Outer Drive for coffee and doughnuts every morning before you go to work."

His temper flared then. Had she been watching him? Or was one of her partners keeping an eye on him? "Yeah, I stop there periodically. Why?"

"You call me tomorrow after you get off work. I'll tell you my theories then." She kissed Peyton, handed him his snack, and left.

Isaac had no idea what the woman was talking about.

The moment he stopped by Tas-T Donuts, he couldn't believe his eyes. Taped against the window of the print shop next door was an eighteen-by-twenty-four-inch flyer. Upon further inspection of the area that crisscrossed Six Mile Road, he noticed that the same posters were even stapled to telephone poles.

The picture of eleven-year-old Becky Cullors was everywhere. Typed in bold letters beneath the photo was a slogan that had obviously been concocted by Governor Lake's campaign team: MY OWN NIECE WAS A VICTIM OF CRIME.

Twelve years of penitence at Jefferson hadn't mattered. Everyone still acted like the tragedy happened yesterday.

Isaac felt pain at the pit of his stomach. He threw the coffee and doughnuts he had bought in the trash can at the curb. It was so cold out this morning, his teeth were chattering. He felt foolish when he started up his Harley; he could have used the warm fluid to jump-start his morning before heading to work.

Isaac had no idea that Dawn, Becky's mother, was livid about the posters that were issued without her permission, and she told the governor so.

Isaac tried to put the incident behind him. What could he do anyway? An ex-convict who felt he was being slandered? It would make a good joke in the comics section of *The Detroit News*. He was still on probation and it wouldn't help his case any if he did anything idiotic at this point. He had only five more months to serve and then he'd be off probation.

The Remmey Grease Company was faring well this autumn season, and they were back on six-day shifts. Isaac prayed for relief. It was tough trying to be perky during performances at the Grille on four hours of sleep.

His job at Remmey's was tenuous, until he could buy a car the following month. His salary had increased from $8.25 an hour to $10.57 an hour. It wouldn't have made a difference to Isaac what his salary was. But it did matter when the men he worked with seemed to take pleasure in letting him know that they were making $15.00 an hour.

Isaac let it pass. Though he was angry, he held his peace. But some of the men wouldn't let him be. They started in on his ponytail. Again, Isaac ignored the jokes. They implied that he was gay, even though several of the white males had ponytails longer than his. By the end of the week, Isaac was ready to explode and his coworkers knew it.

It was during lunch that the shit began. Someone had left a pile of the flyers on his workstation. "Murderer" was written on the pages with red ink.

"He's a child killer," one man said to their boss. "I'm not working with a child killer. Either move him or move me."

Other workers began to agree with him: Pretty soon, Isaac's boss was looking at him funny. Before he knew it, Isaac had grabbed the man and punched him in the mouth.

An hour later he found himself fired and repeating the incident to his brother-in-law. He was relieved to find that Rosemary was at a board meeting and wouldn't be home until six. He knew she'd be furious with him for getting fired. "I lost my temper, Jesse." Isaac removed his jacket and hung it on the back of the chair. They were sitting at the kitchen table with a large bowl of water in the center. Jesse was in the midst of peeling potatoes. It was his turn to prepare dinner this week.

Jesse surprised Isaac by laughing. "Must be in the air. I lost my temper today, too—came home early for the first time in ten years." Jesse told Isaac to follow him outside to the garage. Hidden in the far right corner under several moving and storage quilts was a small refrigerator from which he removed two cold beers. He handed one to Isaac, and both men took a seat on a chair near the edge of the garage.

Isaac was constantly amazed by the way Jesse handled his prosthetic leg. He tried not to stare at it, but at times he couldn't help himself.

Jesse downed half his beer before he spoke. "Detroit is a different kind of city since you left, Isaac. Nobody cares about anyone else anymore. Not even the mayor."

Except, possibly, Rosemary.

Isaac thought back on the last conversation he had had with Rosemary. Lately, she'd undertaken a new crusade, the Covenant House, and wanted Isaac to join forces with her. This program would help ex-convicts function in a community setting. They would have to take weekly urine and drug tests. If they needed clothing or medical attention, the program would provide it. After working six months, they would be given fifteen hundred dollars for a down payment on a new car. The program also matched inmates with mentors. *Me, a mentor? No way,* Isaac thought. He felt he was doing great just trying to maintain a good relationship with his son.

"I haven't listened to the news or read the paper since the primaries began—unless you count the classified sections."

"That's not surprising. Everything else is so depressing. When the problems in the morgue are on the front page of *The Detroit News,* that signals the city is in big trouble."

Isaac laughed. "Can't say that I'm anxious to know what's happening in the morgue, Jesse. But I'll listen."

"First off, the city spent a fortune building a new morgue. It was a waste. This new morgue was supposed to offer world-class facilities and equipment. Not so. Many of the same practices that led to trouble at the old facility are occurring at the new one."

"How so?" Isaac was becoming intrigued.

Jesse went and retrieved two more beers. "Don't tell your sister about my stash, you hear?" When Isaac nodded his head, Jesse continued. "Their first mistake was keeping the same people in charge. They should have hired a whole new staff. These people caused inefficiencies in billing, and mishandled dozens of bodies. Unclaimed bodies are lying around in unsanitary conditions. Some of the cadavers are left in the morgue for weeks at a time. Identification tags are missing. And what's worse is the employees' attitudes. They have shown a blatant lack of respect for grieving families."

"Wow. That must be kind of tough on you, Jesse."

Jesse finished his beer, and found a plastic sack to place the empty cans in. "For the first time in my career as a funeral director, I hate going to work. My job is so stressful, I no longer enjoy it."

Isaac had to control his humor. How in the world could a man enjoy a job as a funeral director? But Jesse was an honest man. One of a few whom Isaac knew. If he was worried about the city, there must be a lot going on he hadn't considered before.

"It's not just the morgue, Isaac. Look at the city airport—outdated radar equipment, potholes all over the parking lot. There's overcrowding in the jails, and the prisons. The streets haven't been cleaned since who knows when. And the garbage pickup—don't mention it."

Isaac tossed his empty can in the sack. "How can our mayor, who is black, stand back and basically do nothing to save the city? And how can its people, who are eighty percent black, let him?"

Jesse paused. His voice was sad when he spoke. "I ask myself that question every day when I listen to the news." When he rose, his small body appeared heavy and tired. "All I know is the next time I vote, it won't be for Edwin Prescott. Two terms is enough time to make some noticeable chances for the good of the city."

"You know, I'm thinking, maybe I should leave Detroit, Jesse." Isaac leaned against the metal door frame. A cool breeze passed over his face. "Maybe Canada. I can't seem to find a decent paying job here. Peyton and I are doing okay, but I'm not sure if he'd be better off living with his mother. Though he's not complaining, my studio apartment is way too small. And Kennedy, well, I'm not sure what Kennedy wants." He ran his hand across his eyes as though he could shut out her picture. "Definitely not me."

"Don't give up so soon, Isaac. You haven't been home that long. The tide will turn your way soon." He stood beside Isaac in the growing shadows.

"I would like you to reconsider voting, though. Personally, I don't really care for Clyde Miller, but he's really dedicated to helping the black youths. Ask your sister."

Isaac laughed under his breath. He'd heard all about it.

"Peyton has asked me if he could come down to the morgue. I didn't know if it was for fun or not. A few times a year I get a few college students touring the place—you know, future doctors studying forensic medicine. But not Peyton. I felt that he was too young to see such grim images. Death is so final, to a child it might seem artificial."

"Thanks, man."

"At first I wanted a son to follow in my footsteps, become a mortician. But not now."

"Are you serious, Jesse?" Isaac was surprised.

"As serious as that Chihuahua on the Taco Bell commercials. Heck, yes. I'm ready to get out of this business. Being a funeral director was never my preference. It was my family's business, and I felt obligated to carry on the tradition." Isaac helped him pull the garage door down. "Not now. I'm young. I want to live, Isaac. Not feeling this numbness being around the dead all day."

Isaac was flabbergasted. Nothing *was* as it seemed. Things were changing all around him. Once they were back inside the kitchen, Isaac put his jacket on and retrieved his keys from a pocket. He hesitated a moment before he left and asked Jesse if he'd seen the flyers. "I can't see how I can fight the governor, man. This wasn't necessary. Lake was going to win anyway. Why use me? Why disturb the dead?"

They both turned around when they heard Rosemary's sharp footsteps coming up the back stairs. Obviously, she'd heard their conversation when she added, "Don't be too sure that the incumbent governor will win next term. Matter of fact, Mother Bethel is sponsoring a fund-raiser dinner for the congressman next month. The timing is perfect, because right now Clyde's moving up in the polls." She set her purse on the counter and went to the sink to wash her hands.

"Baby," Jesse asked, looking inside the freezer, "did you say you wanted green beans or corn?"

The timer on the oven went off. "Green beans," Rosemary said, checking the spicy meat loaf that smelled of hot sausage and sage. She turned the temperature down, then closed the door and reset the timer. It was 6:10 P.M., and looking out the kitchen window, Isaac saw that it was already dark outside.

Rosemary placed an apron around her waist. "I've been invited by the congressman to sit in on his debates with the governor. It should prove interesting. Clyde has a list of questions ready that I don't believe the governor will be prepared to answer."

Watching Jesse empty the bag of frozen green beans into a saucepan, Isaac asked the question that everyone was thinking. "If the governor's already so far ahead in the poll, as he suggests, then why would he stoop to such low tactics as using the tragic mistake of his niece's death to further his own campaign?"

"Sounds like the governor is worried about something," Jesse said profoundly, taking a seat at the table.

"Hiding something might be a better choice," Rosemary suggested. "Move out the way, Jesse." She took the bowl of potatoes and began peeling. "I'll finish this." Rosemary picked up where she'd left off. "Lord knows the man's a gifted speaker, but I wouldn't trusted him with a wooden penny."

Dangling his keys and preparing to leave, Isaac left them with one final thought. "I can understand how much he loved his niece. Possibly close to how I feel about my own son. But I don't appreciate him bringing up the past at my expense. I've paid my dues twofold."

Town Without Pity

It was strangely warm for late October. The temperature had climbed to 70 degrees before noon, and by one o'clock the sky looked as though an angel, in his upward flight, had left his mantle floating in midair. A light sprinkle of warm rain began to fall. The droplets in the clouds acted as prisms, dividing the light into different-color bands. A brief interface of color, like an autumnal rainbow, swiftly streaked the sky. Rosemary had rarely seen anything so beautiful.

185

She'd prayed all week for a sign from the Lord that times were changing for the Colemans for the better. The rainbow was a start. She couldn't remember when her heart had felt so burdened. Isaac still hadn't managed to secure another place of employment. And the governor's flyers had been brought to the attention of the Motor City Grille. His chances of having his short-term contract renewed were slim. It appeared they were keeping him on only until they found a replacement.

Jesse had cautioned Rosemary about worrying so much lately. He didn't have to add, especially about Isaac. But she knew what he meant. If she didn't worry about him, she wondered, who would?

How could she make Jesse understand that she worried about Isaac not only as a sister but as his minister? Physicians, psychiatrists, dentists, and attorneys all have explicit job descriptions. Rarely are they compelled to make a professional decision on the basis of emotion and love. But her job as a pastor was clearly about emotions. It was about joy, ecstasy, fear, dread, guilt, loneliness, and personal involvement in all of these.

Last night she prayed more for Loren's soul than she did for Isaac's. She had no idea if he realized how much his blatant cruelty had affected a man's livelihood. He didn't realize, Rosemary thought, that even if he was elected governor, one day his Judgment Day would come. One day the trumpet of fame will be mute; admiration, desire, and success shall lie down in marble slumber, and nothing will survive to judgment but the character that he has formed on this earth.

When she closed her Bible this morning, a Scripture from Matt. 12:35–37 was on her lips: "A good man out of the good treasure of the heart bringeth forth good things: and an evil man out of the evil treasure bringeth forth evil things. . . . For by thy words thou shalt be justified, and by thy words thou shalt be condemned."

This Scripture was still on her mind when she rushed into the City-County Building just after noon the following day. Her task was to try to locate the correct geographical survey for the property Gary Reynolds planned to purchase for the new prison. The grant for the facility was nearly completed, and Gary couldn't contain his excitement.

While she was there, word was all over the building that the mayor was in a bad mood. After the drug bust last month, a young boy was raped in a local prison and subsequently committed suicide. The public was outraged and called on the entire community to take the necessary steps to remove Prescott from office.

On page 5 of *The Detroit News*, Cassandra Reisen, a resident who lived across the street from the prison with her husband and two kids, spoke out: "My understanding was there wasn't going to be any hardened criminals."

In 1989, with a population of 493, the Remedial Corporation of America, RCA, purchased eighty acres in Cement City for $140,000. Cement City watched as RCA extended water, electrical power stations, sewer lines, and built and opened Cement City Penitentiary in a span of ten months.

Initially, as discussed in 1989, the facility was supposed to be a detention center to house drunk drivers, nonviolent offenders, and inmates awaiting trial.

Not so.

One $2.7-million improvement in 1996 added maximum-security cells, an addition approved and developed simply by obtaining a $700 building permit from Lenawee County officials. There was no public hearing. They totally misled the board members of the town as far as what kind of prison it would be and what type of prisoner it would house (they hadn't mentioned murderers, child-molesters, and rapists).

Public prisons, on the other hand, faced numerous government hurdles, and it could take years for them to win approval for expansions. Not so with private prisons. There is no state law to regulate private prisons that import out-of-state prisoners. All that was required to expand the prison was the $700 building permit.

Six months later, prisoners began coming in from Youngstown, Ohio; Montana; and Hawaii. The states sent their convicted felons, who were too hard-core to remain in the medium-security prisons there to the Cement City Prison.

RCA employed about two hundred people, and even paid the city $800,000 to cover the demand on utilities, and paid the county $52,000 in property taxes.

The constituents of RCA believed that the private prison had done a lot of good for the town. Until they came on board, Cement City was a rural community with a decaying downtown and a steady exodus of youth.

About 220 federal inmates remained at Cement City Penitentiary, but as the prison expanded to include the inmates from Hawaii and Montana, the figure was expected to expand to 600. That would mean that the convicts would outnumber the residents.

Was that cause to worry? Rosemary wondered. She believed that 200 of the 200 residents had come to realize that it did.

Rosemary was finally beginning to see Gary's position on the danger of private prisons. No one could stop the political machine. However, a faith-based private prison stood a better chance of being a success in rehabilitating the inmates, as opposed to the money-hungry executives at RCA, who viewed each inmate as potentially funding twelve thousand dollars in annual profits.

Before she left the building, she caught a glimpse of Tempest being escorted to the mayor's limo. She and the mayor were scheduled to attend today's debate.

Rosemary felt sweat running down her back as she raced across Jefferson Avenue before the light turned red.

When she paid the parking attendant, she felt as if steam were rising from her forehead. *It's this jacket,* she thought. *I shouldn't have worn this outfit today.* The weatherman had forecasted rain, but not the unusually high temperatures. Pulling over to the right, she removed the turquoise-and-teal-plaid wool-and-rayon-blend coat that she'd bought at Lord & Taylor's for today's event. She'd recently lost three additional pounds, and the teal A-line dress that she wore beneath it made her look as if she'd lost twenty.

Just over an hour and a half later she arrived in Lansing. Rosemary turned her car into Michigan State University's Communication Arts and Sciences Building parking lot. This facility housed WKAR-TV, the public broadcasting television station in Lansing. The governor's limousine was by the door. Rosemary recognized Dawn's and Miracall's nearly identical black Benzes. Their cars were parked side by side, as if they had trailed each other there.

They were supposed to be in Studio A by two-thirty P.M. The taping would begin at three.

Once inside the building, people were bustling around like sheep. Rosemary had no idea where Studio A was, so she approached the information desk. Rosemary gave her name, and a young intern asked if she would follow her. Just ahead, Rosemary could see the mayor, his security people, and Tempest. They were being led by two female students through a separate wing where the classrooms were located. A metal strip along the floor led around the west hallway of the building to the studio area, which had a specially designed foundation of sand and rubber that provided protection from the vibrations generated by the nearby railroad tracks and physics lab.

The intern and Rosemary stopped at an eight-hundred-pound door. The thick door was the entrance to the soundproof Studio A, where Governor Loren Lake and Congressman Clyde Miller of Mt. Clemens, Michigan, were already being miked for the debate. Miracall, Dawn, and two other people whom Rosemary didn't recognize were already seated in the few chairs appointed to guests.

While introductions were made among the politicians and the television crew, Rosemary spotted Gary and took a seat beside him. She waved at Dawn and Miracall, who were motioning for her to join them. Rosemary shook her head no, and she was sure that Miracall understood why. It was the Republicans against the Democrats tonight. Friendship would be waiting back on the other side of the thick door.

One surprising tidbit was that Tempest and Edwin hadn't sat on the right side of the room with the rest of the Democrats. They sat one row back from the first line of guests, in a section exclusively for them but squarely in the middle.

Rosemary learned that Clyde Miller's wife, Ethel, as well as Clyde's brother, Henry, were also there to support him.

"Hello, Rosemary," Ethel Miller said, smiling. The Millers were new members to Mother Bethel. Rosemary felt it was no coincidence that they had joined the church just months before Clyde announced his candidacy.

"Nice to see you, Ethel. You look lovely today." Rosemary knew that's what the woman was waiting to hear. She spent all the man's money shopping. Everything they owned was the best money could buy. Ethel never made it to church until everyone was seated. She wanted the entire congregation to see her newest Neiman's outfit.

"Thanks, Rosemary." She exhaled, looking bored. "I don't understand why these debates can't be held on Saturday, instead of during the week," Ethel complained. "I'm exhausted."

My Lord, the woman was already acting like a spoiled aristocrat. She hadn't offered to lift one finger for Clyde's fund-raiser this Saturday. Rosemary glanced at the woman's impeccable nails and hair, and knew she didn't know what the word exhausted meant.

Ethel excused herself to freshen up, and Rosemary was thankful for the salvation. She dreaded hearing Ethel complain and brag all evening.

"I'm glad to see you're on time, Rosemary," Gary said. He nodded in the direction of the stage, where Clyde was sitting. "Clearly Clyde is glad to see all of this support for him in the audience today."

Rosemary thought about the Herbert Street property that the church wanted zoned for more low-income housing. It would be such a boost to so many of her younger members. After all, Miller sought her out so that he could get the support of the church behind him. He was looking for votes wherever he could find them. If Clyde was elected, he promised thousands of dollars to help the community and said he would do everything he could to revitalize the downtown area.

"Does Clyde have a copy of the flyer?" Rosemary asked Gary.

"Mm-hm. He's going to wait until the proper moment. We've even managed to get a statement from Dawn Cullors."

Rosemary was shocked.

"Off the record, you know." Gary turned around and smiled at Dawn. "She's the general manager at the Mall of Detroit. I hired her three years ago. We're not exactly friends, but she's really down to earth and knows her business."

"I hadn't made the connection before, Gary. A white woman working at an inner-city mall. Why would she do that?"

Everyone seemed to be talking, ignoring the reason why they were all there. The noise had gotten so loud, the cameramen were motioning for the crowd to be quiet.

Gary whispered, "She's not cut from the same cloth as Big Ben and Loren. I think she's sorry about what happened to Isaac, and she's trying in an odd way to do something for the community."

Then why was Miracall so upset about Isaac's release? And what did Dawn mean when she warned Miracall about Loren's unscheduled visit when she was at her home last spring? Nothing made sense. Was Loren more personally involved in Isaac's situation than anyone let on?

When the moderator, Rick Gates, a reporter from WWJ news television station, introduced the opponents—incumbent Republican Governor Loren Lake and his Democratic challenger, Congressman Clyde Miller—he laid the rules for the time allotted for answers, and covered the guidelines for questions. Afterward, the studio was as quiet as an icehouse. The lights over the stage were so bright, she couldn't see the whites of their eyes. Roughly six feet away, in the second row, Rosemary could feel the heat from her seat. She could even smell the expensive cologne that Loren had on.

Rosemary was impressed. Clyde Miller didn't have a bead of sweat on his face. As a matter of fact, he looked as if he had a Crane air conditioner in his pocket. He was impeccably dressed in a black pin-striped wool suit, white monogrammed shirt cuffs, and red-and-white-striped tie. He looked eager for the event to begin.

With its strong labor base, Michigan was supposed to be a Democratic state. But Republican Loren Lake, seeking a third term, had built a popular reputation as a tax cutter, and as having zero tolerance for criminals. He was favored to win again.

Loren seemed a little nervous. Certainly, he was as debonair as his opponent was. And no one could dispute that Loren wasn't equally decked out in a silver suit and pale blue shirt that brought out the cornflower blue in his eyes. He completed his conservative ensemble with a silver, white, and blue paisley silk tie.

Rosemary caught Gary's sly smile. Maybe this wasn't going to be as bad as they thought. Maybe Clyde did have a chance to whip Loren's butt.

The moderator spoke loudly into the microphone. "I'll begin this evening, gentlemen, with Congressman Miller." Rick turned to Governor Lake's opponent and said, "I'd like to ask your opinion, Congressman Miller, of what is the one thing that impresses you most about Loren Lake or his record as governor?"

Clyde's campaign manager was just inches away from the platform. His eyes told Clyde to answer—they'd discussed this before.

Mr. Miller replied: "His consistency. He's been a governor who firmly believes in trickle-down economics, trying to impress the Reagan-Democrat people in the western region of the state—the third wealthiest area in the nation. His belief that if you protect the most powerful and wealthy, give them the largest tax breaks, and let them own the majority of businesses, the rest of society will do better. He's out there fighting for the rich people, and the large corporations who have huge tax abatements guaranteed by the state over the next ten years."

"Is that true, Governor?"

Governor Lake replied: "Absolutely not. That really sums up the congressman's campaign. It's been a campaign of attack against me without stating exactly what his position is on anything specific. He's a liberal congressman who has spent a lot of time in Washington. His record is unblemished. However, his entire campaign has been spent reviewing my last term in office."

Gary had excused himself and was now in the corner on his cell phone, but his eyes were riveted on the platform. Knowing Gary, he was speaking to Clyde's assistant campaign manager so that they could plan their next move. Rosemary was so intent on checking out the mixed messages going on between Gary and Dawn, she almost missed the moderator's next question.

"A few years ago, Webster's Academy, a private school, was located just outside the city of Detroit. The Academy received government grants that totaled millions of dollars. Why would the state support a system that is in direct conflict with the public-school system?" He turned to the governor. "I'll ask you to go first this time, Governor."

This was getting interesting, Rosemary thought. She wondered if Miller had all of his information correct. Gary told her that the word on the streets was that the governor might have benefited personally from the program.

Loren hesitated a few seconds, gathering his thoughts. "It's a fact that the Detroit school system is in trouble. All three superintendents have been fired or quit. The district is ten million dollars in debt. The teachers' salaries are among the lowest in the state. I feel the only way to solve the problems in the city is to implement a private system that would control unnecessary spending and provide a better staff of teachers who are motivated to excel by incentive programs and high-paying salaries. I have also introduced a voucher system that would allow parents to send their children to the school of their choice, whether it be in the city district, Bloomfield district, or your neighborhood public school."

"I beg to differ with Governor Lake," Clyde interrupted. "This program would give the state control of the schools instead of the city. The governor failed to mention that the Webster Academy spent eight million dollars the

192

first year. He didn't mention that the student enrollment count was falsified. Teen mothers who were dropouts were paid to come to school on the first day." Miller's voice reflected the disgust that showed on his handsome face. "He also failed to mention that only twelve of the fifty seniors who enrolled in the school graduated. The private program was a disastrous failure. It's a proven fact that when the government intervenes in the school system, it fails." When Governor Lake tried to respond, the congressman interrupted him. "And may I add that the director walked away from the defunct program with nearly four million dollars! I wonder, where did that money go, Governor Lake?"

Loren's face was as red as bull's blood. Rosemary turned when she heard a gasp escape from Dawn. The poor girl looked as pale as the angel of Loren's grave that his opponent was now digging.

"I won't dignify that question with an answer." Loren removed a handkerchief from his inside jacket pocket and mopped his beaded forehead.

Rosemary was proud that Clyde had done his homework. He was very well informed. And he knew Loren's past campaign platform as well as he did his own. Each minute was like a noose tightening around Loren's neck. It seemed they were all getting a lesson in seeing a black man in complete control—a black man who was confident enough to question the governor's platform.

For the next forty minutes, Loren and Clyde debated over the tax breaks that General Motors received from the city, the $70-million-dollar sale of the Renaissance Center that should have been sold to GM for at least $250 million, and giving General Motors the City-County Building and moving the city employees into the old General Motors Building that didn't have the infrastructure for air-conditioning or computer networks.

Loren smiled when he told Mr. Miller that he felt he should be talking to Mayor Prescott, not to him.

Congressman Miller responded by asking Governor Lake if there weren't plans on the table now for the state to purchase the General Motors building for the consolidation of state employees in the downtown area. Loren was speechless. Congressman Miller then asked if the governor shouldn't be concerned about the city, since that's where the biggest block of his votes would come from.

Rosemary noticed that when Loren mentioned the mayor's name, the mayor shifted uncomfortably in his chair. She also noticed that Miracall and

Dawn hadn't said a word to each other in more than half an hour. Loren was being crucified by Congressman Miller, and everyone, including the moderator, knew it.

However, Congressman Miller was so passionate in conveying his criticism about the Detroit police and prison system, she wasn't sure if he realized that he was undermining Edwin's efforts as mayor. She wondered: *Would that hurt his chances to win votes in the inner city?*

Rick Gates asked another question: "Gentlemen, we're about to conclude the debate. I'd like your final thoughts about the privatization of prisons in the state. You have five minutes to reply, Congressman Miller. Will you begin?"

"I'll not mince any words, Governor. The prison system is corrupt. Services are being privatized in Jefferson Penitentiary, in Marquette, Ionia, et cetera, the largest prisons in the state. These services go to a select few who have become millionaires in the process.

"The citizenry of Detroit is being told that crime is high. It's not. Crime is down, but the jail count is up because the corrupt judicial system has changed the rules. There's a disparity in the way the white judges sentence our black men for drug possession as opposed to our white brethren."

Loren tried to jump in, but the moderator tapped his watch, silencing him.

"Black men are given life sentences for three ounces of crack, while white men who are convicted of possessing the same amount of cocaine are merely given three to five years. Governor Lake tries to make the public believe that black folks are a threat to their livelihood, their safety. I submit to you that most of the crimes that blacks commit in the city of Detroit is against other blacks. Not whites! In short, I believe the governor is guilty of using taxpayer money for his own personal gain. For this reason, the state is guilty of encouraging the public to establish a highly profitable prison population." Miller raised his voice. "I say to you this evening that the new plantations in the twenty-first century are prisons! Where a tired body has been replaced with a corroded mind. And the cracking of the whip has been replaced with the slamming of steel doors."

"That's a lie!" Loren screamed.

"May I also say," Clyde said, removing the flyers from his briefcase, "I don't know why a man ahead in the polls would stoop to such low tactics." He placed the bulletin in full view of the camera.

194

"How dare you criticize me—"

"Isn't this a picture of your niece who was killed by a drunk driver? A man who, I might add, was just released from prison after serving twelve years."

Loren looked at Dawn. She looked away, embarrassment showing on her face. "I didn't authorize the printing of those flyers," Loren yelled. "I told—"

Clyde yelled louder, "You've caused unnecessary grief to this man. He's done his time. This man has been fired from his job because of your personal vendetta. Tell me, Governor Lake, what do you plan on doing about it?"

Dawn got up, apparently crying, and left the room. Afterward, everyone in the entire studio was holding their breath. It was obvious that most of the people there knew about the flyers.

"I can't be responsible for others' actions."

Rick Gates broke in. "That's all the time we have." He was as red as a Michigan apple, and avoided eye contact with the governor.

The heavy soundproof door shutting off Studio A was opened, and the sound of thunder was immediately heard.

As they headed out of the studio, the thunder outside cracked so hard, the office windows rattled like castanets.

The cracking of the thunder had an effect on Rosemary that she hadn't anticipated. She felt a pang of fear for her brother. If the governor wouldn't refute an obvious injustice to a citizen on public television, where did that leave Isaac?

Rosemary stepped outside, letting the pounding rain beat against her shoulders. She felt tired. Defeated. Checking her watch, it was now 4:05 P.M. The weathermen had predicted wrong. Even though it was eerily dark outside, she laughed. Driving home would be an Alfred Hitchcock kind of night.

It seemed that all of the weight of Hell and eternity and the coming of Christ in glory on the day of judgment were converging at this moment to condemn Isaac once again.

The Prayer for Mercy

Judge Us

It is of the Lord's mercies that we are not consumed, because his compassions fail not. They are new every morning: great is thy faithfulness.

—Lam. 3:22–23

Compulsion

"She didn't have on a dress, she had on a rubber glove," Peyton kidded. A young teenage girl swinging her hips in a provocative manner had just walked past them.

"Yeah, and one made for an infant." Isaac laughed. The girl turned back around and winked. "What a flirt. What's up with these young broads?"

"I'm thinking, you know, like, they're too desperate. Broads like that turn me off." Peyton took a sip from his soda, then looked at his watch. "You want anything else? My break's nearly over."

They were at Rally's on Seven Mile Road and the John C. Lodge Freeway, just a mile from the apartment. Known for their spicy fries and juicy burgers, the restaurant was always crowded—usually with young folks like Peyton.

Isaac couldn't have been prouder of his son. When he was fired two weeks ago, Peyton had managed to get hired at Rally's working four hours a night after school and full-time on the weekends. Isaac hadn't even mentioned that he was low on money.

"I'm good, Peyton." They cleaned up their greasy wrappers from the burgers and fries they'd eaten for dinner and tossed them into the wastebasket. Isaac patted his son on the shoulder. "I'll see you around nine, then?"

"Yeah. We've got time for one game of chess before I go to bed." He placed his Rally's cap back on his head and smiled. "I did my homework in study hall today."

"Okay, hurry home." The words felt good on his lips. Even though he was experiencing financial problems, he would have never thought he'd enjoy having his son living with him this much. Kennedy, he figured, knew exactly what she was doing.

Isaac started the Harley and gunned the motor a bit, acknowledging a final good-bye to Peyton, who was watching him from the window. He waved, and left the parking lot.

Without a porch light on, the driveway and house were dark. He parked his bike near the garage door, locked the gate behind him, then placed the clear plastic cover over it that Jesse had given him. In another four weeks he wouldn't be able to ride it—it would be too cold. Buying a car at this point seemed crucial. There was still Eli, but now that he was fired from Remmey's, he didn't think Eli would take a chance on him with just the temporary income from the Motor City Grille's salary. It wasn't dependable.

He looked up the flight of stairs, and decided he didn't have the motivation to practice tonight. It was exactly two minutes after six. Buttoning his jacket, he turned toward the twenty-seven steps that led to the back door of his old home.

"Hey," Kennedy said after opening the door. "It's good to see you. Come on in."

Kennedy looked inviting in a pink and yellow floral nightgown and a fluffy yellow chenille housecoat. Even covered up as she was, he could still see clearly the outlines of her high-slung breasts, her curvaceous hips, and her long, sultry legs.

He followed her back to the kitchen, where they usually sat. He knew she would offer him a beer.

"How you feeling? I came by to see if you needed anything." Isaac guiltily looked around the yellow and white room, trying to spot any signs of someone having come by or spent the night—a cigarette butt in the ashtray, an empty bottle of beer in the trash can, the lingering scent of a cologne that he didn't wear.

Because of the expense and Rosemary's nagging, Isaac had quit smoking a month ago.

"Ain't nobody been here, Isaac." She blushed, and laughed at little.

Her smile showed to perfection the lazy flutter of her large brown eyes— he'd never seen a woman look so effortlessly sexy.

"What am I going to do with you, man?" she murmured in caressing tones. "You don't give up. Listen, even though I'm back to work, I'm still in pain. I hurt so bad when I get home, I wouldn't go to bed with the doctor, let alone a man."

They both laughed.

"You can get me a glass of water, though." A spasm crossed her face when she removed the prescription bottle from her pocket. "I hate taking this stuff. Makes me sleep too much. A couple more days and, pain or no pain, they're going in the trash."

He got a glass from the cabinet, filled it with water, and watched her wince as she downed the medication. Prison was tough, and at times tormenting, but he had no idea what it felt like to be shot. Looking at her now, he felt like Jesse, a chauvinist. Being a cop was no job for a woman.

"I'm glad you stopped by," Kennedy said, taking a seat at the table. "Peyton's nearly out of his medicine. He called me this afternoon."

Isaac had gone to look in the refrigerator for a beer. Upon hearing the word *medicine*, he stopped dead in his tracks, slamming the refrigerator door shut. "What medicine? I ain't seen him taking nothing."

"Peyton didn't tell you that he was on Ritalin?" Isaac did a slow burn. "It's my fault, really. I should have told you."

As close as he and his son were becoming, he wondered why Peyton hadn't mentioned it to him. "I read about that stuff when I was locked up. It's just like dope. And I heard that most of the kids using it are black. Why would you put our son on some shit like that? Don't you know that they don't even know how the kids will react when they finally get off that drug?"

"I see you *have* indeed been reading."

"I know dudes in prison who had this same argument with their spouses. I never thought that I'd be having this conversation with you."

Just then his cell phone went off. It was Peyton. "Dad, I just saw something weird. Is your bike parked where you usually keep it?"

"Yes," Isaac said slowly, "but I'm not upstairs. I'm at your mother's." He thought about all the work he'd put into that bike. Plus it was the only transportation he had.

"I'm not certain, but one just like yours just passed here. I knew the chances of someone having a bike painted like that was real low. I got a pretty good look at the two guys that were on it when they stopped at the light. Anyway, I called the police and gave them the information. Told them which way they were heading."

Isaac relayed the information to Kennedy, and she snatched the phone from Isaac. She asked Peyton for a description of the two men—the type of clothes they were wearing. After she hung up, she immediately got on her phone and called the precinct. "Let me speak to Detective Royale, please. Hurry, it's an emergency."

Less than an hour later, they'd recovered the bike. It hadn't been stripped, but the ignition was broken. The two young men were being held in custody at the Fourteenth Precinct, and Isaac would have to come down the next day to press charges.

The officer told Isaac that his bike would remain at the station until he could call a tow truck the next day. The Harley shop was on VanDyke Street in Center Line, fifteen miles away. He had only property liability and property damage coverage on the bike. And no road service. His mind began calculating the costs. A new ignition and the cost of the tow would cost close to a hundred fifty dollars. He'd be broke by Saturday, but he didn't have a choice, he thought irritably. Before he left, he told Kennedy that their conversation about Peyton and Ritalin was far from over. He wanted the name of Peyton's doctor who had prescribed the drug. And he wanted to know when she could take a day off work to go with him to see Peyton's physician and discuss his so-called behavior problems.

That night, he didn't bother to ask Peyton about the Ritalin. Making sure he understood what drugs did to a black man's future was more important to him. By drugs, he meant alcohol—beer. Black males who gave in to their weaknesses usually ended up flipping burgers for a living or living on the streets. Not his son. Peyton's job at Rally's was definitely a temporary gig.

When Peyton came home from school the next day, Isaac was waiting for him. It was time for a man-to-man talk. Peyton wasn't due at work for two hours. In that time, Isaac decided to talk very honestly about the night that he'd left their home upset, broke, unemployed, and drinking. It was the night that he had accidentally killed Becky Cullors.

"That's what drugs will do. Screw up your entire life." Isaac was trying to gauge Peyton's thoughts.

"I appreciate you telling me all this. But I don't drink. And I don't use drugs." He showed his impatience by angrily tossing his book bag on the couch. "Can I go now? I'm supposed to go in early today."

It was a bad lie. And it hurt Isaac.

Fifteen minutes later, an overnight letter from the post office arrived for him. He tore open the cardboard envelope and removed a single-page letter. It read: "Don't give up. Music is the way to melt a person's heart. I know it has mine." Anonymously signed, Isaac had no idea who'd sent it. He thought about Kennedy, but knew that she was still fuming over Peyton's appointment next week.

Isaac was shaving the next morning when the telephone rang. It was his boss at the Motor City Grille, Rex Martin. "I have a proposition for you. My partner and I would like you to play here four nights a week. Two hundred dollars a night."

Isaac was shocked. Eight hundred dollars a week! He could buy a car, move to a two-bedroom apartment. Something warned him to stop and think. "Rex, I'd love to. But why?" he asked suspiciously. "I don't understand. Last week I was certain you were considering firing me."

"To be honest, my partner and I talked about it. Everybody knows about the girl getting killed. Man, it's mystifying—but the calls have been coming in every day since the governor's debate. People want to see you. People want to hear your music."

"What? After all that's happened?"

"I respect you, man, for telling me about your record before I hired you. In my past experiences," he continued with exaggerated emphasis, "most people would lie. Honest people are a rare breed these days. I feel that I can trust you, Isaac. Aside from that, you're the biggest talent that we've had here since we remodeled."

"I don't know what to say. I accept your offer, of course. Still . . ."

"Stop worrying." And Isaac could hear the warmth in his voice. "Listen, Isaac. I'd like to ask you a favor. You've got a bonus coming if you can play an additional set this coming Friday and Saturday nights. The reservations are overbooked on both nights." He paused. "Another thing, word is that a local recording producer is going to be here on Saturday."

This was the first real break he had had since he was released from prison. He felt like crying. Things were changing. Someone was finally giving him a chance. "Rex, is that pay effective immediately?"

"Guaranteed."

"I've got a thought. I know this young guy and his band . . ." Isaac went on to tell him about his talented friend Bernie, whom he would love to do a duo with on special occasions. Bernie even had a singer, he went on to tell him, whom Isaac had heard a few times. When Isaac told Rex that he would pay their fee, Rex was all for it.

"I'll see you on Thursday, Rex. God bless you, man." It was the first time Isaac had ever said those words. Especially to a man.

When Isaac put the receiver back, he jumped up and down like he'd just won a ten-million-dollar lottery.

On Friday, Bernie showed up at Isaac's apartment four hours early. They'd practiced a few times that week, but Bernie felt that they needed another crash session just to be safe. Isaac suspected that Bernie had learned about the record producer's impromptu visit and wanted to showcase his talent.

Peyton was in a better mood and even gave Bernie, Heather, and Isaac a few pointers.

Isaac chose to wear jeans. He added a belt and a jean shirt that spelled out HARLEY in rust and black lettering. He'd bought it way back in the summer when the fall clothes were on sale, and had never worn it before tonight.

"I still feel that we should have added 'Make a Joyful Noise' to the set, Isaac," Bernie said as they began to unload the instruments from his van.

"We're playing jazz, Bernie, not holding a revival." He knocked at the back door of the Grille and the security guard let them in. Bernie and Heather followed behind him to his designated dressing room.

For the first time since the drive over, Heather spoke up. "Bernie's got a point, Isaac. In my opinion, I think we should do 'He Touched Me.' It's a spiritual piece and it's also very sexy."

"I'll give it some thought," Isaac said, still bothered about Peyton's use of Ritalin. He didn't have the energy to argue with them when it was painfully obvious that both Heather and Bernie wanted to perform the songs that displayed *their* personal talent.

Both looked stunning, dressed tastefully in black and silver. Isaac was impressed. Their costumes appeared to be designed and sewn by a professional. The silver trimming that ran along the split and cuffs of Heather's floor-length dress was also sewn around the lapel of Bernie's jacket.

Heather was a very attractive young girl, around twenty-eight years old. She had an Audrey Hepburn type of appeal, with an extremely long neck and wide, exotic eyes. Her a cappella voice was like that of an angel, and she habitually pressed her middle fingers against her throat as if she were straining to reach that higher note.

And tonight, she hit every one of them. They began with a medley by Sam Cooke. Next they improvised a set from B. B. King's greatest hits, and moved into duets by the Chi-Lites. Isaac and Heather had the audience on their feet when they finished singing "Have You Seen Her."

The place was packed, like Rex said it would be. It was standing-room only, and people were still coming in. Isaac talked to the crowd during sets, and even made a few jokes about his brother-in-law's funeral parlor. It was the best night of his life.

During the break, Isaac agreed to play "He Touched Me." Heather was so happy, she kissed him.

Isaac had written several songs since he was fired. He performed three of the solo numbers tonight. It didn't matter if the guests talked loud while he performed, or if a waiter who was serving drinks clinked glasses, or if anyone got up and left. Isaac remained focused on his music.

Much later, when two expensively dressed men took empty seats in the front row, Rex managed to get Isaac's attention. They were the record company executives.

Call it compulsion. Call it selfishness. But Isaac was determined to put on the best show he could. He felt as if his life depended on it.

"Isaac?" Heather gently called from behind him. "It's time."

Bernie began the introduction. Sitting on a high stool, he leaned forward and began plucking the large instrument to a soul-jazz spiritual fusion, leading into the beginning overture to "He Touched Me."

Near the end of the song, Isaac spotted Miracall just to the right of the producers. Her arms were held high, and she was clapping and smiling. He looked around for her friends. For Dawn. Tempest. He wondered what she was doing here alone. At that moment, the emcee announced that the next song would end the show, but that they were welcome to come back tomorrow. Instantly, the two men stood and clapped. Isaac put all thoughts and Miracall behind him.

Heather nodded at Isaac, and he began singing the opening to what he knew would always be his trademark song—"Fire and Desire."

The crowd went wild.

Isaac felt like life was finally giving him another chance.

Devotion

Success was like the sunshine; it brought all the rattlesnakes out. A selfish snake is probably the term that Kennedy would use to describe him if she knew where he was headed today.

Maybe he was wrong. Maybe he should have put more of an effort into finding a white-collar job—unlike the one the Grille provided. But his subconscious wouldn't let him. It was all or nothing.

Catching the city bus to the House of Music on Woodward Avenue, Isaac felt triumphant. He hadn't been in this store since he was Peyton's age. Once inside, he noticed customers near the back, testing out their instruments, which he assumed had been brought in for service.

He scanned the walls, admiring all the brass, until he spotted the saxophone section. "Looking for a new instrument?" the salesman asked.

Isaac was so excited, his fingers itched. "I'm looking for a saxophone." The saxes came in four different sizes: soprano in B-flat, alto in E-flat, baritone in E-flat, and Isaac's instrument of choice—the tenor sax in B-flat. He pointed to the Yamaha Sixty-two Tenor first, then spotted the real treasure. "Matter of fact, that Selmer Mark Six, right there."

The Selmer was the top of the pro-line horn, he told Isaac. They usually kept only one in stock.

Isaac had bought his first hardly used 1968 sax in 1978. He'd been working two jobs to save enough money. His old one was purchased from the pawnshop for forty dollars.

It wasn't that his current sax didn't sound good; it weighed a ton. He had no intention of trading it in because, like the Harley that was still in the shop, his 1968 Mark Six was a collector's item. Back then it cost twenty-two hundred dollars. This beauty, he thought, turning the lighter instrument over in his hands, cost forty-five hundred dollars.

Touching the base felt cool to his fingertips. "Can I try it?" The salesman said they didn't usually do that, but since he had his own reed, why not? Without hesitating a second, Isaac inserted the slim chip and began to blow. He played an old tune that he remembered that would test the range of all three octaves. The soft, rich tone that came from the polished instrument sounded like the ghost of music melting on a rainbow spray of sound. He had to have it. But it would take him six months to save up that much money.

"Do you finance?"

"No, but we are affiliated with a company that we use for outside financing. I'll get the form." While he filled out the application, Isaac casually mentioned to him where he was working weekends. The salesman was impressed. Isaac hoped that it would make a difference when they learned he didn't have any recent credit history.

Back at home, he called Bernie at work, he was so excited. "It's Isaac, man. You still need a sax player for the bar mitzvah on Saturday night? I'm available."

He spent the remainder of the day looking for an agent. It wasn't widely known that a small group from Motown had moved back to the city. Bernie had hipped him to the fact that they were here looking for local talent. Working with Bernie in his spare time was good for now. However, he'd never led Bernie to believe that he wanted to be a part of a band. His long-term goal was strictly to be a solo performer.

That same afternoon the House of Music called. Isaac could pick up his horn with a five-hundred-dollar down payment. Isaac assured the salesman that he'd have it by the following weekend.

He played with Bernie Saturday night and was paid a well earned $120.

On Monday, Kennedy was finally able to accompany him to the Sinai professional building on Outer Drive, where Peyton's doctor was on staff. Kennedy picked Isaac up at eight, an hour after Peyton left for school.

They arrived at the professional building thirty minutes before their appointment. "Want to wait out here or go inside?" Kennedy asked.

He pressed the play button on the CD player. The sound of O'Landa Draper and the Associates' "Reflections" was playing. A sixty-voice choir swelled in the background. He and Kennedy hardly ever agreed on the same type of music, but this was one that he'd heard and liked. "Let's wait here."

She began slowly. "Isaac. I know you. You've got a hot temper. I don't want you to get upset when we talk with the doctor. She's highly recommended."

"A woman doctor? You couldn't find him a male doctor? Preferably a black one?"

"Dr. Allbright is black. And she's the best in the field of ADHD."

"What?"

"Peyton was diagnosed with Attention Deficit Hyperactivity Disorder when he was twelve. I got opinions from four different doctors. They all recommended Ritalin."

"You mean dope." He was so angry, he felt his nostrils twitching. "My son is not going to wind up a junkie." Again, he wondered if Rosemary had known and kept this from him.

"You didn't see how he was back then, Isaac. It took months before we were able to get the dose right. He was so hyper back then, I couldn't calm him down. I found dozens of activities to enroll him in—karate, kickboxing, and even wood-shop classes. He ended up fighting with the other students or arguing with the teachers." She spoke from a spirit that was long exhausted. "Do you remember that day at the principal's office a few months back?" Isaac nodded. "I found out that he hadn't taken his medication in weeks."

While Kennedy continued to talk, Isaac kept his thoughts to himself. It didn't matter to him what the doctor told him today. He'd already made his mind up. Peyton wasn't taking any more Ritalin.

"Isaac, are you listening?"

"Yeah, I heard you."

Her voice was kinder when she said sweetly, "Do you realize how much of a negative impact you've had on our son's life?"

Isaac felt as if he'd been struck a low blow. While his blood raged, he kept his eyes steady as she turned her face slowly to his.

"I made decisions. I'm not saying I was right all the time. Only God knows the answer to that. I couldn't continue to live in a dreamworld. For so many years, I did," she said, tears rising in her throat. "Remember the good times, when we would dream together? Meet each other in our dreams?"

"Yes, I remember." He looked deeply into her moistened eyes. Even with the problems they were experiencing now, he knew he could never stop loving her. "Those were the days when we lived as one. Felt as one. Breathed as one."

Kennedy leaned over and kissed him on the cheek. "It can still be that way." She slid over on the seat, pausing to rub his inner thigh, stroking his growing hardness. "It's a love that I sometimes regret. But one that I can't forget."

Placing his arms around her, he pulled her toward him, kissing her deeply on the mouth. Kennedy moved her body closer until she was inches away from straddling him. The kiss deepened. He stopped when he felt her stiffen. "Baby, did I hurt you?"

Before she could answer, a security guard was tapping on the windshield.

"We'd better go in," Kennedy said.

After exiting the car, Isaac asked, "Can I come by later?" She nodded yes.

Thirty minutes later, dreams and lust were forgotten. After hearing the doctor's prognosis, Isaac had blown up in her office. He was ready to slap Kennedy's face for being so gullible. How could she let these people basically experiment on their son? He was told it could cause cancer. It could also cause Peyton's hearing to decrease. Even knowing those consequences, Kennedy still wanted Peyton to remain on the drug.

Isaac stormed out, leaving her there with Dr. Allbright. He caught a taxi home and waited for Peyton. It was time for another man-to-man talk.

Isaac felt so strongly about getting Peyton off drugs, they both attended Mother Bethel on Wednesday night. They went down front to kneel at the altar, and Isaac asked Rosemary to pray for Peyton. He needed strength in getting this drug out of his system. Together, they would work out another alternative, a healthier way to control his problem.

Afterward, they went to Rosemary's home and Isaac explained the entire situation. Peyton sat quietly listening. Isaac could tell he was embarrassed. While they were seated at the kitchen table she offered him a bowl of banana pudding that she'd just made for Jesse. After Peyton left, Rosemary made a suggestion that Isaac consult a doctor to help Peyton while he began this new life change. She cautioned Isaac that this was a tough decision, but a good one, she felt.

Isaac never mentioned his thoughts about believing that she'd known and kept yet another secret from him. Watching her with Peyton earlier today, he was convinced that she was as shocked by his use of the medication as he had been.

Thursday was payday, and Isaac picked up his final check from Remmey's. After paying his bills, he had three hundred dollars left.

Peyton was doing okay so far. No outbursts. Not even the mildest of character changes.

Though Isaac had no idea that Peyton was still sneaking out at night to meet his friends, things were still strained between them. Neither had completely let go of his past.

Still, Isaac wouldn't feel completely comfortable until he managed to find a Peyton a decent doctor. When he did, the earliest appointment he could get was in two weeks. Upon hearing that, Isaac finally got on his knees; he didn't want anything to happen to his son. Otherwise, he would never be able to look Kennedy in the face again.

Thursday night, Isaac went to work at the Grille and Peyton left for Rally's.

The Grille was packed, just like Rex had keep assuring him it would be. Even so, Isaac noticed a familiar face in the crowd. She was to his left in the back. Dressed in a navy blue pantsuit, he didn't recognize her at first. She applauded throughout his entire first set. He was flabbergasted. Should he go out and talk to her during the break? No. During the second set, she was still there, standing and applauding just as hard as the rest of the crowd. When his performance was over he decided to stop by her table and say hello. But after he changed his clothes and the soft music from the master tape was playing, she was gone.

The following weekend it was the same thing. She arrived after his second number. He felt extremely upbeat because he was using his new Mark Six. Even if the crowd didn't seem to notice the difference in his music, he could. Peyton was still working every day and had even managed to get a decent report card—all B's and an A in wood shop. There'd been no outbursts, no obvious change in his behavior, and Isaac couldn't feel happier. His thoughts went back to the woman. He wanted to speak to this femme fatale who appeared, then disappeared like a mist of smoke. Tonight she left before the first break.

Forget it, he said to himself. *I'm too old to be playing games.*

The following weekend was Halloween. The Grille had gone all out advertising the costume party. It was by invitation only, and Isaac's first time attending one. He had no idea what to wear, or where to rent a costume.

His son simplified his dilemma by picking up the telephone book and finding A-Zakoor Novelty Company on Woodward Avenue. He wrote the address down and offered to go with Isaac. "Zorro! That's the perfect costume," Peyton stated. "Come onstage with your sword in one hand and your sax in the other." He imitated the pose with a broom from the kitchen. "Dressed in all black, and wearing that wide-brimmed mannish hat. Women love that kind of stuff, man."

Isaac would have preferred Peyton to call him *Dad* instead of *man.* For all intents and purposes, the Zorro costume was an excellent idea. A part of him could identify with Zorro. Because, like him, he was trying to do good, but was constantly fighting for his life. For some odd reason Isaac felt like Peyton was testing him. Even though he and Kennedy weren't seeing each other, Isaac felt that Peyton knew how much he cared for his mother. Isaac never tried to hide or deny it.

When he stopped by the novelty store, Isaac was surprised to find that no one had rented the Zorro costume. The owner altered the outfit to fit him, and he left the store feeling strange. What if he looked out of place up there? What if the audience laughed instead of applauded? Until now, the record producers hadn't called him. Rex kept assuring Isaac that they were interested and said they'd be back for another show—just to be sure.

Isaac couldn't shake his continuously growing nervousness, and called Jesse. "Hey, brother-in-law. I'd like to invite you to a party. Would you be my guest on Saturday night? The Grille's putting on this big costume party."

"That sounds like fun. Yeah. I got it now. I could come as an injured Vietnam vet. Complete with missing prosthesis."

"How many beers have you had today, Jesse?"

Jesse laughed. "None. What time, brother?"

Nervous as a cat perched on top of a light pole, Isaac blew the first two numbers that night. The audience barely clapped. Every other minute he was scanning the room, wondering when and if the producers were going to show up again, and all the while keeping an eye out for the mystery woman. Jesse was sitting in the front row, frowning at Isaac. They both knew he could do better. Bernie was onstage with him, along with Heather, the female soloist. Isaac's respect for Bernie was steadily growing. A true professional, he covered for Isaac beautifully.

Then he saw her. *I know it's her,* he told himself. People were looking at her and complimenting her choice of costume with nods and smiles. Isaac had to laugh—it was ingenious. She wore a gray leotard with strips of rags tied around her feet. Covering three quarters of her body was a beat-up metal trash can. Pieces of trash, paper, food, beer cans, and some items not so clearly identifiable were glued around the can. The top of the dented can was on her head, with a rotten banana peel leaning over the side. A black mask covered most of her face, but he could see her eyes smile when she took a seat. Isaac signaled Jesse with his eyes. His adrenaline began to pump up as vigorously as if he'd taken an overdose of steroids.

He thought, *Now the show will truly begin.*

With Bernie's and Heather's help, they rocked the house. He received a nod from Jesse. Isaac wasn't sure what time the producers had finally arrived, but they had. Isaac could see Rex giving him the thumbs-up from the bar at the opposite end of the room.

After the show, Isaac didn't bother to change. He rushed out into the audience. "Did you see her?"

Jesse didn't hear him. He was engrossed in a conversation with three other men. Apparently he'd found his fraternity brothers, because Isaac noticed that two of them wore watches with the Mason emblem.

"Who?" Jesse said, excusing himself from his friends.

"Miracall. She was wearing the trash-can costume."

History Is Made
at Night

Rosemary had no sense of impending drama on the chilly Friday afternoon when Gary phoned her on her cell phone. It was the weekend before the gubernatorial election. She had taken a temporary break from politics, concentrating more on Peyton's daily progress without his medication.

Gary seemed so excited. His sources had learned about the fabulous deal Loren was about to make with the state. As Gary continued, Rosemary was shocked to discover information about Loren and a certain judge in Bloomfield's circuit court. The judge had been a fellow classmate and personal friend of Loren's when he was circuit court judge. *That was around the same time Isaac was sentenced to prison.*

"People are beginning to ask questions," Gary said.

"Isn't it a little late? The election's on Tuesday."

"You might have heard that Clyde is having problems raising money. His financial report came in at the worst time in his campaign. Five days before the election. That same day, his campaign manager quit, citing that he hadn't been paid since August."

Things are only getting worse for the Democratic candidate, Rosemary thought. "Can the church do anything to help?"

What Gary suggested didn't seem unnatural to Rosemary. She agreed. She had no idea that this small generosity would come back to haunt her administration.

Gary appeared irritated. "It's beyond me why candidates, primarily Republicans, place more emphasis on how much money is in their war chest than the real issues of the state. Should it make a difference that Loren has 8.2 million dollars on hand, while Clyde barely has 1.1 million dollars? No."

They were silent for a moment. Both knew that the most competitive period of the entire campaign was the final leg. And even more crucial, it was the last weekend. Money was needed to sway the uncommitted. The television time and newspaper ads cost big bucks. They didn't work on credit. No, it wasn't fair. But it was a fact.

"Everyone knows that Loren is the hometown favorite," Gary continued. "He's got endorsements from powerful judges, and a host of other influential politicians. Even though Loren is attacking MichCare as 'fraudulent and deceptive at the core,' he hasn't addressed the problems with the state's healthcare system in four years. He doesn't even understand what's going on. The latest attempts to restructure MichCare Partners still overlooks the central underlying problem: that you're giving money without accounting for it to some people who are operating for profit. It's putting the mentally ill on the streets or in the jails."

The conversation began to turn serious for Rosemary when he mentioned jails. Gary told her that he wanted to meet for lunch if she was available.

"Jesse's business is just a few blocks away. It's time for his injection." She paused until she completed a left turn on Puritan. "I can meet you at your office in an hour."

Forty-five minutes later, Rosemary was in Gary's office on the twenty-fifth floor of the Penobscott building planning a last-minute strategy for Clyde's campaign. During that time, Dawn had called twice. Rosemary was mystified at the way Dawn and Gary's relationship was building. Surely, they would be voting for opposite parties, she thought. Her friendship with Gary meant more than politics.

They ate a catered lunch of Cajun chicken salad and fresh fruit. Gary had remembered that she loved spicy foods. Afterward, the table was cleared away and it was back to business.

"I can't believe Loren is this insensitive to the mentally ill." Rosemary watched his face. "I don't care much for the governor, but I'm wondering if he doesn't have a heart. Would he sacrifice MichCare, the health of those needy people, some too ill to vote, or may possibly never vote for him, for a few dollars? I would hope that he's a little more human than that."

There was a buzz on his intercom, and Gary picked up the phone. "Okay, I've been expecting her."

Gary shrugged and continued, "Either Loren doesn't understand it, or doesn't care."

The door opened and Clyde's new campaign manager came in and intro-

Wonderword

CAMPING WITH KIDS

Solution: 9 letters

```
B D R A Y S K N M S E I L F
E S E V A C H O T S P D A D
A R A E A A O O O O P R N A
C E A R R R V C R C M U N A
H L T F T E G C Y S O T O G
G I U S T N H A R R E F O R
N A E B I E S R G R E D O R
I R W R S R K B N T T P E O
M T I O E A C I U O E D P T
M T A W L C O K H R I I A I
I X O N A E L I I P G O U U
W H A N S S B N S B B E R Q
S A V L I G N G E W E N R S
B A R B E C U E R K C A N O
S U M M E R S B S S T O R M
```

Barbecue, Beach, Bear, Below, Biking, Boats, Bu
Burger, Burn, Canoe, Canvas, Caves, Clubs, Co
Deer, Farm, Flies, Food, Grounds, Groups, Heavy, H
Horse, Hot dogs, Hungry, Lantern, Mosquito, Pe
Quiet, Races, Raccoon, Raft, Relax, Restroom, S
Scare, Showers, Spiders, Storms, Stove, Summer, S
block, Swimming, Tans, Tiring, Tonic, Track, Tra
Warm, Yard, Zipper. **Yesterday's Answer: Thirst**

duced herself. Rosemary sat there listening for a while, offering what little help she could. After a couple of hours of brainstorming, she excused herself and went home.

Rosemary never understood Gary's interest in politics. He was a very rich man. He had recently purchased Northland Mall in Southfield. He'd never been married, as far as she knew. And it was obvious that he could pick and choose from the most intelligent and attractive women in the city. Still, he had never mentioned a woman to her in the ten years that she'd known him. Now, all of a sudden, Dawn. It didn't make sense to her.

When Rosemary made it home that night and prepared a quick dish of spaghetti and meatballs for supper, it was the fifth night that week that she was too tired to eat. The irony was that when she weighed herself after showering, she'd gained two pounds. How could that happen?

Every pound of her body ached when she got on her knees that night. She began from her first memory of hearing about the Bible.

In the beginning, God created the heaven and the earth. Rosemary was told and made to understand by age thirteen that these four nouns—beginning, God, heaven, and earth—were the primary four elements—earth, air, fire, and water; the four directions—north, east, south, and west; and the four seasons—summer, winter, spring, and fall; thus producing the cross as an emblem of the four elements and symbol of the sublunary physical world.

Soon after Rosemary turned fifteen, when she was able to earn enough money baby-sitting, she purchased her first cross. That was forty years ago, and she still owned and prayed with the same cross today.

The next day, Rosemary spent time in her office at Mother Bethel, preparing the sermon for Sunday's service. It was the last big bash they would have to bolster support for the congressman. Clyde, his wife, Gary, and several other dignitaries would be attending as well. When she finished, she printed a copy of her sermon and left it on her desk, then locked the door behind her.

A woman whom she thought she recognized appeared to be waiting for her. "Yes?"

"My son knows your nephew, Peyton," the middle-aged woman said. Down the hall, choir practice had just ended. Rosemary assumed that the woman was one of the choir members. There were three adult choirs and two youth choirs that totalled more than three hundred members. It was hard to remember all the faces. Rosemary had been prepared for a nice compliment. But when she saw the frown growing on the woman's face, she should have guessed that the conversation would be negative. "I'm so disappointed. I would have thought that our pastor had more control over her own blood. He's been influential in encouraging my child to skip school. My boy's even joined a gang because of his constant badgering."

Rosemary was appalled. She didn't know how to respond or if the woman was actually telling the truth. Her first mind was to call Isaac. She'd heard from Jesse how well Isaac was doing down at the Grille. Kennedy had been put on some kind of special case that she didn't want to discuss. Rosemary knew that Kennedy and Isaac were both bull-headed. Because of that fact, neither would admit how their careers were affecting their son.

Someone had to do something. She decided to call each of them and arrange a short conference. Both agreed to meet Rosemary at her house on Monday night. She timed it so that Jesse wouldn't be home; he would be at a Mason's meeting until eleven. If he was home, Rosemary knew that she wouldn't make any ground with Isaac; Jesse was so protective of him.

When they arrived, the spicy aroma of pears cooking greeted the estranged couple. She led them back to the kitchen.

"What's cooking, Rosemary?" Isaac asked.

"Spiced-pear preserves. They're Jesse's favorite." She stirred one of the large pots on the stove. "Have a seat, you two." She glanced over her shoulder, eyeing them, then stirred the eight cups of peeled and finely chopped ripened pears. "We might be here long enough for both of you to take a few jars home."

She measured and poured four cups of sugar, one teaspoon of ground cinnamon, and one-quarter teaspoon of ground cloves into the pot and waited. After that mixture was brought to a boil, she reduced the heat, stirring occasionally.

Kennedy was sitting at the right end of the table, drumming her fingers along the place mat. Isaac was sitting on the opposite end, fiddling with the glass jars lined up in the center of the table.

"Well, that needs to simmer for about two hours," she said to herself. She checked the recipe for the final step. Yep, she was right. She had to pour the preserves into hot jars immediately, leaving one-quarter-inch head space, and then wipe the jar rims. Then she had to cover them with metal lids and screw-on bands, then process them in a boiling-water bath for ten minutes.

"Who's going to talk first?" She took a seat in the middle and glanced back and forth, her temper flaring, while she waited for one of them to begin.

Kennedy looked annoyed. "I think Isaac should speak first. He's the one who wouldn't listen when I told him not to take Peyton off Ritalin."

"If anything is wrong with Peyton, Kennedy, it's because you put him on that mess," Isaac said defensively.

Even though she'd been back to work for only a few weeks, Kennedy's body didn't show a trace of the injury. To Rosemary, Kennedy seemed like a different kind of cop now. Colder. Indifferent. She didn't understand, but something serious had gone on between her and Isaac. Neither one of them wanted to talk to the other.

The evening proved to be fruitless. She sent both Kennedy and Isaac home with three jars of preserves and nothing accomplished.

After they left, Rosemary cleaned up the kitchen. Jesse came home exhausted and barely noticed her. "What in the world was going on?" he asked. She shook her head dismally, signaling that she didn't feel like talking.

She wasn't a bit sleepy. So, by eleven-thirty, she was back in the kitchen making a batch of tri-berry lemon jam. Christmas would be here soon, and the preserves would make perfect gifts.

By the time she finished, she was starved. Though she knew better, Rosemary ended up turning on the oven and slipping in a cookie sheet full of fluffy Bisquick biscuits. She stayed up till three, eagerly consuming the hot bread loaded with melted butter and pear preserves.

On Sunday, both the eight o'clock and the eleven o'clock services were jam-packed. Her message was from a sermon by Emerson that she paraphrased: "These . . . are a law unto themselves: Which show the work of the law written in their hearts." It was taken from Rom. 2:14–15. Rosemary especially loved the phrase "our evil angel," and she sprinkled that term throughout the sermon.

.   .   .

To Congressman Clyde's surprise, it was nothing short of a miracle when he defied all the odds hours after the polls opened on Tuesday. The congressman was well on his way to upsetting the incumbent, Loren Lake. Rosemary's phones at home and at Mother Bethel hadn't stopped ringing.

Now that the political link had been eliminated from the equation, Gary was on another mission—his plans to build a new prison seemed imminent. His pal, Clyde, was in the position to give the go-ahead for the prison project.

Not so. Less than a week after the election, Clyde didn't return any of Gary's calls.

According to Miracall, the ex-governor wasn't going to step out of office so graciously. Rosemary patiently listened to Miracall's spiel about her renewed relationship with Loren. He needed her now more than ever. Miracall wasn't sure how to handle this man who was trying to reenter her life. Rosemary merely cautioned her.

Gary was next in line. His calls to Rosemary for advice came three to four times a day. He felt as if Clyde had used him and he didn't want to be intrusive. He wondered if he should continue to call Clyde or wait until the governor-elect called him.

Peyton presented another problem. He visited his aunt at home on the Wednesday night after the service. Clearly, he had something on his mind, but after an hour's time, he still hadn't opened up. Rosemary sensed that it was about he and his father's argument about the Ritalin. This wasn't the time to usurp Isaac's parenting decisions.

The one person whom she was genuinely concerned about was Kennedy. She hadn't heard from her in a while. She was worried that Kennedy was feeling the loneliness from not having her son around her. It had to be a major adjustment.

Consoling the people she cared about left Rosemary exhausted. The following week, she canceled all of her meetings. She felt certain that the Premarin the doctor had prescribed for her was causing severe side effects. She was more irritable and depressed than she'd been in years. Unknowingly, she'd gained fifteen unwanted pounds, and her hot spells had gotten worse than ever.

Deciding to do as a church member suggested, she stopped taking her prescribed medication and bought ten herbal products that would help her get through this phase of menopause. Her body went through a major metamorphosis. She began craving foods, like a woman did in her first trimester of pregnancy—in three weeks, all the spicy pear preserves and tri-berry lemon preserves were gone.

On top of everything, early Friday morning of that same week, her assistant minister, Don Scott called her at home. "I thought you'd like to know that the church's financial status is being investigated."

"By whom?"

"The Americans United for Separation of Church and State. They've asked the Internal Revenue Service to do a thorough audit of the church's financial records."

"Why?"

"The group charges that our church, which is affiliated with the Christian Coalition, violated the federal tax law prohibiting nonprofit organizations from distributing partisan campaign material."

Then she remembered feeling strange when Gary had asked her to put together a fund-raiser at the last minute. She had felt hesitant about the entire ordeal, but wanted to show her support and ignored her instincts that something about the affair just didn't feel right. "Thanks, Don. I've gotta go." She hung up and immediately called Gary.

"Mother Bethel is being audited by the IRS, Gary." She didn't hide the irritation in her voice.

"I planned on calling you today. Clyde's assistant apprised me of the petition an hour ago."

"How did this happen?"

"I'm not sure. At this moment I'm looking at a copy of one of the flyers. They were passed out during the fund-raiser dinner that Mother Bethel sponsored for Clyde last month. The person that gave me this one found a stack of them on the tables in the lower vestibule at Mother Bethel. I didn't pay any attention to the flyers. They looked just like all the other campaign material for Clyde." She could hear him thinking. "But none were endorsed by a church, like this one is." He paused a moment. "You know, Rosemary, doesn't this sound vaguely familiar?"

"You mean Loren." Loren had demanded a recount of the votes. The state was in an uproar. Loren would not concede the governorship until all the votes were recounted. That would take weeks. Until then, everyone was a target.

"Bingo. I smell a rat. I think we were set up."

She felt a wave of dizziness and closed her eyes for a moment, praying that it would pass. This was all too much for her to absorb: the flyers, Isaac, Clyde, Loren. Lately, she hadn't given the campaign a second thought. *Would Loren's vengeance stoop so low? Would I also be a target of his barnyard politics?* She had more important things on her mind. Anyway, what difference did it make now? "I still don't get it. Even though Loren lost, no damage was done to him personally."

"It doesn't matter; they don't want the church to be involved in how a person votes."

That night, Rosemary fell to her knees. While she was on her knees beside her bed, her head began to throb and ache. Not one to give in to pain and run for medication, she prayed for relief. A few minutes passed and she began to feel more strength than she had in months. She thought about the heroic women in the Old Testament and their courageous witness to the integrity and holiness of womanhood as God's gift to the world.

And she believed, even without God's presence to reinforce her thoughts, that history is made not by the weak at heart but by the strength of those souls humble enough to get down on their knees and give thanks. Those same souls unashamed to be humbled by being human.

Rosemary thought about Isaac, and prayed for him out loud. "Learn and know that your strength comes from God, down on your knees, and that's why throughout the world, history is made at night."

Flesh and the Devil

"Rosemary?" Gary asked. "The waiter's been waiting to take your order." He politely asked the waiter to come back in a few minutes. They weren't ready to place their order yet.

220

"Excuse me, Gary." She began fanning her face with the menu. "I don't understand what's wrong with me. One minute I'm fine, full of energy, and the next minute my head is aching and throbbing."

Sitting in a booth in the center of Fishbone's of Southfield, the two had agreed to meet for dinner before ending their conversation last Friday. Politics aside, they had business to discuss.

Gary leaned over and touched her affectionately on the arm. "I'd say you're overworked."

"You're wrong. Just overweight." She smiled, then set the menu down beside her. "I already know what I'm going to have."

"A chicken salad, with low-calorie ranch dressing."

Rosemary blushed. "You know me too well, Gary." When the waiter returned, she ordered the salad and asked for a glass of iced tea. Gary placed his order of spicy shrimp gumbo and a virgin margarita.

"Well, Rosemary, the governor's recount is official. Now Clyde has won by a larger margin than was first reported. He apologized for not returning my calls. He said the recount thing had him in a tailspin."

"Whew," Rosemary breathed. "That's a relief. After all the work we've done. I would hope that he didn't plan on shunning us altogether."

"My sentiment exactly," Gary began. "Just this morning, I was contacted by Clyde's secretary. He takes office sometime in January. Once they've made the transition in office, they said that they would consider our grant along with three others. I believe that it's going to be between our Development Corporation and Detroit Initiatives Support Corporation, DISC."

Gary was the president of their company, the Christian Development Corporation. There were nineteen other members on the CDC board of directors who held important positions in the Detroit community and were also long-time members of Mother Bethel and other local churches.

Rosemary agreed to be a part of CDC strictly as a consultant. She'd never voiced her apprehension to Gary about using the prisons to turn a profit when he had asked her to invest in his new business. She had merely declined, citing that she had enough investments for an old woman.

But she did assure her young friend that she would stay involved to help implement the Bible based programs they'd discussed. For eighteen months, Rosemary, as well as other volunteers, would visit the prison, teaching the

Bible six days a week to groups of inmates. They would also help the prisoners complete high school course work, fortify drug-abuse counseling, offer support groups, and take a hand in family and marriage counseling as well as community-service work.

"I realize that you're a pastor, Rosemary, and you may not totally agree with this venture of ours. But this is a chance to make millions and do a great service for the prison population as well." He leaned to the side as the waiter placed the margarita before him. "Mahlik did an excellent job on our proposal. We submitted our bid for thirty-two million dollars to build and maintain a prison for seven hundred of Michigan's most violent offenders. The price tag should be thirty-seven million."

"So you think the bid is a fair one?" Rosemary's palms were moist and she felt her fingers tremble slightly as she sipped on her tea. "That's still a lot of money to ask for, any way you look at it." Her heart began pounding so loudly that she could hear it in her ears. Then, all of a sudden, it stopped, and she felt completely normal. She had to laugh at herself for worrying so much.

For the past hour, the restaurant had begun to fill with the eight o'clock Saturday crowd—their busiest time of the week. People were lined up against the walls waiting for an open table, impatient and hungry.

"Realistically, though, the governor-elect knew that a company with a moderate amount of knowledge of running a private corporation, like Jefferson, knows that there's going to be a twelve-million-dollar drag, because they know they can run the prison for nineteen million anyway. That's why I'm waiting to see how much the governor's office is looking for before they assign the bid."

Rosemary was horrified. "Are you talking about kickbacks?"

"Absolutely. Of course, the governor wouldn't dirty his hands and get personally involved, but no matter how the situation is handled, the governor's office is going to receive two to three million from the company that gets the go-ahead."

Gary talked as if the former congressman were already ensconced and wielding his newfound power.

"No wonder our taxes are so high. The only thing that isn't inflated these days is the Lord."

Gary laughed. "Amen, Pastor Jones. At any rate, the final payment on the land contract is due in January."

"You know, the CDC purchased twenty acres of farmland in Flint, Michigan, in March 1997 for the sole purpose of building a prison. The grant money will only cover the costs of things like beds, staff, food, clothing, and classrooms for GED."

"Does everyone have their money?"

"Surprisingly, yes. It boiled down to about ten thousand dollars apiece." He nudged her chin. "Perk up, the private corporations that build, supply, or run prisons is a market worth thirty-five billion dollars a year. Everyone should be able to recoup their investment in less than six months."

He'd never said what they would do with the property if they didn't get the grant. She wasn't even sure if they could sell the property for what they paid for it. Still, it wasn't her money. She couldn't believe how many people were willing to risk so much of their own money for something so uncertain. She hadn't withdrawn any cash from her account in more than fifteen years. That money had always been for one purpose, Isaac's and Peyton's future. Deep down she wished that all of Gary's efforts were to build colleges instead of prisons.

This prison was only the beginning, Gary was telling her. He had plans to build several more private prisons in clusters of three, not only in Michigan but in California and Oklahoma and Illinois. In Mount Clemens, Michigan, alone there were eight prisons within a ten-mile radius. In three years, he felt, the CDC would be soluble enough to become a publicly traded company.

"There is clearly a growing need for supplying detention and correctional services to governmental agencies." He picked up his drink, but changed his mind and set it back down. "Other correctional services focus on maintaining order only. Our success will be counseling, work opportunities, academic and vocational education, structured leisure programs, and stuff like that. We have an advantage over those other private corporations." He collected his thoughts for a moment, then said, " 'I say unto you, that likewise joy shall be in heaven over one sinner that repenteth, more than over ninety and nine just persons, which need no repentance.' "

"Luke fifteen-seven." She smiled. "Gary, I think you stole my line   " An

223

older gentleman had walked up to her and was rudely shifting from one leg to another, staring at her. "Excuse me. We're not finished with our meal yet."

"Hey, there, I recognize you." He leaned on the table, planting his palms a few inches away from her. "Say, aren't you a Coleman?"

"No. My name is Rosemary Jones," she stated matter-of-factly.

Gary looked at her oddly. Of course he knew that her brother's last name was Coleman. But for some reason, it bothered her today. She hadn't been referred to that way since she was twenty.

The man craned his neck, eyeing her suspiciously. "Naw, I'd know that Coleman nose anywhere."

That nose. Her mother had talked about Isaac's little bulldog nose nearly forty years ago. Her mother had laughed when Isaac was barely three months old. "This child's nostrils are so large, I can see clear through to his brain." Rosemary didn't think it was funny, because she had the same type of nose. It was then that she knew . . .

"Rosemary!" Gary said, nudging her. "Are you okay?"

Rosemary couldn't explain to Gary why she was so upset. She immediately felt uncomfortable and began to gather her purse and gloves. She had no intention of discussing her personal business with Gary, as he'd done lately about his relationship with Dawn. It was none of his business.

"Excuse me, sir, but I don't know you."

"No? But I know *you.*" He laughed wickedly and left.

She'd never been so humiliated in public. "I'm ready to go, Gary." They hadn't even eaten dinner yet. A waiter was carrying a tray of smoking spicy shrimp gumbo to serve to the table beside them. The tantalizing aroma made her stomach grumble. She was starving, but it was pointless now to eat. The food wouldn't even taste good to her. The stranger had left a sour taste in her mouth that no amount of gumbo could remove.

Gary looked confused. "What was that all about?"

"Nothing." Rosemary flushed. "Let me pay the tab, Gary. You'll embarrass me if you don't."

When Rosemary showered and got into bed that night, Jesse was still at his Mason's meeting. It seemed like hours before he came to bed. She snuggled close to him and prayed for sleep.

It came as deep and hard as the push of death.

Two hours later, she felt burning sweat coursing down her breasts and peeled back the covers. Checking the alarm that was set to go off at 5:30, she knew that she needed to get some rest. She turned onto her side and watched Jesse snoring softly, hoping his easy slumber might lure her back to sleep. Every now and then she turned over and checked the clock. The last time she remembered checking the time, it was 4:55.

She began to dream. Back to when it could have been . . . back to when it should have been . . . before . . .

"Help me, Rosemary!"

It was pitch-dark outside. She could see the outline of her mother's body, lit by the shadow of the moon, running toward the barn. Dressed only in a black bra and half-slip, her mother glanced back over her shoulder like someone was after her.

"Rosemary! Help me! Help me!" she screamed again. Rosemary knew something was wrong. Fear gripped her by the bowels and she thought she would defecate on herself right then and there. She fought back the urge and immediately began to run after her. In no time, she was out of breath. Getting her bearings, she recognized that they were more than a hundred yards away from the house. Suddenly she heard another set of footsteps. Someone was following them!

"Somebody help me!" she screamed.

Her mother's petite body was getting smaller and smaller. The distance between them was lengthening by the second. Just then she felt the heat from a flashlight in the middle of her back. She turned and was blinded by the person holding the light. There was a sound, like the thud of a person falling. Turning back around, she could see in plain view the man wearing a black raincoat several yards ahead of her, but she couldn't make out his face. She panicked. Her mother's screaming voice became faint. Looking behind her, the man had disappeared. She was nearly out of breath from running. "Mother! I'm coming! I'm right behind you!"

There was another thud. It seemed to echo through the woods and boomerang back around to pierce Rosemary's heart.

Rosemary screamed her mother's name once more, and jumped up with such a start that she nearly fell out of the bed. Her eyes scurried frantically around the room, registering immediately that she was in her own bedroom, and in her own house; she'd had a bad dream.

Reaching behind her, she felt for her pillow and tucked it beneath her chin. It felt cold from the tears she was certain she'd shed during her dream. She looked at the alarm clock on the nightstand. It illuminated 5:08 A.M. in its bold red block LED numbers.

Maybe I should wake Jesse? No. This was the third night she'd had this horrible dream. Reaching over to touch his shoulder, she heard a soft, small voice, then stopped.

"No, he wouldn't understand," the small voice pleaded. "He'll judge you."

"But he's my best friend."

"You lost a mother and a father. You've never gotten over the shame. Remember, he has a family. He'll never understand."

"Still. I trust . . ."

"Shhh. Don't tell anyone."

"I promise I won't."

Rosemary couldn't believe that she'd said those words. She was hiding something from Jesse. Not really, she told herself. They'd never discussed her parents before.

Outside, she heard the patter of a fresh rain falling. She was lazily turning over in her mind several options that centered on one thing—the flesh. She hugged herself, feeling a rush of chill cloak her resplendent body. Suddenly, an overpowering compulsion came over her like a fever. Turning over, she rubbed a hand over Jesse's warm cheek and neck, then kissed him just above his bare collarbone.

She thought back to thirty years ago, minutes before she was to be married. The pastor discreetly whispered to her, "When the devil cannot reach us through the spirit . . . he reaches us through the flesh." And the pastor had been right. Sex was the primary motivation that had held her first marriage together for twenty-one months. It wasn't the same with Jesse. She loved him. She desired him. But not in the same way that she had her first husband. This was a more mature feeling. A more complete one. The feeling was voluntary, not requested.

Reaching over, she touched Jesse's shoulder, shaking him gently.

226

It was 5:16 by then. Rosemary knew that her entire world could change in less than fourteen minutes.

She began removing her gown, then slightly nudged his shoulder until he awakened. "I need you, baby. Hold me for a moment."

The Defiant Ones

Peyton had been off Ritalin for a month and Isaac was beginning to see positive changes in him. They'd seen Dr. Lynetta Andersen on five separate visits, and she assured Isaac that even though it would be difficult at first, he had to wait it out. Isaac knew his son's future might depend on it.

To borrow the phrase from his sister, "the devil was working overtime" appeared to be appropriately significant in their case. He wondered why, though, the devil won most often. Maybe that's why so many people were on his side.

"The devil called and I answered," Bernie had told him one night after practice. Bernie had laughed, but Isaac didn't.

From Monday through Thursday afternoon Isaac was free to plan and carry out inexpensive activities that he could do with his son. He believed that he had to keep Peyton busy, busy, busy, until he was too exhausted to think about any medication. From going to the pet shop to view the sly movements of pythons to watching the aggressive behavior of the husky puppies, Isaac tried to spend time with his son. Peyton showed more interest when they went to check out cars at used-car lots. And Isaac tried to show his youthful nature when they visited Planet Groove on Woodward Avenue. He painstakingly dropped forty dollars playing video games with Peyton and one of his friends.

Isaac assumed that things were going well. He thought that he had found the best weapons to fight the devil—prayer and faith. But soon, he found himself being overmatched.

Over a short period, things continued to get worse. Isaac finally managed to get a telephone installed, and when he did, one of the first calls was from Peyton's school. They'd sent home two letters requesting a conference, but hadn't heard from either parent. If Peyton's absenteeism continued, he would be suspended.

"I don't understand you," Isaac said when Peyton finally came in. Isaac had been picking up a few things around the apartment, realizing how cramped they were, and at the same time trying to figure out how to get a larger place for them, especially since things weren't going too well with Kennedy. "Why do you keep lying to me?"

"What you talking about now?" Peyton plopped down on the sofa bed. His lanky body was decked out from head to toe in oversized shirt, pants, hat, and shoes that looked like they came from the Goodwill.

Isaac went over to him and stopped. "First, the school called today. You haven't been in days. Secondly, where'd you get those raggedy clothes?"

"My friend gave them to me."

"Why? Are you trying to embarrass me and your mom by going around looking like a bum?"

Peyton shrugged his shoulders, then fixed his angry eyes on Isaac's and stared until Isaac thought that he would literally melt from the heat.

Isaac poured himself a glass of cold water from the refrigerator. He took a seat at the kitchen table and gathered his thoughts. Peyton's eyes had never left him. Parenting was difficult. He knew the boy was lying. He also knew he was confused by the feelings that touched his heart and mind at the same time. He realized that he would have to be the disciplinarian that he needed to be, and be a loving father at the same time.

Peyton took a deep breath, followed by another. "Look, I didn't ask to move in here. I tried to do good. I got a job. I kept away from the so-called bad kids—even my friends like the one that was killed by my mom. But I didn't trip on that. I still went to school every day. But it didn't pay off. You don't know what it feels like to lose a true friend. Nor does Mom. Both of you should understand that your friend doesn't have to be enrolled in Harvard to have some merit in life. That's why I'm bored with school. The teachers don't like me, and I don't like them. And boy, oh boy, am I sick of this itty-bitty apartment. I'm sick of watching television with a fuzzy screen. This is the nineties—we just got a phone. My road dogs couldn't even call me until now."

Isaac stared at him in disbelief. There were truths in what he had said. But he couldn't say that he asked for him to come here. Kennedy had forced this situation on him. He'd done his best and apparently it wasn't good enough. That hurt him.

"Peyton, I'm trying my best to keep you from making the same mistakes I did. I want you to get an education so you won't have to live in the streets or jail. Remember this, son, mistakes are so unforgiving—once you make them, they're yours for keeps."

They retreated into their own worlds of silence, each trying to figure out which move to make next.

The sound of Kennedy's Mustang pulling into the driveway immediately captured Peyton's attention. "Mom's home. If she says it's okay, I'd like to spend the night." His eyes asked, *Do you mind?*

Isaac nodded okay and watched his son leave.

Words would end up hurting much less than seeing his son's life spiral down into the world of crime.

A week later, Isaac received a call from the unlikeliest of people—Dawn Cullors.

"Mr. Coleman," she began. He could hear the trepidation in her voice. "My name is Dawn Cullors. I'm the general manager at the Mall of Detroit. There's been a problem. I have your son in my office. Could you come down here as soon as possible?"

He'd heard the woman on the radio and caught a glimpse of her at the trial twelve years earlier and more recently at the Grille. He'd forgotten her face. But now he imagined her older, colder. He'd never imagined having to face this woman in a private situation.

Calling Kennedy was not an option. A short time later, he found himself being led to Dawn's impressive office on the top floor of the mall.

Dawn was all about business. "Hi. I take it you're Mr. Coleman. Peyton's father."

The pretense of not knowing each other threw Isaac off-kilter. He felt as if he were living an episode of *The Twilight Zone*.

Isaac couldn't speak. There was no way that she didn't recognize him. He was the same Coleman who was convicted of killing her daughter. Surely, she couldn't think there was another Coleman who looked just like him.

Peyton was sitting in Dawn's outer office, handcuffed and being watched by two police officers.

"I'm sure you're busy, as am I," she said, walking past Peyton and into her huge office, "but I felt it was my duty to inform you of your son's intentions." She nodded for the police to leave her office. "Your son is here because he attempted to steal a four-hundred-forty-dollar Pelle leather jacket from The Leather Factory."

"Man, she lying!" Peyton hollered from the connecting room.

Isaac was embarrassed. First him, now his son. "Shut up, Peyton. I'll deal with you later." His laser eyes rested on Peyton's. They said, *I have never beaten you before, my son, but don't test me today.* Peyton looked away. "Go on, Ms. Cullors. And please excuse my son."

"I don't want to bore you." Dawn rested her buttocks against her desk. Suddenly she appeared younger and Isaac could see traces of Becky in her face. "I remember my first attempt at stealing. I botched it."

Isaac tried to hide his smile.

"It's not funny. My family was well off, but all kids steal, Mr. Coleman. My father's money and influence covered it up. I realize that you're not in that same position."

He was stunned. What could he say? These words confirmed that she knew exactly who he was.

"Times are different. Peyton is black, and angry. I can tell. I can't say I know why. But I can do one thing." She pointed to the handcuffs. "Let him know that stealing is not a joke and that anything over two hundred dollars is considered a felony." She turned to Isaac. "I don't want to see your son's life destroyed, Mr. Coleman."

Again, Isaac couldn't speak. Who was this woman? No one had ever given him a chance in his youth. And now this. All he could say was, "Thank you. Thank you, thank you."

"Because this is his first offense, I'm letting him slide." She paused, getting on the intercom to call the officers back. "But he is no longer welcome at the Mall of Detroit until he reaches the age of twenty-one."

After the officers removed Peyton's handcuffs, Isaac turned to Dawn and said, "That's more than fair. And again, thanks."

Isaac made a decision. He called his parole officer to talk to him about the problems he was having with his son. He told Isaac about a weekend program that the city offered to help young men who were on the verge of becoming criminals.

Taking the time to go to Pershing High School and speak with the assistant principal was a godsend. Isaac told the young man about Peyton's four-year dependence on Ritalin. When Isaac told him that he was doing everything in his power to wean Peyton off the drug, the man was moved. He had a four-year-old son who had just been put on the medication. He didn't have the nerve to go against his wife. With this common bond, he agreed to give Peyton one more chance and let him return to school on Monday. Isaac managed to get makeup work from Peyton's teachers for the homework that he'd missed.

The next day was Wednesday. Peyton wasn't due to go back to Pershing until Monday. Isaac knew he'd have a problem convincing him to go, so he didn't tell him.

That same morning, Isaac took Peyton to a Scared Straight program. The program picked up a busload of young men and women from the Seven Mile YMCA along with the parents who wanted to attend, and drove them to Jefferson Penitentiary.

During the ride, two parole officers, male and female, outlined the reasons for the trip. They also did their best to describe these youths the seriousness of being locked up. The officers didn't miss a beat in telling them the horrors of being incarcerated, from the inception of being indoctrinated into the system until they were released. The outing was three hours long. It was usually two hours longer than necessary to scare the shit out of most of the boys. Not Peyton.

To Isaac's chagrin, Peyton laughed all the way back home.

Ashamed of himself for toying with the idea of putting Peyton back on Ritalin, he decided it was time for something stronger.

Together, he and Rosemary enrolled Peyton in every youth activity that Mother Bethel offered. When Isaac was at work, Rosemary picked up Peyton and made certain that he not only attended but participated.

The Thanksgiving and Christmas holidays were fast approaching. Everyone seemed to be in an accommodating mood.

For a while, things weren't faring bad or good. It was an interim period when neither of them had the courage to call a truce. One Friday night after work, Rex pulled Isaac aside and told him about the cruise that the nation-wide chain of Grilles was sponsoring. The Detroit chapter had recommended Isaac, and they had just gotten word that the application was accepted. The two-week Caribbean cruise would begin the second week in December. He'd have about a month to prepare. Could he be ready to go on time? His pay would triple. All meals, sleeping accommodations, and tips were included. The question was, could he afford to be away from his personal responsibilities for that long?

During the next week Isaac managed to corner Miracall at the university before she left. They talked in the parking lot for hours. It was strange. He couldn't confide in Rosemary; he felt that she was too close to him. And even though she denied it, she was too judgmental. On the flip side, Jesse acted as if Isaac were Tarzan—able to conquer any path that he wished to cross. If only, Isaac thought, he'd had such a positive factor in his life twenty years ago, he might never have gone to prison. And then there was Kennedy. He still didn't understand her. She had professed her love on numerous occasions, but there was never a commitment. What was he to do?

Finally, there was Miracall. During his bimonthly trips to his parole officer, his impromptu visits with Miracall had become a good routine over the past weeks. Oftentimes they would find a moment to grab a coffee and a bagel. All she talked about was her mother. It was easy. He had no idea what a mother meant. So most of the time he listened to her talk. It was still so fresh for her.

But on further introspection, he realized that his conversations with Miracall were mostly about Rosemary. Isaac was astounded at how well Miracall knew his sister. Those cherished memories seemed to bring them closer, much sooner than he'd expected. They never mentioned Becky. Nor did Isaac mention his encounter with Dawn at the mall. It was too early to expect miracles. Besides, he liked this woman and was glad to let Kennedy cool off and miss him again. Maybe then things would be right between them. He never saw himself feeling anything but sorrow and friendship toward Miracall.

When she invited him to her home a week later, things changed. During that time, Isaac had talked to Kennedy. She was furious at Isaac for not telling her about Peyton's theft at the mall. She needed more time, he thought.

It was cold out, this third week in November, and the last week for riding his Harley. He'd been turned down by the bank to purchase a car. He nearly froze to death driving his Harley to Miracall's house in Southfield.

Her taupe and beige contemporary home was fabulous, just as he'd expected. Rosemary was right, the furniture and artwork on the lower level alone cost more than every item in Rosemary's home. But somehow he felt completely relaxed, and that all these expensive items that filled her home didn't matter. She cherished the pictures of her mother, Sadie, and the montage of photographs of Rosemary and Sadie together.

The entire rear wall of her tri-level home was made of tempered glass. What fascinated him, once they went down to the lower level, was Miracall's extensive butterfly collection.

"It's a work of art, Miracall." He walked around the ledge built around three quarters of the room. The surface was covered with an assortment of butterflies that were encased in glass display boxes. He stopped at the Silver-spotted Skipper.

"That's one of my favorites."

"I don't know anything about this type of stuff," Isaac said, admiring all the glass cases, and finally paying attention to the huge mobile in the upper left corner, "but this seems so time-consuming." Instantly, he felt brainless. He'd temporarily forgotten that she didn't have children.

"It is. And tedious. But I enjoy it. They're so fragile," Miracall said, smiling.

Like you, he wanted to say. Even so, they were beautiful.

"I've never given any away; they're like my children. I couldn't part with any of them without feeling like I betrayed them." She looked up at him oddly. "Does that seem childish to you?"

"Of course not." Isaac was dumbfounded. He had no idea about butterflies. But anything so beautiful would always get his attention. Just as she had.

After she'd given Isaac a tour of her home, and let him see a more personal side of herself, she took him into the kitchen, where she'd been washing some fresh figs.

"Stop it," she teased as Isaac popped one of the delectables into his mouth. "You're eating them all!"

233

"Mmm," said Isaac. In his thirty-nine years, he'd never tasted figs before. "I'm not accustomed to this. They're so creamy. They melt in my mouth. I can't wait for the grill, Miracall. What can be better than this?"

Miracall continued placing the fresh figs on the tray beside them. "You ain't tasted nothing yet. Just wait and see." She grabbed his arm and urged him to follow her outside to the patio.

"But it's so cold out."

"Shhh, it'll put hair on your chest."

I don't need any more hair on my chest, he thought. He relaxed. This woman was starting to get under his skin.

Smoke, the color of an absent ghost, was wafting through her small patio area. A thread of the grey mist wafted through the screen door, carrying the sweet smell of figs and charcoal inside her immaculate home. They'd already dined on finger food—crab legs and butter. "Bring that bowl of apple juice, will you, Isaac?"

They talked about Isaac's upcoming tour to the Caribbean while Miracall put the skewers on the grill. Afterward, they sat side by side on the patio rocker and pushed off.

Isaac lost track of how much time it took for Miracall to coax him into transferring the paper plates on their laps, so they could eat dessert with their fingers. He couldn't remember having so much fun.

"I haven't had this much fun in years," he told Miracall before he left.

"Me either."

They left it at that, platonic friends. No kisses. No hugs. Just thanks and good night.

The next night Isaac felt guilty. He didn't trust the emotions he was feeling. He paid a visit on Kennedy and was abashed when she greeted him so dispassionately.

Her lackluster eyes judged him from head to toe before she said a weak hello. The bitter smell of Jack Daniel's whiskey blew across his face. She stumbled, caught herself, then giggled. Obviously she'd been drinking, and he didn't like it one bit. He'd never seen her this way before.

"When are you planning to come see your son?" Isaac began. "He hasn't seen you in weeks. You claim to be working hard, but I see your car in the garage when you're not supposed to be home. What's up with you? Are you on drugs, too?"

"That's unfair, Isaac."

Instantly he placed his arms around her. They embraced. Instinctively, he hesitated. Judging her now was irrelevant. "Tell me you don't remember the good times we had together as teenagers. The fun we had. The love we shared before we made love for the first time. Getting high on that illusory quality of what it could be like if only . . ."

"Those are beautiful memories," Kennedy admonished. "I'd nearly forgotten."

"Better now than then." Isaac hesitated. Those were not the words he wanted to convey. But he was stuck. "First you love me, you want me back. Then . . ."—he picked up Eli's black leather cap—"this shit. I want you. I want our family back together."

Kennedy moved inches away from him. He could smell the faint traces of Opium cologne, see the powder tracks on her neck, leading down to the crevice between her breasts. "I still care for you, Isaac."

"You're changing all the time. You're all shadows and smoke. I can't hold on to you." He pulled her toward him and held her tightly. "I don't know how."

East of Eden

Still pushing his luck, Peyton was sitting around at the clubhouse on the corner of Joy Road and Hubbell with J-Rock and three other Prophet gang members. Constantly watching the time, he knew he had a couple of hours before Isaac left the Grille, where he was performing.

J-Rock sat down beside him. "Hey, man, I heard that you and your old man are shacking up together. How's this thing going?"

"Well, I'll tell you, man, it's not what I thought it would be like. Hell, I don't need no daddy now. I need some money. He's trying to make up for the past, but I'm grown up now. I got you guys. You all is all the family I need. But I tell you, man, I can remember when I was a kid about five years old, I kept asking my mom where was my dad. All she would say was he's gone away and won't be coming back."

"No shit."

"Yeah." Peyton accepted the beer one member offered him and popped the cap. He guzzled down half the brew. "I used to sit in my room for hours looking out the window at every black man who passed by the house. Just hoping one of them would come to our door and say he's my father. Nobody ever did. In those days I was doing good in school. All I had to do was do my homework and study. Sometimes I would do my homework two or three times just to have something to do. You know, keep my mom off my back."

He smiled, not realizing he looked as vulnerable as a three-year-old.

"I didn't have any friends. So my mom bought me all the latest video games. I played them until they wouldn't play anymore. Later, she began to question me about going out for football, basketball, track—anything, just to get me out of the house. It got so bad with her till I started lying. Telling her I was trying out for some of the teams until she started to press me, telling me that she wanted to come and watch me. I just told her I got hurt or I got cut. That went on for a couple of years. She seemed to give up on me—just let me be."

Peyton gulped down the last of the beer, then pounded the counter for another. He was feeling better than he had in weeks.

"What she didn't know was just how lonely I was. You know, man, I used to sit in my room listening to the kids playing outside and just start crying. I wanted so much to have one friend to play with. I remember one time Mom came home, I was doing what I always did—playing videos. She reached down and picked up my gym shoes and told me to put them on. 'Get up and get out of the house,' she said. 'You act like you're some kind of mole or something. Like you want to stay underground.'

"I didn't say anything. I could tell by the tone of her voice I better get out of her way. I told her I was going up to the playground to walk around. The park was about a mile from our house. About halfway there was an empty building. No one used it and it looked like it was about to fall down. I went into that old warehouse and found me a corner. I sat there for about six hours until it started getting dark."

J-Rock's eyes bored into his, and Peyton had to look away.

"I never told anyone about this before. After that, I used to hide in the basement for hours to make Mom think I had been out playing. Those were some dark times." He took the Miller Lite and gulped it down. He felt the golden liquid burning his throat, and the sensation felt good. "I'm glad that now I have a friend like you, J-Rock, along with the rest of the guys around here."

J-Rock extended his arm, and they did a power embrace with their fists. "I'm always here for you, bro. You know that." They both looked at the clock at the same time. "Say, Little Caesar, you'd better G-up before Pops gets home."

Peyton was feeling his oats and barely paid attention to J-Rock's warning. "Man, I often think what it would have been like to have had a dad around to teach me things, to take me places. I tell you, J-Rock, you don't ever want to be without friends." Peyton didn't realize that his words were beginning to slur. "You know what else? I'll tell you what really broke my water was when after all this time Pops shows up. Man, I was so pissed off at Mom for not telling me the truth about my father. I know she was trying to protect me. But in reality, man, I think that fucked me up more." Peyton swiveled off the stool. His legs felt weak beneath him. He vaguely remembered what his dad had said about drinking and driving and the accident that had gotten a young girl killed. He laughed to himself as he guzzled the remainder of the beer. Hell, he wasn't even old enough to own a license.

"Hey, dog"—he shook J-Rock's hand—"I'll see you tomorrow . . ."

Cause for Alarm

"Isaac, this is your sister, Rosemary."

Something was wrong. He had only one sister. Why did she feel it was necessary to preface it by saying this?

"Can you come to the hospital? It's Jesse."

She couldn't say whose fault it was. Lately, Rosemary's duties were becoming so demanding that Jesse had offered to medicate himself. Rosemary should have been monitoring him, but she was too busy. It would make her day a whole lot easier. Stopping in mid-stride at one in the afternoon and again at four caused a severe halt in her schedule.

Rosemary was unaware of how much pressure she was under when the twenty homes they'd promised to their congregation hadn't been completed. The final date now was March thirtieth. There were families who'd counted on moving in in December, and who were now trying to find temporary housing in the dead of winter. Rosemary felt like opening her home to anyone who needed one to lessen her guilt, even though she knew it wasn't all her fault.

She had had no idea that Jesse was having a problem. She watched him inject himself for days, making sure he was doing it right. It didn't matter; less than a week later, he had a severe diabetic attack. The doctors told her that Jesse hadn't been injecting the correct dose into his system.

The assistant director from the funeral home called Rosemary on her cell phone. Jesse had passed out, of all places, in the room where the new caskets were displayed and purchased.

An ambulance took him to Mount Sinai Hospital and Rosemary met him there. He'd been in a coma for two hours. She called his mother and father, who lived in New York, and told them what happened. They had never liked Rosemary and had barely had any contact with them since Jesse married her. Rosemary did her best not to feel hatred toward these small-minded people. When Jesse wasn't feeling well, he always talked about his mother. Even though she'd been distant since their marriage, Jesse never gave up hope that his mother would one day come around.

As she'd expected, his parents couldn't come at this time, but their son would remain in their prayers.

Rosemary wished that she felt that encouraged. She had met them after the wedding, and felt the devil's presence until they left to go back home. She secretly prayed that they would never have to go to New York again. And now, three years later, their only contact was an annual Christmas card.

Isaac arrived in no time at all. Rosemary felt comforted. Her brother, after seeing Jesse and coming back to reassure her that her husband would be okay, wrapped his loving arms around her. It was just like old times, when she used to hug him and reassure him that one day things would be good. Better.

"Did you eat today, Rosemary? You need something in your stomach. What if Jesse wakes up and he sees you looking so worn-out."

"You're right, Isaac, I haven't eaten today."

"The cafeteria is on the lower level. We can eat dinner and rest a minute. The doctor said he'd contact us the moment Jesse's condition changed."

It was vanity, she knew, but Isaac hadn't noticed that she'd gained back a few pounds. All the preserves, spicy apple pies, and fatty entrées that she knew she shouldn't have eaten but did.

She told herself since early September that it was the overwhelming duties of the church that fueled her appetite. The membership, thanks to Henry Miller, had soared from three thousand members to fifty-five hundred. They were making preparations to have three daily services as opposed to two. Rosemary had no idea how she would manage. She had to pray daily for strength and rely more on her assistant pastors and deacons.

"Only a salad, Isaac. And a Diet Coke. I'm serious."

Isaac went through the line and brought back food and drink for both of them while she waited in a comfortable booth by the center aisle. It was odd, how she felt—tingly, a little faint. It couldn't be because she hadn't eaten. She'd gone through months of fasting before. Why this weird feeling now?

The cafeteria was half-filled. It was 9:00 at night, and it seemed that every ten minutes at least ten more people left the area. By 9:45 the room was empty. Only a female cleaning person, mopping the floors, remained.

"Jesse has excellent doctors, Rosemary. Even though he hasn't come out of the coma, his prognosis is good. He's young, strong. He'll make it."

Rosemary felt encouraged with each breath. "I know. I'm worried, but I have faith. I'm concerned about you, Isaac. I shouldn't have bothered you with my problems."

He smiled. His words were sincere. "Jesse's my buddy, Rosemary. I would have found out anyway, if you hadn't called me. He's good people. I remember your last husband. A real jerk. Without you even admitting it, I know the reason why you were hesitant about marrying Jesse—because in the beginning he wasn't saved, just like your first husband." He placed his hand over hers. "Jesse's different. Maybe it's because what he's been through losing his leg. But he's still different. I know he cares more for you than I've ever known a man to care about a woman. I don't know if he told you, Rosemary, but he

239

feels less of a man because he never went to war. It bothers him. He used to tell me how he wished he could have been a part of Desert Storm. Maybe you could let him know war don't make the kind of man that he is."

She reached over and touched his arm. "I will. As soon as he comes home." She lowered her head, and closed her eyes. "I'm ashamed of myself, Isaac."

"Why?"

"I never asked you. In all the months you've been home. I never asked you . . ."

"What?"

"How it really felt being locked up. I feel like you need to talk to me. I want to hear in your own words what it was like. If you want to talk about it."

That simple statement seemed to release a dam of emotions that had been built up in Isaac. It didn't take him long to open up.

Isaac sipped on a cup of lukewarm coffee, wishing it was a cold beer. "From the day I arrived home, I couldn't sleep. I'd look at that ceiling all night long, waiting for the guard to call my name—Coleman, Isaac. No one called. I felt disoriented. Disconnected. That night was the first time in years that I allowed myself to think about the first day that I'd been processed into the prison system. It was a day that I wanted to forget."

Rosemary was speechless. She wanted to hear, but another part of her wanted to scream "I don't want to know." But as someone who loved him, how could she deprive her brother of releasing these emotions that she was sure he couldn't share with anyone but her.

"Right off, I received a six-digit identification number, 823497, which would replace my name for the duration of my stay. I was given a series of tests, handed a two-inch-thick mattress, a one-inch-thick pillow, a towel, dingy sheets, and underwear that someone else had worn. This was all before being sent off to my new home at Sedonia Prison in Ionia, Michigan. I lived in a cell that was four feet by six feet, in a facility that I was too old to go to in the first place. Sedonia is a youth prison. It was set up for offenders between the ages of eighteen and twenty-two. Because of the overcrowding at Jefferson, I stayed until I was twenty-nine." He looked up at her. "Maybe you remember?"

She shook her head no, mesmerized, her eyes rarely straying from his.

"In a matter of days, I learned who the big drug dealers were, and which guards were on their payroll. What was worse for me was finding out that some of the men that were locked up didn't want to get out. These inmates felt that a place with three free meals a day, a decent place to lay their head every night, and an unlimited supply of punks that they considered to be their women was the ideal place to be. In short, they loved it there."

She was waiting for him to tell her about the first time he'd met Paps. It was certainly not the same moment when she'd met him. Isaac was far too young.

"I was then sent to Southern Prison at Southern Michigan, at the north side of Jefferson Penitentiary. This section was a medium-security unit. SPSM is the world's largest walled-in prison, with over fifty-five hundred inmates. It was unmanageable, the staff said, and in 1992 SPSM was cordoned off into three prisons with three separate wardens. I hated it. SPSM was a harder core of individuals than Sedonia. Even the north side, where I was transferred from, wasn't nearly as threatening as the men in Three Block. There were gangs of guys with tattoos on nearly every inch of their bodies. These fools were looking at me like I was Tyra Banks."

Rosemary was beginning to feel uneasy. Even a little light-headed. She was positive that she didn't want to hear anymore. *Please stop!* She was about to speak and couldn't find the right words. After all, she'd asked him to tell her.

"I began working out in the weight room and got into the best shape of my life. I was able to bench-press five hundred pounds. But just before I was given my last transfer, I was told that the system was trying to ban weight lifting, because the inmates were too much bigger than the guards. The guards feared for their lives."

"I don't need to hear anymore," she whispered faintly. But Isaac didn't hear her and he continued on with his spiel.

"My spirits lifted when an inmate in the same section that I was in, and soon to be released, sold me his old saxophone. I practiced the old tunes I knew and stayed to myself. Two years later I was moved again. Starting over this time was hard. By now I was thirty-five years old . . . and tired.

"I trusted no one. However, the third morning in my new home I was caught off guard and nearly beaten to death in the shower. Paps Bowenstein, a lifer, known as a buzzard in the prison world, saved me. He's the reason why I enrolled in college. Paps also taught me the rules inside the prison and the rules out in the yard, where big money ruled. Rules I had to respect, if I wanted to survive in this section. Thanks to Paps, for my final four-and-a-half years I didn't have any more problems."

There it was. He'd met Paps. Rosemary was sure that Paps knew Isaac by his last name. But Isaac was too young. There was no way that Isaac could ever know who Paps was. And each time they met when she visited Isaac, Paps's eyes told her that he kept the secret between them.

Rosemary thought that Isaac had finished. At this point, she was too exhausted to comment on his story. Her shoulders slumped forward in defeat, but she managed a small smile and forced herself to listen as he continued.

"Two weeks before I was released, I saw two white boys severely beaten by twenty Indians. One died. One lived, barely.

"The Indians put a lock in a sock and busted their heads open. This took only about two and a half to three minutes. The prison guards left the blood all over the walls in the TV room for two days. Flies were everywhere and it started to stink. The entire prison was on lockdown until the officials finished their investigation of the murder."

"Where were the guards?" Rosemary asked, her voice as sharp as a straight razor. "Do you mean to tell me that they leave all of you alone together?"

"No. But, sis, there's only one guard for a hundred twenty inmates in a minimum security—" He paused. "Sis, this is what Peyton is headed for unless I can find a way to get him turned around."

"Mrs. Jones?" the nurse said. "The doctor wants to see you."

They stood and followed the nurse. Rosemary felt even more troubled than before. Isaac had managed to get her mind off Jesse, but her heart was still heavy. She wondered, *When would be the right time to tell him the truth?* To tell him the one thing that she'd been keeping from him all his adult life.

A Warm December

Isaac caught the bus to Eli's collision shop on Woodward Avenue. It was 5 degrees, and the roads were icy. Fat flakes of snow had fallen from the sky the day before and now covered the streets like Betty Crocker's instant mashed potatoes.

"I need a car, man," Isaac said to Eli after he was seated in his well-heated office. "Can you help me out?" He'd been procrastinating for weeks. Isaac had more than two thousand dollars stuffed beneath his mattress, and he still didn't want to make the commitment to have yet another monthly bill. It seemed so ghettolike to him.

"I'm sure I've got what you need, Isaac. Dozens of like-new vehicles just came in. Let's go take a look."

Eli wore more gold than he did clothes. His tiny body was weighed down with jewelry. He glittered so much, you almost missed the background of black-on-black clothing.

They looked over the lot for more than an hour. Isaac could hardly make up his mind. He found it strange that the 1996 Pontiac Firebird that he had set his eyes on five months ago was still available.

Odd or not, he claimed it. It was a rich champagne color, and looked brand new. He had the cash in his pocket, though Eli insisted it wasn't necessary for a down payment. He signed the title with a thousand dollars down, and felt good driving the car off the lot. He couldn't wait to show Peyton. His sixteenth birthday was in a couple of weeks.

Some people thought it was stupid to keep money beneath a mattress, but Isaac had heard lately that many banks had closed up and moved out of the city, and he felt it was a whole lot safer for people like him, more than most would acknowledge.

Even though Jesse came out of his coma in six days, the doctors kept him in ICU for nine.

During Jesse's stay at the hospital, the doctors thought they'd lost him a total of four times. They told Isaac and Rosemary that Jesse appeared to be giving up. He didn't seem to have any fight left in him.

Not Jesse, Isaac thought. Immediately, he felt guilty. Jesse had used up so much of his energy on Isaac and Peyton, he didn't have enough strength left to save his own life. Besides Isaac's sister, no one had ever given him anything in his life. The Harley meant more than anything to him. Jesse was definitely a man he respected and cared for. He hadn't realized how much until now.

Kennedy came the next day, keeping a silent vigil with Isaac. To his shock, Miracall appeared. Isaac didn't know how to introduce her to Kennedy.

Thank God, Jesse was finally able to awaken the following morning. Maybe it was the syrupy smell of the cinnamon French toast and sausage that he and Miracall had shared for breakfast, Isaac thought.

"What's that smell? Apples?" Jesse propped his body up on his elbows. His eyes were still closed. His voice was so weak, they barely heard him. "Rosemary, bring me some of that."

Isaac and Miracall fell out laughing. Jesse was coming around. Isaac knew it wouldn't be long before he was back to his usual self.

Kennedy was another matter. She called Isaac on a daily basis. For some reason, he mildly put her off. At this point, he turned down the invitations that she constantly offered. No, he didn't want to come over. She still professed her love, but, he wondered, did she *really* know him? Was she in love with a memory from so long ago? Or did she really care about the man he was now?

The more time Isaac spent with Miracall, the more he realized that he didn't know Kennedy anymore. Kennedy never discussed her job with him any more. Miracall couldn't stop talking about her position at the college.

What she did at Wayne State was boring at first for Isaac. *Doing research in the archives department? What exactly did that mean?* He'd never even heard of anyone earning a degree in library science. But here was this educated woman who took the time to share with him her knowledge of so many things. He felt a kind of spiritual awakening. Other than the heroes in Elmwood Cemetery, he learned more about Detroit and the famous people who resided there from her than he would ever learn from reading the newspaper or taking a history class. Miracall truly made him rethink his son's education more than he ever had before.

December crept up before he had time to prepare. Isaac realized that he'd forgotten to get the permission from his probation officer to leave the country.

"I'll be honest with you, Isaac," his probation officer said. "Our office has received some complaints about the publicity regarding your tour. Folks familiar with the law know that you're not supposed to be out of the country. You keep that to yourself, you hear."

"What?"

244

"In all my years as a probation officer, I never received a request like this before. I'm not going to tell you what it said. I just want you to know, you've got another six months before you're off probation. Don't blow it. Otherwise, I can't help you, man." He extended his hand and said, "I love to see my men making a liar out of the system. You're one of few that's been through here in years that has done that. I wish you all the success in the world, man. But you get your rusty butt in here and check in with me the moment you get back in town."

That left him feeling strange. Oddly enough, Isaac received a letter from Paps. They rarely wrote to each other but Isaac knew that he'd never forget Paps. Things had definitely changed. Isaac was certain that Paps felt it, too. The letter was short. He told Isaac that Rosemary had told him that he was doing well, and even complimented Isaac on his growing popularity as a professional saxophonist. He ended the letter by saying that word was going around in the joint that there was a hit out on him, and to be careful.

That night, his eyes shut tight, closing out the rays of blue moonlight, Isaac drifted into an endless space. His foremost thoughts were on Kennedy— on the woman who'd been his driving force since he'd been released from prison. At three in the morning, he got up, dressed, and left the apartment. As he headed downstairs to Kennedy's house, two questions took center stage in his mind. Who would want to kill him? And why?

There was a car parked in Kennedy's driveway that he wasn't familiar with. Eli drove a gold Mercedes. The car he saw tonight was a four-door Plymouth. Definitely not a car he recognized. It didn't matter; all the lights were off and there was obviously something going on. Isaac sat on the steps and waited. Three hours later, a man left the house. By the way he held his shoulders back and his hips rigidly forward, it was obvious that he was a professional man—possibly a policeman. Faintly lit by the overhead porch light, Kennedy stood in the doorway, half-dressed in a thin wrapper, waving good-bye.

Isaac went back to his apartment with questions creeping into his mind every two seconds. Why didn't she just file for the divorce and get it over with? Why was she continuing to lead him on? Why did she make him think that she still loved him? If she did, how could she be intimate with another man?

She knew that he would never end it. It had always been her call. In all the years they'd loved each other, he never intentionally hurt her. Why would she want to torture him this way?

Isaac was set to leave the following week on Sunday, December thirteenth. Peyton's birthday was four days later. He needed to go shopping for himself and for Peyton's gift. He didn't have a clue about what to wear on the cruise. To his delight, Miracall offered to take him shopping.

"I thought I'd buy some tropical shirts and matching shorts."

"No," she said flatly. "You don't want to blend in with the tourists. You're the star, you should stand out." They were at Saks Fifth Avenue in Troy and Miracall was checking out the designer collections. "You should wear pale, cool colors. Light blue. Pale pink. Light purple."

"Purple?"

"Yes, purple."

While she tested the fabrics' textures, Isaac checked out a few of the price tags in the men's department. He was shocked. Miracall must have noticed because she quickly reassured him that he could mix and match these clothes into several different outfits during the length of the trip.

When they left the store, Isaac had spent more than a thousand dollars. Miracall had even insisted on purchasing two outfits for him. It was the first time a woman had bought him anything. He had to admit that he was flattered.

The plan was that Peyton would spend the first five days with his aunt Rosemary and uncle Jesse. The second week, Peyton would be home with his mom. Isaac suspected that Peyton and Kennedy weren't getting along too well. He wasn't sure, but he guessed that Peyton disapproved of the time Kennedy was spending with "the stranger." Isaac cautioned Rosemary to try to keep tabs on Peyton while he was there, without appearing too nosy.

They'd already discussed the flavor of birthday cake that Peyton wanted. Rosemary was so excited to have her nephew staying with her, she'd fixed up Isaac's old room extra special. She purchased a bright red and royal blue spread and matching curtains. Jesse helped her with the latest CDs, and even splurged on a new television set.

The day before Isaac left, Miracall called him. "You sure you're going to be okay? I couldn't sleep last night worrying about you."

Here was this gorgeous woman worrying about him. Why? He still didn't get it. They hadn't been intimate. Their relationship was totally platonic. And when she said, "I was thinking that I could go with you," he was so shocked he couldn't talk. "I've got some vacation time."

That's how it began. Though he didn't know it then, Miracall was trying to wean herself from the powers that be, just like he was. Isaac had no idea how much pressure Loren was putting on her. His career virtually stalled in politics, she'd become his main focus again. Knowing full well that she was being used, Miracall countered his bullshit and stuck her neck out, designating Isaac as her savior.

Isaac felt a little easier being with her. He was definitely not her savior, and never told her that he would be. His plan was for Kennedy to hear about his tryst with Miracall and make a decision either to go through with the divorce or to realize that she was losing him.

Before he knew it, Miracall had called the cruise line and made her reservation. She paid big bucks for first-class accommodations, and her quarters were on the same deck as Isaac's.

He felt ashamed to tell Rosemary. So, he didn't. When he dropped Peyton off on Sunday afternoon, he gave her Peyton's gift, a brown-and-black Fubu leather jacket, while Peyton was taking his things downstairs. It had cost more than the Pelle jacket that he had claimed he wasn't trying to steal. Isaac still didn't believe him. But if his son wanted a leather jacket, he should be the one to buy it for him.

They were all standing awkwardly on the front porch. The cold air brought a clatter to their teeth, but no one seemed to object.

"Don't worry about a thing while you're gone," Jesse said, shaking his hand.

"I won't forget this, Jesse."

"I see you bought yourself a car." He looked past him at the shiny automobile parked in his driveway. "A Firebird, isn't it?"

"Yeah. I paid too much for it, though." Isaac shrugged his shoulders. "A man's got to do what a man's got to do."

Rosemary heard the tail end of their conversation. "Peyton told me that you've been teaching him how to drive. That child's old enough to have his driver's license. When you plan on doing that?"

"As soon as I get back." He winked at her. "Don't want to give the child too much responsibility too soon." They both knew that he meant that he didn't trust Peyton, who still acted a little hyper sometimes, behind a steering wheel. He could do what Isaac did years ago.

"I spoke with Kennedy this morning. She's taking a few vacation days off work next week to spend with Peyton. I invited her to come over for"—they heard Peyton coming upstairs, and she whispered—"you know what." This time Rosemary winked at Isaac.

"Thanks, sis." He hugged her, and even though Peyton objected, he hugged him, too.

"I'll call you, son, when I get there. You mind your aunt and uncle, you hear?"

"Sure." For some reason Peyton looked uncomfortable to Isaac. He retreated back into the house, his steps slow, like he was bored already.

"Say, Isaac," Jesse said, "why don't I drive you to the airport? You can leave your car here. It costs a fortune to park at the airport these days."

"I hadn't thought about that, Jesse. Thanks."

Isaac parked his car on the street, locked it, and Jesse helped him move his luggage to his car. On the way to the airport, Jesse assured Isaac that he would make sure Rosemary stayed on her diet. Not once did he mention his previous illness. Isaac couldn't remember a man ever being so unselfish. And he wished that he could be that way, too.

He knew that his sister was in good hands. She was one of the few women who could depend on their man. But Peyton was another issue. In all their conversations over the past months, Peyton had never called him "Dad." He would sometimes give him the respect of adding "sir." Once he even called him "Pop" when he needed some money. It bothered him today more than it ever had before.

They arrived at the airport twenty-five minutes later, and Isaac hadn't been able to shake the feeling that Peyton was troubled about something and obviously didn't want to confide in him what the problem was.

When Jesse saw Miracall handing over her ticket at the American Airlines check-in counter, Jesse didn't act the least bit surprised. He even paid the attendant while Isaac checked in and had his luggage tagged.

An hour later, he and Miracall were boarding the plane. Isaac felt like a kid.

He hadn't told anyone, but it was the first time that he'd been on a plane and he was scared to death.

Miracall was a godsend. She made him feel relaxed from takeoff to landing. They stopped in Atlanta for a two-hour layover, and she and Isaac shopped for souvenirs for Peyton, Jesse, and Rosemary.

The next leg of the trip went smoothly. Isaac had had a few beers by then and was feeling lighthearted by the time they landed in Miami—the departure point of the Yuletide Caribbean cruise.

The heat was overwhelming. All around them were people laughing and hugging each other. The atmosphere was misty beautiful. And seeing all the lovely couples, some of whom, he was certain, planned on getting married during the cruise, made him miss Kennedy a little. They'd never had a real honeymoon, and he knew that she would have loved this.

They were bused to the ship, then shown their cabins. He had not anticipated a ship this huge. He learned that Miracall had been on three cruises prior to this one. She knew all the ins and outs, and walked him all around the ship, and promised to get him something so that he wouldn't get seasick. It was obvious that the woman was rich. But what impressed him about her was that she didn't flaunt it.

"You've been extremely helpful, Miracall. I'm speechless."

"It's nothing that a friend wouldn't do for another." She left him standing on the sundeck with his mouth wide open.

Surely, he hadn't expected anything different. They were friends. It was a kind of friendship that he had never had with a woman before. But still, he couldn't say that it wasn't anything more. And he did enjoy her company.

He had the first night off. He and Miracall, dressed casually, enjoyed the moonlight for a few hours on deck. Afterward, while she went to her cabin for a nap, he took the majority of the evening to go over his music and practice. The second captain met him in his cabin and gave him a schedule of the times and days that he was to perform. Two hours a night, eight out of the fourteen days they'd be on the cruise. The rest of the time was his.

By day three, Isaac felt like a big star waiting to be discovered by the right record company. The tourists loved his music. The temperature was a comfortable 78 degrees. It was the warmest December that Isaac remembered.

With each performance, he gained confidence. Miracall, looking gorgeous, sat in the same second-row seat to encourage him. By then, he didn't know how he would have gotten through the cruise without her.

On Christmas Eve, the lights were set to stay on all night. The mood was cheerful and everyone seemed to be handing out gifts. Gifts were being opened at all times during the day.

Instantly, Isaac felt ashamed. He hadn't bought Miracall anything. Luckily they had a well-stocked gift store on the huge ship, and he bought her something not too expensive but nice.

To his dismay, she beat him to the punch.

"Here," she said, handing him a mid-sized slim box. They were on the promenade deck, feeling the warm air touch their faces.

Isaac was speechless. Excitement wasn't too far behind. Tearing at the wrapper, he felt like a kid. What was inside warmed his heart. How could one woman be so considerate? "Do you like it?" she asked.

It was a three-inch-thick black neck strap to hold his sax. What was special about it was his name: ISAAC COLEMAN was printed in white bold letters. Never having invested in a nice band, he was overwhelmed. His old one, solid black, was around his neck now, holding his instrument.

He could only nod his head as he stared at the custom-made band. "What made you think to buy this?"

"In my job, I'm paid to pay attention to the details." She smiled. "Besides, stars need to look like stars." When she wrapped her arms around him, Isaac thought she was going to kiss him. "Now, let's try it on, okay? You've only got five minutes before you're due to go onstage."

That night, he played a new song. He felt bold and the song he chose that night showed it. The room was full of beautifully dressed people of all ages. It was the night the captain hosted the dinner. It seemed that everyone had had such a great time, just as he had. Most regretted that the cruise was coming to an end.

It was tonight that Isaac chose to sing. He started with "Ain't Nothing Like the Real Thing," by Marvin Gaye. The crowd went wild. The momentum continued when he began playing some of Sam Cooke's old tunes and "Joy Joy," by the great Isaac Hayes. He ended his performance with Keith Sweat's "Girl,

You Need to Get with Me." This is when he went to the edge of the stage and prompted Miracall to come up onstage with him.

She blushed, whispering in his ear, "I didn't know you could sing so well."

"People thought that George Benson couldn't sing either."

Later, after Isaac's performance, he received a phone call from Rosemary. It was Isaac's fortieth birthday. She was crying.

"I'd hoped to lose fourteen pounds for your birthday. I didn't make it, Isaac."

He stifled a laugh. "I love you, sis. No matter what size you are. And I know that Jesse loves you, too, no matter what. The best birthday gift you can give me is to cut down on your salt and take good care of yourself, Jesse, and my son. I'll be home on Sunday. Tell him that I miss him. I'm a coward, Rosemary. I don't have the nerve to tell him myself."

Miracall knocked on his door a little while later. "Come on in, girl, I'm celebrating."

He had never told her about his birthday. She couldn't have given him a better gift if he'd told her about this day previously. And right now, it didn't matter. His son was okay. His sister was doing fine, and so was he.

"You've got gray hair!" he teased when she took a seat on his bed.

"Um-hm. And I've decided that it's time that I let it show. No more dyeing."

He was impressed. They both had grown since they'd gotten to know each other. He didn't know how to feel. He cared for her. It wasn't a sexual thing; it was a kind of feeling that he'd never felt before and couldn't label.

"I remember that day I saw you at the cemetery. Remember? You were so withdrawn back then. It's not the same woman that I see before me now. You've got strength in you that you don't even realize that you have."

"I've noticed that about you, too." Miracall fell back on the bed, gauging him. "But I have to admit that I was judging you then, too. Too harshly. Rosemary helped me to see that."

"That's a special woman, isn't she?" Isaac could understand now why Rosemary had taken to her so. Truthfully, he'd judged Miracall too harshly in the beginning as well, and was definitely jealous of the time and effort that Rosemary spent with her. It was time now to put all their hypocrisies in the past.

There was a bottle of champagne on ice sitting on his dresser. "Wait," he said. "Let's make a toast." He exaggerated the motions of popping the cork, and getting two glasses together. "Cheers."

"Happy birthday, Isaac."

"How did you know?"

"Rosemary told me years ago. Who could forget a Christmas Eve baby? That means you're special." She moved closer, but didn't touch him. "You're a quiet man, but a tender one." She kissed him lightly on the forehead, and Isaac felt completely naked. "There's nothing stronger in the world than tenderness."

It was the best birthday that he could remember.

The Blue Angel

Less than a week after Isaac returned from the cruise, the newspapers splashed headlines about gang wars breaking out in the city. More surprising was that the gang violence in the Detroit public-school system was just as bad.

Because of Peyton's past actions, Kennedy and Isaac had chosen to put him in a private school for the second half of the school year. The tuition was forty-five hundred dollars a semester. Putting Peyton in an environment that was more positive and where the students' primary goal was to attend college was the selling point for them. Peyton, they felt, had finally found a home—or so they thought.

Peyton never told his parents that the first week he attended Frederick Douglass Academy, a gang leader had approached him—he had to choose whose crew he was going to side with. It was a well-known fact, the kids said, that the administration knew about the gangs. The lofty tuition that FDA received was the motivation for keeping their mouths shut.

Clad only in his briefs, Isaac was in his bedroom practicing a new song when he heard the buzzer go off. He and Peyton had moved to their new apartment downtown a week after Isaac returned from the cruise. "Just a minute," he called out, and slipped on his pants.

"It's me, Isaac," Kennedy spoke into the intercom.

Minutes later, after he'd buzzed her in, he stepped out into the hallway, listening to the elevator starting and stopping until it reached the eleventh floor. He spotted Kennedy. He was surprised to see his son's tall frame a reserved two steps behind her. When Isaac stepped aside to let them inside, he checked his watch. Barely noon, he knew that it was too early for Peyton to be home from school.

"Peyton?" Isaac called out. The child didn't answer him but pushed past him, half-running to his bedroom, slamming the door behind him.

"He's suspended." Kennedy took a seat on the narrow sofa, shaking her head. "We've run out of options, Isaac."

"What happened?" Isaac tried to keep the annoyance out of his voice. "Don't tell me he's been fighting again." *I'm going to whip that boy's butt*, he thought as he removed a sweatshirt from the laundry basket and slipped it on.

"No, drugs," she said dryly as her pager beeped. "Hold on."

She made a quick call, saying that she'd be there as soon as she could to meet someone named Royale.

"Sorry. I'm still on duty," Kennedy said to Isaac, turning away from him.

So, the professional dude has a name—Royale. This was the person who was keeping time with his wife in the middle of the night. Isaac scowled as she ended her conversation.

"The short story is Peyton was caught smoking marijuana in the school's bathroom. You might have wondered why he hasn't been experiencing a lot of withdrawal symptoms since getting off the Ritalin. The marijuana is the reason why."

"How? Where'd he get it from?"

"Gang members at the school. There was a shooting at the school today. A fifteen-year-old kid shot another student today. He was high on marijuana that was laced with cocaine. My partner and I were close by, so we answered the call. I can't tell you how embarrassed I was to find out that Peyton was involved with the gang members who sold the boy the gun, who said that he bought the marijuana from Peyton."

Isaac jumped up. "Peyton, get out here!" he yelled. He waited a moment, then stormed into his room. It was empty.

Kennedy was right behind him. "He left out the rear door." After swiftly removing her cell phone from her hip, she pressed the redial button. "Royale, can you do something for me? It's personal. My son has just left the house. He's wearing a pair of Damon Stoudamire sneakers, brown pants, a brown-and-black Fubu leather jacket. If you spot him, call me."

"Tell him to put the boy in the car." Isaac was fuming. How dare that child leave the house? Where did he think he was going?" His unspoken thought was, *to that damned clubhouse*—where they hung out, he had no idea. At this point, there was nothing left for Kennedy to say to Isaac. She left without another word. The moment she did, Isaac called his sister.

"Have you heard from my son?"

She hadn't heard a peep.

Next, he called Jesse at the funeral parlor to tell him to be on the lookout for Peyton.

It was Tuesday night, and Isaac's day off. He had promised Kennedy that he would comb the streets looking for Peyton. Whoever spotted him first would call the other one.

No luck.

By eleven that night, Isaac was exhausted. He chastised himself for not knowing any of Peyton's friends. He did remember one, though.

At eleven-thirty he found himself knocking at Windy Fulsom's door in Birmingham. "Excuse me, Mr. Fulsom, but is Windy home?"

"Who are you? Do you know what time it is?" The little man appeared overly irritated as he tied the housecoat around his thick frame. In the background he could hear the man's wife asking who was at the door.

"Sir, I realize it's late. But my son is missing. I wanted to know if he contacted Windy."

He wagged a finger in Isaac's face. "Hell, no! And tell your son to stay the hell away from my daughter." When the man slammed the door in his face, Isaac felt the breeze reverberate through to his toes.

Isaac drove around for another two hours. He was so out of touch with the young people, he had no idea where his son would hang out. He tried the video arcade, where they'd gone last summer. It closed at ten during the week. He was so frantic, he began stopping kids on the streets.

"Have you seen a black boy around six foot three wearing a black-and-brown leather jacket?"

The group of kids laughed. "Man, we don't talk to strangers. You could be a cop."

"I'm just like you—a black man on the run from the man. It's my son, Peyton Coleman. He's missing. Maybe one of you knows him?" He waited, while they one by one said, "Never heard of him, man. Sorry."

It was no use. Isaac went home and sat on the living room sofa, praying that his son would come home. He wouldn't be mad. He would sit and listen to the problems the boy was having. No, he would hit him. Then he'd listen.

Kennedy called around three. "No luck, Isaac. He's hiding out. I'm not sure where. But I've got a lot of my people on the lookout for him. He can't hide forever."

She was wrong. A week went by and still no Peyton. Isaac went through the motions at work. Rex noticed and asked him if he was feeling well. Isaac told him about Peyton. He asked Isaac if he wanted to take a few days off. Isaac thanked him and said no. Kennedy didn't have to tell him that even if Peyton was suspended, they still owed the remainder of the forty-five hundred dollars. He couldn't afford to be off work now.

"I'm not kidding you, Rosemary," Isaac said after he called her on Sunday after church. "I'm going to whip that boy's butt when I see him." No, that wasn't true. He wanted to hug his son and tell him how much he loved him. Whatever it took, together they would work things out.

"I don't know what else to do. What if he's hurt? What if some fool shot him and he's lying in some ditch somewhere?"

"Stop it, Isaac. I've got the entire congregation praying for that boy. Ain't nothing happened to him. He's just stubborn, like you and Kennedy. He's trying to worry you two, that's all. I believe in my heart ain't no harm come to him."

"It's all my fault. I shouldn't have taken him off the Ritalin. Kennedy warned me. I didn't listen. Can you believe the boy's been using marijuana? I

255

noticed something different about him that day when I left for the Caribbean. Now that I think about it, I believe the boy was high."

"Now, don't go jumping to conclusions. We ain't sure of nothing right now." Rosemary was back to her usual self when she asked, "Have you been eating?"

It was just like Rosemary to think of food. "Yes. Stop worrying about me," he lied. Every time he looked at food, he lost his appetite. He missed eating at Rally's with Peyton. It was one ritual they'd managed to be consistent with. They ate dinner together every night. Isaac just didn't feel right eating alone anymore.

Monday morning, Isaac hit the pavement again. He parked his car on Greenfield and Chicago and set out on foot—stopping to talk to anyone, and showing them Peyton's latest school picture.

"Has anyone seen him? Please, he's my son. If you see him, tell him that his father is looking for him."

By Thursday night, Isaac was exhausted when he left for work at the Grille. To his surprise, Kennedy showed up in his dressing room before his first set began.

"A young man fitting Peyton's description was spotted near a known gang hangout on Hubbell, near Joy Road."

"What was he doing way over there?"

"I can only guess. I found out that he's a member of the Prophets. My partner and I responded to a call by an unidentified person who had spotted a dead body in a ditch near Joy Road. My partner and I visited the crime scene and found that the male victim, approximately twenty-two years of age, was shot eight times in the back of his head. Six cents was left in his otherwise empty pockets."

"What kind of shit—!"

"I just feel that Peyton's in trouble somewhere." Her voice was so hoarse, she could barely speak. "We were able to track down and talk to some of the known members. They admitted that Peyton was a member of the Prophets, but told us that their gang was only involved in car washes and barbecues." Kennedy pulled up a chair and rested her foot on it. "Of course they're lying. The Prophets have killed at least twelve people this year—execution-style.

Sometimes, when members try to leave, or break their code of silence, I'm told that one member holds the violator's arms up in a full nelson while others beat him in the face. This kind of violence is sometimes called 'a pumpkin-head' because of the swelling later involved. They also sell drugs and occasionally rob convenience stores."

"What!" Isaac said with pain showing all over his face. "When did all this take place?" He began taking off his outfit and changing back into his jeans. There was no way he could perform tonight.

"An hour ago."

The condescension in her voice made him feel like she was a prison guard and he was still locked up.

Isaac eyed this woman, still wearing her blue police uniform. Here she was, calmly telling him that his son was involved with known killers and felons. Here was a woman whom he'd loved beyond redemption. Here was a woman whom he trusted more than life itself. Here was a woman who always appeared to him in his dreams like a nightingale. Here was a woman whom he thought of as a blue angel—half mortal and half spirit. And now here was this same woman telling him that unless Peyton was found and soon, there was a good chance he would be a second-generation con living the same horrors of prison life that he had. Without a doubt, he knew he had to do something to break the chain.

In that split second, he hated her.

There had to be a time when situations had to change. Change for the better. His son would not be a victim. No. No. There was no damned way.

Seconds passed like hours. The hours like days. It seemed forever since Isaac had seen Peyton. He knew that time was running out.

Sitting in his apartment in the dark, he tried to think of something that he'd missed. He'd tracked on foot and in the car a fifty-mile radius of Detroit. Nothing. When the telephone rang, he didn't bother to answer it. After the sixth ring, he got to thinking: *It could be Peyton!*

"Hello," he said, his voice hinged with excitement.

"Hey. It's me, Miracall. I know you're not feeling like company. I just called to see if you heard anything, and if I could be of any assistance."

She was right. He rubbed his hand across his face, not realizing how thick his beard had grown. Flicking on the lights, he looked in the mirror. *My God, I look like I'm homeless.*

"No, we haven't heard anything yet. I'm okay."

"I figured as much. I've been talking to Rosemary. She's worried that you haven't been eating lately. Would you mind if I bought dinner for you?"

Why was everyone concerned about feeding him? He couldn't just sit home and have dinner like nothing had happened. He'd just read in this morning's paper about the number of suicides among black youths between the ages of fifteen and nineteen. The rate had nearly doubled since 1980. It said that the roots were often the same for teenagers—depression, a lack of self-worth, a sense of hopelessness, a crushing despair about one's future, and one's dwindling reverence for life. Funny, Isaac thought, that description fit him better than it did his son. "Thanks, but no. I need to be here in case Peyton is found."

"I was thinking that I'd come over there," she said.

Isaac didn't know what to say. He was lonely, tired, and finally beginning to work up an appetite. His relationship with Kennedy right now was even more strained.

Yeah, he thought, an objective person was just what he needed right now. "Miracall, you're right, I'm starved. Stop by Steve's Soul Food and pick me up one of those large ham hocks and something sweet."

"That sounds good. I think I'll have the same." He loved to hear the laughter present now in her voice. "I don't know where you live. What's your address?"

When he hung up, he cleaned up the place and took a shower. By the time he buzzed Miracall up and she knocked on his door, Isaac had showered, shaved, and had a pot of coffee brewing.

Miracall brought just what he was craving for—ham hocks, mashed potatoes, fried corn, and his favorite—a whole sweet potato pie. Afterward, he sat back on the sofa and relaxed for the first time in nearly two weeks.

Tuning in the radio to 92.3 FM, he and Miracall talked about Peyton's problems. Primarily, about the Ritalin, the marijuana, and his alleged affiliation with the Prophets. Isaac was honest about the kind of relationship he was trying to build with his son. He told her about Kennedy getting pregnant and him marrying her back in the eighties. When he explained that he had loved Kennedy but had resented that she'd gotten pregnant, he tried to gauge her reaction.

Revealing a part of himself seemed to make Miracall open up, and she began to talk candidly about her eleven-year marriage to Loren. How embarrassed she had felt when he divorced her before he became governor. How hard she'd worked over the past two years helping him during his reelection campaign, even writing some of his speeches. During that time he had promised her that they'd announce their remarriage after he was elected this term. When he lost, she knew it was obvious that he'd been using her.

"That's why I went on the cruise with you. Not to make him jealous. But to do some soul-searching myself. I had to make a decision. It's time for me to think about *me* for a change."

Isaac wasn't sure how to say it, but it came out anyway. "You don't have any kids. Didn't you ever want children?"

"I did. I don't think Loren ever did. He loved Becky like his own child. You see, I was jealous of the little girl. Dawn and I talked about it. Of course, I loved Becky—I couldn't help it—she looked exactly like Loren. She was smart, well mannered, and a gifted piano player. She'd taken lessons since age three. Loren predicted that she would debut at the Philharmonic Symphony Orchestra Hall before she turned fifteen. He insisted she was a child prodigy before we found out that she actually was one. Her father, Dwayne, never took time with Becky. I think because Loren never gave the man a chance to be a father. That was Loren's job. I believe he was the main factor in ending Dawn and Dwayne's marriage."

"I had no idea that the child was so special. But to a parent, whose child isn't?"

"I agree."

"Funny, I didn't want a child until I was at least thirty-two. Maybe thirty-five. I had big plans. Now that Peyton is here, I can't see my life without him. I have so many dreams for his future. Plans that he and I never discussed. I wanted to get my career established first. Make consistent money. I wanted him to understand that I would be there for him."

Miracall stood up and began cleaning off the kitchen table. Even when Isaac objected, she waved him off. "I've never been a mother, but I know that having a child run off for more than two weeks would drive me crazy.

I'm not trying to appear negative. But tell me, have you been through his closet?"

"Yeah. But not thoroughly."

"Doesn't matter. You should check his pants pockets."

Isaac popped himself in the head. Why hadn't he or Kennedy thought of that? They'd been so busy concentrating on the drugs, they forgot about the small things.

He and Miracall went through every item Peyton owned. It took two hours to do a decent search. They didn't find a thing, except a pack of matches. The name on it was the Chestnut Lounge on Fenkell Avenue. The bar was less than five miles away.

Miracall got into Isaac's car and they went to the bar. They looked around inside and didn't see him. Miracall suggested that they wait outside until the bar closed; he could still show up. No such luck. Miracall assured Isaac before she left to go home that night that if he continued to frequent the bar, he'd find Peyton.

On day seventeen, Isaac felt encouraged. He learned from a few young men standing outside the bar that a young man fitting Peyton's description had indeed been there on Friday night. He didn't come every night, but they'd seen him, all right.

That Saturday afternoon, he called Bernie and asked him for a favor. Next he called Kennedy. "We've got a break! Peyton's been seen at the Chestnut Lounge. We should synchronize our days to monitor the place."

"I'll ask the patrolmen to keep an eye on the bar."

"No, Kennedy. If he sees the squad cars and the lights, he'll never go in. I think we'd better do it this way."

Reluctantly, she agreed.

That night, Isaac had the first watch. He felt so confident about finding Peyton that he called Rex and asked if he'd mind if Bernie stood in for him.

His heart was beating like an overworked alarm clock when he started the Pontiac. In just a few minutes, he might be able to see his son.

Barely a mile down Eight Mile Road, he spotted flashing lights behind him. At first he thought it was Kennedy.

Not so. The officer told Isaac to get out the car and spread 'em. His car was searched and they found a pound of marijuana hidden in the trunk.

Now he understood why the Firebird had been waiting for him.

Isaac was livid. All he could think of was Eli. Eli.

He was taken to the station and booked. Rosemary was there in no time, posting bail and getting him released.

Force of Evil

For more than four hours, Peyton had been thinking about getting himself something to eat. He realized that he hadn't had a decent meal since he ran away from home. After he and J-Rock entered the small bar on Fenkell, J-Rock did his swaggering walk, slapping high-fives with everybody he ran into, and they each took a seat on a stool at the bar.

J-Rock ordered a shot of rum and a Coke. Peyton ordered a hamburger with everything and a Miller Lite.

Roscoe, the regular bartender, always served all the gang members without asking for any ID, the reason being they slipped him a couple of joints to smoke. And for a good marijuana joint, Roscoe would serve the Pope if he came in. Presently, Roscoe was running an errand for the owner. Sonny Boy Washington, the new tenderoni, was tending bar tonight, and he refused to serve them.

"I need to see your ID," Sonny Boy said.

Peyton started to leave. He had volunteered to carry half a pound of marijuana for J-Rock and would be in all kinds of trouble if the police were called.

But J-Rock, already smashed from smoking a joint before they got to the bar, jumped back off the bar stool. He pulled out his .357 magnum Colt, waved it at the bartender, and told him, "This is my ID. Actually, I've got six of 'em." J-Rock aimed the gun at Sonny Boy, cocked the trigger, and shot him in the chest. "This is one piece. I don't think you need another."

At that point, Peyton was overwhelmed. All hell broke loose. Fighting to get to the door, people began to run out of the bar. J-Rock was shoved in the back and dropped the gun. With so many people running for the exit, he had no chance to recover it.

Peyton, already afraid, grabbed J-Rock and dragged him out of the bar behind him.

Unbeknownst to them, a couple of Kennedy's police friends were nearby and keeping an eye on the bar—on the lookout for Peyton Coleman. Just as they were driving by, they spotted Peyton running down Fenkell, half-dragging J-Rock. The officers apprehended Peyton and J-Rock before Peyton could ditch the marijuana. They were spread-eagled on the ground and searched.

Peyton knew that he was in big trouble. Being caught with that much marijuana was stupid. Though he'd been carrying it for J-Rock, it didn't matter. He was trying to prove he belonged to the gang. He was a fool. And the words of his father reminded him, *"You don't want to go to prison, son. It's hell. Hell is Jefferson Penitentiary."*

Why hadn't he listened?

4

The Siege of Detroit

Deliver Us

The Lord hath accomplished his fury; he hath poured out his fierce anger, and hath kindled a fire in Zion, and it hath devoured the foundations thereof.

—Lam. 4:11

Body and Soul

It seemed that the work she did for the prisons was taking up more of her time than her church duties were. Not once did Jesse complain. Rosemary was flattered when she was asked to join the Pastors to Prisoners advisory board. She was the first black ever asked to join the staff.

She was also instrumental in helping PTP receive their status this year as a 501(c)(3) nonprofit organization by the Internal Revenue Service. It had taken just eight months. Requests of this type usually took a year or longer, and the board realized that God truly does answer prayers.

Their slogan—"Helping Broken Men Put the Pieces Together"—was one she believed in. Her prayers lately were that Peyton wouldn't be one of the men who were trying to put their pieces back together. His trial was set for March 15. She prayed that his family would keep him safe.

Each and every February, the fiscal year ended for the Metalcase workers, the union corporation whose jobs were being threatened by the prison work. They took that opportunity every year to picket Jefferson Penitentiary. After all, over the past ten years, Metalcase had lost thousands of jobs to Jefferson because of the excruciatingly low salary that Jefferson paid its employees. Thus far, nothing had been done about it.

When Rosemary returned home from Jefferson Penitentiary, she found that a curt message had been left on her answering machine by the bishop: "Please be at my office at 9:00 A.M. Monday morning. It's extremely urgent." Apparently her pastoral obligations hadn't gone unnoticed.

The bishop's office, which was located in Monroe, fifty miles away, was a gallows trek away from hers. It took two hours to make the trip to his meager surroundings. Standing outside his door, she felt like a criminal.

Once Rosemary entered his office, the bishop immediately made his thoughts clear about the feelings of the board. Membership had declined for the first time in nearly a year. To make matters worse, the money collected from the Sunday offerings was down by two thousand dollars.

"Why wasn't I told of these problems earlier?" She felt blindsided by her board of directors.

"There have been several letters and numerous complaints lately, Rosemary," the bishop told her. "Too many to mention."

"How can I defend myself if I don't know the charges?"

"The problem stems from your sermons. A lot of members believe that you have depended too much on the secular view of the world instead of using Scripture quotations."

Rosemary was furious. "I use the problems presently crippling the world and our people today as the topic of my lessons. I take the exact Scriptures from the Bible and apply them to the current issues. After all we're seeing today, events that were already prophesized in the Bible, I'm not too surprised with what's going on these days—in the city and around the country. Our problems today are the same problems that our ancestors dealt with years ago. Our congregation is smarter these days. More educated. I'm not just a pastor. I'm a marriage counselor. A principal. A woman. Not to mention the savior of the people. My strong suit is getting more young people to understand how history repeats itself. Especially in the Bible. If I can't show them how today's times mirror dates and events in history, especially our spiritual beginnings, I'll lose them."

"I'm not saying that your heart—"

"Isn't in the right place!" She cut him short. Right then, she felt her temper flare. They could keep this job. It was more responsibility than she'd anticipated. No wonder the other pastor's health had broken down. All this pressure would make anyone ill. "I must have complete control over my message. If I can't have that, give this job to someone else."

"Sister Jones, you're getting yourself upset for nothing. I am not objecting to your sermons."

"No. No!" she shouted. "I will be judged by no man or woman. God will be my judge. And now these same hypocrites dare to tell me how to preach? I've dedicated forty years of my life to the Lord. There aren't but a handful of people in this church who can honestly say the same." She picked up her purse and Bible and left.

It seemed that everyone was complaining, Rosemary thought as she drove home through hectic traffic. Mother Bethel had finally managed to be cleared of the IRS investigation. Gary was instrumental in saving the church's reputation. He proved that there was an attempt to set up the church. The culprits were never uncovered, but that wasn't necessary. The damage was done and all they could do now was to move forward and count their blessings that the church was exonerated.

Even the mayor was under fire. Legal proceedings were in place to impeach him. It was no longer a theory. It was a fact. And with Peyton just being released on bail, and the threat of the implication of drugs being added to his sentence, Rosemary didn't have much sympathy left for the mayor.

When she returned home, there was a message from Gary.

"I know you've heard the news. Things are crazy in the city, the mayor's impeachment trial. Rumors have it that the gangs have all but seized control of the city, including the bigwigs in the police department. Maybe we need to rethink this prison thing. Governor Miller isn't holding up to his bargain. I think he's changed his position on prison privatization."

Jesse had gone to his monthly Mason's meeting. It occurred to Rosemary that before she became so involved in the church, Jesse had seemed mildly interested in the Masons. Now it seemed to be his life force. Was it her fault?

She decided to wait for him that night, no matter what time he returned. She popped into the VCR a copy of cartoon videos that Jesse watched over and over again. Midway through, she found herself in hysterics. The phone interrupted her laughter.

It was Henry Miller. Rosemary wasn't in the mood for business tonight. But when he talked, she listened.

"I found out a few facts from a reporter who's doing a story on the public's view of Clyde's administration's supervision of the state's penal system. The reporter brags about the story being run on the front page of tomorrow's paper. This is the clincher. The state's four-hundred-ten-million-dollar-a-year prison system has not been under the same scrutiny since the prisons went private. The two private companies that own these prisons are not keeping them up to code and in many instances are violating the civil rights of the inmates by withholding meals and making them work twenty-two-hour days. The private companies also have a poor record of late payments to the service providers for the prisons. Public sentiment that windfall profits are being made has caused unrest in the community as well as inside the prison."

"I know that already, Henry," Rosemary stated.

"But did you know that the escape from Cement City Penitentiary was a direct result of drug payoffs to the prison guards, who, incidentally, used to be employed as Detroit policemen. The mayor's people aren't talking, but an internal affairs investigation has just begun. We'll get to the bottom of this sooner than the guilty anticipated."

"No. And I'm not sure if I care about it anymore. Politics and the church don't seem to jive. If I continue to get involved, I might be out of a job. I'll call you in a few days."

She hung up and pressed the play button on the VCR.

When Jesse finally came home late that night, Rosemary was in a good mood. She'd laughed till she cried. She had put Peyton's situation into perspective and decided that the bishop was a threat to her only if she allowed him to be.

In short, she was tired of worrying about things out of her control. As a pastor she would continue to pray and keep her faith strong. But tonight she needed more. Her body needed consoling. No one else but her husband could fulfill that task.

She smelled like heaven. But she knew that Jesse would smell only the Eternity cologne that was gently splashed over her body. She heard him showering and pretended to be sleep until she felt him remove his prosthesis and fall clumsily onto the bed beside her.

After he slid into the bed, she reached over and kissed him. Turning back on her side, she waited to see what kind of mood he was in. It didn't take long. He turned over and ran his hand across her upper body and then farther down. He was surprised to find that she was nude.

"Darlin'."

Reaching beneath the sheets, she felt his manhood beginning to grow in length and took pleasure in removing his boxers.

Within seconds she felt his passion pressing against her leg. They needed no pomp and circumstance to their joining. Their communication was short and to the point. Touch me. Feel me. Love me.

When he touched her, she heard herself moan. When she touched him, he groaned with pleasure.

She felt his fingers sliding inside her and her thighs gripped tightly together like hoops of steel. Her feelings lasted longer the longer they were delayed.

In the darkened room, she blindly reached for him, her fingers pressed indecently against his back. In no time, she felt him moving on top of her, mounting her. It was an easy fit, because she was wet and ready for love.

Instinctively, she urged her pulsating tightness to envelope him, taking his hardness and length deeper within her.

Jesse's joy of excitement turned into a harsh growl of pleasure.

Within minutes, her eyes had become accustomed to the darkness, and she saw the veins standing out on his forehead, the same type of veins that she imagined were now protruding on the exterior of his love muscle. To her delight, he grabbed her buttocks and worked his hips into a frenzied pace.

She felt the bed beginning to shake, his bony knees pushing, pushing, faster and faster, like a jackhammer. After a few hard thrusts, she heard him exhale. It was over for him, but not for her.

In less than two shakes of a lamb's tail, she straddled him, imprisoning him inside her hot walls. Her hands groped for, then grasped, his, their fingers tightly interlocked as she began to set the rhythm. With deep but low strokes, she gyrated her hips slowly until she felt the thunder building between his legs once again. Their tempo took on that familiar beat. The headboard began to bang against the wall, and with each thrust, she heard Jesse groan like some sad prophet who foresaw the doom. She felt ashamed to be enjoying such carnal pleasures. But she was human. It was the fire of desire that was emblazoned in her limbs. Her body and soul were entwined for a long, sweet, spinning, rapturous moment. She was almost there. She felt her jaws clenching with unparalleled pressure as a splash of white light dazed behind her eyelids. The sheer sensation of that culmination of effects lit up her body like a twelve-foot Christmas tree, as pleasurable as deserting her soul and becoming a slave to her sexual desires. Without any further hesitation her brain gave way, and she felt pulverized, even driven at times, without one glimpse of reason, or of heaven, as she rocked them toward dementia.

Satisfied, she rolled over, completely fulfilled.

Her last thoughts were that everything had come too late. Her ministry—Isaac—Peyton—Kennedy—Miracall. How could she continue to be everyone's savior when her own sould needed so much?

Persuasion

The snowdrifts in February were as deep as Rosemary's dreams. In Michigan it was the month with the worst weather, and most workers began to look forward to any sign of the coming of spring. By the first of March, the ice had finally begun to coalesce like spiderwebs. Fog, rain, and warmer suns were gradually melting the snow; the days were finally beginning to grow longer.

On Wednesday, March 3, Jesse turned thirty-six years old. Rosemary convinced him to take the remainder of the day off after she'd given him his noon insulin shot. The previous weekend she'd purchased thirty-six presents, all inexpensive except for the Mason's gold watch that he'd wanted and was too cheap to buy. She hid the presents throughout the house, and laughed during the hour and a half that it took Jesse to find them all.

Afterward, she watched Jesse stuff himself with strawberry ice cream and a fresh strawberry cream cheesecake. Rosemary felt slightly jealous as she settled on a bowl of fresh strawberries; she was still fourteen pounds overweight.

On a more positive note, the twenty members of Mother Bethel had moved into their homes. Oddly enough, they'd had to stoop to pulling names out of a hat to determine who would move into the renovated houses. But even so, everyone seemed satisfied.

That same afternoon, a letter arrived from Jefferson Penitentiary. It was from Paps Bowenstein. She hadn't seen him in two months. During that time she'd received several letters from him. He never asked when she was coming again, and she never mentioned when she'd be back in the letters she wrote him.

"How's he doing?" Jesse asked after Rosemary began reading the letter.

Flipping through the pages, she said, "Fine, judging by the length of this letter." It was eight pages long.

Paps's left arm was broken when he slipped and fell in the Metalcase Furniture factory. He told her not to worry—his old bones were healing nicely over the past few months. She had no idea, though, that he was recovering from a recent heart attack.

Rosemary went on to summarize the contents of the letter after reading it halfway through. "He's concerned about Isaac. Paps says that he's written Isaac numerous letters and Isaac hasn't written him back."

"That's not like him," Jesse said, wrapping up the remainder of the cheesecake with aluminum foil.

She continued to read, then stopped, pressing the pages against her chest. "God in Heaven!" she swore. "Paps says there's a hit out on Isaac."

"Don't upset yourself, darlin'. All that medication you're taking ain't working as good as you think it is." He went over beside her and read the remainder of the letter along with her. "I'm not too sure about this kind of stuff. How would Paps know if someone was trying to kill Isaac?"

Rosemary didn't even want to think about it. What did it matter how? She was concerned about who. "Isaac told me about the convicts in there. Some are cold-blooded criminals."

Jesse looked incredulous. "Ain't that why they're in prison?"

"This ain't no time to be funny. I got a bad feeling about this." She glanced at the phone, wondering if Isaac was home. "They've got more money in their accounts than we do. For that reason, I have to believe that anything's possible."

She turned and studied her husband's handsome face. There was a certain tenderness in him that made her wonder what he ever saw in her. With all the pressures that she was dealing with lately, she was glad that God had sent her a friend as well as a husband.

Was this the right time, she wondered, to share a part of her past with him? Or was it better to keep the past in the past? None of their lives would change for the better or worse. Then she thought about Paps and his soul. One day he would die, and the past would haunt her once more. She thought back to the time just five years earlier when she learned that Isaac was moved to a cell right next to Paps.

"Have you forgiven yourself yet?" she had asked Paps.

"There is good and evil in all of us, Rosemary. Either one can lead to God. I've learned to fight evil through faith. I didn't have the strength to know that then." His eyes were moist with tears when he said, "I've tried, but I can't." If only she could have truly understood his demons.

"It's time, Seymour. We've all been through enough. I don't know how much longer I can keep this between us."

Rosemary reached for the phone. As she did so, Jesse read the last lines of Paps's letter: "I realize that Isaac's concerned about his son. But he can't help Peyton if he's dead."

Her breath held in her throat as she dialed the number. Isaac picked up on the fifth ring.

"Hello, Isaac. Jesse and I are on our way over."

Isaac sighed wearily. "I take it you've heard from Paps."

Rosemary told him about the letter.

"Don't pay any attention to that nonsense. Why would anyone want to hurt me?"

She thought about Loren. Since he left office, no one had heard a peep from him.

"I'm not sure, Isaac. I can't help but worry about you, that's all."

She thought back to the small child who had gone to bed every night giving her a big hug and saying "I love you, Wosy." And *he* wondered, *Why would anyone want to hurt me? She* wondered how she could survive if anything happened to her brother.

Normally, the first Sunday service was a long one. Not today. It was Mother Bethel's turn to serve somewhere else. Rosemary, along with dozens of volunteers, were at St. Phillips Catholic Church on Forest Avenue downtown, two blocks off Warren. St. Phillips fed the homeless every Sunday from eleven-thirty to three o'clock in the afternoon.

Getting more involved with the community had never been more fashionable than during the mid-nineties. With so many large corporations vying for their turn to serve, time to offer their services was at a premium—especially for the homeless. The dates allocated to each of the fifty-five corporations were designated to just under one Sunday a year. Mother Bethel's turn had finally come around.

When Rosemary and twenty-two other members arrived at St. Phillips, there were at least forty sleeping people forming a line outside the front doors of the church.

She found out later that each one of them held a ticket, like the lottery, that they'd received from a homeless shelter. Otherwise, there wouldn't be enough food to go around.

By eleven-fifteen, everything was ready. There were soup and sandwiches, chicken and gravy, pork roast, milk, and iced tea. Besides Rosemary and her group, there were six other servers from St. Phillips who would help out today.

When the doors opened at precisely eleven-thirty, the line looked unending. Rosemary saw several men steering their children with one arm and trying to balance a tray with the other.

"Can you fill this for me?" one man asked, handing the man beside Rosemary a plastic bag.

"Sure."

"Can I get some extra milk?" a woman asked. "My baby ain't had none in days."

There were people who seemed like they'd lost their minds. She'd been prepared but was still shocked that the largest core of the crowd were alcoholics and drug addicts. At one point Rosemary had to step back, their stench was so strong.

When she looked up more than an hour later, she took an assessment of the crowd. They had served nearly three hundred people. Only a few out of that number were white. Her guess was that maybe thirty-five or so were women.

"What you got back there, sweet?" the next man in line asked.

"Hot apple pie," offered the woman beside her.

For early March, it was cold—27 degrees. Rosemary noticed that less than half of the men, women, and children there today wore coats. Most wore sweatshirts or had a blanket wrapped around them.

A little later, she heard a man ask a server for a quarter for bus fare. The server, barely three feet away from her, said no.

"How could you turn him down?" Rosemary hollered so that no one but the ones behind the counter could hear.

"He'll probably buy crack with it."

"Since when did crack cost a quarter?" She removed her apron and went to find the young man.

While she looked for him, she realized that the majority of men in line were between the ages of twenty-five and fifty-five.

She thought about Peyton, and knew that she'd lose her last breath before she allowed him to end up like this. Even Isaac, who appeared to be nonplussed about the hit out on him, was a candidate for this very situation. He was too bull-headed to listen to caution.

Finally, Rosemary found the man. He was trying to gather his kids, his threadbare clothing barely covering his thin body.

"I'm Pastor Rosemary Jones." She extended her hand and the man merely embraced his children tighter. "I heard you a while ago. I'd like to give you a dollar if it won't offend you."

She reached inside her apron pocket and handed the man the money.

"No, thank you."

"I thought you needed the money."

He turned up his nose like he smelled something foul. "No, not from church people. Y'all kind of folks scare me—all cleaned up, wearing nice clothes, smelling good, shoes shined, with their Rolexes on. Not like the folks on the street. They let you know up front that they don't like you. But church people, they work behind your back. They'll drop a dime on you in a minute to the man to bust you."

Rosemary was speechless. "Please don't put me in that category. You don't know me."

Slowly, the man turned and looked at her. His eyes seemed almost angelic then. It seemed like an eternity before he spoke. There was a hurt look on his face when he said, "What would happen if Jesus passed you by because *you* were raggedy. Because *your* hair wasn't combed. Because *you* didn't have decent clothes to send your child to school in. Because *you* were living in a sugar shack and using a chitlin' bucket as a commode?"

Rosemary was speechless. The news was all over the radio. Governor Miller had just signed the proposal for the state to take over the Detroit public schools. The poor test scores, high dropout rate, and crumbling school build-ings had prompted the state to take action. Mayor Prescott had less than sixty days to elect a panel to take over the school board. She had come down here to help, and now, looking at the man's children, felt helpless.

"These people claim to be religious. Christ-like. They're not. They look at us like we're aliens or something worse."

"Not me. Please not me," she begged.

The clatter of serving spoons scraping the bottoms of the aluminum pans seemed to strike up interest in the line. People stood on their toes, straining to see if the food would run out before they reached their turn in line.

"Sister, I haven't given up on faith." His smile crucified her. "Just on worldly people representing themselves as Jesus' servants and ain't. I still have faith in the Lord. In Jesus. Otherwise, me and my children here might be dead," he said, shaking his head. He took a few steps around her, his hands behind his back. "I'm so glad that Jesus stopped by to see about me when other folks thought that I wouldn't make it. I'm so glad that Jesus stopped by when I didn't have two cents in my pocket and I hadn't ate in three days. I'm so glad that Jesus stopped by to see about me!"

He left, leaving Rosemary standing in the midst of confusion, realizing that half of these hypocrites today would go home bragging to their loved ones about how much they helped their community by feeding the homeless. But in truth the homeless felt sympathy for them, because a large number of them knew that these people standing behind the counter were standing in judg-ment, and really didn't have any sympathy for them at all.

She held all this in her heart until her Wednesday night sermon. Isaac was getting his life back together after being acquitted of drug trafficking. Her nephew was still out on bail and doing well. His trial would be starting soon, and would determine his fate.

She remembered the general idea of what Jesse Jackson had said a few years back; "You wouldn't see the states' jails filled with young white boys. No, some-thing would be done about it. But obviously black men are expendable and dis-posable."

Rosemary thought about that on Wednesday night. And she fought to keep the tears out of her words.

"You women say, 'Where are all the black men?' You wonder where they are? I'd like you to take a moment on Sunday afternoon to visit the soup lines at St. Phillips Catholic Church on Forest Avenue."

A woman in the congregation shouted, "Preach, sister!"

"That's where our men folk are. As a pastor, I wish that most of them weren't strung out on drugs. But truthfully, a lot of them are. Some of them are experiencing psychological problems. Most are without hope." She paused, fighting back tears. "I'd like to know, where are the families of these people? Have they turned their backs on them?"

A young woman in the back, who she'd noticed was weeping, had just run out of the church.

"I could no more turn my back on any of you than I could a drunk laying on the side of the road. I pray, my Christian sisters and brothers, that you might open up your heart to do the same."

Summer and Smoke

When Isaac had come home from jail that fateful night in January, he had seen a bottle of Cristal champagne and three pounds of king crab legs tucked inside a basket. And covered in pink plastic was a lone orchid in a pot. Both had been placed close to his apartment door. There hadn't been a card. But Isaac had known that they were from Miracall.

That night was the beginning of a change in their relationship. Their friendship was blooming with promise, like an apple in the month of May. It had begun, oddly enough, in a cemetery, then moved into understanding at the Motor City Grille, then into respect by the unfortunate circumstances of his son's incarceration.

He couldn't be sure, but he felt the person responsible for planting the drugs in his car was Eli, or someone who worked for him.

When they had finally arraigned him and he stood before a probable-cause hearing less than forty-eight hours later, it was over. Rosemary had contacted his parole officer before he even asked her to do so. Isaac realized that if he didn't beat this rap, he'd be convicted of parole violation and would be on his way back to prison. Thank God he had a decent parole officer who really liked him and recommended a good attorney whom he could afford.

The Fourth Amendment requires that a police officer have reasonable suspicion that a person is involved in criminal activity before detaining that suspect. However, the police may stop a car if they reasonably believe the car had violated a traffic law.

The policeman who arrested Isaac claimed that he had a reliable informant. Conveniently, the police didn't have to reveal this person's identity.

It didn't matter. The case was thrown out. The prosecuting attorney didn't have any direct evidence that the drugs were Isaac's. After receiving the lab reports, which concluded that Isaac's fingerprints weren't anywhere on the drugs, the prosecutor had known that his case was weakened.

Also, Isaac's attorney successfully argued that the drugs were planted, thus shedding reasonable doubt on the prosecutor's case. Even though Isaac was found innocent of the crime, another black spot remained on his record; it showed that the case was dismissed because of insufficient evidence. But the blemish remained.

Isaac was reminded of the book by Donald Goines, *White Man's Justice, Black Man's Grief.* Everyone he knew in prison had read that book—including Wide-eyed Willy. Goines died years ago, but the bigotry in the prison system was still as pervasive as when he first penned the novel twenty-six years earlier.

Peyton's trial was set for three weeks after Isaac's. He was still free on twenty-five thousand dollars that was promptly paid by Kennedy. During those weeks, Kennedy took a leave of absence and took Peyton home to stay with her. Isaac hid his disappointment.

During those lonely days, Isaac received a letter from Paps. Wide-eyed Willy had died of cirrhosis of the liver. The poor man's only crime in his adult life had been two counts of breaking and entering. Both incidents had occurred while breaking into liquor stores.

With Willy's death fresh on his mind, Isaac was even more despondent when he heard Peyton's charges.

The youth was initially charged with being an accessory before the fact, which meant that he, the accomplice, had acted with the intent to aid or encourage the principle, Johnny "J-Rock" Johnson, in the commission of the crime. However, before his arraignment, the prosecutor's office was trying to trump up Peyton's crime with two more counts of aggravated assault, and send a message out to all gang members who thought they could continue to get away with killing innocent people.

Isaac, Kennedy, Rosemary, and Jesse listened intently in Peyton's attorney's office as she calmly explained to them, "If Peyton and J-Rock had gone into the bar with the intent to rob the bar and they had guns, but during the course of the robbery they shot and killed the bartender, Sonny Boy Washington, then they're also guilty of murder under a couple of theories—one, he could be guilty of accessory before the fact; or two, felony murder, which was a killing that occurred during the course of a felony if it is a foreseeable result of the felony."

"Excuse me," Kennedy said, annoyance snapping into her voice. "What is all this bullcrap? We've got three witnesses that can prove Peyton didn't pull the trigger."

"Please, Kennedy!" Isaac blew out a stream of breath. "Can't we please listen to the woman."

Peyton held his mother's hand in his. Each time the attorney spoke, Isaac noticed that Peyton was clutching hers a little tighter. Kennedy turned to look at Isaac and cut her eyes at him.

Meanwhile, Rosemary broke out crying. It took both Isaac and Jesse to console her. Minutes later, Isaac felt Kennedy's dark eyes peering at him once more as the female defense attorney continued.

"The burden is on the prosecutor to prove beyond a reasonable doubt that Peyton acted with intent to aid or encourage J-Rock in the murder of Mr. Washington. Our defense will show that Peyton had no intent. Nor did he have any prior knowledge that J-Rock was going to do this. I feel confident that we can prove this. But I don't believe we'll be as lucky with the possession charge."

The defense attorney knew what she was talking about. They managed to clear Peyton of all charges in the felony murder. J-Rock was sentenced to fifteen to twenty years and sent to Jefferson Penitentiary.

Unlike Isaac's case, Peyton was taken into custody during a lawful arrest. In those cases, the police don't need a warrant. The search was deemed contemporaneous—possession of an illegal drug. They found eight ounces of marijuana on Peyton's person. Even though his attorney argued that Peyton was using the drug because of withdrawal symptoms from Ritalin, they found that it was not a sufficient excuse. Nor did Dr. Allbright's testimony help—Peyton was sentenced to a year in prison.

During those trying times, Isaac couldn't feign the pleasure of riding his Harley. The best he could do was polish it and place the cover back on top of it.

Isaac originally thought that Peyton's incarceration might bring him and Kennedy closer. It only widened their already existing problems. When he called her, he got the answering machine. When he went to her house, she didn't answer the door.

He had to get her out of his system. Work became his passion. He had to believe, as work began to pour in, that the gods were on his side again.

The dream of becoming a journalist was ever-present. He never lost sight of that. But at the moment, his talent as a musician was paying the bills. He had to keep things in perspective.

Invitations began to come in for interviews with local agents. With Miracall's assistance, he chose an aggressive twenty-six-year-old female named Ginger Ruffin, from the west side of Detroit.

"I don't know, Miracall, she hasn't been in the business too long. I checked her references."

"Look, she's friends with the owners of Motown. That means more than any reference. She'll get you work. She doesn't get paid if she doesn't."

It turned out that Miracall was right. Ginger was booking engagements and had him performing all over the city of Detroit. Her contacts even extended to Chicago and Ohio. Ginger was confident that the jazz market would broaden out even farther. It was a fact that jazz music was on the upswing and interest was stronger than it had been in prior years. He was now working seven days a week. Correspondingly, his income increased dramatically.

It began in May, with the Atlanta Caribbean Festival. Then, between practicing new songs and working at the Grille, he drove to Baltimore in late May, and to the *Boston Globe* and Jazz Wine Festival in June. He headlined at the Charlotte Smoking' Grooves tour of 1999 in mid-June. And, closer to home, he played at the Chicago Blues Festival at the end of June.

He would be home for two weeks before he was back on the road to Ohio for the Cincinnati Smokin' Grooves Tour of 1999 and the Cleveland Jazz and Rib Festival, which he'd appeared at the previous year. In July, he would, for the first time, headline the Detroit Afro-American Festival.

During his hectic schedule, he never missed a weekly visit with Peyton; they'd grown closer. Isaac was sure that Peyton was completely and finally drug-free and appeared to be doing much better.

He thought about his Harley again. And the firm belief that Jesse held that he wanted him to pass down this beautiful machine to his son. It was then that he knew that he would never ride the Harley again. Not until Peyton was free and he was able to hand over the reins to him.

Peyton was scheduled to move to the new youth penitentiary in Bad Axe in August. Until then, he had to persevere in the confinements of an over-crowded jail. Isaac hated that he had to be in jail so long.

"Dad, this place ain't cool. I mean, there are criminals in here, man. I ain't like them." Peyton looked like a caged animal that was trying to find a way out when he knew there was none. "The other day this dude my age was raped. I heard the whole thing. It was like listening to a horror movie. The guy cried big time afterwards. I knew he wouldn't make it," he continued with emphasis. "They removed his body this morning. The dude hung himself with a sheet."

Isaac pressed the phone firmly against his right cheek, trying to hear Peyton's voice as best as he could. He didn't know where to begin. There was so much he could tell his son. But there was also a lot that he wanted to leave out. Things that he didn't ever want his son to know about.

"Listen to me, Peyton. I know you didn't intend to be involved in the circumstances surrounding that bartender's murder. The whole thing is unforgivable. It was my fault that I took you off the drug before you were ready."

"No. I could have told you I was still having problems."

"I'm the adult here, Peyton. We're going to get past this. I know you're clean now. Even though you'll be in a youth facility, I've already got it set up for you to take classes to get your GED. We can still get you in the first semester of college in January."

"Dad, when did you do all this?"

"The same day they sentenced you." There was conviction in his voice.

"You will not be some lost soul without an education. You will not be an une-ducated casualty." Isaac swallowed back tears. "Your family loves you, Pey-ton, and we want to see you succeed."

When Isaac wasn't performing, he loved watching videos. It had taken him nine months to finally buy a videocassette recorder. And for three days, he rented twenty videos and enjoyed watching every one of them.

One of his favorites was *Ransom.* It was while watching that movie that he thought about Eli. All along he believed that Eli was the perpetrator, but he couldn't prove it. He knew he had to keep this theory to himself until he had proof.

After all, Eli was the one who had sold him the car, and the one he believed had set him up with the drugs in his trunk. One hot summer night, when he couldn't sleep, Isaac began taking night rides by Eli's chop shops. On a hunch, he even drove by his home in Birmingham off Woodward Avenue.

When Eli spotted him one night, Isaac was pumped. It was like *Gunfight at the O.K. Corral.* The show was on.

Isaac waited. Two weeks went by and nothing happened. He still had to work, but he wasn't crazy; he did fear for his life.

"I've got good news, Isaac," Ginger Ruffin told him one cool June after-noon. "We have a firm commitment on a two-week jazz gig in Rio de Janeiro and Bahia, Brazil. I think this event could even land you the record deal you've been waiting for."

When he called Miracall, she was ecstatic. "Rio! I've never been there."

That information alone made Isaac feel empowered. Finally, somewhere that she hadn't been before.

With hours of help from Bernie, Isaac was finally able to get a wardrobe de-signed and sewed specifically for him. There were no hard feelings between them, even though Isaac's career had soared and Bernie's struggling quartet appeared to remain stagnant.

The day that Isaac was set to leave, Kennedy paid him a visit.

"We haven't talked for a while. I stayed away for a reason. There's been a four-year investigation going on in the city—my partner and I are part of the undercover team working on the case."

Undercover or under the sheets. "Detective Royale?" She nodded yes. *So that's who's been keeping late hours at your house.*

Kennedy walked over to the sofa and casually eyed the visible contents of his suitcase. "A west-side drug and money-laundering organization is currently under siege by the FBI. Primarily because the drugs have been coming in from Miami, Florida, and up to Michigan. The feds feel that Eli is a major player, but they think that there may be bigger fish controlling this operation. The investigation will continue until they are identified and prosecuted."

Who was this woman? Didn't she fear for her safety? "What does this have to do with me?" There was so much he wanted to say. Like, *Baby, let someone else deal this case. Come with me to Brazil. We can have the honeymoon that we've always dreamed about.* Instead he said, "Why are you telling me this now?"

"You were set up. We know that. Peyton was a casualty because of the Ritalin. Still, you're the one with the heat on him. The word is still out that there's a hit out on you."

How did she know? Did Rosemary tell her? "It doesn't matter. I'm leaving tomorrow for South America."

"I know." She turned to leave. "But be careful. I can't help you over there."

From the moment he took a seat on the plane, Isaac felt uncomfortable. He remembered Kennedy's words, *"I can't help you over there."* Had she been keeping an eye on him all along?

Rio was great. But Bahia, Brazil, was even better.

Bahia was rich in black history and culture. Related by their Nigerian ancestors, the Afro-Brazilians were blood cousins, and proud of it. The commonality of their roots was evident from the slave routes from Africa in the seventeenth century to North America, South America, and the Caribbean. The Nigerians brought with them their faith in the Yarbu Gods, which was also practiced in Bahia.

Their faith and culture also carried forth to foods; white and yellow yams, rice with smoked meat, okra, and collard greens were the favored dishes. The exotic flavors of the Bahian cuisine also included Portuguese and African influences; *acaraje* and *moquecas* were favorite seafood dishes.

The sweet scent of coconut groves filled the air as hundreds of tourists, along with Isaac and Miracall, enjoyed viewing the mythical land of happiness.

The grueling trip on the plane and long ride to their hotel hadn't tired her. She shopped for clothes the moment she learned from the hotel attendant where the best shops were. Exhausted, and experiencing a mild case of heat stroke, Isaac was grateful that she allowed him to nap.

"Miracall," he called after her just before she closed the door to their adjoining rooms, "don't buy me anything. I mean it."

Peeking her head back inside his room, she said, "Not even a shirt? I'm sure I could find a cheap—"

"No. You've bought me enough nice things already." He smiled at her. "Now promise me you'll do as I say."

She mouthed "I promise," and headed back out the room.

Restless, he wasn't able to sleep from the moment Miracall had left. His mind was sharp, taking every precaution to check out every hotel attendant who spoke to him or dared to enter his room without invitation.

Isaac was on the telephone discussing tonight's event when he heard Miracall enter her room. He hung up and, after knocking first, opened the door. The amount of packages piled on her bed was a sight to see.

When he managed to lock eyes with her, guilt was written all over her face. "I bought a few gifts for my secretary. And a white-on-white religious garb, celebrated by the ancestral Nigerian women, for Rosemary. Then I thought, I can't go home without buying outfits for Dawn and Tempest."

"What's that?" he asked, pointing to a heavily wrapped burlap package lying against the wall.

"Two masks. The smaller one is a rare wooden dance mask, trimmed in monkey fur and white pigment. The other is a hand-sculptured face that's supposed to ward off evil spirits."

Isaac complained to her that he had no idea where she would put these items in her home; they didn't match her decor at all. And besides, they must have weighed a few hundred pounds and would probably have to be shipped back home. He tried to hide the irritation in his voice when he turned and caught Miracall reaching inside a bag.

Her voice was apologetic. "I'm sorry. I couldn't resist."

Isaac threw her a warning look, but smiled, realizing that he could have guessed she'd buy him something anyway. Inside was an antique hand-carved African ring that was made of silver, ivory, and black onyx.

"The woman said that it's an exact replica of a ring belonging to King Benin from the West Coast of Africa, during the sixteenth century."

She helped him slide it onto his right ring finger. Besides his wedding ring, he'd never owned a piece of jewelry before. Taking her in his arms, he kissed her. "Thank you. It's beautiful."

He couldn't have asked for better company. And God knew, he truly hadn't wanted come to Brazil alone. Though Miracall didn't admit to it, one of the reasons she had agreed to come was something small that was close to her heart—Brazil boasted the largest species of rare butterflies in all the world. And before he left, he'd find the perfect gift to show her his appreciation.

On their second night in Bahia, Isaac and Miracall watched a group of men and women dance the Capoeira. Capoeira was a sort of martial arts dance, and not hard to follow. Both he and Miracall were able to join in, dancing and enjoying the excitement with the townspeople. They didn't speak much English, but everyone was very friendly. And when it came to dancing, no further communication was needed.

"Wow!" Miracall said when they arrived in Pelourinho. "One of the guides told me that the city has been completely restored." She removed her camera from its case and began shooting picture after picture. "There's so much history here, I could stay for a month gathering information for the library, and that still wouldn't be enough time."

Isaac was secretly proud of Miracall. People who walked by stared at her as if she were a celebrity. She had on her new colorful clothes; she was dressed in a hot pink skirt and head wrap, and an off-the-shoulder cotton blouse that showed off her bronzed tan. Several beaded necklaces rested against her firm breasts. Large silver hoops with assorted beads dangled at her ears. Even though there were dozens of very beautiful women whom he was attracted to and who even flirted with him, he could barely keep his eyes off Miracall. She seemed to radiate a clean spirit of energy that he wasn't used to.

"The locals call the city Pelo," she said as she coaxed Isaac to pose for her. Isaac stood in front of the Eletricos nightclub, where he would be performing that evening.

When Miracall learned that *pelourinho* meant "Whipping Post," which originated from the slavery years, she wasn't as impressed with the city.

Trying to change her mood, Isaac said in a perky tone, "Listen to that beat," while he snapped his fingers. Music coming from the small cafés and nightclubs created a festive mood. "Come on, let's go inside." They ate and danced for hours, and caught a taxi back to the hotel.

That night, Isaac was set to perform at Eletricos, and it was extravaganza. There was standing room only. After performing fifteen numbers, the crowd didn't want him to leave. Isaac had never felt so embraced by a people who had no true idea of who he was. No other performance in the States could compare to the freedom and love that he felt in Pelo.

Even more exhilarating was the moment he left the stage. Miracall welcomed him with open arms and led him outside. Hundreds of people were in the hot streets, dressed in scantily clad outfits, dancing a provocative dance. It was the calypso. She'd been taking lessons in Michigan and hadn't told him.

The brick-layered street was flooded with couples. Very few were experienced in dancing the calypso, and the ones who weren't didn't care. Everyone was having a good time. By the third song, Isaac was into it. His and Miracall's bodies blended in one long and delicious tremble, like a chord.

No wonder nothing mattered in Pelo. The music was enchanting, and his partner was even more so. It was only natural that on the night before they were to return home, he began to feel a renewed passion toward Miracall.

He had to take it slow, though—for his sake as well as hers. With the pretense of giving her a pedicure, he lured her into his room.

"I noticed that your dogs were killing you today," he said with a laugh. "Even wearing the most expensive sandals don't hide ashy feet." Carrying a bucket of hot water, he poured the liquid into the shallow tub and squirted into it a healthy helping of foaming footbath.

She bopped him in the head with a hand towel. "Don't talk about my feet. I'm sensitive in that area."

"Shut up and lay back on the pillows. I won't be long."

Everything he needed to complete the job had been readily available in the hotel's gift shop, even the plastic footbath. After her feet had soaked for ten minutes, he lifted her left leg over his shoulder and began to manipulate the toes and muscles of her right foot, up and along her calf, until she exhaled her pleasure.

"When did you learn how to do this?" she teased.

He smiled a shy smile and gathered her small feet into his hands. "One day I'll let you in on a few of my secrets." He massaged her ankles and played with her auburn-painted toes before placing them back into the tepid water. She moaned graciously.

"Sit back and relax. You'll spoil the treat."

Miracall grabbed both handles of her chair and rolled her head back against the back of the seat cushion, then closed her eyes.

An hour later, the peppermint sloughing lotion and foot and leg conditioner lay turned over beside the vacant footbath.

For the life of him, Isaac couldn't remember who touched whom first. Who removed whose clothing first hadn't mattered. They were together, in another climate, another place, where no one and nothing could touch them. Not even their pasts.

Miracall sat up straight, with her legs cradling his. Isaac's spread knees were beneath her thighs. They sat facing each other for a long time, touching each other's bare bodies, stroking one another, until they inched closer together, letting his fingers touch her moist entrance.

He watched her head fall back when he entered her. Her body slid forward, their thighs rising up, buttocks touching, grinding. Reaching as far back behind him as he could, he grabbed the sheets, clutching deep into the mattress to support her body pushing and grinding firmly against him. Together, they climaxed, falling forward, foreheads touching.

They disengaged for what seemed like a long second. Then his arms fell down to her waist. He felt her stomach muscles tighten as she rolled her hips slowly and the soft muscles rippled all through her body.

Her body began to sway like a water plant in a wave, in the most complete display of sexuality that he'd every witnessed. When she shuddered seconds later, he could see the muscles standing out along her neck. Completely out of control, he came with her, with slow, wrenching spasms that seemed to go on for eons. Miracall was still coming when he'd finished. He was surprised by the steady growl of almost unbearable joy issuing from between her clenched teeth. It sounded line a train whistle when she fell against him, trembling.

Unlike his moments with Kennedy, Miracall didn't ask for more. She merely laid her body upon his. Relishing in the moment. Not saying a word until he moved.

"No, please, don't move yet." She stroked his face lovingly. "Stay inside me a while longer. Please."

When he saw her eyes close, he reached over and pulled the covers over their love-soaked bodies. He heard her whisper his name as he stroked her face, then he kissed her.

Her thighs held him close inside her as they fell into a peaceful sleep.

Late that night when he was awakened by the roar of the ocean tide, Isaac thought about their lovemaking. He didn't want to, but it was unavoidable that he would compare it with his special moments with Kennedy.

Isaac felt relieved that Miracall didn't pressure him the next day. He needed time to think. After all, they weren't teenagers, and if the relationship was going to work, time would be the ultimate aphrodisiac.

The afternoon they returned home, Isaac learned from Rosemary that random fires were breaking out all over the city.

"It's not right, Isaac. The men in the Covenant House are being blamed for the crimes. Certain neighborhoods are supposed to be on the lookout for a group of black individuals who were seen fleeing from a recent incident on Freeland Street."

"Stop taking this so personal, Rosemary," Isaac warned. "You can only do so much. Everybody has to take some responsibility. How do you know that your men aren't guilty?"

It was like a slap in her face. Isaac knew why Rosemary was so involved in the Covenant House—primarily because of him and Peyton. Still, she couldn't save the entire black male race in Detroit. And somebody needed to tell her so.

Weeks later, Isaac was walking home from the party store, just a block from his apartment. He had been out of razor blades. Even though Peyton's calls and letters were encouraging, Isaac knew that his son was suffering.

On his way back home, just three houses down from his apartment complex, he spotted a group of teenagers sneaking into the backyard of his neighbor's property. He casually walked up to them. One of the men was lighting a match to a Molotov cocktail. He held it in his hand as he viciously puffed on a cigarette.

"Son, you don't want to do that," Isaac said, trying to reason with the youngster. "Say, let's walk down to the corner. We can talk about what's bothering you. It may be something I can help you with."

He had no idea if his words had any effect on the young man. Isaac felt a flicker of fear, but consoled himself with the knowledge that they were just teenagers. He couldn't help but visualize Peyton's face in each and every one of theirs.

"Man, you should get out of here," one of them said.

Then another spoke up. "Yeah, this ain't none of your business."

"Say, y'all don't want to get in no trouble. Ain't you heard, crime don't pay." Isaac was trying to be funny. Obviously they didn't think he was. Isaac felt a hard blow to the back of his head a few seconds later.

It felt like slow motion, but in real life it was fast-forward. He was hit in the head with a brick. Who were these boys? Then he noticed the emblem on their sleeves. It read: GANGSTER PROPHETS. The teens gathered around him as if he were a science project. What did they plan on doing with him? He felt a kick in his abdomen, then another in his head. Why were they trying to harm him? He was only trying to help. Someone was going through his pants, feeling for his wallet. He felt a blow from an iron pipe against his head. Instantly, all the lights went out. All his previous thoughts were gone as quickly as the scent of a vulture.

"That's for J-Rock. Tell your son he should've kept his mouth shut." He felt someone rummaging through his pockets and inserting two coins. The last thing he heard was someone saying that Peyton had broken rule 1919—the code of silence, in gang parlance.

Isaac vaguely remembered seeing a quick flash of red. But he didn't see or hear a man snicker in the alley, then stealthily walk away.

Less than thirty minutes later, when he was transported to Grace Hospital, he had no idea that his skull was fractured. He felt numb. What he did remember was someone lighting a cigarette. No. It was the sour stench of a cheap cigar. He remembered seeing the curl of blue smoke in the alley just moments before he became unconscious. In those few seconds, he thought about the last conversation that he had had with Peyton.

"No one understands us, man. We never meant to harm no one." Isaac's thoughts intertwined with the memory that he had never intended to hurt Becky.

Why couldn't people understand that most criminals saw themselves as victims?

A Breath of Scandal

"Why Miracall? Of all the women he could be dating, why her?" Rosemary fumed.

Gary was sitting in a chair against the wall, near the end of stage. His legs were crossed and his hand was tucked under his chin. He hadn't provided any thoughts to her continued questions about Miracall. She had the distinct feeling that Gary knew something but wouldn't say.

For the past thirteen days, Isaac lay in a coma at Grace Hospital. His skull was fractured, one of his lungs had collapsed, and the walls of his sinus cavity were broken. He looked like he was two seconds from death. It hurt Rosemary to see him lying in that bed so helplessly.

She thought, *At least he's alive.* She was reliving the pain and sorrow she used to experience every time she went to Jefferson. To see him, an unidentifiable numbness settled in her stomach.

Twelve days passed before the doctors gave Rosemary any hope that the comatose Isaac would survive. To Rosemary's chagrin, Miracall was there every moment she could be, crying like a newborn baby.

Upon seeing this woman at her husband's bedside, Kennedy had confided in Rosemary that she would say her prayers at home.

The following Friday, Rosemary was knee-deep in the second round of rehearsals. Tomorrow, the Fashion Share Day for homeless, addicted, and needy women would be held at Mother Bethel. Rosemary was the emcee, and she wished that she could gracefully bow out at this time. She had entirely too much on her mind.

However, one look at the church classrooms and she had to feel encouraged. Donations from businesses and church members filled every available space. The wares included everything from lotions and perfumes to belts, hosiery, jewelry, shoes, and purses. And, of course, there were tons of clothes.

But this was no ordinary clothes closet filled with secondhand finds. Many of the items were brand new, purchased especially for the occasion. The women would also receive makeovers and haircuts donated by several large chain stores. As part of the program, the physically and emotionally challenged women shopped for free at the church "galleria."

Rosemary remembered telling the sponsors, when she asked for assistance, "Just because they've lost a bit a their self-esteem and are having difficulties making ends meet doesn't erase the need to feel pretty and put on a flattering dress. These women need to know that they're special, too."

Mother Bethel's church bulletin stressed the previous month that the event would not be the typical church fashion show and tea. "One hundred best-dressed ladies of the church will not parade across the stage to show off their designer dresses," the bulletin read. "Our desire is to share the love of Jesus Christ with these women so that they can ultimately feel good about themselves."

Early on Saturday morning, church members, including Rosemary, picked up women from various shelters and brought them to the church, where they had a cookout and fellowship together. Rosemary could see that the attention the women were given was overwhelming, they were fussed over so.

Later, a woman nearing the end of her six-month treatment program told Rosemary, "Detroit has been good to me. I came here to get my life together. But I'm told that the real recovery doesn't begin until you're out of the program."

Rosemary thought about Isaac. Even though he'd had a few bumps and hadn't become a journalist like he'd planned, he was still making it just fine.

"Do you trust in the Lord, Sister April?"

"Yes, Lord," the young woman said with conviction.

Rosemary wrapped a consoling arm around her. "Then, you get out there today and strut your stuff. Know that God is blessing you, today and every day that you abide by his word."

Tears filled the woman's eyes, "Thank you, Pastor Rosemary."

An hour later, the show began.

"Look at her," Rosemary said, smiling. "Who would believe this woman has five children? Her stomach is so flat she could bounce a tennis ball on it." She nodded to the young girl of twenty-four, all the while praying for her strength to kick a drug habit that had destroyed her life and left her homeless since age fourteen.

One special moment took Rosemary by surprise. A forty-eight-year-old woman took Rosemary's microphone just after she'd been introduced.

Dozens of stitches from a recent stabbing were still red and swollen on her pretty face. "I'm only here by God's grace." She walked onstage and strutted as if she were auditioning for the Miss Universe contest.

"Hold up, people. We've got a drama queen here tonight. Check out Sister Lamika," Rosemary said, shuffling her cards. "She's selected a floor-length pastel-pink chiffon gown. Sister Lamika has even picked out the perfect rhinestone earrings, matching silver pumps, and has even found a positively striking silver-feathered boa to complement her ensemble. My, my, don't she look lovely tonight?"

The audience began to stand and applaud. Rosemary clapped her hands and encouraged the young woman to take a second strut across the stage.

"Now look at this one," Rosemary said, feeling full of joy. "Her name is April Blanchard. Ain't she fine, strutting her stuff up here tonight? April is wearing a conservative black-and-white houndstooth two-piece suit, with an orange, green, and black print scarf adorning the jacket." She paused as the audience clapped. "She has on black basket-weaved patent-leather loafers by Gucci." They clapped again. "And girls, the loafers are a size six. Tell me who's even heard of a woman wearing those itty-bitty shoes these days. Now, ladies, wouldn't you agree that this outfit is a winning combination? You know, I swear this child looks just like I did when I was twenty-five. Don't y'all agree?"

The audience clapped and cheered and Rosemary began to feel better. She knew that what the church was doing for these individuals tonight couldn't be measured in words, or money.

Afterward, Rosemary felt rejuvenated and exhausted at the same time. It reminded her of the last time that she and Jesse had made love. A broad smile eased across her lips until she spotted an unfamiliar car parked outside her home.

Kennedy didn't bother to get out of her car—she waited for Rosemary to come around to her open window. "I hope I didn't scare you. But I've been waiting for you to come home."

"Has something happened to Isaac?" When Kennedy shook her head no, Rosemary relaxed. She was terribly exhausted and couldn't wait to get into bed. She especially wanted to feel Jesse's arms around her right about now. "I can call you in the morning."

"No!"

The alarm in her voice frightened Rosemary. "Come on inside, Kennedy, so we can talk about what's bothering you."

"It's too late." Her hands were shaking. "Too late. Things are getting ready to blow up. My partner, Lindsey Royale, was indicted on drug charges." Rosemary could smell the ripe scent of alcohol on her breath. Still, she respected her sister-in-law enough to listen. "Back in the eighties, Royale was a guard at Jefferson Penitentiary. He was accused of buying drugs for the prisoners. They're holding that against him, even though it was never proven that he actually did it."

"I don't understand why you're telling me all of this." And she really didn't want to discuss Kennedy's lover. She tried not to sound annoyed. "Maybe you should be talking to an attorney."

"You don't understand. The same person that set up Royale also set up Isaac with the drugs that were found in his car. This stuff is so deeply connected, even judges are implicated."

Rosemary remembered that Loren had once been a circuit court judge before he became governor. It was scarier than she wanted to think about.

"We were this close, Royale and I," she said, crossing two fingers together. "Now I have to go on by myself."

"What do you mean, Kennedy? Don't jeopardize your life. Nothing is worth that."

"Yes, something is—my family."

"What are you planning on doing?"

Kennedy started the motor, drowning out Rosemary's protests.

"If it takes my last breath, I'll find out who implicated Isaac and Royale."

Heroes for Sale

Rosemary scooted her chair closer to Peyton and placed her hands on his shoulders. She brought him toward her, intending to hug him, but stopped and stared at him. He reminded her so much of Isaac. She gasped, then grinned, pulling him toward her again. They hugged each other, both holding back tears. She could hold him forever. She pulled away and reached for her purse, which was close to her chair, and removed a tissue and a mint. She wiped her burning eyes and popped the mint into her dry mouth.

It was the first Sunday before Labor Day, the day when most kids were looking forward to starting school. Not so for Peyton Coleman, and the hundreds of young men who were also locked up in this spotless new facility. Their lessons would be taught behind bars. He'd been transferred to the Bad Axe Youth Correctional Facility five days earlier, and it was the first time that Rosemary had been able to physically touch her nephew.

"How's my dad doing, Auntee Rosemary?" Peyton asked.

He wore the regulation blue jeans and jean shirt. They hung as loose as negligence on his lanky body. It hurt her to see him so skinny. *Isaac can object all he wants to,* she thought, *but this child is going to stay with me at least a week so I can put some meat on his bones.*

"He's still healing. The doctors said that it's going to take a while before he'll be back to normal. During that time, he has to undergo physical therapy for his shoulder three times a week."

"I didn't realize how much I'd miss him." His brows nearly touched at the center before he spoke again. "I miss my mom, too. She keeps sending me money and clothes. That's cool. But she's only been down to see me a few times. That's not like her. Do you know what's going on, Auntee?"

She felt trapped into keeping more secrets. Kennedy believed that Isaac was set up in a drug deal, and that even the beating Isaac had received was related. Rosemary kept silent about what she knew; she'd made a promise to Isaac that she wouldn't mention what she knew to Peyton or Kennedy.

"I know your mother's working long hours on a special case right now. I can't say any more. I promised her that I wouldn't." Rosemary could feel the sweat building on her palms, and wiped them with the tissue. "Why don't you call her tonight?" She checked her watch and didn't notice that when she did, her hand was trembling.

Peyton eyed her suspiciously. "Why are you acting so nervous?"

She stood up and began to gather her things. "I've got to go, son."

"Auntee, talk to me, please. I'm not a little kid anymore." There was urgency in his voice. "Is my mom in trouble?"

In her entire life, she'd never felt so burdened. She could feel the blood in her heart beating, pulse after pulse. What words could she say to comfort him? The Bible said that one kind word could warm three winter months. *"Let the words of my mouth . . . be acceptable to you, O Lord, my rock and my redeemer."*

She took a deep breath and said, "Your mother is a policewoman. A very good one. It would not be right if I told you my thoughts without your having spoken with your mother first."

"How can I become a better person, Pastor Jones?" April asked Rosemary. "I have habits and traits that I want to get rid of, but I don't know where to start. You know me. I know you know that I'm trying. But it's *so* hard."

Rosemary thought for a moment. Just as she was about to leave the shelter that afternoon, April had pulled her to the side and asked if she could spare her a few moments.

"Begin by realizing you cannot become the person you should be without God's help; then ask him to help you become the person He wants you to be." She thought about Peyton and Isaac. Though they didn't realize it yet, they both were becoming the people God wanted them to be. "God has a plan for each of us, and the greatest thing we can ever do in life is to find His plan and then do it. You might ask, What is God's plan for me? His plan for you is to become a part of his family, because he loves you and wants you to spend eternity with him in Heaven. Christ came into this world so we could be forgiven for our sins and reconciled to God."

Tears filled April's eyes when she looked at Rosemary.

Realizing the woman was on the verge of a breakthrough, Rosemary ran a soothing hand up and down April's arm. "The most important thing you can do right now is to ask Christ to come into your life and commit yourself to him. The Bible says, 'To all who received him, to those who believed in his name, he gave the right to become children of God.' Don't miss taking that first step, but open your heart to Christ today. You need his forgiveness, and you need the help he alone can give."

April fell on her knees, crying. Rosemary began to pray, asking God to save her. When Rosemary heard the young woman begin to speak in tongues, she got on her knees and began praying. She had no idea how much time had passed when April showed all the signs of receiving the Holy Ghost.

Rosemary's heart felt so full when she drove home, she couldn't wait to share her joy with Jesse. Once home, the morose look on Jesse's face told her that something was seriously wrong.

"I got bad news, darlin'."

"Oh, my God, not Isaac!" she quietly screamed. Jesse helped her to a seat at the kitchen table.

"No." He wrapped an arm around her shoulders and pulled her close to his chest. "It's Kennedy." His arm tightened. "Now, don't! Don't! We can handle this together."

Rosemary didn't want to believe the worst, though her gut told her that she was gone. "Is she hurt? What hospital is she in? Are you going to drive me? Hurry up, we've got to go."

"Wait." He shook her shoulders gently and looked deeply into her eyes. "She was shot. Gary called and gave me as much information as he could. Very few people knew that Kennedy was working undercover on a narcotics case. It went down in Highland Park, near the Kowalski Sausage Plant on the east side of Detroit. He said things had gotten so crazy that the police were shooting at the police."

"You mean beasts," she mumbled under her breath. Rosemary barely heard his words. But the words of the Lord were much stronger: *"And God saw that the wickedness of man was great in the earth."* Who's going to tell Peyton?

Jesse's voice was flat. "Apparently Kennedy knew all about the crooked cops. She never realized that these same cops would retaliate so openly."

"My God. Don't say any more. Where is she?"

"I think they're taking her body to the morgue at Grace Hospital."

"The morgue!" Even though her husband worked as a funeral director, she'd never gotten used to that word. It was the final insult to a human life. Kennedy was dead.

295

Jesse drove Rosemary to Grace Hospital. Together, they identified her body. When she'd called Isaac, no one answered. She left a message and had thought that he would meet them there, but he hadn't shown up yet.

Only moments after viewing her bullet-ridden body, the reports began to come in on the eleven o'clock news. The story from her captain, who was still at the scene, said that they weren't sure whether the officer's death was in the line of duty or not. She had not been authorized by her supervisor to be at this establishment tonight. Another officer was already handling the case.

"What difference does that make?" Rosemary was outraged. "How dare they try and degrade this woman by saying that her death was in vain. Would she be less dead if she'd died off-duty?"

At that moment, a man came in. Rosemary had never seen him before, but instincts said that he knew her. He was heading straight for her. There were tears in his eyes. This man had been Kennedy's lover.

"Hello, I'm Detective Royale." He took the empty seat beside her. "You must be Rosemary."

"That I am." She introduced him to Jesse. Afterward, she had to wipe her eyes with a white handkerchief, trying not to lose sight of reality. Peyton was in prison, Isaac was nearly killed, and now Kennedy's body lay prone in a cold, refrigerated drawer. It was too coincidental. It looked like someone was trying to destroy an entire family.

She thought about Loren and Becky. Could a man that high up in office still be stirring the pot? Could he still be holding a vendetta thirteen years later?

"I know this is hard for you. Somehow, I've got to make you understand. Kennedy knew who put the hit out on Isaac. She figured it out, but wouldn't tell me. She left today on a tip from an informer."

"Alone?"

"Yes. It so happens that I'm still suspended from duty. But there was no way, even if I was fired, that I'd let her go meet an informer without backup."

"Why would she take a chance like that?" Jesse was silent beside her. She was sure that he was thinking the same thought.

Royale looked brokenhearted. "Because of your brother. She loved him, Rosemary. I was just filling in for a while. It didn't matter, I still loved her."

"I'm sorry." What else could she say?

"Before Isaac left for Brazil, Kennedy had a good idea who had set him up. Now she was sure. For almost a year now, Kennedy and I, as well as two other policemen, have been running a secret investigation. Some heavy hitters are the subject of the inquisition." He shook his head and breathed heavily. "These days, you can't tell the elected officials from the criminals out on the streets." He began crying tears nearly as thick as blood. His last words thundered. "That's why most of the officers don't know who to trust."

"But you and Kennedy did, I take it?"

"Yes. For the most part, we did."

While Royale spoke lovingly about how he would miss Kennedy, Rosemary found herself getting angry.

"Most people don't realize that, on average, the female cops bring more honesty to the job. They're less willing to take bribes. And Kennedy was no exception."

"Tell us something we don't know," Jesse spoke up.

"There's still a problem, though. Isaac's life is still in danger. So take care. Trust no one. Especially cops—you never know."

When he got up and left, Jesse and Rosemary looked at each other as if they'd just seen a ghost.

Immediately, Rosemary went to the phone and tried Isaac again. She could hear the tears in his voice and knew that he'd gotten her message. All she could muster to say was, "She's gone."

Isaac listened as Rosemary described the morbid details of identifying Kennedy's body at the morgue.

The moment she said the words *Kennedy's body,* Isaac felt a sharp pain beginning to wrench his body. The pain felt like someone had stabbed him with a large screwdriver and was turning it ever so slowly, wrapping his intestines around it till his body felt as empty as a nine-millimeter shell.

Kennedy's funeral was set for the following Saturday. Rosemary helped Isaac with the arrangements. Kennedy had named him and Peyton as her beneficiaries. It took a while to contact her family, who lived in Minnesota and Arkansas. They had to wait until the majority of them could get time off from work either to fly or to drive to Detroit.

The nights were becoming cooler, and the air took on the color and tang of harvest time. The sound of people raking leaves could be heard during the day. And the autumnal evening suggested a chill absent in summer.

When the day of Kennedy's funeral arrived, Isaac seemed more disoriented than usual. Rosemary felt that, as sick as he still was, he was taking matters into his own hands to find Kennedy's murderer.

Since the mid-nineties, a fee was charged for two officers to escort an inmate to a funeral service. All of their expenses had to be paid for in advance: breakfast, lunch, gas money, as well as their time. It didn't matter when the two officers delivered Peyton to Mother Bethel Church. Rosemary said her prayers for the umpteenth time when she saw that they had removed the handcuffs. Isaac did remember to send ahead the clothes that Peyton would wear today. He was dressed in a black suit, white shirt, and black and silver tie. She'd never seen him look more like a man before.

"You've got to be the strong male in the family now." Rosemary hugged her nephew, then stood on her tiptoes to kiss him on the forehead. She told him that his dad and mom were both heroes—Isaac for trying to spare the teenagers who beat him from going to jail, and his mom for trying to save his dad's life, despite putting her own in jeopardy.

"Did anyone ever tell you that your father's name came from the Bible?" He shook his head no. "Look in Genesis seventeen-nineteen. It says: 'And God said, Sarah thy wife shall bear thee a son indeed; and thou shalt call his name Isaac: and I will establish my covenant with him for an everlasting covenant, and with his seed after him.'

"So, you see, your dad is special, and so are you, Peyton." When she saw the tears in his eyes, she hugged him again. "Now, you go on over there and meet your relatives. They haven't seen you since you were just a little thing."

The church began to fill. Most of the officers from the Fourteenth Precinct came. Kennedy was given the full honor of a policeman's funeral.

Jesse came up beside Rosemary. He seemed to anticipate lately when she couldn't hold herself together. It was all too much. "I'll get Peyton. It's almost time. You ready?" She nodded.

When Peyton joined them, he said, "Aunt Rosemary, I'd like to read a poem that I wrote last week about my mom . . . if it's okay."

A soft thud from the front doors opening made everyone turn around. It was Isaac. He was leaning on Miracall, and appeared to still be in pain.

"Hi, son," he said, extending his arm. "Come over here and give me a hug. I ain't seen you in so long."

Tears blended into love. Nothing but God's grace could have kept Rosemary standing. She dropped to her knees, and she felt Jesse strain to lift her back up. Even Jesse had tears in his eyes.

The music began to play, and Rosemary took a few seconds to hug her brother before she hurried up to the pulpit.

Kennedy's beautiful face looked so angelic lying in her casket. Jesse had taken special care to make sure she looked like herself. She wore a cream suit with an off-white ruffled blouse, similar to the outfit that she'd worn at Rosemary's confirmation. She didn't look tired or worn out. With her hands crisscrossed across her chest, she looked at peace.

"Let us stand."

The choir behind her sang two selections before Rosemary read Kennedy's eulogy. She thanked everyone for the beautiful flowers and the loving telegrams.

For fifteen minutes she talked about the soul lying before them now—her sister-in-law. She watched Peyton's and Isaac's faces as she recounted several memories about Kennedy that she'd never shared with them. She had begun crying midway through her speech, and now she was losing her voice.

Then, remembering Peyton's request, she extended a hand toward her nephew. "Come on up, son." She wiped the sweat from her forehead and took a sip of ice water that was placed beside her. "Her son, Peyton Coleman, would like to read a poem that he's written about his mom."

Peyton didn't appear to be the least bit nervous. He looked down at his mother and smiled. Rosemary could see him whisper, "I love you, Mom."

When he began, Rosemary saw Isaac brace himself. None of them had ever seen Peyton so outspoken before.

"I had a dream about a dove." Peyton's voice was loud and strong:

> I had a dream about a dove. Some people say
> That mourning doves are a sign of death

Or that they mean tragedy
Or danger.
Doves,
I think are beautiful
And,
Why would a beautiful bird mean such terrible things?
But I did have a dream,
I was in a world of clouds
I was floating around in heaven's atmosphere
And there were doves
Everywhere
Beautiful birds.
In a beautiful dream, they couldn't mean terror
Maybe happiness
Joy
Love

Half the congregation was crying by now. Isaac was openly crying, unashamed and proud. Peyton was crying, too, but his voice was filled with conviction and strength.

I had a dream about a dove. And it was beautiful
Maybe one day, I'll prove wrong of those people
Who think such things of beautiful birds.
But even if I don't I'll still remember,
My dream about doves
They somehow show truth
And loneliness
But at the same time courage
They glide through the wind
Like cookies through milk
There're many things that I could say about doves, about my mom
But I'd run out of words of elegantness

He paused, then said, "I love you, Mom." He walked down from the pulpit and went to kiss his mother before returning to his seat.

Isaac stood, tears in his eyes. Anyone could see the love that was expressed between father and son. Rosemary couldn't remember anything more beautiful until she heard her nephew say: "No matter what, we've got to keep the family together—stay together. We have to get past the lies, the untruths."

Without saying so, Isaac knew that Peyton had taken on the responsibility of keeping all of them together. "We're a family. Nothing is more important than that."

A solo was sung by a member of the youth choir while the congregation paid their last respects to Kennedy. To everyone's surprise, including Isaac's, Bernie and his friends played "Nearer, My God, to Thee," while Isaac shook his head to the beat.

It was one of the most beautiful ceremonies she'd ever conducted. Beautiful because so much love had been shared in such a short period of time.

She called for the funeral director to close the casket. The weeping became louder, and Rosemary prayed silently that she wouldn't fall victim to her emotions.

With hope for the future in her heart, Rosemary took another look at Peyton. Then at Isaac, Jesse, and, finally, Miracall. She envisioned a proud smile on Kennedy's face, and felt comforted. She gathered her wits about her, lifted her head. Her smile shone through her tears.

"All heads bowed and every eye closed."

Forever and a Day

Isaac rode in the car with Peyton when he was being escorted back to prison. He remembered his son saying: "Man, right before I ran away from home, I found those letters you wrote my mom while you were in prison. I read them. I was so confused. How could you love her that much and not come home? The more I read, the less I understood. I mean, thirty and forty pages long, Dad—that's real love. Your letters are what gave me the encouragement to write that poem about Mom. Some of the words came from your letters, you know."

Isaac smiled. It was the first time he'd heard his son call him "Dad."

Later, he and Miracall were relaxing at his apartment, drinking hot chocolate with marshmallows, watching a video. Miracall had changed her clothes and was wearing one of Isaac's gray sweat outfits. It fit heavily on her small body.

Isaac was dressed in comfortable attire, wearing black-and-white-striped pajamas and a tailored royal blue housecoat with the initials I.C. emblazoned on his left chest pocket. Warming his feet were a pair of royal blue suede slippers.

"You know, Isaac, Rosemary's sermon today was really inspiring. I'm impressed by the title she chose, 'The Flip Side of Sin.' It seemed to tie in perfectly with what's happening in today's society. There's so much corruption in the police department, one doesn't know who to trust anymore."

"In Genesis three-fifteen, God gave us hope for life," Rosemary had begun. "A savior will take away the sins of the world and give each of us a right to the tree of life. Sin is the cause for our many failures in life. It brought destruction without favor. It is the only thing that we as a people come into this world with, according to Psalms fifty-one-five. And it will be the only thing that we take out if we don't make certain changes before it's too late.

"Sin is the transgression of the law, first book of John three-four. But there is a flip side of sin. The only thing that can make wrong right is God's grace and his unmerited favor for us; it lies between all of our problems. Grace can bring about peace where there was confusion. It can pick us up out of a mired and unsettled lifestyle.

"God's grace can give us a heart to forgive those that hurt us in the past." Looking directly at Isaac, she had finished by saying, "The down side of sin is God's wrath and his Judgment."

"I watched you, Isaac." Miracall crossed her ankles and folded her hands tightly on the table. "That sermon hit a chord in you. I felt it, too. Even Jesse was visibly moved."

Isaac did feel moved when Rosemary spoke. And he remembered her words. He couldn't get the phrase *the flip side* out of his mind. Those words had another significance that he couldn't put his finger on. When the telephone on the wall rang, he was deep in thought. "Hello."

"Hi, Isaac, it's Rosemary. I need to talk to you."

He could tell that she'd been crying. "Sure. I can be there in fifteen minutes." When Miracall flicked off the set and rose to clear the coffee table, he motioned for her to stay. It was odd, he thought. Lately, the couple spent more time at his house than they did at hers. He wasn't positive, but she seemed so comfortable here. "I'm all ears, sis."

"No. I should come over." She was crying again. "Jesse's sleeping and I don't want to wake him."

Miracall had brought over the old movie *The Glenn Miller Story*. It was Isaac's first time viewing it. It was nearly over by the time Rosemary knocked on the door.

"I've got company I hope you don't mind, but we'd already made plans for the night." Isaac couldn't look her in the eye. Fornication even at forty seemed sinister in his sister's eyes. Still, he was grown and his life was truly his business.

Rosemary said a polite hello to Miracall, who immediately excused herself and headed for the bedroom. "No," Rosemary said to her, "don't go. It's time that I accepted the fact that you two are serious about one another."

Rosemary walked over and stood in front of the couch. She looked around, observing the candles on the dining room table. Dozens of colorful butterflies were suspended in a mobile above it. On the corner of the table was a small cup of half-drunk hot chocolate. The apartment definitely had a woman's touch. It was much different than she'd ever seen it before. She fell back onto the couch, taking a pillow into her lap as she looked up at Isaac.

He had no idea what she was going to talk about, especially in front of Miracall. He knew that she was still hurting about Kennedy.

Rosemary began by talking about the funeral, even reciting specific lines from Peyton's poem. Every sentence seemed to make her break down more, and Isaac wasn't sure what to do. Miracall's eyes seemed to say, *"Let her get it out. She'll be okay."*

"Have you two been listening to the news?" Rosemary asked.

"No," Miracall spoke up. "We've been watching videos."

"The Mayor's mansion was burned to the ground this evening."

Isaac picked up the remote and flicked the TV on to the local news. It was 11:05, near the beginning of the broadcast, and they were showing the live-cam pictures of the destruction.

"For those of you who've never seen the mansion," the reporter began, "it's located a little east of the Belle Isle Bridge. The five-thousand-square-foot Italianate mansion overlooked the Detroit River, and had a breathtaking panoramic view of Windsor, Canada, where a ten-story Canadian Club neon sign landmarked the spot where the famous whiskey was manufactured." Pictures were shown from behind the house before it was burned.

"The seventy-year-old mansion looked entirely different after its remodeling in 1994, when Mayor Prescott was first elected. There were seven bedrooms, nine bathrooms, two patios, a bowling alley, an outdoor swimming pool, and a private boathouse. Nearly two hundred thousand dollars was donated for all the renovations that took six months to complete. Four hundred gallons of paint were needed to repaint walls that hadn't seen fresh paint in decades. Next, the main focus began with the purchase of new furniture for the living room, dining room, and lower family room by Henredon, and oversized contemporary pieces in sage green and toasty taupe by Marge Carson. Custom Kraft Maid cherry cabinets, with bone-colored Corian countertops and Thermador appliances were provided to create a live-in kitchen. Honeywell donated a computerized security system. Flame Furnace was responsible for replacing an old boiler with five new furnaces. The master suite received as much attention with the purchase of an Aqua Glass octagonal whirlpool and glass enclosed shower by Masco. Even valuable African-American artwork was loaned to the Prescotts to make their home a showpiece."

"That's all gone now," Rosemary interrupted, looking as if she were in a trance. "It's nothing but smoke and ashes."

Miracall said, "I'm forgetting my manners. Let me fix you some hot chocolate, Rosemary. Or maybe you'd like some tea?"

"Nothing, thank you. I'll never sleep tonight." Rosemary's eyes and mind wandered again. Turning, she spotted a snapshot of Miracall and Isaac pegged next to Isaac's work schedule on the kitchen wall. The scenic backdrop, she assumed, was when they'd gone to the Caribbean. She was alarmed by their closeness, and turned quickly to look out the window at the sounds of horns blowing. It seemed as if even the cars were angry these days. Trees shed auburn leaves, making a short flight through the air, dying away like the peal of cathedral bells. She picked up the pillow that sat in her lap. "I don't know if you know how many rumors I hear. It's been rumored since the mayor took office that he's changed loyalty. He and Loren used to fight in public, but personally, I'm told, they're very good friends."

Miracall spoke up. "I wouldn't say they're good friends, Rosemary. Loren doesn't befriend anyone unless money is involved."

"This is over my head, ladies." Isaac went over and sat beside his sister. "Sis, I never understood politics. What I'd like to know is what is the police department doing about finding Kennedy's killer?"

Even though he was crying on the inside and his tears were begging to be shown, he kept his feelings hidden.

Miracall spoke up. "The Democrats in the city are embarrassed by Mayor Precott's administration. And because of all the obvious corruption going on in the police department and Kennedy's murder, well, all hell has broken loose."

Just then the news replayed, once again, the smoke and rubbish left from the destruction of the mayor's mansion.

"Some people probably believe that it's a righteous destruction," Miracall said. And both Isaac and Rosemary were astounded that she could be so objective. "The feeling is that the punishment of his sin will so exactly answer the sin that was committed and will be visible in the punishment."

Rosemary looked amazed. No, *dazed* was a better word.

"Sis, you've got to relax. The doctors warned you about getting excited."

"I'm not the one who's been beaten." Her words stung and Isaac felt his heart lurch.

"Look at me," he said, getting up from the short sofa. He got down in the middle of the floor and did twenty-five Chinese push-ups, clapping his hands between each one. "I'm strong as instinct. It will take more than a few teenagers to get me down."

"It's unbelievable how quickly he's healed," Miracall said.

Rosemary's tone became grave. "If we didn't believe in the unbelievable, what would happen to faith?"

The cuckoo clock struck twelve. Time had been their fashionable host, and now quietly shook Isaac by the hand.

305

"You'd better get home, Rosemary. If Jesse wakes up, he'll be worried. We can talk tomorrow. I'll be over early."

"No. I need to say this now." She started to cry fresh tears, and Isaac thought that he would break down crying himself if she didn't stop soon. "I never told you how much I worried about being alone. I wondered, What if something happened to Jesse? Who would take care of me? Who can I depend on?"

"Don't say things like that, sis. You know Jesse and me will always be there for you."

"I've resented for so long not being able to bear children. I'm proud that you were able to, Isaac." She paused. "I treated you like my child. In the beginning, I resented Kennedy. She took you from me. But when she said she'd divorced you after you went to prison, I felt like I had my child back. I began to feel needed again. Then I found out that you weren't divorced. I felt that same emptiness all over again."

Isaac was overwhelmed. His eyes filled with tears, and for the life of him he didn't want her to go on. Now he understood why she was so opposed to his dating Miracall. It was like losing him all over again.

Rosemary turned toward him. "Jesse warned me to let you live your life. I wouldn't listen. I kept right on trying to dictate what you should do, where you should work. And then, when you started dating Miracall, I felt you were making a mistake."

Miracall said, "I never meant to come between you two."

Rosemary rose to leave. "It's not your fault, Miracall. I've been extremely selfish. Being a pastor, I couldn't hold this burden on my heart any longer. I thought I'd be the center of your life forever, Isaac. Forever and a day. I was wrong. I've kept too much from you already. I'm sorry."

Miracall was openly moved. "I wish I had a sister that cared as much for me." She went over and hugged Rosemary.

Isaac watched his sister leave, too emotional to speak. *What did she mean, "I've kept too much from you?"* It didn't make any sense.

5

The Prayer for Restoration

Restore Us

The joy of our heart is ceased; our dance is turned into mourning. The crown is fallen from our head: woe unto us, that we have sinned! Turn thou us unto thee, O Lord, and we shall be turned; renew our days as of old.

—Lam. 5:15, 16, 21

Imitation of Life

"I know everything about you, boy. The problem is that some folks have been lying to your stupid behind for years."

"I didn't come here for a history lesson, Eli. I came here to talk about Kennedy. I believe you know why she was killed."

They were in the back of Eli's garage, the money-maker of his chop shop. It was 7:15. All the workers had gone home for the day. When Eli welcomed him in, Isaac could tell the man was stoned out of his mind. Instinct told him to leave right then, but his curiosity wouldn't let him go.

As the beneficiary, Isaac didn't have the heart to drive Kennedy's new Cadillac. It would be parked in the garage until Peyton decided when and if he wanted to keep it. The insurance had paid for everything—the house, the car—and even left some cash for Peyton when he reached the age of twenty-one. Isaac had had no clue that Kennedy had been prepared in case she died. He wasn't.

Eli took a seat at his desk and exposed the jumbo joint that he'd obviously been enjoying before Isaac arrived. "Kennedy's dead. There ain't no bringing her back." He snickered. "She wasn't nothing. A ho, just like your mammy was."

Isaac grabbed Eli's bony body and lifted him up from his seat before he'd realized what he'd done. He popped him in the mouth and dropped him back in the chair. "Now, you watch your mouth. You're talking about my son's mother."

"It's cool, man. Cool it. You been gone a long time, man. I ain't gonna lie. I tried to get it on with Kennedy. She thought I was stupid, that I didn't know she was leading me on to get information about my business. The police know who's dealing drugs in the city. I ain't nobody's fool. Shit."

In his imagination, Isaac visualized Kennedy trying to come on to Eli. The thought sickened him. It was a comfort to know that she hadn't succumbed to seducing him. He had to remind himself that even though Kennedy was gone, he was sure Eli had been involved in her murder in some way. Isaac got up. "That shit smells awful." He frowned. "I'll be seeing you around. I'm outa here." He was about to go when Eli broke out in uncontrollable laughter.

"Like I said, man, Kennedy was a ho, screwing that partner of hers every time she got a chance. I seen them sneaking around town several times. She thought she was so slick," he snickered. "Yeah, like I said, just like yo mammy was."

What was this fool talking about? Resting his hands on the desk, he looked down into Eli's ugly face. "I realize you're high, but, man, you don't know a thing about my mother. I'll remember this, Eli. I'll see you when I get off probation."

Eli was nonplussed. "Hey, cool it. I thought you knew about your infamous mammy. Obviously Rosie-tosie ain't told you doodley-squat."

"I don't need to hear about my mother from you, fool. Just know I'll be keeping an eye on you, Eli."

Eli ignored him. "I heard that she looked like a black Lana Turner," Eli hissed. "You know, long legs, narrow hips, smoky, eager eyes, and that deep, husky voice that men died for. Yeah, she's the reason why men go to the bars to see sexy women like her, because they got pretty at home. Yes, sir, she would have been a real star today."

"Shut up, asshole!"

"No, you should know, back in the day, women weren't that tough then. Then again, I'm forgetting Kennedy. She fell into that category, too."

It was then that Isaac reached over the desk and punched him in his mouth. Eli didn't even try to fight him. He just looked at Isaac pitifully and smiled. Isaac said, "You're a low-life garter snake. And if I live to be forty-one, I'll make sure that you get what you've got coming to you, even if it means rotting in hell!"

"That's where your mammy is. She's the one that set up Paps. Lied to the poor man."

"Shut up." Isaac backhanded him across the face. It didn't do any good. Eli was out of control now, laughing like a parrot who was trying to convince a patron to buy him.

"Thirty-nine years ago. That man killed your mama, but it was brought out in court that she had it coming."

Once again, Isaac slapped him. This time Eli fell to the floor. Blood oozed from his mouth, and slowly, Eli smiled and, with the back of his hand, licked it. "Nothing like true-blue blood. Unlike you, my brother. You ain't nothing but a half-breed black Jew."

Isaac raised his hand to hit him, then stopped. What good would it do? He was so high, he probably wouldn't even feel it.

Nothing made sense. He didn't understand. Until he heard Eli's final words: "Ask your sister, Rosemary. She knows."

Isaac's first thought was Miracall. She would know exactly how to go about finding information. After all, that was her job. But no, he didn't want her to know that much about him. He wanted to keep the dark secret, if it was one, within their family.

He checked the clock on the dashboard. It was eight-thirty when he backed out of the collision shop. His first thought was to head downtown to the main library. From all the time that he and Peyton had spent there last year, he remembered that the library closed at five-thirty on Friday nights.

Common sense told him that Eli was lying and he was wasting his time. Then, he thought, if he didn't check it out, he would never know the truth. And he had to know. Even a drunk couldn't conjure up facts like he just did.

The next morning, he arrived on the Cass Street side of the Detroit Public Library, where the Burton Historical Collection was located. There were at least five librarians on duty. Every one of them was busy. When one finally gave him a few minutes, she seemed so short-tempered that Isaac was just about to give up on the whole endeavor.

Isaac told her that the information he needed was approximately forty years old. He was looking for a woman's name in particular—Ellen Coleman. Remembering the year that was engraved on his mother's grave, he told the woman that a murder was involved.

311

"We don't keep that type of information out here. I'll have to go back into the archives." She rolled her eyes at Isaac. "That will take a while. Excuse me."

If she didn't find anything, he would ask her to cross-reference his father's death a year later. Something had to turn up. It had to.

Just after two that afternoon, the librarian found the clipping. Isaac had spent five laborious hours with three different librarians. Two had given up. The same thought had occurred to Isaac. His fingers ached, and his back hurt from bending over the computer. Fortunately, the last woman, about Rosemary's age, felt sympathetic toward Isaac and refused to give up.

"Sorry it took so long. The story didn't make front-page news." She handed him the paper and said, "I hope this is everything you need. Several others are waiting."

"Thanks," he said, and meant it. The room was full of college students, a quarter of whom appeared to be waiting to be helped just like he had been.

It was a short article. No pictures, but informative and to the point. "Man kills woman in love triangle. Seymour Bowenstein fatally kills Ellen Coleman after arguing about their two-year-old son."

Astonishment was too mild an emotion. Isaac could see only the words "their son." His heart ached so much at that moment, he couldn't move. Even when they began turning off the lights, he still couldn't move.

Paps hadn't told him. That hurt. But Rosemary—keeping this a secret crucified him. How could she?

Eli's laughs about being a black Jew were apparently true. He looked at his arms, touched the curly hair on the surface, and felt repulsed. He removed a knife from his back pocket and cut off the ten-inch ponytail that he'd always been proud of. It was a joke, just like he was.

Isaac stood. And for a moment he couldn't feel. The world stood still. He felt as if he were dying inside.

When he left the library not feeling in complete control of himself, he tried to remember every conversation that he had had with Paps with every ounce of strength that he could muster. He thought back on the time when Rosemary first met Paps. Looking back now, their meeting had been awkward. Why hadn't he noticed it before? What kind of fool did they take him for?

It was all a bunch of lies and secrets. Worse than lies. They were dark truths. How could anyone be so cruel?

When he made it home, he thought again about calling Miracall, then hesitated. She and Rosemary had been good friends for more than seven years. What if Rosemary had confided the truth to her and Miracall hadn't told him? No. That was irrational; Rosemary wouldn't have told Miracall. Still, his life, his son's life, being proud to be a Coleman, were all lies.

Coleman . . . a strong name . . . a name that he'd always been proud of . . . a name that was replicated on his marriage license, his son's birth certificate, his prison records. The thought of his name possibly being Isaac Bowenstein sickened him.

Is this what Rosemary meant when she said, "I've kept too much from you already"?

Key to Time

Tonight she slept on praying hands, tucked neatly under her cheek. She was dreaming about Peyton and his homecoming in a few short weeks. She thought about the corned beef and cabbage that he would refuse to eat but would finally give in to upon her promise of a decadent dessert. She felt a warm smile touch her lips when she was awakened by the phone.

"I'm sorry to bother you this early in the morning, Mrs. Jones, but I didn't know who else to call."

Rosemary reached for her glasses that were next to the telephone. Turning on the light, she felt Jesse stirring beside her. She whispered, "Excuse me, who did you say this was?"

Glancing at the clock, it was 4:40 A.M.

"I'm Mrs. Sullivan. I work in the infirmary at Jefferson. It's Mr. Bowenstein. I'm afraid that he won't make it through the night."

"What?" She pulled back the covers and reached for her robe. "Hold on a minute, please." She pressed the hold button, and went into the kitchen to retrieve the cordless phone. "What in the world happened? I was just there two weeks ago. The doctors said that he was doing just fine."

"He's had a series of attacks since that time, Mrs. Jones. We've continuously tried contacting his family. I left messages and even sent several telegrams, but they haven't answered any of our correspondence. His health began to deteriorate quicker at that point. Afterward, Mr. Bowenstein refused to let us call anyone else."

Images were flashing through her mind about her mother on that fatal night. The nightmares had been more frequent lately. Maybe now, she thought, the nightmares would finally end. "I'll be there as quickly as I can."

Taking a moment to prepare a pot of coffee, she wondered if he'd left a will. If he hadn't, how would she know what to do with his body or his personal belongings?

"Ouch!" she said after burning her lips on the dark liquid. Pangs of an oncoming headache pounded at her temples, and she realized that she was being punished for her evil thoughts. She said a short prayer and asked the Lord to check her spirit, because she knew that the will of God went against that type of thinking.

Isaac should know, she told herself. Today was Tuesday and he didn't have to work at the Grille. Funny, she thought, she hadn't heard from him over the weekend, like she usually did.

"Hello."

"Hi, Isaac. It's me. I'm sorry for waking you, but it's important. The nurse at the Jefferson Penitentiary just called. Paps is dying. I wondered—"

The phone line went dead. She redialed and the line was busy. She continued to dial, checking her watch, watching the clock continue to beat faster with every try. It was five o'clock by then, and she had to get dressed.

By 5:20 she was ready to head out the door. Leaving a note on the nightstand for Jesse, she grabbed her purse and keys. She headed for the back door, then backtracked to the dining room. Standing in the doorway, she took a final look at her mother's treasure. It was always so beautiful. She wondered, had Paps forgotten how many times he had sat at that table? How many times her mother had laughed along with him when he filled the pink punch bowl with money he'd won gambling—the same bowl that sat in the center now?

It didn't matter now, she thought, after leaving the house and getting in her car. Glancing back over her shoulder, she pulled out of the driveway, and kept a watchful eye out for Isaac. She waited a moment in front of her house, then rationalized that he could be driving himself down, or running late getting here. Whatever the reason, she couldn't wait any longer. She put the car in gear and sped down the vacant residential street. Turning west on Six Mile Road, she popped in a tape by O'Landa Draper and the Associates, and sang a familiar old spiritual along with him.

"There's a wickedness in God's mercy, like the wickedness of the sea;/ There's a kindness in his justice, which is more than liberty./There is welcome for the sinner"—she felt tears touch her lashes—"and more graces for the good;/There is Mercy with the Savior./There is healing in his blood."

The drive seemed much longer this time. In twenty minutes the sun would be coming up and she wouldn't feel so terribly alone. Halfway there, she turned over the tape and continued to sing the words that she could remember. She prayed that Isaac would show up. And she had to weigh the consequences of finally telling Isaac the truth against avoiding it altogether. No one had been harmed. All the damage had been done years ago, and nothing would bring their mother back.

Even though they'd never discussed it, she still believed that Paps still hadn't forgiven himself. At odd times, when he thought she wasn't looking, she'd see the suffering in his eyes, and she knew why.

But today, both she and Paps knew that because of his strong belief in the Jewish faith, he couldn't die in peace until he asked for forgiveness for his sins and believed that he'd been forgiven. Otherwise, he would not be able to enter into heaven. She thought about how pain played a significant if not an essential part in the liberation of the human soul from the bondage of desire, the limitations of physical existence, and the mortality inseparable from it.

An hour and ten minutes later, Mrs. Sullivan led her to the infirmary, her hat and coat resting on her arm. The nurse explained to Rosemary that she'd been off-duty for a while, but had tried to stay until Rosemary arrived. Her reddened eyes told Rosemary that Paps didn't have much time left.

The doctor introduced himself, and cautioned Rosemary to limit her stay to a few minutes at a time.

Even though it was daylight out now, the room was respectfully darkened. She could see Paps's ghostly figure outlined on the narrow bed. Wearing a white gown beneath tucked-in white sheets, his wild white mane fanned out over the white pillowcase, he looked like a sleeping dove.

She scooted the chair closer to his bed. Scanning the medical equipment that pumped life into his body, it reminded her of the time not long ago when Jesse was in a similar situation at Mount Sinai Hospital. Even Jesse didn't look as bad as Paps did here today.

Opening her Bible, she searched for a particular passage, then leaned over and stroked his cool hands. Then she sat back and began to read.

" 'Teach us to number our days, that we may apply our hearts unto wisdom.' " Rosemary spoke softly. "I hope you can hear me, Seymour. It's Rosemary. I don't have to tell you why I'm here. You know why. Time is passing. The little time that's left is not long enough for us to share our sorrow with each other. It's time, Seymour, to prepare your soul."

She closed her eyes in meditation, and silently prayed. The soft light above Paps's bed glowed against her hands, and she could feel a beam of heat.

When she opened her eyes, the room was as still as a grave. Nothing moved beyond time's shadow.

"My heart tells me that you haven't forgiven yourself for what happened so many years ago. During all these years, there is only so much time, so much running of the sand, so many tickings of the clock." A stream of tears hid themselves in drops of sorrow. "This is real time, but life is so much more, Seymour. Life is the being of a soul, of an intelligent, remembering, reasoning, forecasting man; it is the succession of thoughts that run around the universe, that wander aimlessly through eternity; it's the collection of actions, acts, virtues, generosity, devotion, the pursuit of knowledge and hope; the choice of religions and the limited time on this earth that we have to serve the Lord. You've been a blessing to Isaac while he was here; that shows your generosity. You've been devoted to me, to your family. You've encouraged Isaac to educate himself while he was here, as you have. During that time, you've never turned your back on the Lord. This is what life is all about."

She heard him move his head, and she paused to touch his hand. She patted it gently. "If only we all held the key to time, Seymour, there would be no repentance, no saved souls, no hell, and no heaven. But life is not like that. There has to be a balance—good and evil—so there is a natural balance in this world of ours."

The doctor held up three fingers. She would have to leave in a few minutes. "I've only got a few minutes, Seymour. Try and open up your eyes. I know you can do it. Please try."

She stood up and bent over him. Closing her eyes, she began repeating the Lord's Prayer over and over.

Paps didn't move. Just as she prepared to leave, she noticed that his breathing sounded much heavier. His eyelids tightened and she could see that he was making an effort to communicate with her. "Seymour? It's me, Rosemary. Open your eyes! I know you can do it."

The doctor came in then. "You'll have to leave now, Mrs. Jones."

She pleaded with him. "Please, just a few minutes more. Can't you see he's trying to wake up? It may be the last time. Please!"

He nodded respectfully and left. When she turned back around, Seymour's weakened blue eyes were open. They were embalmed with tears. He touched her hand, his fingers tightly closing around hers.

He spoke to her with his eyes. Wise eyes that seemed to ask her the question: *"Have you forgiven me?"*

"Yes, I've forgiven you, Seymour. I'm sorry it took so long for me to tell you that. We should have had this conversation long ago." She felt him grip her hand. Then he pressed harder. "What is it? Are you trying to tell me something?" He nodded his head yes. "Is it your family?" His eyes bore deeply into hers. "Family? Do you want me to call your family in Omaha?" He shook his head no. "Then, who?" She saw the tenderness in his eyes as bloodless tears began to fall. "Isaac." He nodded yes.

Where is Isaac? Rosemary thought, dabbing at her eyes. *He should have been here by now.* Then an eerie thought came over her. *He's not coming.*

She felt his hand again and said, "I'll tell him, Seymour. I'll make him understand."

All his effort seemed to drain from him. Just then, the doctor broke into the room. "Nurse!" The monitors began beeping loudly, and she removed herself from the room.

Seconds later, as Rosemary stood outside the glass wall, she watched the doctors and nurses work on Seymour's tired body. In less than five minutes it was over. He was gone.

"There's a kindness in his justice," she said to herself, reciting an old spiritual proverb, "There is a healing in his blood. When we know Christ, God dwells within us by his Holy Spirit, and . . . the Spirit helps us in our weakness . . ."

On her way home, she thought back to a few years ago, when she'd first learned that Seymour was at Jefferson Penitentiary. She didn't recognize him immediately. Later, she knew exactly who he was. At the time, she was in her last year in theology school. In all conscience, she knew that she couldn't show any hatred toward this man. If she had, she might as well have saved the rest of her tuition and went to work with Jesse at the funeral home. It didn't stop her, though, from asking him a pressing question:

"Seymour, I've always wanted to ask you . . ."

His voice was incredulous. "When did you start calling me Seymour?"

"Shhhh. I'd like your opinion about something. Why do you think that the Jews are the chosen people?" Rosemary asked.

"Because of Abraham! Read Deuteronomy seven-seven carefully. You'll understand why God loves us so."

Abraham, she knew, was married to a woman who was so beautiful and comely, he lied and presented her to the king as his sister. How strange that he would pick this man as a martyr.

She smiled and said instead, "But don't you believe it was because you were the fewest of them all?"

"Possibly," Paps answered.

"Possibly because the Jews are the closest race to black people—and wouldn't you agree that black people are special people, too?"

It had taken him a while to answer. But he finally said, "I have to agree."

Later, Rosemary learned that Paps did leave a will, naming her executor of his estate. There was a sealed note attached addressed to Rosemary Jones. It said, "I always thought of Ellen as my black queen, like Esther in the Bible. Forgive me for my most unforgivable sin, Rosemary. I'll always love her."

This saddened Rosemary. Even though she loved her mother, she was no black queen. Unlike Esther, her mother did not sacrifice her life for her people, or her children. Instead, she'd put her life on the line for her husband—the same sorry man who had introduced her to prostitution. Oddly enough, in Gen. 12:17–20, Abraham didn't tell the Pharaoh that Sara was his wife. Because of that lie, the Lord plagued Pharaoh and his house in Egypt with great plagues. Rosemary's father's lie had led to the death of her parents.

And now, Seymour's.

Rosemary and Jesse claimed his body and made sure that he had a nice memorial service and was buried according to his Jewish tradition. His family in Omaha sent money but refused to attend.

None of this surprised Rosemary, except the final codicil of the will. There was $145,000 in cash and more than $200,000 in stocks. Everything was left to Isaac Coleman.

Blood on the Sun

The ear of his ear was now hearing ever so clearly, and the eye of his eye was now open wide. No words could describe what Isaac felt toward Rosemary.

"I told you that I didn't want to hear from you no more." He held the receiver away from his ear. "Why do you keep calling me?" Isaac's words hissed at his sister.

"Please, Isaac. If only you'd give me a chance to explain."

"I'm no fool. I know what happened to our mother. You're a liar. The biggest hypocrite that I've ever known. How dare you keep a horrible secret like that from me!"

"Isaac!"

Click.

Sure, it hurt hanging up on his sister, but she'd misled him. No, *lied* was a better word. After nearly forty years, she was certain that he'd never uncover the truth. And now, truth, like a rotten apple that sometimes requires it to be cut in half before one could tell which portion contained the worm, had finally reared its ugly head.

He had no idea how she'd gotten his new number. Three weeks after Kennedy's funeral, Isaac had decided it was time to move again. Kennedy's home was just a short seven and a half miles from his apartment. He found himself constantly driving by, imagining that she'd come out the front door and wave to him, or that he'd see her car pull up in the driveway. He was ashamed to think about the way the blue fabric of her uniform stretched so sensuously across her breasts and hips. Even the gun resting high on the side of her waist seemed provocative. It was a powerful image. Right now, too much so.

A friend of Rex's was moving out of the state and wanted to sublet his condo in downtown Detroit for a year. The conservative Indian Village apartment complex housed mostly professionals. There was twenty-four-hour security and a newly remodeled weight room. Isaac planned to utilize the facility fully so that he could completely recuperate from his wounds. Even though the rent was triple what he was paying he knew the advantages were worth it.

He was able to move into the new place two weeks before Thanksgiving. The following week, he'd be bringing his son to his new home, and he wanted to make it comfortable for him.

Living downtown obviously had its advantages. The best restaurants in the city were located there—in Hart Plaza, Chene Park, Greektown—and the constant lure of the new casinos and having access to all the freeways were key to paying the high rent in the spiffy downtown dwellings. But it was the thirty-two-hundred-square-foot four-bedroom, two-and-a-half bath apartment that sold Isaac. Now he'd have enough space to write and practice his music, and even put in a sound studio, when he could afford it. But, more important, Peyton would have a huge room to himself and his own bathroom.

Confused and hurt, Isaac had read his Bible every night since Paps died. It had been three weeks, and still he couldn't come to terms with his feelings.

During that stressful period, Isaac hadn't spoken to Rosemary. She'd sent word by Miracall, even by Jesse. No, he wasn't ready to see her yet. Rosemary had committed the worst offense that a sister could . . . concealing the truth.

He could understand why she did it at first—to protect him. But for the past forty years he had thought there were no secrets between them.

Each time she sent a package, he sent it back unopened. He had no idea what could possibly be in a package that size. He wondered if it was any of Paps's personal things from prison. Or any of the items that Isaac had left for Paps and he was returning. With that thought in mind, he finally opened one and looked inside. He was shocked by the contents. Paps had left him a fortune in cash and stocks. It didn't matter. No amount of money could ease the torment he felt. Nothing could compensate for his mother's life. A mother he was never able to know. He felt robbed, used, by Paps and Rosemary, and the secret they shared between them.

Rare for mid-November, it had rained nonstop for four days. His Thursday night performance at the Grille was canceled because of a leak in the roof. Isaac was relieved and decided to go to bed. Picking up the Good Book, which was lying beside him on the nightstand, he began to read the story in the Bible about Noah beginning his mission of starting anew on earth. John the Baptist was preaching by the Jordan River, calling every soul who would listen to repent of their evil ways and be baptized. Matthew told the story that when Jesus came out of the water he experienced the presence of the Spirit of God like a dove coming down to rest on his shoulder.

Had Peyton gotten any of his inspiration for the poem about the dove from the Bible, he wondered? "They sometimes show truth and loneliness. But at the same time courage." Courage was just what he needed. The courage to move beyond death and begin to plan his and his son's future.

When the phone rang, he was angered. He thought it was Rosemary trying to contact him again. After five rings, he decided to answer it. It was the Realtor asking him if he could meet her at Kennedy's home tomorrow morning. She had a preapproved buyer who seemed very interested in the property.

As he sat in the driveway of Kennedy's house the following morning, waiting for the Realtor to show up with the potential buyer, he began to reflect. He thought about what might have been if Kennedy was still alive. His eyes welled with tears. He could imagine how happy he and his son would be if they hadn't lost her. Although Miracall was good for him, and Peyton was beginning to accept her, he knew deep down that no one could ever take the place of Peyton's mother, the woman he loved more than life itself.

As he continued to wait, he envisioned her smiling face—always less than a breath away. His heart ached when he thought about the wasted years in their marriage. And it ached even more when he thought about what kind of marriage they could have had—a husband and wife who had fought the world side by side, who had borne a child by joy and become aged together, and who were not infrequently found curiously alike in personal appearance, in pitch and tone of voice, just as twin pebbles on the beach were similar that had been exposed to the same tidal influence. He could see her supreme beauty before him now.

Before the Realtor left, she assured Isaac that she'd have a signed deal for him that afternoon and asked if he would be home to look over the offer around five o'clock.

Because of his health, he had had to break several engagements in the early fall. It set him back a bit, but he still had thousands in cash stashed in his mattress.

Fortunately, his agent, Ms. Ruffin, managed to reschedule the most important event—a recording at the local studio in Southfield that was affiliated with Motown. Miracall was right, this girl did have connections. The record would be issued overseas in the Caribbean first, where Isaac hoped to jumpstart his recording career, following his successful South American tour. Next, it would be released in the States.

Daily conversations with Miracall helped to encourage him. When he was finally due to record his first album, he wanted her by his side.

It was near the end of the recordings, when the sound, lyrics, music, and tone were all in sync. Tomorrow, the crew assured Isaac late Thursday night, as he headed for the door, would be the final taping.

"You were great," Miracall said to Isaac after they left the studio. They were walking side by side, holding hands through the packed parking lot. Her car was parked at the end of the row near the far west corner.

He smiled. "Your choice of restaurants: The Golden Mushroom or Alexander's?"

Several other people were leaving the shops nearby. The spicy smell of Italian spaghetti filled his lungs. He wanted to eat right then and there. It wouldn't be fair, he thought. Miracall had been patient, waiting hours for him to finish. He could at least be the gentleman that he told himself he was.

A few feet from the car, Miracall released his hand, reaching for the keys inside her purse. "Neither. Let's try this new restaurant—Fusion, in Farmington. You make your own food."

"Neither one of us are great cooks, Miracall. Anyway, why go out if we have to cook?"

"We don't really cook the food. We go to the market first and select ten to twelve vegetables. Then you have a choice of bases, from noodles, rice, or mashed potatoes. And finally, you pick a sauce. Out of the fifteen available, everyone is usually satisfied with their customized meal." She smiled. "Isn't the concept unique?"

"Hmm."

"And Isaac." She smiled. "It's cheap."

"I love that word, but I prefer to use the word *affordable.* Lead the way." Isaac went around to the passenger side. All of a sudden, bright headlights blinded their vision. The sound of a motor gaining speed alerted Isaac that something was wrong.

Miracall wasn't paying attention. She still hadn't located her keys and was blabbering about dessert. "They've got this apple pie with slithers of apples, a double crust, and a homemade caramel sauce. And they serve it with vanilla bean Häagen-Dazs—"

"Miracall!" he shouted. "Look out!"

The car was heading right at Miracall. By the time he made it around to the driver's side, he managed to grab a handful of her coat. He heard an odd thud, the cloth slipping from his fingers. Miracall's tiny body was knocked a few feet in the air, then fell backward on the asphalt.

Someone screamed.

It was like watching an action movie that you didn't have the energy to look away from, but found yourself involved in the hurried details. Isaac felt temporarily helpless.

When he bent down to lift her up, she was rubbing the back of her head. "I'm okay, Isaac," she stated. "Did you get a glimpse of the license plate?"

"No. But I did get a good look at the make and model. Maybe someone out here will remember the license plate." He reached for the keys that were lying beside her. "Sit still now. I'll call an ambulance."

The small shopping center where the studio was housed was a busy one. It turned out that someone had indeed taken down the license-plate number of the 1996 light blue Plymouth that had hit Miracall.

Fortunately, Miracall merely suffered a broken leg. The police met them in the emergency room of Providence Hospital. Questions were asked and answered. It was only a matter of time, they believed, before the perpetrators would be apprehended.

That night, Isaac went to Miracall's home and packed a bag for her. He told her that she couldn't go back home until the police found out who had tried to kill either her or him.

He couldn't stop thinking about the butterflies—that Miracall was finally free. She'd confessed to Isaac that she had turned down Loren's final proposal of marriage. Though there was a good chance that he could be back in politics by the next voting term, it hadn't made a difference. Loren was making plans to move to Texas. He'd been hand-picked to work on Governor Bush's presidential campaign. If Bush won, Loren was told that he would be given a position in Bush's cabinet. "No, go," she had told him. She was a Michiganian at heart and planned on staying one.

When Isaac returned home, Miracall had just hung up the telephone.

"Some man named Gary called while you were at my house," Miracall called out from the master bedroom. "He said he'd call back in thirty minutes."

"I don't know a Gary. It's some wisecrack calling. Ignore it." He came into the room with two pain pills and a glass of cold water. "Now take this and lay back down."

A little while later, Miracall was fast asleep. Isaac knew that he wasn't too far behind. For a while, he watched her snore lightly in the center of his bed. There was no denying that he cared for her. He was stunned by how their relationship had matured into something more personal, more natural, than he had expected. Indeed, she was a remarkable woman.

She'd been patient with him all during Kennedy's funeral and the trying time afterward. He'd never been in a relationship this uncomplicated. For the first time, he felt some of the same passion for Miracall that he had felt for Kennedy. It was a feeling that he had thought was surely buried with Kennedy, but now he wondered.

The phone rang, interrupting his thoughts. It was Gary Reynolds.

"Look, brother. I don't know you. Where did you get my number? It's private."

"Rosemary."

Isaac perked up. "What does she want? What do you want? I told her to leave me alone."

"It's about tonight. Miracall. I know that she was hurt."

"Why are you calling me instead of the police? Forget that you know Rosemary. She's a pastor, but she ain't God." He was mad at himself for talking so much. He didn't know this man. Why should he tell him about the problems that he and Rosemary were dealing with? It was none of his business.

The man's voice hinted at impatience. "It's the same man, Isaac."

"Are you saying the same person that killed Kennedy tried to run down Miracall?"

"Yes. This was no accident. Listen to me, Isaac. I'm a businessman, not a reporter. Man to man, we're losing the war on crime to the drug addicts and gangs in the city of Detroit. I realize that you haven't been home long, but because of Peyton's recent incarceration, your beating, Kennedy's death, and now this accident on a woman I believe you care about, I assure you, all this isn't a coincidence."

The man had managed to get his attention. Certainly something was up. Isaac's gut instincts said that Gary Reynolds sounded educated and might just be smart enough to know something. He decided he should listen.

For the next half hour, Gary outlined the theory that the police were working on a major drug ring, and that Kennedy had been involved. Something had gone wrong. There was always the possibility of an inside informant. Or possibly a drug dealer who was on their payroll. Whatever the case, it was police corruption at the highest level. Isaac mentioned his theory about Eli's involvement. Gary told Isaac that he was aware of Eli's drug dealings, and that he had people working on it. Some of the information Isaac already knew. This confirmed Gary's sincerity. Isaac continued to listen. In short, Gary knew that someone high up in the police ranks was involved.

"We've got a break!" Gary shouted into the receiver. "Hold on." He paused, and Isaac could hear people talking in the background. "They've got him!"

"Who?" Isaac could still hear someone's voice behind Gary's.

"The guy that tried to run down Miracall. I'm told the detectives are now squeezing him for information, and before the night's over, the junkie will be singing like Della Reese."

They laughed simultaneously.

Afterward, Isaac felt guilty. It was time for him to call Rosemary and try to put the skeletons to sleep again. Skeletons that had caused them so much grief. He hadn't really given her a chance to tell her side of the story. Even though he'd read the clippings, he was mature enough to know that there were two sides to every story. And after some of the hurt and anger subsided, it was time he heard hers.

He picked up the phone four times to call Rosemary, and each time he hung it back up. He wasn't sure how to begin. Should he say that he was sorry first or wait for her to say it?

While he was debating the words he'd use, Gary called back. "The man confessed. He agreed to turn state's evidence in exchange for a reduced sentence. He's named Detective Lindsey Royale. If we get to Ben in time, we'll get the others."

"I don't understand, Gary. What do you have to do with all of this? How do I know what you're telling me is credible?"

"Forget that I've known your sister for over ten years. Forget that I'm trying to open a new prison that would change the entire way prisoners are handled and rehabilitated. Think about this. I love Dawn Cullors. I'm sure you know the name. I didn't know how much she loved me until she gave me a tape two months ago. The tape implicated her father and a captain whose name was one that we could never quite discern. The tape mentioned Kennedy's murder." Isaac felt his heart pound in his chest. "However, we had nothing concrete to tie them into it, until we got this break. There was no way that we could go after public officials without valid proof."

"What's next?" Isaac asked.

"Making some high-profile arrests."

"Which means?"

"Arresting dozens of police officers."

"Can you do that?"

"Not me. Only the prosecutor's office can. You take it easy, Isaac. I'll call you if anything else happens."

How could he take it easy? No arrests had been made yet. What if someone shot through his front door right now? This whole affair was ridiculous. Why hadn't anyone arrested Eli? It was obvious that he was a key figure in this entire ordeal.

When he turned on the TV, everything Gary had said was being reported on the eleven o'clock news. However, a few details were left out. "Big Ben

Lake was arrested on grounds of drug trafficking and conspiracy to commit murder."

When the phone rang, Isaac cringed. He glanced over and checked the number displayed on the caller ID. He still hadn't called Rosemary and secretly hoped that it was her. It wasn't, it was Gary. Though he knew the information from Gary was useful, he had no desire to speak with this man right now. Given that fact, he hesitantly picked up the phone and said a grave hello.

"You won't believe it," Gary said. "They found a map. A treasure map on Big Ben's property up north. Hidden on his fifty acres of property were four point eight million dollars in cash buried in plastic containers."

Isaac thought about the money that he still kept under his mattress. *You're a fool. Someone might think you stole it.* He made a mental note to open an account the next day.

"This is all good information, but I don't see how it affects me."

"The police dug up more than one hundred ninety pounds of marijuana. It had the same wrapping as the stuff that was found on Peyton. Is what I'm telling you becoming clearer now?"

Impatience was in his voice again. "When the officers executed a search warrant at the junkies' northwestern apartment, they found a piece of paper indicating several other locations where money was buried. One place that the map indicated to dig at was in Birmingham, Michigan. Can you guess who owns the property?"

"No," Isaac said too quickly, before he could think.

"Detective Lindsey Royale."

Rhapsody in Blue

Isaac finally finished his first album with a gospel-jazz-fusion style. Even though the local record company appeared to have everything under control, his agent encouraged him to invest in his future. That included spending a big chunk of his savings. He agreed and hired a marketing firm.

Next, he purchased his very first computer and planned on visiting all the local churches to get them to stock his album in their stores. Ministries like Rosemary's, whose membership was now more than six thousand strong, were a market that couldn't be ignored.

His faith in God was growing, even though he didn't express it verbally. He suspected that all of his troubles still weren't over. Call it a hunch. Call it instinct. He wasn't stupid. It wouldn't be daylight until the rooster crowed and he and he Rosemary were singing a happy tune.

Thanksgiving for Isaac and Miracall wasn't the usual holiday setting. They didn't have turkey and dressing and cranberry sauce. They ate cheese grills and tomato soup for dinner. Miracall didn't cook. She made only appetizers— exceptionally well. At this point in Isaac's life it didn't matter. Family did. He and Miracall gave very special attention to every detail in rearranging and purchasing new furniture in preparation for Peyton's homecoming.

The following weekend, he and Miracall painted Peyton's room. They'd chosen china white for the walls and found the perfect size charcoal gray carpet remnant at New York Carpet World. Throughout the next week, they shopped at several department stores until they found the spread and drapes in the perfect tone of deep purple. The room was coming together nicely.

When they finally finished and stepped back to admire their handiwork, Miracall said, "You seem troubled about something. What's wrong? Are you worried about Peyton?"

"Not exactly."

"You know, I've been thinking about you, Peyton, and myself. I've concluded that we're not like most people. No, the three of us are like soldiers. We carry our lives in our heads, and the grace of God in our hearts." Miracall's voice wrapped around him like a warm caress.

"I understand what you mean. But without a doubt, we're survivors."

Isaac turned and looked at this woman as if for the first time.

He hadn't confided in her his trauma about actually being a Bowenstein. There was no one alive whom he knew of who could confirm or deny his heritage, except Rosemary. The more he tried to put it out of his mind, the more it mattered.

All he knew was that all of his life he'd been a proud black man. How in all consciousness could he be proud to be of Jewish heritage? None of it fit. Besides the small things that Paps had told him, he knew nothing about the Jewish culture. He didn't want to be a Jew. The label petrified him.

Common sense took over and reminded him that he could still have a family with Miracall and Peyton.

With these thoughts in mind, he purchased grave blankets for his parents' graves. It was Sunday, the twelfth of December. He'd been praying avidly for days. They'd changed Peyton's release date three times in the past month. Now, finally, his son would be home on Monday.

Miracall didn't question him when he picked her up at six o'clock. The strong scent of pinecones in the trunk filtered through to the front seat, filling the silence as they drove to the cemetery.

A full moon painted every treetop mirrored in the night hazy blue. The cool wind whistled as cars breezed by. Even the untended flowers on the graves radiated a melancholy blue.

In no time, they placed the grave blankets on the graves, anchoring them with foot-long metal pins. Afterward, they sat in the car looking skyward. "In the next life I want to be a flower," Miracall said.

"Why?"

"Because of their innocence. Tenderness. Freshness." She snuggled closer to him, tugged on his earlobe, then kissed it. "Most humans never understand the simplicity of tenderness. They associate it with weakness."

Isaac thought about the years of enjoying cigarettes. Was it a weakness? Yes. Did he need them now? No. He needed something more tender, like the woman tenderly fondling him now.

Here was a woman whose gray hair defied age in its softness and its semi-gray shade of darkness, and yet he, still dyeing his hair black as needed, hadn't let go. Was it weakness? No. It was vanity.

There was a painful meaning here, but one he felt calmly. The tombs of their ancestors, relatives, and friends brought about sad thoughts and poignant recollections which time had assuaged. And together with this cool air of evening sifting through the top of the cracked window, and the moon shining over all with the same faint delight, was a feeling of comfort.

"Isaac," Miracall said ever so softly, as if it were a secret, "Christmas is the time of forgiveness. It's the beginning of a new beginning."

New Year's Day. The millennium. He was silent.

329

"Don't begin this time with an unforgiving heart." In the blue moonlight tears glistened on her cheeks. "Call Rosemary. She's called you so many times, you should be embarrassed. She loves you, Isaac. She's *always* loved you. Whatever she did, she was only trying to do what was best for you. You know that, don't you?" Her lips met his, and she clung to him. He felt her body tremble, and felt her warm words whisper in his ear, "And you know you can't stop loving her either."

"That's true." He pushed her off him. "But not yet."

Miracall was furious. "I'm so disappointed in you, Isaac. You're acting like a woman would. How could you treat your own sister so coldly?"

"You don't understand."

She put her hands on his shoulder and pushed her face close to his. "Oh, but I do. I know all about Paps, the murder, how your sister kept the truth from you. I've known for months, Isaac. We can't change the past. Seymour's gone. Your mother and father are gone. Rosemary is here. She's alive, Isaac. And she needs you."

"I don't know," he stuttered. "She doesn't seem like the woman I always respected. Always trusted."

She gazed at him with her eyes of velvet, wide open, peaceful, mysterious, all the more beautiful for her tears. "Rosemary helped me find my faith again. She helped me to wean myself from Loren's suffocating grasp. Even helped me to finally release my mother's memory. And you wonder about trust? About love? What she's given us is a gift. Her own personal sacrifice of herself that's seldom given by anyone, but always well received by everyone." She pushed him in his chest until he was backed up against the door and glared at him. "Why is it so hard for you to give her a such a small gift? One she deserves."

"She knows that I love her."

"I don't mean that. I'm talking about something deeper. The gift of forgiveness. You can act like a fool if you want to. Take me home."

They were silent all the way to her house. He watched her get out and slam the door, knowing that he should stop her, but his ego wouldn't let him.

Back at home, he rubbed his cheek against the pillow where she'd lain earlier that day. It still smelled of her perfume. He had asked the Lord to send him a lover . . . someone to believe in. Miracall. Someone whom he could hold, who could take away the cold. Miracall. Give him back what he was missing. Miracall. Someone who could give him a new beginning. Finally, he asked for Miracall.

Blue was emblematic of the sky, and also represented not just the light of the northern climate but the deep, dark hue of the eastern sky. Under the Scriptures of Esther, Ezekial, and Ecclesiastes, this color was used in the same way as purple. *Violet.* Princess and nobles were clothed in robes of this color. Even the idols of Bablyon.

Would it be beyond reason that Isaac would view Miracall in this same hue? A rhapsody in blue.

What they shared together tonight was as rare and beautiful as a fallen star from heaven. *Why, then,* he thought, *did I let her go?*

Orphans of the Storm

A two-mile-wide storm came from the southwest and moved northeast at about thirty to forty miles per hour. Several trees in front of the Joneses' house were uprooted. Others were stripped of their leaves and wall-papered homes on the street in a soft green-leaf mosaic. During the thirteen-minute storm, hail, ranging from the size of a nickel to the size of a quarter, broke most of the windows in half of the homes on Stansbury Street as well as homes on four other blocks in their small subdivision.

Five days before Christmas, the Joneses were forced to stay at a hotel until the windows in their home could be repaired. With so many homes to repair, the insurance company thought that it would be at least two weeks before they could return to their home.

In all her years, Rosemary had never witnessed so much devastation. She felt that God was surely speaking to her. Sure, dozens of other homes had been equally destroyed, but Rosemary didn't look at it that way. She believed in omens—retribution. She began to wonder if what she'd done to Isaac was wrong. No matter how much she tried to tell herself that she hadn't lied to him, she now knew that withholding the truth from him was something only God could judge her for.

"Rosemary, darlin," Jesse began, "you're driving me crazy." He took her by the hand and pulled her down on the bed beside him. "I want you to listen to me."

Outside, the rain was coming down in pellets, making mournful music for the mind. It had rained fifteen of the twenty-six days of December. And today, there were no signs of it letting up. Rosemary was so exhausted, she barely heard Jesse's words. She merely nodded.

"I know what's bothering you. Peyton came home yesterday and Isaac hasn't called."

When Rosemary heard Isaac's name, her head turned slightly. She began to listen. Jesse had forgotten that Isaac was a Christmas Eve baby, but she hadn't. Her brother had turned forty-one two days ago. It hurt her to think that he'd celebrated the event without her.

"Mrs. Jones, I want you to go over there tomorrow. I'll go with you if you want me to. After all that's happened between you and Isaac, you should show the man some respect. Show up at his door." He took a blanket off the bed and wrapped it around her. "Darlin, I'm worried about you. In five weeks you've lost almost twenty pounds. I can tell you haven't even noticed. Worried weight loss doesn't look good on nobody."

Rosemary looked in the mirror on the wall directly in front of them. After she got a good look at herself, she had to hold her breath from screaming. She watched as her hand reached up and touched her hollow cheeks. How had she not noticed? Sure, she was small, but she looked older. Aged. Not like the healthy, full-figured woman whom Jesse had married and had always told her he preferred over a petite woman. "I'm sorry, Jesse. I had no idea what I was doing to myself. To us."

Jesse started to turn away from her, then abruptly stopped, wagging his finger in mid-air. "You just reminded me of something." He went outside and came back with a CD and inserted it in the portable player on top of the bureau. Within seconds, the song "I Believe I Can Fly" by R. Kelly flowed through the small room.

"Jesse?"

"Shhh," he said, placing a finger on his lips. "Just listen."

When the record was over, Jesse played it again. His words were soft when he spoke. "When I lost my leg I was devastated. When I went through therapy with this prosthetic limb, I didn't think I'd ever be able to walk. I quit. Refused to try anymore. Then a nurse brought me this record. She told me about her daughter, born without a hand. By the time her child turned one, she was able to use her prosthetic hand like a normal baby. They called it 'the helper.' I envisioned that child, and this strong mother volunteering her time to help other people. I stopped feeling sorry for myself. Listening to that song gave me courage. And then I met you, Rosemary. You taught me to love in heart and in spirit. But unlike you, I believe my relationship with God is personal. That's why I don't talk about it much. And like you, I *do* love the Lord. And I know that he's real."

"This is so strange. We've never talked like this before."

Wrapping his arms around her, he pulled her close. "I know. And it's long overdue."

"Tell me, Jesse . . . do you feel differently about my ministry now? Be honest. At one time I thought about quitting."

"In the beginning I didn't believe you were sincere. You told me that the Lord had called you into the ministry. Still, I wanted you to quit. I didn't believe. But since then, I've become so proud of you. The Lord has indeed called you, Rosemary."

His words touched her so deeply, she couldn't speak.

"Do you remember that day we went to church and you wore those pretty roses? That, to me, was a symbol of your ministry, sweetheart. God doesn't promise a person a bed of roses when they're called. But you wore yours proudly just the same. But if more people understood more fully that you're human, just like us, many of the thorns would be removed. Our Christian folks don't intentionally mean no harm. And during your short ministry you've cultivated beautiful, blossoming, fragrant roses. Sure, there are some jealous people who would rather send you roses that are dead, wilted, withered bouquets of failure. But you know, Rosemary, those members are as dead as the roses they send. You can't save them all, darlin'. But God knows that you've done your best."

She squeezed her eyes shut, waiting until she was sure that she could speak without a quiver in her voice. "Thank you, Mr. Jones."

"You've got to trust me, Rosemary. And darlin', you've got to trust in the love that Isaac has for you, even though he isn't showing it now."

"I hurt him, Jesse. I should tell him the whole truth. I don't know what he's thinking about me now. I only know that he doesn't trust me anymore." Sad tears rolled down her cheeks as a wave of guilt for her sins washed over her. "It's all my fault."

The pelting rain outside silenced her screams.

"Talk to me, darlin'. What happened? Can't you finally tell me what happened between you and Isaac? Tell me about this dark family secret that has all but destroyed my lovely wife."

When she turned to look at her husband, his eyes so dolorous, she cringed with shame. How in the world could this man still love her after all this? In the four years they'd been married, she never hid how much she loved her brother. Jesse knew that before they were married. And with Isaac seemingly turning his back on her, what opinion did he have about his loving wife now? It was time that she told him what she should have told him after they were married. After all, she trusted him, loved him as the man she wanted to share the rest of her life with.

"Never mind, darlin'," Jesse said patiently, patting her on her thigh. "I can wait until you're better."

Leaning back against the headboard, she closed her eyes. Her mind went back to a night thirty-nine years ago. But it was a night that she would never forget. "It was raining that night, Jesse. Just like tonight." She opened her eyes. "Isaac was just a toddler. He'd just learned how to say my name right. Mind you, he couldn't say the whole thing. He shortened it, saying 'Wose,' for Rose. It was so sweet, hearing that little boy say, 'Wose, I hungry. Feed me.' " She smiled, remembering. "Mama was outside, I can't remember why. Then, I heard the squeech of windshield wipers in the driveway and knew it was Seymour's car. He was early. At seventeen, I was old enough to know that early meant bad for Mama. I didn't know until later that Dad was in the backyard with Mama. Seymour must have suspected something was wrong, because he didn't listen to any of the excuses I made about Mama. He ran out back in the pouring rain and I couldn't stop him."

"Darlin'," Jesse said, wiping her eyes with a tissue, "you don't have to say any more. We can talk about this some other time."

Rosemary hadn't felt the tears. She had no idea what she looked like—only what she felt. And she felt empty now, as if she didn't have an ounce of blood in her body. "No, I've got to explain. You should know the truth. I should have told you years ago. But I was too afraid." She lowered her head, shaking it as if trying to clear it of all the evil memories. "Anyway, I fed Isaac as quickly as I could, and then laid him down on my bed. I could sense that something was wrong. I told Isaac not to move until I came back. I felt that something bad was going to happen. When I opened the back door, I heard my mama scream. At first, I was rooted to the floor, holding on to the door, afraid to move. I couldn't move. Mama screamed my name, 'Rosemary! Help me! Help me!' It seemed like an eternity before I heard Seymour's car start up and leave. I checked on Isaac once more, who was asleep by then. Then, I left the house and headed for the barn. The hard rain rinsed my tears as I imagined the unimaginable. But I knew before I got there. My mama was dead. I slung open the doors, and after stepping inside a few feet, I saw my mama's bloodstained body lying dead on the floor. She wore a black bra and torn black slip that was awkwardly hanging off her nude body. I turned at the scent of a burning cigar. It was smoldering on the wet barn floor, along with a large set of footprints that had unsuccessfully tried to stomp it out. I realized that my father had been there, too.

"Isaac never woke up, never heard the screams that I heard. Later, after the police had gone, I picked up Isaac and began to walk around with him. I knew he was too young to understand what had happened. I knew one day I would have to tell him the whole truth about our mother and father. I sat down and told him everything about our mother's death and Seymour's thoughts about being his father. This way, I felt, I had told him. Although I knew he didn't understand anything I was saying, I knew I would never repeat this again. So Jesse, I never lied to Isaac. I told him the truth—he just doesn't remember."

Rosemary didn't realize that she was shivering. When she rolled her head back, she felt Jesse's fingers gently caress the veins on her neck. She sighed with pleasure as he began to knead her knotted shoulders. Praying for a grip on her emotions, words caught in her throat.

335

Reaching back, she gripped his hands hard. "That night," she said, "Isaac and I became orphans. We never saw our father alive again. And our lives changed forever."

Misty

The rain had not ceased, and Rosemary was beginning to wonder if it ever would. Her mood was as somber as the rain. She didn't stop by Isaac's place, as Jesse had suggested. Instead, she went and talked to the bishop the following day. A week earlier, he'd left a message on her machine asking if she could stop by his office when she got a chance.

"When the New Year begins, Mother Bethel will finally be debt-free," the bishop said after Rosemary took a seat in his office. "The future of the church looks bright."

"Thank the Lord." The membership had more than doubled since Rosemary became the new pastor. The Lord had truly blessed the church, and now Rosemary hoped that some of those blessings would come a little closer to home. "I won't take up too much more of your time."

"And, yes, yes. Donations for food and blankets have been overwhelming." He consulted the book on his desk. "My wife is really looking forward to the event. Especially the music."

Since June, most of the churches in the inner city had agreed to make their buildings available as shelters in the event that the rollover to 2000 triggered a major power failure. Mother Bethel had been turning away folks since Thanksgiving. Even though the utility companies assured that they were ready, most people still didn't believe them.

Rosemary listened to the bishop go on and on about the affair, but she barely heard him, until he mentioned her brother's name.

"He's still performing, right?"

"I haven't spoken to him." Her eyes went blind. "Bishop, the spirit of Lucifer is making rounds, stirring up ill feelings between me and my brother. I

336

know the Lord will work things out. Meanwhile," she said, rising, "you say a prayer for us. Please."

It was on the third day after she and Jesse had spoken that she finally found the courage to go to Isaac's home on Jefferson Avenue. The relief she felt was overpowering. Finally, she'd be able to clear her conscience. To her dismay, the doorman told her that Isaac wasn't at home. She waited in the parking lot for another two hours. She had no idea that Isaac had taken Peyton to the Dave Bing Institute to enroll him for the winter term.

She decided to leave and try again tomorrow. It was time to go to work, but before she did, she made a U-turn and drove by Kennedy's house. Surprised to see a FOR SALE sign on the front lawn, she wondered if Isaac had decided to leave the city and not tell her. The thought of not seeing him and Peyton again killed her. Life was moving forward. Moving on. She wondered if she'd waited too long to make amends. And maybe now it was too late.

Hunger pangs rippled through her abdomen. Thankful that she was beginning to regain her appetite, she stopped at the New York Bagel Shop on Woodward and ordered a caraway seed bagel with vegetable spread and a large coffee. Her nerves were buzzing as she headed toward Mother Bethel.

A little later, she had finished her snack and was midway through writing her letter of resignation when Miracall walked into her office.

"I've been looking for you all afternoon." She closed the door. "We need to talk."

Rosemary felt Miracall's eyes scanning her body from head to toe when she offered her a seat. Even in a sitting position, it was obvious that she'd lost a lot of weight. When their eyes met, they communicated the same thought . . . *Why?*

In the same breath, Rosemary's eyes zeroed in on Miracall's hair. She couldn't remember seeing Miracall look so beautiful. Every strand of her hair was steel gray. The silvery highlights seemed to capture the glow in her cheekbones and eyes. "I love your hair. How long have you stopped coloring it?"

"A little while after I saw Isaac at the cemetery last year. I understood what a hypocrite I was. The bourgeois lifestyle, designer clothes, hundred-thousand-dollar cars, all meant nothing. I wasn't happy. And I also realized that I would never be able to bring my mother back from the grave. You helped me with that, Rosemary. And today, I want to try to help you."

"How? Where's Isaac? Peyton?"

"They're at the Dave Bing Institute. It's a newly built private high school that specializes in honor students who've had problems excelling in a regular school. It wasn't easy getting him enrolled. The student has to be recommended by a former teacher. Even my influence couldn't get him in. But somehow Isaac's boss, Rex, was well acquainted with a board member and was able to get Peyton in."

Rosemary felt a flutter of relief. *So they weren't moving away.* "I was at his apartment today for hours."

"I know. The guard told me." Miracall crossed her legs and let out a big, cleansing sigh. "I'd like to begin by dropping all barriers, Rosemary. To make a long story short, I know everything about your mother's murder."

Rosemary's face went nearly translucent with shock. "How?"

"Research. I've known since this spring. You probably never understood my job as a library director. Few people address me as Dr. Lake. It was never important. I have a job most people have never heard of or even aspire to. It's boring. My work consists primarily of research. Working on preserving the archives of Wayne State University. In early January I was asked to conduct the research on a famous alumni—Mr. Gil Banks.

"Mr. Banks was a 1957 alumni from Wayne State University. He passed in 1997. At the time, Wayne was compiling an extensive biography about his life. My office was the obvious choice to help with the biography. I was able to get transcripts from trials that he worked on during his thirty-year career.

"That's when I first saw the name Coleman. I only heard you mention your mother's name once—Ellen. You never said anything about her. Only that she died in 1960. Coincidentally, I thought it strange that a woman named Ellen Coleman was murdered that same year."

Her lips parted in surprise, and when the phone rang, Rosemary ignored it. "Still, that could have been someone else." She suspected that Miracall knew some things, but she couldn't possibly know *everything.*

"No," she went on. "Not when I remembered that the accused man was Seymour Bowenstein. *That* name is very uncommon. I went to the public library downtown because I wasn't able to retrieve the newspaper article on microfiche. It wasn't front-page news like I expected. A black woman from Arkansas, now living in Smith's Creek, that was murdered by a man from Omaha wasn't a major concern by the taxpayers of Michigan. Obviously, the community didn't care about nonnatives."

"The story made page three." Rosemary's laugh was stifled. "I remember reading it and feeling sick to my stomach."

"That long ago, who would remember?"

I do. Like it was yesterday. "A name was missing from that article. It was my father's: James Coleman. I look just like him. Isaac favors my mother's brother, Daniel." Her expression was impassive. "When I was twelve I learned about prostitution. My mother was one. My father couldn't get a job, and he was using heroin before it became fashionable. They came from the South in the early forties. Racial tensions in Detroit were at an all-time high at that time."

Miracall interrupted, "I remember reading about the 1943 race riot. Most people think the '67 riot was bad—they're misinformed. If they knew the circumstances that brought about the '43 riot, they'd know that it was much worse. The thirty-six hours of rioting claimed thirty-four lives, twenty-five of them black." Miracall skimmed a finger along her jaw. "I'll bet your family lived in the Brewster projects." Rosemary nodded. "It's ironic that the Housing Commission named the new projects in 1942 after Sojourner Truth—a facility that was initially for black families, and until the riot it had been changed to let whites move into the new site. It's a crying shame so many lives were lost. And what did Detroit have to say in its defense? They offered one of their timeless mottos: *speramus meliora*—We hope for better things." Sarcasm whipped in her voice. "Yeah, right."

She was right, Rosemary thought. Back then, most of the blacks who believed they were heading to a promised land found northern bigotry every bit as pervasive and virulent as what they thought they had left behind in the Deep South. Ellen and James Coleman were two of those hopeful folks.

"Yes, we lived in the Brewster projects," Rosemary said wearily. "Even with the low rent, my father could barely feed his family. He was always laid off. But he was weak. He frequented the bars, even though he couldn't afford it. The activity of tourists coming in from Canada seemed like a lottery to him. He decided to use his wife to help him make a bundle of cash.

339

"My mother was coaxed into the business by her husband. Although I can't remember hearing her complain much. I *do* remember that they pretended to be brother and sister when he took her out. I remember them laughing one night while they were counting the money that Mom had made that night. This went on over a two-year period. My father was maintaining his drug habit, and my mother wasn't complaining—she was able to buy her first mink coat. Not long afterward, my mother bamboozled a big fish with plenty of money. He was in town temporarily from Omaha and was spending money like he owned First Security Bank."

"Seymour Bowenstein?" Miracall quizzed.

"Right. In no time at all, he was living with us. He wanted to marry her. It didn't matter that she'd been acting as a prostitute. He loved her, especially when she told him that she was pregnant. Seymour had no idea that the child, Isaac, was my father's. I think my mother convinced my father to leave, because he was gone for about four months. Then, one night, he was back. It was the night that Seymour caught my mother and my father in a compromising position. He left, and stayed away for a week. Then he came back, mad as a pit bull. I overheard my mom telling a friend that people were teasing Seymour because Isaac wasn't his son. He came back again that rainy night and shot my mother. He'd intended to kill my father, too, but I assume he ran away. Mom was three months' pregnant. I found out a year later that my father had overdosed on heroin. I didn't have an ounce of sympathy for him.

"My mother's cousin, Lucy, took care of Isaac and I until I turned eighteen. I married a man I didn't care about, just to get us out of her house. It didn't last long.

"You may think badly of me. But Isaac was only two years old. He didn't remember a thing. I was seventeen, and hadn't been to church in my entire life. That's when I decided that our life had to change. I had to change. I went to church and prayed. I asked the Lord to help me and my brother. He had to be special."

"He is special," Miracall said, "and so is his son."

"You have to understand. I always wanted to tell Isaac when he got older. I didn't want him to hate his mother. I've never been a mother, but I know, I know, that I wouldn't want to hear these truths about *my* mother. Over the years, I wondered, Miracall, should I spoil his illusions? Tell him the truth?

Then I thought, what good would it do? All I could hope is one day if he ever found out, and I put more emphasis on that *if ever*, that he would forgive me. Because chances were, he never would.

"I wanted him to make the Coleman name mean something. I don't know, Miracall, but I feel that black people don't care about their name anymore. They don't carry on tradition. They don't think about the future. They live for today. That's why we hang on to stories that tell us about the past, like Alex Haley's *Roots*. It changed the whole look of Black America."

"I remember. It was the most successful miniseries ever to be televised. And Steven Spielberg didn't have nothing to do about it."

Rosemary queried, "Why do we need white people to tell our stories?"

Miracall thought for a moment. "We don't. We can tell our own stories."

They turned when they heard a knock at the door.

"Afternoon, Miracall," Jesse said apologetically.

"Hi, Jesse. I'd better get going. I've got tons of work to finish this afternoon." Miracall went over and hugged Rosemary and whispered, "Please come and speak with Isaac. It's not right for me to tell him the truth. You have to tell him—I think he's ready to listen." She kissed her on the cheek and left.

After she'd gone, Jesse spoke words that she hadn't ever expected to hear. "I know that you go down to the prisons, and that you spend time at the shelters. But you need to listen to black men who are just like me—plain, poor, honest men. You never asked me, for instance, Rosemary, how I feel about my name, Jones. It's not important that my family wasn't rich. My father left me a legacy. It may seem small, even embarrassing, that it's a funeral home, but I'm proud of the Jones name just the same."

"Jesse, I didn't mean *all* black people." She felt so embarrassed, realizing that while he was waiting outside her door, he must have heard every word that she had said to Miracall.

"No. I didn't say you did. You don't understand, Rosemary. There are men who work for the city of Detroit. Sanitation workers, for example, who know they'll never be more than that. But they're proud, just the same. They've provided an honest income for their family. Should we think less of them because money doesn't bring instant recognition to their name? I would say no. These men are proud of their name. Proud of the sons they bore, knowing that they will continue to carry on that name."

Outside, the rain had let up, but it was still misty. Looking out the window now, Rosemary felt melancholy. In the background she heard a crack of thunder and shuddered. The sky was pale porcelain blue and looked as if another thunderclap might shatter it into a million pieces.

Rosemary began to feel woozy, and her ankle felt tight. She looked down and noticed it was beginning to swell. Turning slightly, she felt the edema creep up along her thigh, hip, and shoulder. She wondered what was wrong, and began to feel extremely tired. Reaching down, she massaged her legs, then tried to stand up. Her head felt so heavy, she held on to the edge of the desk for support.

An odd feeling of numbness crept over her left side. She couldn't feel her face, primarily her mouth being drawn down. Edema began to creep upward from the toes. Her body began to swerve, and all she could manage to say was, "Oooooohh."

"Say what?" Jesse asked, looking at her funny.

"Excuse me. I've got to go . . . I've got to go tothewesstwooom." She wavered slightly, and didn't feel her mouth pulling even more downward as her body began to lean over like a weeping willow.

It took all of Jesse's strength to catch her.

Cries and Whispers

All she could think of as she began to lose consciousness was that she had a christening service to perform tomorrow.

Seconds later, a whiz of white jackets talking fast, moving faster, was all around her. She felt several arms lifting her onto a gurney, and thought she heard someone ask Jesse what had happened to her. Another voice said something about the ruddiness of her complexion. Yet another voice cautioned that she could be having a stroke.

Not me! she screamed to herself.

She struggled to stay awake, and felt herself losing the battle. The weight of her head seemed so incredulously light—a somewhat dizzying but happy

342

kind of light, like those dream-smiles, which were the speech of sleep. Darkness sluiced through her body and she began to fade like the sunset.

When Isaac entered the hospital room, Jesse jumped up from the chair and embraced him.

"I'm glad you're here, Isaac," he said quietly, seriously. "She needs us both right now." With red-veined eyes, he braved a smile and left the room, giving Isaac a moment of privacy.

It was no surprise to see the room filled with fresh flowers and colorful balloons. Cards and telegrams came, it seemed, every five minutes. Isaac hadn't realized before how many lives his sister had touched.

He only had a moment, he thought, after the nurse left, to speak with his sister.

Placing her hand in his, he leaned over the bed. "Sis, I don't know how to tell you how sorry I am—how selfish I've been. I won't attempt to put it into words because I can't. So all I can do is ask you to forgive me. I was wrong. I know now it was the demons that were attempting to manifest hatred in me toward you, knowing all the time the heavy burden it would put on you." His eyes welled, a steady stream settling, then dripping, down quivering lips. "Sis, I'm sorry."

The missionaries came to his aid, praying for him in the hospital waiting room.

"Brother Isaac"—Sister Jackson gently touched his shoulder—"would you like to come to the revival with Sister Walker and I tonight?" Isaac nodded. "We'll pick you up at seven."

That evening was like an awakening of his soul. The sisters in the church embraced Isaac like he was a saint. They helped him to the altar, and prayed for his sister, his departed wife, and Peyton. Finally, they prayed for Isaac.

When the assistant pastor laid his hands on Isaac's head, Isaac felt a peace come over him like he'd never experienced before. Tears stung his eyes, and he whispered, "Thank you, Jesus."

During the following day and night, Isaac enjoyed attending the revival services with the saints from his sister's church. When others went out into the aisle to form the prayer line, Isaac stepped out and joined them. Later, when they went to the altar, Isaac got down on his knees, too, and prayed for his sister's speedy recovery.

343

While Rosemary was still unconscious, Isaac sat next to her bed and held her hand. Even as he told her how wonderful he now felt, he scanned the various tubes and needles going in and out of her body. Machines monitoring her comatose body beeped and bleeped. It was the common sound in the intensive care unit that reminded the healthy of the complexities of all living beings.

Seeing Rosemary in the hospital was the worst time in his life. For two days, she couldn't speak; she merely stared at him. Tears dripped from his eyes that he didn't bother to wipe away.

"Rosemary has a blockage in the renal artery," the doctor explained to Isaac and Jesse the first night. "This is the artery that comes off the kidney. It could be genetic—we don't know."

"But she's never—" Jesse began.

"Sir, your wife is fifty-seven years old. She's had a massive stroke. And I have to caution you, she is dangerously ill. I realize, after checking her medical history, that she's never had any *serious* health problems before. It doesn't matter. The primary culprit in these instances stems from an overuse of sodium."

"Salt?" Isaac said, stunned. Rosemary exercised five days a week, and was just fourteen pounds overweight. It didn't make sense.

"Yes—sodium—not necessarily in the form of salt. Her blood pressure is two-twenty over one-forty. We're working on bringing her pressure down, but be prepared for a long night. She'll be in the hospital for two to three weeks. Then rehab for weeks afterward. Rosemary has to learn how to use her extremities again. She also has to learn how to speak again. It's called physical therapy. She will also have to go through occupational therapy."

There were tears in Jesse's eyes when he spoke. "Will she fully recover?"

"Some people fully recover—others will always have that weakness."

Isaac wondered how a woman as strong as his sister could possibly have a stroke. He didn't know a woman on earth who exuded more strength. He hated to admit it, but it was he who felt weakened now. Jesse didn't show any signs of being much better off.

What would they do without her?

Isaac went back into her room and looked at his sister's body lying there, helpless. She looked as if she were in perpetual pain. He felt the same way.

Pain, the outcome of sin. Isaac wasn't sure if it was his sin or Rosemary's.

The doctors prescribed Procardia and one aspirin a day, and assured them that Rosemary was receiving the best possible care.

On day three, Rosemary was coherent, though she could barely talk. Most of what she said wasn't audible.

That afternoon, when Isaac came to visit her, she'd fallen asleep with the Bible resting on her chest. She opened her eyes when he kissed her forehead. Her loving eyes filled with tears. No words were needed when he reached out and caressed her arm, then leaned over to hug her.

Pushing him back, her eyes led him to a piece a paper that was tucked in the folds of the Bible. It read: "I LOVE YOU, Isaac."

He laid his head on her chest and felt the arms that had rocked him as a child embrace him lovingly.

"And I love you, Wosy."

On a Clear Day You Can See Forever

Isaac eyed the registered letter lying on the bureau. The return address was from the Emperor Record Company in Bahia, Brazil. Emperor had made him a six-figure offer if he would relocate to their country. They would guarantee him a five-year recording contract, and set him up in a comfortable home, complete with furnishings and a brand-new upscale car.

This is the sort of thing that I've been working for. I would finally be financially independent for the rest of my life.

Then he remembered the other letter in his jacket pocket that he'd carried for two weeks—it was a letter from an editor at *The Detroit News*.

Nervous sweat ran down his armpits when he tore open the letter. As he began to read the contents, the telephone rang.

"Morning, Brother Coleman," the assistant pastor at Mother Bethel said cheerily. "I'd like you to know that your family is in our prayers."

Isaac couldn't remember his response when he hung up the phone.

The news of his job offer—career change—came as a shock to him. Eighteen months ago, it would have been a dream come true—the most important compliment he could have gotten—but not now. After all that had happened lately, he realized his music career was secondary. Nothing could be more important than being there for his son. Seeing to it that he didn't continue to make the same mistakes Isaac had. There was no way he could accept the possibility of his son becoming a career con.

The calls continued to come in from Mother Bethel. Now Isaac had the peace of mind to listen.

"Brother Coleman, I'm a friend of your sister's. I'm praying for you and your family. May God continue to bless you all."

Dozens of cards came in the mail. Beautiful flowers were left at the security desk. Scores of meals were elaborately wrapped and placed in front of his door.

Isaac was somewhat confused. Then he remembered what Rosemary had said at Kennedy's funeral:

"Those that repent, and of their first works, shall rejoice, and recover their first comforts. God's mercies to his people have been ever of old, and therefore they may hope, even then when he seems to have forsaken and forgotten them that the mercy which was from everlasting will be to everlasting."

"Forgive me, Lord."

And he thought back on Rosemary's prayer when he was in prison. He opened his Bible and read Jer. 31:3. "The Lord hath appeared of old unto me, saying, Yea, I have loved thee with an everlasting love: therefore with loving-kindness have I drawn thee."

In that quiet moment at home, he knew that he had felt "everlasting joy."

Later that day, Isaac, along with his son, walked up the high steps to Mother Bethel. Not a threat of rain in sight, the sky was suddenly as crystal clear as diamonds, so clear and clean that he could see forever.

Peyton stopped midway. "Dad, I'm scared. We haven't had any snow in nearly two months. That's real weird. I'm worried that when the clock strikes twelve tonight, on January first, 2000, the world will end."

"I used to think about that when I was fourteen. I don't think that way anymore. You know why?" The sparkle of learned wisdom shone in his eyes. "Because I stopped looking toward the future—to what might happen next. I began to enjoy the small things, like getting to know my son—my sister's life being spared—finding a friend in someone I've learned to love. By putting my trust in the Lord, I began to feel better about myself."

Isaac thought back to Loren's belief about convicted felons. "A man once said that he believed that every man accused of a crime who is not behind bars is a danger to society, and that these individuals have failed to realize the love of God. He was so wrong, son. God's mercies are new each and every morning."

"I understand what you're saying, Dad. That God is the source of our hope and our strength."

"Rosemary taught me that you and I are two prime examples of living hope, Peyton. Hope that does not merely change the conditions of life but life itself. Christ does not only offer that hope; he is that hope."

"I didn't know that Aunt Rosemary was that smart. She's getting old. But what about Miracall?"

"I believe we've got what it takes to make a lifelong commitment to one another." He chose his words carefully. "She's right for me, Peyton. I don't want to take anything from your mom. I loved her. I'll always love her. And Miracall knows that. That's what's so beautiful about our relationship. If your mother hadn't died, I believe that she and I would still be together."

"I'm glad, Dad. I really loved my mom. And I sort of figured that she still cared about you, too, because she never said anything bad about you—not to me, that is. And you know what? I expected you to talk about her when you came home. You didn't. That's when I knew that I had special parents, and I had to do something with my life to show you that I appreciated you two."

Father and son entered the church together. A duffel bag rested over each of their shoulders. The entire congregation planned on spending the night, to start the year off right.

Isaac immediately spotted Miracall sitting in the front pew and headed up front to join her.

Dawn, Gary, Tempest, and Edwin were there to show their support. The bishop spoke on Rosemary's behalf. Afterward, Isaac provided several spiritual selections on his saxophone that he dedicated to the loving support he received from his sister.

"Without her," Isaac said, "I wouldn't be the man I am today." He lowered his head in respect. "But she also taught me the most important lesson of my life—forgiveness. We expect God's chosen people to be perfect. But I know now that no one is perfect."

A single snowflake spiraled down just outside the back window, and Isaac caught Peyton's smile.

He stepped to the center of the stage and began to play "Make a Joyful Noise."

The tune moved the congregation so much that half of them got up and danced in the aisles. In the interim, more flakes began to fall from the sky. The year 2000 was coming in with a Michigan snowstorm. The new millennium was going to be just as normal as any other New Year.

Glancing out into the congregation, Isaac became aware of the dwindling numbers of older members in the congregation and the abundance of young people who filled the church. Their wisdom was irreplaceable, and could never be exchanged for the eager minds of the youths of today. He wondered, did they understand the history of the Bible? Did they know that one couldn't repeat a dream that took place in the past?

He thought back on his dreams of becoming a huge success. They were still so fresh in his mind, and always seemed close enough to touch. He didn't realize then, as he did now, that success meant being loved and showing love. He'd come a long way to this peace.

It was befitting, then, that he ended his song with a prayer.

"Hope—that is our bright tomorrow. But I believe in tomorrows. Our tomorrows lighten our load and brighten our way. Oh, yes, I've got my sights set on tomorrow. Tomorrow I see souls being saved. Tomorrow I see miracles waiting to happen. Tomorrow I see the full manifestations of God's grace working in the church. Yes, Lord. We've made it to the millennium, praise God. Some didn't believe that we would." He took a moment and smiled at his son. "I leave you today and ask that you trust in God's grace today and in all of your tomorrows. Believe it! Celebrate it! Know that Christ is in you, because I know that he's in me."

"Amen!" someone shouted.

Isaac concluded by saying the words that he knew Rosemary would say: "All heads bowed and every eye closed."

Isaac and Peyton had made plans to have breakfast at the International House of Pancakes on Jefferson Avenue after service ended.

"Do you remember watching the playoffs between Indiana and New York last year?" Peyton asked his father as he followed him to the parking lot. When Isaac shook his head no, Peyton continued, "During half-time they showed an interview with Indiana's Jalen Rose. He talked about his dad whom he hadn't seen in so many years."

"Had his dad been in prison?"

"No. He used to be an NBA player. One of the best number-two guards I've ever seen. To make a long story short, Jalen tried to contact his dad a few times without any success."

Isaac stopped and turned around to face his son. "Oh, yeah. I vaguely remember reading that article. The basketball player carried the unopened letter from his father for weeks before he read it."

"Mm-hm. Jalen was angry with his dad for leaving him. That's how I felt about you, Dad. Most times I was lonely, but angry, too. You were a man I'd only known in my dreams." Images of Easy Boy's cold death flashed through his mind and he shivered with shame. "Then I got to thinking," he said, taking hold of his shoulders and hugging himself, "what if something happened to you?" Peyton swallowed several times, then looked directly into Isaac's chestnut-colored eyes. "I told myself, I ain't nobody's Little Caesar. My name is Peyton Coleman. And I know that my mother would want me to tell my father while he's still living that I love him."

"*God has set you free,*" Isaac heard the Holy Spirit say. "It's all right now. Raise your hands and begin to say yes. It's your day of Deliverance! Break through it. Break through it. Be set Free! Hallelujah! In Jesus' name—you'll never be the same again."

"I love you, Dad." He felt Peyton's hands trembling as he hugged him around the shoulders. "I need you in my life. I don't ever want to live without you."

Isaac hugged his son tighter than he ever did. "I love you, son. And I don't *ever* want to be without you."

349

The wind blew thick flakes across their faces, then suddenly shifted, now coming out of the south. Looking up into the sky, Isaac thought, even as the wind changed, he knew that God would never change. He realized that friends change. Relatives change. Employees change. But not God. And Isaac knew that nothing would change the love that he would always feel and show toward his son.

About the Author

Rosalyn McMillan was a Ford Motor Company factory worker for twenty years. After two serious car accidents, which ended her career in the auto industry, she used the drama unfolding in her own life as the basis of her three successful novels: *Knowing* (a national bestseller), *One Better,* and *Blue Collar Blues.* She lives with her husband and children in Tennessee.

Visit the author's Web site at: www.rosalynmcmillan.net.